Cruel Intentions

Eastern High Series Book One

Eve Campbell

CHAPTER 1

AUBREY

The thought of going back to my dad's house after a year and a half feels like some sort of cruel joke, especially after everything that made me leave in the first place. When my mom finally left him, I really believed things would be different. I thought she would change. I thought I knew who she was. Turns out, I didn't know a damn thing.

When we left, I swore I'd never set foot in that town again. Never did I imagine I'd be back on this damn road, heading straight toward the past I fought so hard to leave behind. But here I am on that fucking road, with all the memories of the boy next door that still continue to haunt me.

He wasn't just a boy. He was my everything. My first crush-my first kiss-my first sexual experience-my first heartbreak. And now, the weight in my chest is unbearable. Breaking his heart still feels like a fresh wound, one that's never stopped bleeding.

I can already feel Noah's resentment hanging over me like a storm cloud, heavy and inescapable. Mom thinks it'll be simple—that we'll hug it out, or some bullshit—but I know better. His anger runs deep. Deeper than I probably deserve. And I can't blame him. Because I left him.

I tried to explain, tried to make him understand why I had to go. That I needed a fresh start. That I had to get away from my alcoholic, abusive father. I thought going with Mom would fix everything.

Noah warned me it wouldn't work. He begged me to stay. But I didn't listen. What I didn't realize was Mom wasn't taking me far—just to a neighboring town. Close enough to remember, but too far to reach him. And I never got the chance to tell him the hardest truth: I wasn't coming back.

But none of that mattered anyway.

He ignored me—like the girl he once swore eternal love to had vanished without a trace. And it fucking destroyed me. He wasn't just some fleeting crush—he was the only person who ever made me feel truly seen, truly loved. His promises burned like fire, fierce and all-consuming, while the rest of the world blurred into nothing.

And now?

Now, I'm walking back into the ashes, and I don't even know if there's anything left to save.

To him, I was everything—more precious than any jewel, held so tightly in his arms it felt like nothing and no one could ever break us. Our bond wasn't just some shallow connection; it was a tapestry woven from our lives, stitched together with every laugh, every tear, every whispered secret beneath the stars.

But time has a way of unraveling even the strongest bonds. My love for him was boundless, reckless, wild, and it was matched only by the fire in his own heart. It wasn't just love; it was chaos. A wildfire that devoured us both. And we didn't care if it burned us to ashes.

And now, as I head back into the wreckage of my former life, the memories cling. Sharp and painful. Clawing at my mind, leaving behind a hollow ache that no amount of time can dull. Every mile pulls me closer to the ghosts of what we were—closer to the day it all shattered.

That fucking day. The day I got in that car and left him behind. It's a bitter reminder of the love we once had and the way it all came crashing down. Because of me.

If only I'd listened.

Noah warned me. He told me things wouldn't change, but I was too damn stubborn, too desperate to believe in something better. I thought maybe, just maybe, I could finally belong to a real family—my mother and me, together.

But now?

Now, I regret that choice with every fiber of my being. I regret climbing into the sleazy asshole's car that day, the one who picked us up and smiled like he was doing us a favor. He was just the first in a long, miserable parade of my mom's boyfriends—men who always came first. Men who looked at me in ways they had no fucking right to.

There were nights when I couldn't take it—nights I'd pick up my phone and hover over Noah's number, my chest so heavy with regret it felt like I was suffocating. I wanted to tell him everything. To pour out the love I never stopped feeling. To say I was sorry. To beg him to come get me. But I never did. Because deep down, I knew the truth: I didn't deserve him anymore.

Sitting in the stifling hellhole that is the backseat of my mother's latest boyfriend's car, I feel the resentment boiling inside me—thick, heavy, and toxic, like poison in my veins. This place they're dragging me back to—the place she swore I'd never have to see again—looms ahead like a cage. A cage she expects me to step into and call home.

It's unbearable. Infuriating. Watching her sit there in the front seat, carefree and oblivious, that hollow smile plastered on her face like nothing's wrong. Like her choices haven't shattered my life over and over again. She doesn't see the wreckage she's left behind—or maybe she does, and she just doesn't give a shit.

And then there's him—the puppet master, sitting smugly next to her in the driver's seat, pulling the strings of my life without a single thought for the damage he's causing. Every word he speaks, every decision he makes, drips with cruelty. And what pisses me off the most is that she just sits there. Silent. Always silent.

Her refusal to stand up for me, to protect me from the wreckage he creates—it hurts. Her silence isn't just cowardice; it's betrayal, a wound so deep and gut-wrenching that it cuts far deeper. Because no matter how much shit he throws my way, it's her choice to let it happen.

All these eighteen years, and all I've ever wanted was to matter to her. To be the fucking center of my mother's world for once, to feel her attention and devotion without having to fight for the scraps. But here I am, in the one moment I need her the most, and of course she's choosing *him*—choosing some asshole who will move on eventually when he gets bored—over me.

No fucking surprise there.

It stings like a bitch, and I hate how much it fucking hurts to admit that. I can't wrap my head around why she just won't let me finish school at home, especially when it's my last year.

The thought of going back to my old school, knowing Noah will be there and facing him every day... I'm not sure I can do that. The social media stalking I couldn't stop myself from doing has been like a slap to the face—a constant reminder that while I've been drowning, he's been thriving. Noah's somehow gotten even hotter, like the universe just had to rub it in, and his popularity. It's off the charts now.

Every photo I see hurts like a bitch—him at parties, surrounded by girls throwing themselves at him, desperate for his attention. Once, it was me he looked at like I was his entire world, like nothing else mattered. But those days feel like a lifetime ago now, buried beneath the weight of what's become of us.

His mom left when he was just seven. She didn't even give him a second glance before she walked out that front door, never to look back. I can feel the weight of that now, the years of heartbreak he's already carried, and now I'm just another person who walked out of his life.

I know what's coming when I see him. The confrontation. The anger. The hurt. And I'm ready for it, even though I'm not sure anything I say will ever make up for what I did.

From the front passenger's seat my mother lifts her hand, runs it through her dickhead boyfriend's hair, and then leans in to kiss him like it's the most natural thing in the world. I can feel my stomach churn. If I wasn't stuck here in the backseat, I'm sure he'd pull the car over so she could straddle him and take his cock for a ride, like that's just an everyday occurrence.

Nothing about her actions surprises me anymore. Not after the shit I've had to listen to, the noises coming through the paper-thin walls of our shitty apartment.

When she pulls away and settles back into her seat, the asshole glances at me in the rearview mirror with that smirk playing on his lips. It takes everything in me not to punch the seat in front of me. I fucking hate him with every ounce of my being.

I turn my head away in disgust as my mother gives directions and we turn onto our old street. It's hard to miss how little has changed since my last visit to my father's house six months ago. The memories come rushing back — the forced small talk, the uncomfortable silence. My dad slumped in front of the TV, numbing himself with beer, while my mother pretended to have fun with old friends. That day, it felt less like father and daughter and more like strangers coexisting in the same house.

Since I've been gone, my mother has dragged me back to visit my father twice. Each time as awkward as fuck. She never warned him, just dropped me off like it was another errand, leaving him blindsided each time. And now, as we head back, I'm certain my mother wouldn't have said a single word about me living with him again.

Just thinking about it makes everything feel ten times worse, and I can already feel the nerves crawling under my skin. What the hell am I walking into?

"There it is," my mother says, pointing ahead.

The asshole parks the car right in front of my father's house, like he owns the damn place.

I glance out the window and notice nothing's changed—the paint on the siding's still peeling, the windows cracked, the yard a jungle of overgrown weeds slowly swallowing the house whole. My gaze shifts to Noah's house next door, and for a moment, I wonder if he's inside. Probably not. Not with all the shit he's been up to lately. I've seen enough on social media to know he's probably out partying, being tagged in endless photos of his latest bullshit antics.

My mother opens the car door and steps out, leaving me alone with the obnoxious dickhead.

He kills the engine, and the silence settles in, thick and suffocating. My throat tightens, the weight of the moment pressing down harder than I ever expected. This isn't just some temporary mess—it's a nightmare. She's dragging me back to a place she once swore was too dangerous for us. But here we are. It's happening, whether I want it to or not.

I reach for the seatbelt, but before I can undo it, my mother's voice slices through the silence. "Aubrey, come on, get out of the car now. It's time to go," she whines, her voice high-pitched and laced with impatience, like I'm just some annoying chore she can't wait to be done with.

It's obvious—she's just itching to start her new life with the asshole sitting there with that shit eating grin plastered on his face. The one who's caused nothing but tension between us.

"Don't let the door hit your ass on the way out," he says, with that smug smile on his face.

Fuck. I hate this guy. I can't stand him. If I were the type to throw punches, I'd happily shove my fist right into that smug, twisted grin of his. I snatch my bag from off the back seat and push my mother's seat forward to get out of the car. I don't care if I scratch the fucker's sports car, him and his mid-life crisis can go fuck themselves.

When I slam the door with a hard thud and turn, I know his eyes are burning a hole in my ass as I walk away. A wave of disgust rises in my throat at the thought of it. Fucking Creep.

Halfway up the front path to the house, I notice my mother's posture—stiff, uncomfortable, like she's bracing herself. Her body language screams tension. As I get closer, she lifts her head, and our eyes lock. In that brief moment, I see it. The guilt. It's clear as day on her face. She knows exactly what she's doing. She knows this whole situation is fucked up, and it's that asshole behind the wheel pushing her into it. That much is painfully clear.

"Please, Mom. Please don't do this," I beg, my voice trembling with desperation.

She swallows hard, her throat tightening, and I can see the internal struggle in her eyes. She wants to say something, I can tell, but nothing comes out.

"Come on. Hurry the fuck up," the asshole yells from the car.

My mother turns her head away, her eyes fixed on the old house, like it's some kind of sanctuary, like staring at it long enough will make everything somehow fine.

I silently pray, hoping—no, begging—that she'll snap out of whatever trance she's in and stand up to that asshole. Tell him there's no way she can do this; there's no way she can leave me here. But as the seconds stretch on and she doesn't say a word, a cold fear creeps into my chest. A fear that maybe—just maybe—she won't change her mind at all.

"It's only going to be for a year, Aubrey," she says, as if her words will make it okay. As if a year can be dismissed with a single sentence, like she's already made up her mind. She then strides down the front path choked with overgrown weeds.

Anger burns, hot and unforgiving. How could she do this to me, after everything we've been through. How could she just throw me back into this mess like it's nothing? Where the hell is the mother who was supposed to protect me? The one who promised to always have my back? Instead, she's walking away, ready to drag me back into the lion's den—into the world of that drunken asshole, who's volatile, alcohol-fueled rage could explode at any moment.

I want to scream. I want to rip everything apart as I listen to the sound of her heels clicking on the uneven pathway—like she's already moved on from this whole situation.

I can't take it anymore. "What the fuck? Are you seriously leaving me here after everything we've gone through? Goes to show how much you fucking care." I shout as I trail behind, barely able to keep my feet moving. She won't change her mind—not with that asshole waiting for her back in the car.

She halts, but only because she has to. "Aubrey, I *do* care," she snaps, spinning around to face me. Her eyes swim with guilt, tangled with something else I can't quite place—something that's so far from the love I'm desperate for right now.

If she actually cared, she wouldn't be dragging me back to this goddamn circus. She wouldn't be forcing me to wade through every brutal, soul-crushing memory like it's no big deal. Like it's just another fucking Tuesday.

"Yeah, your actions speak louder than anything you could say," I spit, sarcasm dripping from every word like venom. "Picking *him*—that asshole—over your own flesh and blood. Over your own daughter for Christ sake. That tells me *exactly* how much you give a shit," I snap, my voice sharp enough to cut. The anger boiling inside me isn't something I'm even trying to hide anymore. It's raw, blistering, and goddamn relentless. I'm done pretending it's not eating me alive.

She stumbles over her words, trying to defend herself. "You know it's not like that, Aubrey," she says, her voice shaking with weak resolve, as if anything she could say would ever make this okay.

"Don't," I cut her off, my tone sharp. "Just don't." My patience is gone, burned down to ash, and I'm done wasting breath on her bullshit excuses.

As we reach the front step, my mother knocks on the door, the sound sharp and unforgiving, slicing through the dead silence of the neighborhood. My chest tightens, that familiar knot of dread twisting tighter, squeezing the air from my lungs. Is he even going to bother answering? Or are we about to find him buried in yet another haze of booze, using it to smother whatever shred of responsibility he has left?

It's after four. Prime happy hour for him. And let's be real—I'm not expecting anything else.

The seconds crawl by, each one dragging like nails on a chalkboard. When the door finally creaks open, there he is—my so-called father, bleary-eyed and unsteady, like he just stumbled out of some booze-soaked fog.

His eyes land on me, surprise flickering across his face for half a second before they dart to my mother. And I see the unspoken question hanging in the air. *What the fuck is this about?*

When his gaze shifts back to me, it's empty, cold, no flicker of anything resembling fatherly concern. Just that detached indifference he's worn like a second skin for all these years. Like he's a goddamn stranger with the unfortunate title of being my father.

He stands there, silent and unmoving, like a figure sculpted from stone, waiting for my mother to finally speak. To explain why the fuck we're here.

"I've been carrying this shit alone for far too long," my mother hisses. "Now... It's *your* damn turn." Before my father has a chance to protest, she turns around and walks away.

She doesn't glance back. She simply walks away, calm and resolute, as if she's finally free.

The engine roars to life, as she strides toward the car parked on the street—toward him—the bastard who set this all in motion. It's like she can't get to him fast enough, leaving the rest of us to pick up the pieces of her destruction.

"Yeah, actions speak louder than words, Mother!" I shout, my voice cracking with bitterness. But it doesn't matter. She won't hear me. She's too wrapped up in her shiny new life, with her shiny new boyfriend, to care about me.

My father stumbles past me, his breath ragged, eyes burning with something I can't place. He moves down the front path, and when he catches up to her, his hand shoots out, grabbing her arm and yanking her to stop.

"What the fuck do you think you're doing?" he spits, his voice sharp and full of venom, making it clear that there's no way in hell she's leaving me here.

"I've already made that clear," she says. "She's your responsibility now. So grow a pair and raise your daughter. I've done my part, and now it's your turn."

The brutal truth of how little I matter to her cuts deep. I've always known my father didn't give a shit but hearing it from my mother rips me apart. She might as well have slapped me, because that's exactly how much it fucking hurts.

I can hear their voices, muffled and sharp, cutting through like a soundtrack to my life. They're arguing over whose responsibility I am, like I'm some unwanted possession. It's sickening. To them, I'm nothing but a burden, a piece of trash to toss around between them.

My mother yanks her arm free from my father's grip, like she can't stand his touch. She doesn't even look back, just walks to the car, done with everything—done with me. My father stands frozen, staring at her as she climbs in, regardless of everything that's left unsaid.

It doesn't even matter that the passenger door is still half-open. The asshole just revs the engine and tears down the street. No goodbye. No nothing. Just the deafening scream of the tires, like he can't wait to get the hell out of here fast enough.

My father stands there, his eyes fixed on the street as if he's waiting for her to return, as if something will magically change. But it won't.

Finally, he turns, his eyes meeting mine and in that moment, there's an understanding between us—a raw, brutal kind of connection. It's not the kind that promises things will get better, or that he's glad I'm here. No, this is the kind of understanding that makes it clear we're both trapped. Stuck in the same broken mess, in a house that doesn't feel like home anymore—just a cage I can't escape from.

After what feels like an eternity, he finally moves into the house. His steps are slow, deliberate, as if he's measuring every inch of space between us.

"You know where your room is, right?" His voice is cold, barely rising above the harsh sound of the screen door slamming shut behind him.

I don't answer at first. I just stand there, staring at the door, wishing it was different.

My chest tightens, every breath a struggle. I clutch the strap of my bag like it's the only thing holding me together. This fucking bag—it's all I have left. Everything I own, everything I am, packed into this small space. My entire life, reduced to a few scraps, a few broken pieces. And it feels like I'm standing on the edge, watching everything slip away.

When I finally take that first step inside, the old floor creaks beneath me, louder than it should, like it's calling out to me. Like it knows how much I hate being here. Nothing's changed, not since the last time I was dragged back here months ago. The mess, the dust, the neglect—it all still clings to every corner.

I remind myself it's only for a year. One fucking year. But the question claws at me, relentless, like a beast trapped inside my chest. What the hell happens after that? When the year is over, when I've somehow dragged myself through this shitshow, where do I go until my scholarship kicks in?

I stop by the door, stalling.

"Do you want something to eat?" he calls out from the kitchen.

"No, I'm fine," I mutter, my voice flat. I don't want anything from him—not food, not some pathetic attempt at comfort, not any of those empty gestures he thinks will fix everything.

"I'm sure you remember where everything is," he mutters, barely looking up as I step into the kitchen. His voice is stiff, like he's trying to pretend I'm not even here. I catch the flicker of discomfort in his eyes, like I'm just another burden he's been forced to tolerate.

Without a word, he moves forward, eager to escape this reality. He grabs his half-empty bottle of beer and downs the rest in one angry gulp. No fucking surprise there.

I stand frozen, not knowing what the hell I'm supposed to do.

He walks past me like I'm invisible, opens the fridge, grabs two more beers, and retreats to the couch. He flicks the TV on and watches some football game, cranking up the volume like it's the only thing that matters in the world.

That's my cue. Time to get the hell out. I turn away, each step heavier, than the last. The walls close in, suffocating me with memories of every second I spent trapped here.

When I reach my room, I open the door, and the memories come flooding back. The good ones with Noah—how we grew up together, how he was always there when my parents' fights forced me out of the house. He'd come running whenever he heard them shouting, always checking to make sure I was okay. But that's gone now. There's no Noah anymore. I'm just... alone. Alone in a place that's never felt like home.

I drop my bag on the bed, sit on the edge, and suddenly, the tears come. I've never been the type to cry, but it's like the floodgates open and I can't stop.

I bury my face in my hands, wishing the room would just swallow me whole, and take me away from all of this.

CHAPTER 2

NOAH

My body feels heavy, weighed down by the haze of last night—too much booze, too many regrets, and the fading warmth of a girl whose name escapes me. The memories stab through the fog in sharp, fragmented flashes: her on her knees, eager, desperate, and the way I took what she offered without feeling. It was rough—too rough—but that's the only way I seem to know how to touch anymore. Every girl is just another body to lose myself in, another face I'll forget by morning.

With two major schools in town, the possibilities are limitless—girls eager to offer whatever I want, no strings attached. It's not just for me but for my boys, Jace and Reece, though they always follow the unspoken rule: I get first pick. I decide who's off-limits and who's worth the risk. No one dare challenges me, not even the football team. They know better. Crossing me is a mistake you only make once.

But it's all starting to blur. The faces blend together, the bodies merge, and the emptiness creeps in after every conquest. Eastern High's been played out for a while—every girl just another notch, another meaningless fuck. Last night was supposed to be different—new blood, a fresh distraction—but even that's already slipping into nothing. The thrill doesn't last anymore, and the satisfaction never sticks.

All that's left is this gnawing ache, this crushing weight of wanting something more—something real. Something like I used to have. But now, I don't know how to stop.

The hot water cuts through the numbness, washing away the dull ache in my body but doing nothing for the deeper wounds. I linger too long, hoping the heat will drown the thoughts I shouldn't be thinking.

Twenty minutes later, I emerge with a towel slung low on my hips, the haze in my chest as heavy as the steam clinging to the mirror.

I snatch last night's shirt from the floor and toss it into the overflowing laundry basket, my movements mechanical, thoughtless. But, as always, my eyes wander—drawn toward the house next door. It's instinct, a pull I can't resist, no matter how pointless. No one's there anymore. I know that.

But I look anyway.

Aubrey.

Her name is a ghost that clings to the jagged shards of a past I can't escape. She didn't just leave behind an empty house—she left me with a bitterness that poisons every memory and regret that festers like an open wound. I once believed she was everything, that what we had was unbreakable. But she shattered that illusion, walking away as if it all meant nothing—as if I meant nothing.

And now here I am, standing in my room, towel wrapped around my waist, getting ready to drown it all in another night of reckless indulgence. Another night where my dick finds solace in strangers, but my heart remains trapped in the wreckage of what we had. The bitter irony is almost laughable. I've spent years trying to forget her, trying to bury the pain, but it never fully fades. It just lingers—like a shadow—waiting for the moment I'm alone again.

Aubrey's rejection didn't just break me—it rebuilt me into someone unrecognizable. A man who demands attention, takes control, and never lets anyone close enough to hurt him again. It's armor, a defense mechanism so solid I've almost fooled myself into thinking it's who I've always been. But the truth? I owe it all to her—the girl who shattered my heart and unwittingly gave me the blueprint for survival. She carved the man I've become, forged in the fire of her absence.

Sometimes, late at night, when the silence cuts deeper than I want to admit, I wonder if she ever thinks about the boy she left behind. The one who would have done anything—everything—to make her happy. I would've moved mountains, rearranged the stars, if it meant seeing her smile just once more. But to her, I was just a passing memory. Something easy to let go of, something not worth holding onto.

The thought stings, the bitter irony twisting the knife deeper. She's the reason I've built this fortress of dominance and detachment. Yet she'll never know the power she gave me to change when she walked away. Or maybe, if she did, she wouldn't care.

As I glance out the window, a familiar sight freezes me in place.

Aubrey.

Sitting on her bed, her head bowed, hands covering her face as her shoulders shake with silent sobs. The world tilts, disbelief crashing over me like a tidal wave. What the fuck is she doing back here? And why now, after all this time?

My chest tightens, old instincts roaring to life before I can stop them. That unshakable need to protect her, to shield her from the chaos that's always loomed next door, claws its way to the surface. For a fleeting moment, I feel it again—the boy who would've done anything to keep her safe. But then reality hits, hard and unforgiving.

She left.

She made her choice. I've spent years trying to bury the wreckage she left behind, building walls so high not even the memory of her could climb over them. And now, out of nowhere, she's back. Crying. Alone.

Whatever's broken her, she'll have to fucking deal with it on her own. I'm not that guy anymore, and I'll be damned if I let her undo everything I've worked to become. Let her live with the consequences of the choices she made—because God knows, I've been living with them.

I force myself to turn away, to walk back to the life I've created without her—but my feet refuse to obey, frozen in place as if they've forgotten how to move. It's pathetic, honestly. After everything, after all the walls I've put up and the bitterness I've buried myself in, just seeing her is enough to break me.

She lifts her head, her eyes drifting to something in her room, and for a moment, it feels like no time has passed. She's still as beautiful as I remember—long black hair falling around her face, soft and wild all at once.

My chest tightens with the memories of how I used to run my fingers through her hair, not because she asked, but because I needed to. Just to touch her, to feel close to her in a way words never could. It was the kind of closeness I thought would last forever.

But forever wasn't in the cards for us. And now, standing here like some ghost haunting her shadow, I'm reminded of everything I've lost—the girl, the touch, those quiet moments that once felt so damn perfect. And yet, despite it all, I can't make myself move. She doesn't even know I'm here, and still, she holds me the way she always did.

I drag a hand over my chest, trying to ease the ache that's been there since the moment I saw her. Memories I thought I'd buried claw their way back—her smile, her laugh, the way she made me believe in something I never thought I deserved. But those memories don't belong here anymore.

She's just like my mother—walking away without a second thought, without giving a single fuck about what they left behind. I was seven when my mom disappeared, and it felt like the world shattered. I swore I'd never let anyone do that to me again. But Aubrey? She slipped through all my defenses, made me believe I might actually be worth staying for. And then she left, proving I was a goddamn fool for thinking any differently.

I clench my fists, forcing the anger to drown out the ache. Fuck them both. Neither of them is worth my time, my pain, or the pieces of myself they took when they walked away. I've survived without them, and I sure as hell don't need her back now to remind me of all the ways she broke me.

But then I see it—the way she wipes the tears from her face, her shoulders shaking like she's trying to hold herself together. And just like that, something inside me cracks.

It doesn't make sense. The Aubrey I knew would never have cried. Not even with all the shit that went on in that house. Not even when the world was crumbling around her. She was steel and fire. But seeing her now—broken and vulnerable—it feels wrong, unnatural, like the universe is trying to turn her into someone I don't recognize.

A surge of tenderness floods my chest, uninvited and unwanted. And fuck my weak heart for still clinging to a past that almost destroyed me.

I've spent too long trying to forget her, trying to outrun the person I used to be. Now, I'm the king of Eastern High—untouchable, ruthless, ready to take whatever I want. If she came back looking for the boy she left behind, she's about to find out he doesn't exist anymore.

She turns her head, and for one brutal, soul-crushing moment, time fucking stops. Our gazes meet, and all the things I've been running from, all the truths I've been too scared to face, come crashing down. The pain in her eyes—so raw, so undeniable—it cuts through me. I can't breathe, can't think, because seeing her like this—so shattered, so empty—makes something inside me coil tightly, impossible to unwind.

She rises from the bed, hesitant, as if she wants to reach for me but knows better than to try. Her eyes stay locked on mine, her face caught somewhere between hope and despair. God, I want to make it right. I want to run to her, hold her close, tell her everything will be okay, like I've done so many times before. But I can't.

The vulnerability in her eyes is so raw it cuts through me. Every inch of her body seems to scream for something—something I can't give her. I move across the room, each step heavier than the last. That old, hopeful smile tugging at her lips, the kind that used to make everything feel right between us.

She walks toward the window, the place that used to feel like our safe haven, where we'd whisper our secrets into the night, finding solace in each other's company when sleep wouldn't come. But as I get closer, I don't want to remember how we were—how we'd sit by our bedroom windows, talking for hours.

Instead of opening it like I used to, I reach up and pull the curtains closed—sharp, cold, and final. It's as if I'm shutting the door on everything we were, on everything I can never be for her. A move to push her away, to lock away the last remnants of us that still remain. And I can't tell if I'm doing it to protect her... or to protect myself.

I throw on some clothes in a hurry, not bothering if they match, and head downstairs. I push thoughts of her to the back of my mind, focusing on the one thing that matters now—partying, the booze, finding some distraction to drown out the memory of her.

Walking into the kitchen, I find my dad sitting at the table, eyes glued to his phone. The second I step in, he flips it face down, like he's hiding something.

"Hey, Dad," I mutter, grabbing a piece of fruit from the bowl and biting into it, barely tasting it.

"Hey, son," he says. "Heading out?"

My dad has always been my anchor—the one thing that kept me grounded when everything else fell apart. Not in some clichéd "he's a great guy" way, but in the kind that makes you believe in something unshakable, even when your world is falling to pieces. When my mom left, she didn't just walk out on me; she walked out on him too. He carried it all—her absence, my anger, the heaviness of a home that felt too quiet without her. I could see it in the way his shoulders slumped when he thought I wasn't watching. But he never let me see him crack. Not once. He turned himself inside out trying to keep me safe, trying to keep me whole. And for a long time, I thought he was invincible.

"Yeah, the guys and I are meeting up, then there's a party across town," I say, my words muffled by a mouthful of food. I toss the half-eaten apple into the bin without a second thought, then head to the fridge to grab a bottle of water.

His phone rings, and I expect him to pick it up, but he silences it quickly.

He's been doing that a lot lately. The buzzing and ringing have been constant these past few months.

"See ya later, Dad," I say, heading for the door.

"Yeah, be safe, son," he says, like always.

As I yank open the front door, my thoughts spiral to Aubrey. We were two halves of a whole, spending endless hours together, roaming each other's backyards, finding peace in the secret refuge of my treehouse. I can still feel the echo of that kiss I pressed against her lips on her thirteenth birthday—soft and innocent, but somehow it haunts me now. I've loved her for as long as I can remember—from the sweet, naïve days of childhood to the tangled mess we became. I swore I'd love her forever, whispering promises into her ear like time was on our side.

And she—she promised the same, vowing no one would ever take my place in her heart.

We were each other's firsts in everything, growing up side by side. But then... I watched her change, blossom into something so beautiful it terrified me. Every day, my love for her grew, pushing against the walls I'd built around it, afraid that even a whisper of what I truly felt would shatter the fragile thing we had—our friendship. I thought I could protect it. Protect her from the life in that house.

But now?

Now that same friendship I tried so hard to preserve is twisted beyond recognition, morphing into a cruel reminder of what we once were.

I slide into my car, the engine rumbling to life, desperate to get the hell away from here—away from her, away from everything that threatens to tear me apart. My hands are already gripping the wheel, my mind racing, counting down the seconds but as I press my foot down on the brake, ready to shift into reverse, something stops me.

It's not fear. It's something far worse. A pull I can't name, an invisible force holding me in place. My hand hovers over the gear shift, trembling, as though it knows, deep down, I can't drive away. It's her. I can feel her presence next door, a shadow that clings to me, refusing to be ignored. It tugs at my heart and and I fucking hate it.

I should just leave. Put her behind me, lock her away in that box where I don't care. But for some reason, I can't. And the longer I stay there, the clearer it becomes—I can't drive out of this driveway, not yet. Not until I figure out why the hell she's back here.

Why does she still have this hold on me? And why can't I shake her, no matter how hard I try?

"Fuck!" I mutter, slamming my fist against the steering wheel, pissed off at myself for being so goddamn weak. I should've left by now, should've gotten the hell out of here. But instead, I'm still sitting here, stuck in her orbit.

Irritation claws at me as I kill the engine—Reece is waiting, and I'm already late. But I can't ignore this. I need to get her out of my head before it drives me crazy. Without thinking, I push open the car door, my feet already moving, dragging me toward her house like I don't have a choice anymore.

I step into her yard, walking along the side of the house, my pulse pounding in my ears, drowning out the sound of my footsteps as I reach her window.

I glance inside, and there she is, sitting on the bed, her face empty, eyes hollow. No tears, but a silence that screams louder than anything. This isn't her. Not the Aubrey I remember—the one who'd laugh in your face and tell you to go fuck yourself if you even looked at her the wrong way.

Part of me wants to turn around, walk away, let her deal with whatever shitty mess she's got going on. I don't owe her a thing. It should be easy to leave. Hell, she did it without a second thought, without looking back. But something claws, a darkness that tells me if I don't figure this shit out now, it'll eat me up for the rest of the night—maybe longer.

I ball my fist, ready to knock on that glass, ready to tell her exactly how it is. I'm done playing the game. I'm ready to tell her she means nothing to me. That whatever this is—whatever we were—is nothing more than a mistake.

As I knock, she jumps at the sound, her eyes wide as she scrambles to get off the bed. What the hell does she have to cry about, anyway? Wasn't she the one, chasing some "better life," acting like I wasn't enough to keep her here? Like none of this—us—meant a damn thing?

I can't stop looking at her as she moves closer, my eyes drinking in every detail. My cock stirs at the sight of her, and I hate myself for it. Her tits are bigger now, fuller, and those long legs in denim cutoffs—damn. I shouldn't even be looking at her like this, but I can't stop. She's always been beautiful, but now... Now she's mesmerizing—too perfect, too *real*. Every inch of her is a siren's call, dragging me under.

I hate that my body reacts to her. I don't want to feel anything anymore, especially not this. I try to tear my eyes away, but every curve, every detail pulls me in harder. It's like she's taunting me, reminding me of all the things I tried to forget. I remember the way she moaned and how she felt beneath me, so perfect. The memory hits like a goddamn drug, and I'm fighting it, fighting *her*, but fuck, it's useless. She still has this hold on me—this pull I can't shake, even if I hate myself for it.

She reaches the window and slides it open like it's the most natural thing in the world.

"Hey, Noah," she says, her voice smooth, almost too calm.

Hearing my name on her lips again... it stirs something deep, something raw and ugly. I used to love the way she said it, the way it felt when she screamed it loud in the heat of the moment—when I buried myself deep inside her, when she begged for more.

But now?

Now, it hits like a goddamn punch to the gut.

"What the fuck are you doing here?" I snap, my voice sharp, the words coming out like a warning. My irritation flares hot and fast, a reflex more than anything else. Nothing but silence since she left and now she just pops back into my life like it's nothing.

Her casual "hey" feels like a slap in the face, and it makes my skin burn with rage.

Her demeanor shifts instantly at the irritation in my voice. There she is—the Aubrey I know—the one who doesn't take shit from anyone, who's never afraid to call you out. Her eyes go serious, intense, as she crosses her arms over her chest, pushing her tits up, like she's taunting me on purpose. It's a goddamn trap, and I walk right into it.

I can't stop my gaze from dropping to them, and the memories flood back—vivid and overpowering. How I used to suck on those tits, kiss them, touch them. I shove the thoughts down, locking them away, pushing against the craving that's rising in my gut.

"Just so we're fucking clear, you don't belong here anymore," I spit, the words coming out like venom, thick with emotion I'm too pissed to hide. "I'm not your goddamn friend anymore. So go back to where you belong. You mean nothing to me."

I turn away before she can speak, knowing if I don't, I'll fall apart. I keep my back to her, walking to the car without once looking back. She needs to see it—that I've changed so much that the guy I used to be is now a complete stranger every time I look in the mirror. Now I'm just someone who's closed off, chasing any warm pussy or willing mouth to fill the emptiness, drowning out the need for anything real.

I slide behind the wheel, firing up the engine, its growl matching the storm ripping through my chest. I slam the accelerator, reversing out onto the street, trying to outrun the shit inside me.

As I drive, my grip tightens on the wheel, a desperate attempt to hold myself together.

CHAPTER 3

AUBREY

T oday is the day I've feared. Sleep eluded me, leaving me instead with hours of staring at the ceiling, consumed by the storm of anxiety swirling in my chest. Noah's words from last night echo in my mind, each one cutting deeper the more I replay them.

I've never seen him like that before—so vulnerable, so angry, so... not him.

When he appeared at my window, I thought, maybe, just maybe, it was the Noah I once knew—the boy I trusted with all my secrets. But the moment he opened his mouth, he shattered any hope I had left. His words weren't just harsh; they were crushing, a painful reminder of how much he's changed. Now I don't even know if I can even face him. But today, I'll have to—and I'm not sure I'll make it through the aftermath.

I can't help but wonder how Tia, my old friend, will react when she sees me today. I've tried reaching out to her so many times, but all I've gotten is silence. The two people I trusted the most ghosting me as if I don't exist. I get it with Noah—he was upfront with me; said he couldn't do this if I walked away.

At least he was honest. But Tia? I don't get it.

Maybe she was never really my friend to begin with.

One thing I'm sure of, though, is that she's always had a thing for Noah—just like every other girl back then. And now, every time I creep through his social media (yeah, I know, I'm pathetic), there she is, always in the background, smiling. With how much hotter he's gotten over the past year, I know she's still all about him.

Maybe that's all I ever was to her—just a way to get closer to him.

The truth's going to come out today when I see her. I'll finally know if she's still got my back or if I was just a pawn in her little game.

Part of me wants to text her now; to let her know I'll be back at school, so I don't have to walk through those gates alone. But then I remember the distance that's grown between us, and I just... I can't. I don't know if I can handle hearing whatever bullshit excuse she's going to throw at me.

I throw the covers off, my feet hitting the cold floor with a jolt. I get up, my body moving on autopilot, but my mind... It's stuck. Without even realizing, my gaze drifts toward the neighboring house, my eyes landing on Noah's window.

The curtain is still closed.

It hits harder than I want to admit.

It's not just a window—it's a symbol. A barrier between us.

It used to be open, just like mine, like we were part of each other's world without even trying. But now? Now it's closed, and it feels like I'm staring at the remnants of something that's been shut out.

I throw on whatever clothes I can grab, then snatch my backpack, trying to move quietly, like I'm sneaking out of a place that's no longer mine.

The silence in the house is suffocating. But it's better this way. I don't want to deal with my dad, not with the way things are, not with the awkwardness still hanging between us. Besides I don't know his routine anymore.

I shuffle to the cupboard, my stomach already growling. When I pull open the door, it's empty, just a few tins staring back at me as if mocking me.

With the hunger gnawing at me, I slam the cupboard shut, and move to the fridge, hoping for something, anything.

But it's just as empty. Mostly filled with beer. I guess some things never change. I close the fridge, turning away, ignoring the emptiness that's creeping into every part of my life, and walk to the front door.

After a nine-block walk, I finally reach the front of the school, my feet feel heavy, like they're dragging me toward something I don't want to face. I stop short of the entrance, my eyes automatically drawn to the parking lot. Cars are lined up, a mix of shiny and beat-up, but it's the people that hit me the hardest. Groups cluster together, laughing, chatting, like they all belong. Some head into the school, and I stand there, scanning for someone, anyone, that I might recognize.

There are a few faces I remember from before, but we were never close enough for me to strike up a conversation. I'm not part of this. I'm not part of anything here.

Standing on the edge of it all, I feel invisible, like I'm just a shadow of someone who used to exist.

I grab the straps on my shoulders, tugging them tighter, as if it'll somehow anchor me. I move forward, walking past groups of students who glance at me but say nothing. I'm just a passing blur to them. I push through the towering gates of the school, the noise and chaos of it all threatening to swallow me whole.

My first stop is the administration building. I need to find out if my mother bothered to contact them about my attendance. But deep down, I already know she hasn't. The idea of her thinking about me feels like a bad joke. Just last Friday, I was at my old school, surrounded by people I trusted, people I had real friendships with. I never had a boyfriend there, but I didn't need one. I had admirers. Not that any of them ever caught my eye—they never came close to Noah.

Now that I know the truth about how he really felt about me, maybe I should've let them in, instead of clinging to some twisted fantasy of what I thought Noah could be.

I climb the steps, and push through the door into the building.

The noise hits instantly, like a wall—students moving in groups, laughing, talking, completely at ease. Some linger by their lockers, chatting like they've got all the time in the world, like this is their kingdom and they know exactly where they belong.

I push forward, keeping my eyes on the floor, doing everything I can to avoid drawing attention. But as I move deeper into the hall, the noise shifts. Conversations taper off, one by one, like someone hit a mute button. Suddenly, all I can hear is the pounding of my own heartbeat, loud and relentless in the silence.

I glance up to find every eye in the building is on me.

I can feel their stares searing into my skin, like I've become some kind of exhibit. My breath catches in my throat, and for a moment all I want is to vanish. To turn around and walk right back out the door, leaving all of this shit behind.

But I don't. I keep moving, even though I feel like I'm about to crumble under the weight of all their gazes.

I scan the crowd, my eyes darting over familiar faces. But it's like I'm seeing everything through a new, twisted lens. Some people return my smile, while others glare at me, their eyes sharp, full of something I can't quite place. My presence here, my so-called popularity—it was never really mine. It was tied to Noah, to the connection we had, to the friendship everyone else wanted a piece of. Without that, I'm just... nothing.

I swallow the lump in my throat, trying to push past the sting of realization. I was just a shadow, a fleeting afterthought in a world where Noah was the sun, and everything orbited around him.

I force my eyes to focus ahead, even though every step feels like a weight dragging me under. And then I see her—Tia. But she's not the same.

She's standing there, surrounded by the girls from our old group, and they all seem... different now. Polished. Perfect. Their faces are caked in makeup, their hair flawless, like they just stepped off the set of some fashion shoot. Not at all like the Tia I remember—the girl who wore ripped jeans and oversized T-shirts, who didn't give a shit about looking like she had it all together.

I take a deep breath, and when she turns her head, I raise my hand, offering a smile.

As I watch her face, I catch it—a flicker of shock. Maybe she's surprised to see me, too. Maybe she didn't expect me to show up here again, standing in front of her like nothing's changed. But that's the problem. Everything's changed. I'm not the same. And the smile I was hoping for, the one that used to come so easily between us, never appears.

Instead, her eyes shift. Her attention flicks away from me, and I feel the sudden coldness. She's looking at something—or someone.

I follow her gaze, and my stomach sinks as I spot Noah with a group of guys. Reece Wilson and Jace Cooper—his old crew, the ones who were always by his side. They were inseparable back then, always up to something. And now?

Now, Noah stands there like he's fucking royalty. Leaning against the lockers, his hair falling effortlessly over his forehead, looking like he doesn't have a care in the world. He smiles, talking to Jace, while the others hang around, listening to him like he's the king of this place.

Tia moves toward them, her steps deliberate and calculated as she positions herself directly in front of Noah. It's a deliberate shift, one that pulls her into the center of the group with a sense of ownership.

I swallow hard as a cold; unsettling feeling settles in my chest.

I can't help but remember how Tia used to talk about Noah, how she'd swoon over him like he was some untouchable god. And now, watching her slip effortlessly into his orbit, something claws at me. Are they together now? Is that why Noah looked at me like that last night, like he didn't even recognize me anymore? The thought eats at me, my chest tightening with every second that passes.

I keep my eyes locked on them, hating myself for it, but I can't look away, even knowing it's only going to hurt. Tia says something, and Noah's head snaps up, his attention locking on me. Then Reece and Jace follow suit, their faces unreadable. But it doesn't matter. I'm not part of their world anymore. I'm just the girl standing on the sidelines, watching as everything slips away, piece by piece.

It feels like I'm drowning in this stupid, impossible situation. I want to scream. I want to demand answers, but all I can do is stand here, completely exposed, completely alone, as they all look at me like I don't belong anymore.

I force myself to keep walking, my feet dragging with every step, as the stares and whispers slice through the air. I can feel the weight of their glares burning into my skin, like daggers of judgment, but I push it all down. I have to keep moving forward, even when every part of me is screaming to turn around and run.

The piercing gazes of the girls from Tia's group make my skin crawl. They're scrutinizing me, dissecting every step I take, and I feel myself shrinking under the weight of their judgment, like I'm not even human to them anymore—just a target for their silent ridicule.

But it's Noah's look that hits hardest. Like he's watching me with something close to disgust. Like he's already decided what I am in his mind, and none of it is good. I feel exposed, completely vulnerable, like I'm a broken piece of glass in his hands—fragile and useless.

I quicken my pace, desperate to escape the weight of his stare, to seek refuge in the safety of the office. Anything to stop feeling so damn small.

Standing in the office foyer, I try to steady my breath, but the anxiety claws at me, a suffocating pressure that refuses to let go.

My eyes are drawn to the large photos on the wall. Two former students who have become music legends. Xander Williams and Ace Roberts. Their names are etched beneath their faces, bold and proud. They were just like me once, sitting in these same classrooms, walking these same hallways. And now, they're the biggest rockstars in the world, icons whose names are screamed by millions of adoring fans. Did they ever stand where I am now, facing this place with the same fear, the same uncertainty? Did they ever feel small here, lost in a crowd, wondering if they'd ever make it out? Or did it always come so easy for them, while I'm stuck here, struggling to even survive a single day?

A voice breaks through the haze of my scattered thoughts, and I turn sharply toward it. A young admin assistant stands there, her face a picture of calm composure. Her smile is polite, distant, and I can't shake the feeling that I'm intruding.

"Can I help you?" she asks, her voice a little too sweet, like she's done this a thousand times.

I swallow, my throat tightening. "Yeah, um... I need to update my information. I just transferred back here," I mutter.

"Of course," she replies, her smile unwavering, and I can't stand how effortlessly she falls into that role—like she's never had a second of uncertainty, never felt out of place. She gestures toward the seat. "I just need a few details from you."

I just have to make it through this year—get through it, and then I'm free. School will be over. If Noah and Tia think I'm going to back down, that I'll just let them walk all over me, they're both fucking wrong.

I'm stronger than this. I've been through worse and made it out. They might have gotten to me this morning, but that was just the beginning. I'm not some easy target for them to tear apart.

With my schedule clenched in my hand, I step into the classroom, each breath controlled, the familiar knot of tension already settling in my chest. I approach the teacher, a middle-aged man who glances at me for a moment before looking down at the note in my hand.

"Take a seat," he says, after handing him my late note.

My gaze sweeps the room, my mind already bracing for what's coming. In the back, Noah sits with Reece and Jace, the trio looking effortlessly cool and too damn hot. Tia's in the middle, a queen reigning over a clique of girls. Their eyes flicker over me for a brief moment before shifting away, but I can feel the weight of their judgment, the silent sneers that still linger.

I take a deep breath. I'm not here to back down. So, I stride toward the only empty seat in the room, chin held high, with no hesitation in my step.

As I pass Tia, the all-too-familiar sound of laughter rings out—sharp and mocking. My foot catches on something, and before I can react, I'm crashing to the floor, the room erupting in cruel, echoing laughter.

I don't flinch. I don't wince.

I catch a glimpse of Tia's smirk, her foot still casually stretched out in my path, her eyes gleaming with that same malicious intent. But I'm done playing her game. I push myself up off the ground, glaring at her.

If she wants a fight? I'll give her one.

I dust myself off, straightening, not a trace of weakness in my posture. I don't need anyone's help. I don't need their approval. And I sure as hell don't need to fall in line.

"I'm not going anywhere. So back the fuck off," I mutter under my breath, watching her face falter for a split second.

"I have no idea what you're talking about," she says, her voice laced with fake innocence, her eyes darting to her little entourage as if she's clueless. The words roll off her tongue so smoothly, like she's rehearsed them a thousand times, but I see right through it.

"What are you talking about?" she repeats, her tone thick with mock confusion, before muttering a barely audible "bitch" under her breath—just loud enough for her loyal little crew of fake bitches to hear. And that's all it takes to fuel their judgmental whispers.

I want to fire back, to rip her apart with the truth, but the weight of their eyes on me, the mocking laughter from her posse, makes it impossible to shake the sting of humiliation. It feels like the walls are closing in, the room shrinking by the seconds. I'm suffocating in their attention as if they are waiting for me to break.

I bite down on my tongue, fighting the urge to lash out.

I lift my eyes, searching for a place to sit, and there it is—Noah's smirk. It's not just a smile. It's a threat, a warning, like he's daring me to challenge the unspoken rules of his little kingdom.

I scan the room, forcing myself to ignore the weight of his gaze, and that's when I see her. A girl with bright red hair, sitting by the only empty chair. Her green eyes meet mine, cutting through the noise. There's something in her stare—a quiet defiance, soft but unyielding, like she can see straight through all their bullshit.

Her lips curl into a small, knowing smile, and with the slightest tilt of her head, she gestures to the seat beside her. No hesitation, no fear—like she couldn't care less about Noah, Tia, or their bullshit games.

As I approach, the teacher's voice drones on about politics—or some other boring shit that's supposed to be important— but it's just noise, like everything else in this room. I slide into the seat next to her, my heart still pounding from the shit that just went down.

"Thanks," I murmur, keeping my voice low as I take a moment to pull myself together. I need a second to breathe, to reset. The last thing I want is for her to notice how shaken I am, how much Tia's cruel stunt and Noah's twisted smirk are still tearing at me.

I sneak a quick glance at her, my gaze lingering just a moment too long. Freckles dust her nose, subtle and perfect, like they were painted there to enhance her effortless beauty. Her red hair cascades in loose waves, catching the overhead light as it spills down her back. And her eyes—bright, steady, unshakable—make it seem like nothing in the world could rattle her.

It's a stark contrast to Tia, who slathers on layers of makeup like armor, acting like that's what makes her sexy. But this girl? There's nothing fake about her. No facade. Just raw, effortless beauty that's impossible to look past. And for the first time all day, I feel like maybe I don't have to fake it either.

"You're welcome," she mutters, her voice soft, just loud enough for me to hear while the teacher keeps rambling. She leans in, her words sharper now. "But seriously... You should probably stay the hell away from them. Tia's a total bitch." She lets the words hang in the air for a moment, letting them land, before adding with a slight smirk, "I'm Sam, by the way."

I remember Sam now. We've never really crossed paths before—different crowds and all that—but fuck, I've always admired her hair.

"Yeah, Samantha Carter," I say smoothly, watching as a flicker of surprise crosses her face. She clearly wasn't expecting me to know her name.

"I used to go here, about a year and a half ago," I add, letting the words settle between us. "I'm Aubrey. Aubrey Baxter."

Recognition flashes in her eyes, and she nods slowly. "Ah, yeah, I do remember you now," she says, her voice softer, like she's sifting through old memories. Then her brows knit together, a flicker of confusion crossing her face. "Didn't you used to hang out with Tia and Noah back then?" She pauses, and something seems to click. "Wait—wasn't Noah your boyfriend or something?"

I shift uncomfortably in my seat, that question hitting way too close to home. Fuck, that name, and fuck those memories.

"Yeah, we were," I admit, the words tasting like shit in my mouth. "But that was a long time ago. Things change." The words sting more than I expected, but it's the truth. He's not mine anymore. And he never will be.

Sam gives me a small, sad smile, the kind that's more heartbreaking than reassuring, before she turns her attention back to the teacher. I try to follow her lead, but the weight of Tia's constant, pointed glares presses on me, like they're searing into my skin. Her and her clique—whispering, laughing, plotting. It's exhausting, this game she's playing. I can't for the life of me figure out why she's so hell-bent on tearing me down.

If we're not friends anymore, then fine—cut me out. I don't need her. But instead of moving on, she's dragging me through this shitstorm, like she needs to prove something. Maybe she thinks I came back for Noah.

Doesn't she see how much he hates me? How his stare is colder than a slap every time it hits me? If she's got him now, good for her. She won. But I'll have to live with it, no matter how much it hurts to see them together. So why the hell does she still feel the need to make me her personal punching bag?

Every glance Tia throws my way feels like a spark, daring me to light the fire she's just waiting to stoke. She wants me to react, to slip up and give her the excuse she's been craving. The tension tightens around me like barbed wire, digging in deeper with every snicker and whisper that drips from her lips.

Beside me, Sam leans in. "Just ignore the bitch," she murmurs. A faint smile tugs at her lips, one that screams fuck Tia and her crew of bitches.

I smile. Sam seems like the kind of girl who doesn't take shit from anyone, who stands her ground without a second thought. There's something about her—calm, unbothered, like nothing and no one can shake her.

When the bell finally rings, I shove my stuff into my bag. Tia and her posse of fake-ass disciples spill out of the room, all of them practically stumbling over each other to hang on to every meaningless word she spits.

I roll my shoulders, pushing the tension out, and exhale sharply, relief flooding through me now that she's finally gone.

Sam tosses her pack over her shoulder. "If you want, you can hang with me and a few of the other girls. We get how hard it is to deal with Tia. We've all seen how she taunts Lola, a girl from our group. It's like Tia gets off on tearing her down."

"Thanks, I'd really appreciate that," I say, standing up, but my mind's racing, trying to figure out who the hell Sam's talking about.

Sam doesn't hesitate. "You won't remember Lola. She wasn't here when you were at the school. She showed up about six months ago." As we exit the classroom, she casts a glance my way. "It was her first day, and Tia started on her for no reason. Been at her every day since. Like she has some sick need to break her down."

I can't help but wonder what the hell turned Tia into such a bitch. What did she do—what ruthless shit did she pull to claw her way to the top and crown herself queen bee of this goddamn school? I never saw that side of her when we were friends. Back then, she didn't have that venom in her. Now it's like she's drowning in it.

As I push through the crowded hallways, I can feel Tia before I see her—like a storm, ready to tear me apart. Without warning, she's next to me, yanking hard on the strap of my backpack. The sudden pull knocks the bag off my shoulder, and it crashes to the floor. She kicks it forward, then grabs the bottom, flipping it over so everything spills out through the damn zipper I forgot to close. Pens, notebooks, and random school crap fly everywhere—but it's the personal stuff that makes my stomach drop.

I watch as tampons roll across the floor—just fucking perfect. But it's the roll of condoms that really hits. The ones Marjorie, my friend from my old school, shoved into my bag last Friday, laughing her ass off, telling me I needed to get laid since I didn't give a shit about any of the guys hitting on me. My face turns bright red with embarrassment, and I feel the weight of their stares—every last one of them.

My heart pounds in my chest, my hands trembling as I crouch down, frantically trying to shove everything back into my bag. I can hear the whispers, the footsteps closing in, too damn curious as they gather around to watch this trainwreck unfold. I hate how powerless I am right now.

As I reach for the nearest tampon, Tia's foot connects with it first, sending it skidding across the floor until it crashes into someone's shoe.

My eyes snap up, and I freeze when I see it's Jace's shoe. If he's here, then Noah can't be far behind. And sure enough, there he is, a smirk tugging at the corner of his lips, his eyes practically gleaming as he watches Tia's little show. He's loving this, like my humiliation is his entertainment. Reece stands beside him, arms crossed, his face blank—like he's too good to even care. And, of course, the rest of the school is gathered around, drawn in like moths to a flame.

Before I can even reach for the roll of condoms, Tia snatches them up like she's found her holy grail. She holds them out for everyone to see, her voice thick with sarcasm.

"Looks like someone's got big plans," she sneers, loud enough for the entire hallway to hear.

My face burns with a mix of fury and shame, but the worst part is the way Noah watches me, his eyes flickering with something dark, as if he's documenting every moment of my downfall. I want to scream, to say something—anything—but all I can do is stay here on the ground, helpless, as Tia pushes me further into the flames.

"Looks like she's easy, guys," Tia sneers, her voice dripping with smug satisfaction as her words sink into the crowd.

The smirk on her lips is infuriating. Her words cut deep, their sting fueling the rage in my veins, especially since the only time I've ever had sex was with Noah. To paint me as some easy slut isn't just unfair—it's downright insulting. But the worst part? Tia knows exactly what she's doing. She's out for blood.

Her laughter rings through the air, bouncing off the walls like a twisted melody. The others follow suit, and I can feel every pair of eyes on me—some amused, others just waiting for me to crack. But I won't give her the satisfaction of seeing me break. Not today.

I take a deep breath, the sting of humiliation still clawing at my insides, but I refuse to let her win.

I rise to my feet, my legs trembling, but my resolve steadier than ever. I square my shoulders and lock eyes with her. She wants to play this game? Fine. We'll play. If she thinks she can tear me down, she's going to have to do it face-to-face—not hiding behind her petty insults and the crowd of assholes she has gathered around her.

"Line up, boys. Seems like she's down for it," Tia sneers, her smirk wide and cruel, like she thinks she's won.

Every muscle in my body tightens with rage, and I march toward her, not caring about the crowd watching. Her eyes flick to the group, searching for their approval, but I won't give her that satisfaction. Before she can even react, I reach out and snatch the condoms from her hands.

"You don't know fucking shit, bitch," I snap, stepping right into her space, the words cutting through the air like a blade.

Her eyes widen for a split second, surprise flashing across her face. She wasn't expecting this. She wasn't expecting me to stand up to her. But that hesitation fades in an instant, and she steps back, quickly hiding her shock behind the same smug attitude she always wears like armor.

"Looks like we've got a girl who's ready for all those Fuck Boys," she mocks, her gaze never leaving mine, as if she's daring me to react.

I stand there, refusing to look away, letting the tension between us hang heavy in the air. She doesn't scare me. And if she thinks this is over, she's got another thing coming.

"Enough," a deep, resonant voice cuts through the chaos, and even before I turn, I know it's Noah. His tone is commanding, sharp, like a whip cracking through the air. Within a heartbeat, the laughter and whispers vanish, and the entire hallway falls silent. The shift is immediate. The king has spoken.

Tia spins on her heels, fury flashing in her eyes as she glares at him. She's pissed, and I can see why—he's just ruined her little show, and she hates it. Noah's eyes shift to me next, and there's no mistaking the look he gives me. It's a glare, cold as ice, full of judgment. The kind that makes my stomach knot, but there's something else there too—something dark... and disappointed.

He turns away, that jaw of his clenched tight, like he's trying to swallow whatever the hell he's feeling.

In an instant, the crowd disperses, as if Noah's spoken and it's time to go, Reece and Jace following like loyal shadows. But I stay rooted to the spot. My heart pounds in my chest, the silence heavy around me. Tia may have been the one trying to break me, but Noah? His presence—his cold indifference—cuts deeper than anything.

I try to swallow, the lump in my throat making it almost impossible to breathe as I stand there, feeling like I'm naked in front of everyone. The boy who once meant everything to me—who used to look at me like I was his world—is gone. In his place stands a stranger, his eyes now filled with bitterness and hate, as if there's nothing left of the person I once knew. The warmth, the love, all of it has been replaced with this cold, razor-sharp animosity that cuts through me, chilling me to my core.

And it hurts as I watch him move down the hall.

It's a reminder that we'll never go back to what we had. There's no chance of us being friends again, no way to undo what's been done. I turn my face back to Tia when she speaks.

"He's not yours anymore, bitch," she sneers, her voice dripping with smug satisfaction, a cruel smirk playing at the edges of her lips. "Might as well face it—he'll fuck anyone but you." She steps closer, and I can feel the venom in her words, her eyes gleaming with the victory she believes she's claimed. "He fucked me three days ago, and you have no idea what you're missing out on."

The words hit, but it's the way she says them—so casual—that twists the knife deeper. She pauses, her smile widening, darkening. It's as if she knows exactly how to break me, how to remind me of everything I can't have.

And I'm right there. Ready to punch that smug look right off her face.

But then she drops the bomb. "The way he went down on me... fuck, it blew my mind."

The sting of her words cuts through everything, and I feel the anger surge, hot and suffocating. The thought of Noah, of him touching her, burns like acid in my chest. That's the reality now, and it hurts more than I'm willing to admit.

Suddenly, Sam's hand grabs my arm, holding me back with enough force to stop me from launching at Tia and wiping that smug look off her face. Her new nose, courtesy of daddy's wallet, wouldn't stand a chance if I got my hands on it.

Tia catches sight of Sam, and her gaze shifts, the same nasty gleam in her eyes. "Oh, look, another slut who thinks she has a shot with Reece," she sneers, her voice dripping with disgust. "He fucked Simone just yesterday. He's done with you. Told us all about your little hook-up."

I toss a quick glance at Sam, and for the first time, I see a flicker of hesitation in her eyes. There's something there—something she doesn't want me to see—but it's enough to make me pause.

I don't press it. Whatever the hell has gone down between her and Reece, it's clear it's messing with her. And I'm not about to dig into that kind of pain. Not now. Not when it feels like I'm barely holding it together myself.

I step closer to Tia, getting right in her face until she's forced to take a step back. "Stay the fuck away from me," I snarl, every word sharp with fury.

She laughs—and then her lips twist into a vicious sneer. "You forget who the fuck you're talking to. You're nothing in this school anymore, and every goddamn day, I'll make you regret coming back. Mark my words, bitch."

With that, she spins on her heels and struts her skank ass back to her pack of bitches. Their smirks are as fake as fuck, their overdone makeup trying too hard. They watch me like I'm some ant under a microscope, but I'm done feeling small. They all shift their gaze to Tia like she's their queen. It's pathetic. The crowd parts, and she glides through them, her little minions trailing behind her.

I drop to my knees, shoving everything I can back into my bag. Sam kneels beside me, her hands moving quickly to collect the mess that Tia's made of my things. This isn't over—not by a long shot. If that bitch wants to play, then fucking game on.

CHAPTER 4

NOAH

I've always known Tia was a bitch. Growing up, I saw how she treated anyone she thought was beneath her. She had this way of looking down on people like they were nothing more than tools to boost her own fucked-up ego. Sure, we fucked once—no big deal—but it meant nothing. For me, it was just a way to kill time, to scratch an itch. But for her? She thought it was something more. The next day, she flooded my phone with texts.

I wasn't stupid enough to fall for that shit. I kept my distance after that, made sure she knew that I don't do clingy. But it never stopped her. She's the type of girl who thinks a quick fuck means you want to exchange vows with her. Fuck that.

Since Aubrey tore my heart apart and left it to wither, I stick to casual hook-ups. It's easier that way—no strings, no emotional baggage, no worrying about anyone's feelings. Just get in, get off, and get out. Simple. After that shitshow with Tia, I learned my lesson. Now, I make it crystal clear to every girl who wants to hook up: it's just that—a hook up—nothing more. No dates, no feelings, no fucking strings attached. I don't have time for that. My heart's been trashed once, I'm not doing that shit again.

I'm honestly shocked at how ruthless Tia's being with Aubrey. They used to be friends—or at least, I thought they were. But Tia doesn't know a damn thing about Aubrey's life outside the parties and the bullshit at school. She never did. Aubrey kept all that hidden, and the only person who ever got a glimpse of the mess inside her was me. I heard it all—the screaming matches between her parents, the shattered glass, the way they tore each other apart every day. But no one else knew. She trusted me with that pain. I was the only one she let into that fucked-up world of hers.

But now? Now it's like Tia's made it her personal mission to tear into Aubrey, to break her down like she's some kind of target. Tia's jealous. I know it. She had a huge thing for me back when I was with Aubrey, and she still does. What else could explain why she's so fixated on making sure Aubrey's life is a living hell, tearing her down every chance she gets? Jealous, spiteful bitch.

Jace, Reece, and I slide into our usual spot in the back of the lunchroom, the one where we can see everything without anyone noticing us. It's the perfect vantage point—keeps the bullshit at arm's length. Tia and her crew walk in, and she smiles at me. It's wide, fake as hell, and those eyes... They practically gleam with interest. Like she thinks I'm gonna fall for that crap. Hell no. Not in a million fucking years.

She plops herself down at the table opposite me, her little followers trailing behind, hanging on to her every word like they're starving dogs waiting for scraps. They'd kill for her approval—just a glance, a fucking crumb. And then there's Nicole, practically buzzing for attention, ready to spread her legs for anyone who'll toss her a second of validation. She slides into the seat next to Tia, acting like they're the untouchable queen bees of the universe.

"I can't believe that bitch tried to stand up to me," Tia sneers, her eyes darting around the table, looking for someone to back her up.

Approval—she needs it, always. The words hang in the air like they're the only thing that keeps her going. My fingers itch to throw something, but I settle for grinding my teeth. There are bigger problems in the world than her fucking petty, childish vendettas.

"Did you see the condoms? I bet she opens her legs for anyone," she adds with a pointed smirk, shooting a look at Nicole, who bobs her head in agreement like a damn puppet.

I zone out the second Aubrey steps into the lunchroom, her backpack hanging carelessly over one shoulder like she gives less of a shit about who is watching her. But I'm watching. My eyes lock on her, narrowing as she walks beside Sam, her laughter carrying across the room like a dare. It's impossible not to take her in—those waves of long, black hair cascading down her back, her tight, fuckable body demanding every ounce of attention in the room.

My tongue darts out to wet my bottom lip as my thoughts spiral into places they probably shouldn't.

The way those black fishnet stockings cling to her legs, the curve of that mini skirt riding high enough to tease but not quite enough to satisfy—fuck. It's the vibe she throws off, that bad-girl, untouchable attitude that makes my blood heat and my cock stir to life. She's dangerous in all the right ways, and it only makes me crave her more.

Aubrey doesn't drape herself in designer labels like the rest of the girls, desperate to avoid being ripped apart by Tia's bullshit. No, she's here in her worn-out top that slips just enough off her shoulder to drive me fucking crazy. And those combat boots—scuffed, battered, the same brand she's been wearing since she was thirteen.

Tia used to sneer at them, mocking her for not following the crowd, but fuck that. Those boots are a statement, just like she is.

Aubrey doesn't give a fuck about blending in. She doesn't waste her time pretending to be something she's not, doesn't drown in the bullshit that drips off everyone else. She's raw, unpolished, and unapologetically herself. And God, it's fucking hot.

"You've tapped that, right?" Jace asks, his voice low but laced with his usual smugness.

My jaw clenches as I snap my head toward him, catching the way his eyes linger on Aubrey. In an instant, a wave of protectiveness hits me, hot and unrelenting. My fists tighten at my sides, itching to silence him with a single punch to the throat. I know Jace too well—his games, his conquests—and there's no way I'm letting him anywhere near her.

Yeah, Aubrey might drive me insane, always pushing my buttons and making me grind my teeth, but the thought of him sinking his claws—or worse, his cock—into her? Fuck that.

Tia's grating voice, like nails on a chalkboard, falters mid-sentence; her attention shifting as she follows our line of sight. When her eyes land on Aubrey, they narrow, her lips twisting in that familiar way that reeks of venom.

"Yeah," I say, trying to sound casual, but the words taste like shit in my mouth. I barely recognize her anymore. The image of those condoms spilling out of Aubrey's bag earlier keeps looping in my head, and the thought of other guys touching her makes my stomach churn.

The Aubrey I knew wasn't like that—when we lost our virginity to each other, it was real. It meant something. But now? Now I can't stop picturing her with every asshole who crosses her path, and it makes me want to punch something.

Tia spins around, her smirk sharp and dripping with malice. "I'd say get in line if you wanna fuck her, Jace," she sneers. "Looks like she puts out. What a slut." She glances around for validation, like her words are gospel, and her little pack of starving bitches nod along, feeding off her toxic cruelty.

"Cut the fucking shit, Tia," I snap, my voice sharp and raw with frustration. "I'm done listening to your bullshit day in and day out."

Tia's silence hits like a slap, her eyes narrowing into sharp, deadly daggers aimed right at me. Her pride's bruised, but I don't care—not one bit. She glares at me like I'm the one in the wrong, but I'll deal with her shit later. Right now, my focus shifts to Aubrey as she slides into a seat with Sam and the other girls. When she looks up and our gazes lock, it's like the ground tilts beneath me, knocking the air from my lungs.

Memories flood in, sharp and relentless. The sound of our laughter, the way we'd pass notes between classes like the rest of the world didn't exist. The stolen moments. The kisses that felt like they meant every-thing. All the shit we shared, all the shit left unfinished. But right now, I can't afford to care.

Aubrey quickly looks away, diving into a conversation like nothing happened, but I can't tear my gaze off her. And I swear to God, she knows it. Every so often, she sneaks a glance my way, like she's trying to act oblivious, but I catch it—the way her eyes linger just a second too long.

Lucas Simpson saunters over to her table, and a surge of irritation flares through me. The second Aubrey notices him and flashes that smile, I can feel my blood start to boil. But what pushes me over the edge is when I catch him blatantly checking out her tits, not even trying to hide it.

No fucking way in hell is he—or anyone else on the football team—getting anywhere near her. I need to make that crystal clear: Aubrey is off-limits.

If Lucas or any of his buddies think they have a shot, they're about to learn the hard way just how wrong they are.

"Aubrey's off-limits," I growl at Jace and Reece, my voice low and dangerous. "Make sure everyone knows."

Jace raises an eyebrow, a smirk playing on his lips. "She's that fucking good, huh?" he mocks, then adds, "I knew that mouth could suck cock."

Before I can even stop myself, I'm on him, every ounce of anger and possessiveness in my voice. "You fucking talk about her like that again, and I will end you." I lock eyes with him, and I know he gets it. He sees the rage burning in mine—the kind of rage that doesn't give a damn about consequences.

I turn my head back towards Aubrey, and the second I spot Lucas Simpson still hanging around, I snap. I shove myself up from my seat, and the conversation around the table dies instantly. All eyes are on me, waiting, watching to see what the hell I'm about to do. Jace and Reece follow without a word.

My fists clench, the rage building as I watch Lucas lean in to talk to Aubrey, his head dipping way too close. I know exactly what he's doing—getting a good look at her tits. I see it the moment his eyes drop to her chest. But what really gets to me is when Aubrey leans back slightly, clearly uncomfortable with him crowding her space.

The sight of her leaning back calms me more than it should—knowing she can keep a guy like him at a distance. But even still, I can't shake the image of those condoms in her bag. It fucks with my head. I refuse to believe she's turned into some easy slut just because of that.

As we get closer, heads start to turn, conversations stumble to a halt, and whispers trail behind us.

The curiosity hangs thick in the air, like they're all waiting to see what's going to happen.

But Lucas, that oblivious dickhead, is still crouched over, chatting up Aubrey like he's the only one in the world who matters. The sight of him blatantly checking her out pisses me off, and what makes it worse is that he's too clueless to realize I'm coming for him. He doesn't even catch on when Aubrey glances my way, her eyes flashing like she knows exactly what's about to go down.

Aubrey squirms in her seat, her eyes flicking nervously, and I fucking love it. I can see her trying to stay composed, but I've already thrown her off balance, and I'm not about to let her find her footing again.

I don't waste a second. Grabbing Lucas by the collar, I yank him toward me, hearing the surprised grunt rumble in his chest. His wide eyes meet mine, pure fucking shock written all over his face. Good. He should be surprised.

"Hey, Red," Reece's voice calls out, that stupid nickname rolling off his tongue like it means something. He's always had a thing for Sam—always calling her that dumb name. The fucker's been obsessed with her for as long as I can remember.

I make sure my grip on Lucas tightens, forcing him to stumble with every step I take. I can't let him near Aubrey, not now, not ever. And it's not just him. Any other asshole who thinks they have a shot with her better think again. I'll make sure they know exactly where they stand—away from her, far the fuck away.

I drag his ass toward the large double doors that lead to the field outside, my grip tightening as I shove him through the doors.

"What the fuck did I do, Noah?" Lucas asks, his voice tight, but I can hear the panic creeping in.

I don't give a shit about the curious eyes peeking through the windows. Let them watch. They're all just waiting for something to blow up, and I'm more than happy to deliver.

"Stay the fuck away from her," I growl, my words low and dangerous, making sure he gets the message loud and clear.

"I was just saying hi," he mutters, like he's trying to play the innocent little asshole, but I know him better than that.

"Yeah, right," I snap, my teeth gritted. "I saw you fucking eyeing her tits." I make sure to throw the accusation in his face, watching his eyes flicker with guilt, his posture tightening up.

He swallows hard, looking down at his feet like he's trying to avoid facing the truth. Pathetic.

I step forward, shoulders squared, my gaze hard as steel. "You better tell every other prick on that football team to stay the fuck away from Aubrey Baxter. Got it?" My voice is low, controlled, like a threat barely held back.

He looks up, his eyes wide, nodding like his life depends on it. "Got it."

"Now get the hell out of here and don't come near her again, Asshole." I watch him scramble back into the lunchroom; no doubt eager to avoid my wrath.

I can't go back in there—not with Tia's bullshit hanging in the air, weighing me down.

"Hey, you guys wanna ditch this place, head over to Jace's trailer, and talk some bullshit while we smoke a joint?"

Aubrey being back in my orbit has me completely fucked up, and I need to get the hell out of here before anyone picks up on it. My chest is tight, like I'm seconds away from falling apart, and I can't let her see that—can't let anyone see that. Not now. Not ever.

"Fuck yeah," Reece says, with a smirk. "I've only got Chemistry and English left anyway. Fuck it."

Jace nods, tapping his shirt pocket. "Joint's ready to go."

We cut through the lunchroom, the buzz of voices fading into a low hum as we navigate the maze of tables to grab our backpacks. My eyes lock onto Lucas, sitting with his little football crew, all smug grins and that overpowering cheap cologne. He meets my gaze for half a second before looking away, his jaw clenching like he's been caught red-handed. His teammates notice too, their laughter cutting off mid-sentence. Good. Let them squirm. The last thing I need is those assholes thinking they're untouchable.

Outside, we get into my car, and I floor it out of the school parking lot. My knuckles throb as I grip the steering wheel, trying to force Aubrey out of my head. But she clings, like a ghost I can't shake, the kind that makes it hard to breathe, hard to focus on anything else.

We pull up to Jace's trailer, hidden behind his aunt's house. The trailer is falling apart—dented siding, a window patched with duct tape, and the yard's overrun with weeds. It's not a home, just a constant reminder that Jace doesn't belong anywhere. His aunt keeps him locked away back here, out of sight, like he's some stain she doesn't want to taint her perfect suburban life, her glossy, picture-perfect kids. It's as if he's the dirt on her immaculate floor, a reminder of something ugly she'd rather pretend doesn't exist. Her own blood, and she treats him like shit.

"She still giving you shit?" Reece asks, his voice low as he watches Jace unlock the door.

Jace shrugs, like it's nothing. "Every damn day. Ain't like I'm new to it." He steps inside, kicking some shit out of the way to make space.

I collapse onto the beat-up couch, the springs protesting under me. Jace pulls out the joint, lights it, and takes a long drag like it's the only thing keeping him from losing his shit. He passes it to me, and I inhale, feeling the smoke burning the way down my throat. The calm hits hard, like a veil over everything, and for a moment, Aubrey's image fades, her face not clawing its way into my brain like it always does.

"So, Aubrey," Reece says, slumping into the chair across from me, his eyes gleaming like he knows exactly what he's doing. He takes a slow drag from the joint, savoring it, and then blows the smoke in my direction.

I glare at him, my jaw clenched so tight it's like it might snap, every muscle in my body screaming to throw something—him, my damn fist, anything. Without thinking, I snatch the joint from his hand, my fingers rough, too forceful, as I rip it away from him. I take a hit, a deep, burning drag, my lungs on fire, throat raw, like it's the only thing keeping me from snapping.

"We're not fucking talking about her," I growl, my voice low but cutting.

Reece doesn't back off, his smirk curling like he knows exactly what he's doing. "Come on, man. You don't want anyone fucking her. So that means you're keeping her for yourself."

I feel the weight of his words slam into me, twisting like a knife. I hate that he's right—hate that I can't stop thinking about her, that I care more than I want to. But I won't let him see it.

"I'm not interested in that bitch," I snap, forcing the truth back down, the lie I keep telling myself. I shove the joint back to Jace, praying they don't see through the cracks in my armor.

But they will.

They always do.

Reece's phone pings, and he pulls it out like he's been expecting it. His eyes scan the screen, a smirk slowly spreading across his face. He shoves the phone back into his pocket, standing up like he's had enough.

"Guess I'm outta here," he mutters, his voice oozing with that same smug arrogance. "Got a chick, Nicole. She wants to meet up and have a good time." He's already halfway out the door, not even bothering to look back. "Later," he tosses over his shoulder.

The door slams behind him, and a twisted sense of relief settles deep in my chest. I'm glad he's gone. Glad I don't have to deal with any of his fucked-up questions anymore. Glad I don't have to pretend his words don't sting.

Jace leans forward, passing me the joint like it's second nature. "I was talking to my cousin the other day," he mutters, his voice distant, like his mind's somewhere else. "He was out in the driveway, just riding his bike, you know? Just being a kid." He takes a long drag, the smoke swirling around him.

I stay quiet, waiting for him to finish, but I can feel the weight of whatever's coming next. He doesn't talk about his aunt. Never.

"Fuck, man. She fucking lost it. Like, lost her goddamn mind. She was screaming at him, yelling for him to get inside, telling him to never talk to me again," his voice cracks, but he doesn't stop. "He's just a kid, you know? Then she freaked out on me." He spits the words out like they're burning him. "I fucking hate it here," he continues, his face twisted in something close to rage. "Fucking hate that cunt of a mother for leaving me with her."

I can see it—the rawness in his eyes, the anger that's been building up for God knows how long. His jaw tightens, his hand running over his face like he's trying to scrub away the memory, but it's there. Sticking to him, sinking into his skin, heavier than anything he can shake off. I lean forward passing Jace the joint.

He lifts it to his lips, taking another hit, but this time, it's like he's doing it more out of habit than anything else, like he's trying to cover the cracks he doesn't want to show.

I watch him, the guy who's usually so sure of himself, so fucking untouchable, slowly cracking in front of me.

I can feel the weight of the moment pressing down, like if I don't say something—anything—I might choke on the silence. I've never been the talker between us, but right now, my throat's tight, and I can't stand it anymore. I need to break the tension before it swallows me whole.

"You know," I begin, my voice steady but low, "it's not all on you. It's like you're trapped in the middle of this fucked-up mess, thinking you're the one who has to fix everything. But that shit with your aunt? That's on her, not you."

"Yeah, I know," Jace mutters, his voice low and rough, running a hand through his hair. His face twists into that grimace I recognize too well. "I just can't stand it." His shoulders slump, the weight of everything pressing down on him, making him seem smaller, weaker than he ever lets anyone see. But I see it.

It's not just the aunt—it's everything, piling up, drowning him, and I can see it in the way he's holding himself, like he's one step from breaking.

I don't say anything. I'm not stupid enough to try and fix it. Instead, I lean back, staring out the window, letting him know he's not alone. I'm here, and that's enough.

Time drags on, but neither of us moves.

"Shit, I gotta go," he says, like he's just snapped out of whatever dark space he was in.

He's got to head to the burger joint, the one he works at, just to scrape together enough cash for food. His aunt couldn't care less if he eats, if he's starving, or if he's even alive. Doesn't care if he withers away or ends up dead on the side of the road.

It's moments like this that make me appreciate my dad. He's never made me feel like I'm just some inconvenience to be tossed aside. He's always there. He gives a shit. I'm lucky to have him, even if I take it for granted sometimes—because even though my mom walked out on me like I was nothing, at least I've got someone who actually gives a shit. Jace doesn't have that.

After I drop Jace off at the burger joint, I head back home.

As I pull into the driveway, old habits kick in, pulling at me, telling me not to glance at the house next door. The one I can't seem to ignore. But I force myself to keep my eyes straight, focusing on my front door instead. I need to get inside before I lose my edge and end up staring at her window again, like I've done too many times before.

Relief sets in when I step into the house, but something feels off. The air's wrong. There's no scent of my dad's cooking, no familiar comfort that usually tells me everything's fine.

I freeze, something in my gut twisting. This isn't right. I don't know what the hell's happening, but the hairs on the back of my neck stand up, telling me something's broken, something's changed. And it feels like it's all crashing down around me.

"Dad!" The word bursts from my mouth as I rush into the kitchen, a tight knot of worry clawing at my insides. Stepping into the room, my eyes lock onto him—sitting there, swallowed by shadows. For a second, my heart stops. I don't know if it's relief or panic, but the worry in my stomach eases, just enough to make me feel like I might breathe again. But something's off. That gnawing unease lingers, refusing to let go.

The empty beer bottle on the table speaks for itself. The man I know doesn't drink like this. My stomach churns, but I force it down. I cross the room and sit on the opposite end of the couch, my eyes fixed on him. His face—hell, his whole fucking presence—feels like it belongs to someone else. His eyes don't even move in my direction. Did he hear me at all? This isn't the dad I know, the one who makes me laugh, the one who yells at the TV during a football game. That guy is gone.

"Dad," I repeat, a shaky whisper barely audible, the tremor in my voice sending shivers down my spine. The second it leaves my mouth; I see him snap out of whatever fog he's been in. Noticing the empty beer bottle on the table, he reaches for it and stands up.

"Hey, son," he says, forcing a smile that doesn't quite reach his eyes. His voice cracks, trying too hard to sound casual, but it's all fake, and I can feel it. "How about we grab takeout for dinner?" he suggests, acting like it'll make everything better, like changing the subject will fix this. But the way he tries to play it cool only makes it worse, tightening the tension between us, like he's pretending nothing's wrong when everything seems like it's falling apart.

This awkward, desperate attempt to smooth over whatever just happened. It's not working. Not by a long shot.

"What're you hungry for?" he asks, moving to the drawer and pulling out the takeout menus like it's just another damn night.

"What's up, Dad?" I press, getting up from the couch and stepping over to the kitchen counter, closing the space between us.

He freezes, breath heavy, the silence between us suffocating. I can see the weight of whatever's on his mind, but he won't say it.

After what feels like forever, he looks at me, forcing another fake ass smile.

"So, what're we having tonight? Pizza, pasta—" he starts, but I cut him off.

"Dad, talk to me," I beg, my voice shaky, and I hate it. But I can't stop it.

He meets my gaze, and I see the storm brewing behind his eyes, like he's fighting with something dark and heavy. I don't look away. I can't. My eyes are begging for the truth, urging him to break down whatever damn wall's keeping him silent. It's not like him to drink in the afternoon—hell, that's usually reserved for special occasions, like football games or celebrations. He's struggling, swallowing hard like the words are too much to bear.

After what feels like forever, he finally spits it out.

"Your mother came by today."

The instant he says it, something inside me hardens. My walls slam up, thick and impenetrable. I bury everything behind the silence, shutting it all down.

For years, her absence has been a silent, bleeding wound, a constant reminder of the love she promised but never bothered to deliver. No birthday cards, no calls—just an endless, suffocating void where a mother should've been. The thought of her showing up now seems impossible. I stand there, frozen, as his words hang in the air, heavy and thick, like they're trying to drag me down into the depths.

"She wants to see you," he says.

"No," I snap, my voice ice-cold as I take a step back, needing space between us. "Absolutely fucking not. She couldn't give a shit about me when I needed her, but now she wants to waltz back into my life like nothing happened. Fuck that."

I glare at my father, my fists clenched tight at my sides. Why the hell is he even entertaining this bullshit? The resentment I've carried for years flares up, turning everything cold and sharp. There's no way in hell I'm letting someone who ditched us waltz back into my life like it's all forgotten.

"That's not all, son," he says, his voice low, like he's bracing for impact. "She has a family."

The words cut deep—too fucking deep—tearing through me like a blade. The pain hits harder than any physical wound ever could, dragging me back to that moment she chose to walk away. The bitter irony claws at me: She abandoned us, but somehow, she moved on, started over, while we were left to pick up the broken pieces she left behind.

"Your mother has a son and a daughter," my father adds, each word another slap to my soul. "They want to meet you."

"I don't give a shit what they want," I snap, bitterness crawling into my voice, laced with anger and all the years of resentment. "They're not my family."

I start to turn away, but my father's voice stops me dead in my tracks.

"Noah," he says, gentle but with an edge of something that makes me flinch. "I know she hurt you."

I spin around, frustration bubbling over, ready to explode. "Dad, she hurt both of us. She walked away like we were nothing. And now, after all these years, she thinks she can just waltz back in like everything's fine? Like I'm supposed to pretend I wasn't worth sticking around for?" The heat in my chest burns, but I can't stay here, can't keep talking about this. I storm down the hallway, needing to escape this conversation, this whole fucking mess.

Chapter 5

Aubrey

After one of the shittiest days of my life, I lock myself in my room, shutting out the world—and especially my dad. Talking to him isn't an option. Not about my day, not about the money I need, not about anything. Just the thought of asking him for help makes my stomach twist into knots. I can't even meet his eyes without feeling like I'm drowning. So yeah—time to get a job.

And my mother? Nothing. She didn't even bother replying to the text I sent her last night when I was barely keeping it together. Guess that's the answer I didn't want but should've seen coming. It's clear now—I'm on my own. Completely. Totally. Fucking alone.

I didn't think today could outdo last night, but life loves to kick me when I'm down. Noah's anger at my window should've been the first warning shot, but Tia? Tia took it to a whole new level. She's turned her bitch mode up to eleven, strutting around like she owns the world. And the rest of them? Just her little entourage, too scared of her wrath to do anything but follow her lead and kiss her ass.

It's pathetic, really—the way they look at her, wide-eyed and worshipful, like she's some kind of royalty.

But the worst part? I didn't think their hate could get under my skin. I thought I was tougher than that, above their petty bullshit. Yet here I am, staring at the ceiling, gutted.

I don't even want to imagine how I would've survived Tia's bullshit today if it weren't for Sam. Facing that venom on my own would've been a whole new level of hell. But Sam didn't let that happen. She pulled me in like I mattered, like I wasn't just some afterthought. Her group might be small—just her, Lola, Liz, and me—but it feels solid. Real. Like, for once, I might actually have people who've got my back.

Still, Tia needs to be knocked off her pedestal, and I'm done playing along. She can have her little army of sheep kissing her ass, but I'm not one of them. I'm not afraid of her, and if she keeps pushing, she's going to find out just how serious I am.

As I lie in bed, the darkness closing in, a sudden flicker of light from Noah's window slices through the shadows. His curtain stays drawn, but my eyes latch onto it, unwilling to look away. Somewhere deep down, I'm hoping—stupidly, desperately—that he might pull it back, that he might glance over, just once, the way he used to. But I know that's a lie I can't afford to believe. He hates me now. The kind of hate that burns, the kind I deserve.

The memories creep in anyway, sharp and relentless. I can't stop thinking about us—about what we were and how I destroyed it. The truth is, I still love him. God, I love him with every broken, aching part of me. That fire never went out, not for a second, no matter how much it tears me apart. Every time I see him, it flares hotter, searing through my chest, a constant reminder of what I lost—what I never should've let go of in the first place.

But I did. I broke us. I broke *him*. And now all I have are the ashes of what could've been, and the unbearable truth that he'll never love me like he once did.

I don't know where to begin, how to undo the damage I caused. Fixing us—if that's even in the cards—feels like standing at the base of a mountain I'll never climb. Maybe we'll never go back to what we were, but can't we at least stop ripping each other apart every time we're in the same room? The weight of the tension, the way it crackles like a live wire between us, is too much to bear.

Maybe I need to talk to him. Lay it all out. Apologize. Tell him how sorry I am for every way I messed this up. We were each other's firsts, and that has to mean something. It has to count for more than the pain I've left behind. Doesn't it?

Still, there's a part of me—a small, aching, desperate part—that clings to the memory of the Noah I lost. The Noah who was mine. The one who could make the weight of the world disappear with just a look, who held me like I was the only thing that mattered. But I can't pretend anymore. That Noah is gone, buried beneath the wreckage I caused.

For some fucked-up reason, all I can think about is explaining the condoms in my bag. I don't care what anyone else thinks—let them gossip, let them assume. But Noah? His opinion is the only one that matters. The thought of him thinking I'm some easy slut, someone who'll spread her legs for anyone who looks my way—it makes my stomach turn. I can't let him believe that about me. Not him. Not after everything.

When Tia held them up, smug as hell, I didn't even see her. My eyes locked onto Noah, and fuck, the look on his face tore through me. Hurt. Disappointment. It was all there, plain as day. And I hate it. I just want to fix this. I want him to know it's not what it looked like. I don't even know why it matters so much, but it does. It just does.

Outside my bedroom door, down the hall, I hear my father crank up the damn television. He always does that when he's drinking, like the booze fucks with his hearing and he needs the volume turned up, as if he's terrified of missing something—anything—important.

I've lost count of how many times my mother would scream at him to turn it down. That's when the real shitshow would start—the yelling, the things getting thrown, the doors slamming, the air thick with accusations and name-calling. It never ended well. It never fucking did.

I roll onto my side and see Noah's light flick off. I stare at the wall, my mind racing, hoping that tomorrow might somehow be different. That it'll be better. A fresh start. A clean slate. Because surely, it can't get worse than today, right? But deep down, I know the truth. Tomorrow? It'll probably be just as fucked up as today.

My sleep is shattered, restless through the night, and it's way too early. I don't even bother checking the time on my phone, so I just lay here too tired to care, staring at the ceiling, trying to force my mind to shut the fuck up long enough to get some sleep.

Then, my phone pings. And like clockwork, thoughts of my mother flood in. Has she finally gotten back to me, or is she still wrapped up in her own shit, ignoring the daughter she's supposed to give a damn about?

I snatch my phone from the charger, squinting at the screen through tired eyes. If it's her, part of me wants to ignore it, just like she's ignored me for God knows how long. But it's not her.

It's Sam.

The pain hits hard. My mother's probably lost in her new boyfriend's bullshit, too busy living her new life while she conveniently forgets about me—the daughter she swore she'd protect, the one she couldn't even be bothered to check in on.

Sam: *Need a ride to school today?*

I don't hesitate. I fire off my reply, almost too quickly. It's pathetic how badly I'm clinging to something so insignificant.

Aubrey: *If you're heading past 32 Rocket Street, that'd be great.*

I hit send. The phone sits in my hand, taunting me with its silence. Then it buzzes.

Sam: *Okay, I'll pick you up in about an hour.*

Relief washes over me, almost too good to be true. No bus ride this morning, no bullshit with the usual crowd. I toss my phone onto the bed and take my time getting dressed, as my thoughts scatter in all directions.

The house feels unnervingly quiet. I move through the hallway, trying to stay as quiet as possible, knowing my dad's probably still in his room, nursing a hangover. I don't even bother opening the fridge or cupboards—there's nothing but stale shit in there. Last night's dinner was a dry piece of bread I couldn't even choke down. Moments like this only remind me how badly I need to find a job—anything to make sure I don't starve while I'm stuck here.

I swing open the front door and spot Sam's car parked at the curb. I close the door quietly, skipping the lock—my dad never bothers with it. Maybe that's why he's never given me a key.

Tucking my phone away, I slide into the front seat next to Sam.

She turns to me with a smile. "Ready for another day of fun?"

"Yeah, yesterday was fucking awesome," I say, remembering all the shit that went down. "Looking forward to doing it all over again."

"Today will be better, you'll see," Sam says, but I don't believe her.

She bursts into laughter when I just stare at her, then starts the engine. In a few seconds, we're speeding down the street, the world blurring around us.

"So, what's it like having the hottest guy in school as your neighbor?" she asks, her voice full of that teasing energy.

I stare out the window, watching the houses blur by. What the hell do I even say to that? Part of me wants to tell her that living next to Noah used to be the best, that I loved it, but now it just fucks with me.

"Don't worry, you don't have to answer that," she says, cutting through the quiet. There's a pause before she asks, "Do you think you two will ever be friends again?"

"I don't know. Probably not, especially now that he's with Tia," I say, turning to face her.

Sam looks at me, raising an eyebrow. "You know they're not a thing, right? Him and Tia," she says, her voice light, but there's something off in the way she says it. "It's common knowledge Noah doesn't do relationships. He's all about hook-ups. Same goes for Reece and Jace. Always chasing tail."

I pause, processing that. "But I thought Tia had a problem with me because of Noah."

"Oh, she probably does," Sam says with a smirk. "She's been dying to be with him. Everyone knows that. They hooked up once, but that's about it."

I let out a breath, feeling the tightness in my chest loosen just a little.

Sam flicks on the indicator, waiting for a few cars to pass before she swings into the school parking lot.

My nerves hit hard as I spot groups of students chatting and laughing, their carefree energy only making the weight of today press down harder. But no matter how much shit gets thrown my way, I won't let Tia or Noah fuck with me today. Not this time.

As soon as the car stops, I'm out, slinging my pack over my shoulder. My eyes scan the parking lot, and there she is—Tia, flanked by her pack of bitches, all high-maintenance and bitchy, like they own the place.

Up ahead, Noah leans against a car, all effortlessly cool, talking to some guy whose name I can't even remember. My stomach tightens, and for a second, I just want to turn around and walk straight back to the car. But I can't let them win. Not today.

The second Tia spots me and Sam walking her way, her smile twists into something mean, like she's just been handed a weapon. She edges closer to Noah, like being near him makes her untouchable. I can already see it in her eyes—she's gearing up to start some shit, or maybe she just wants to pull that pathetic "he's mine" routine again.

As we get closer, Noah's eyes flick to mine, just for a second, and my breath catches before I quickly look away. The last thing I need is to lock eyes with him right now—not here, not with everyone watching. I'm not about to air out all our fucked-up history in the middle of the parking lot. If we're going to talk, it'll have to be later, in private. That is, if I can even manage to get him alone.

But Tia? Tia doesn't give a shit about subtlety or privacy. Of course not. She turns to her group, smirking like she's already won, and says loud enough for half the lot to hear, "Oh, look, everyone. It's the new school slut and her loser friend."

Her words slice through the air, full of venom, and I can feel the weight of everyone's eyes on me. The laughter starts to stir, just like I knew it would. My hands ball into fists, my face burning with anger. Fuck Tia.

I'm done with her shit. My mouth opens, prepared to tell her exactly where she can shove her bullshit. But before I can get the words out, Noah moves. His arm wraps around Tia's waist, pulling her in close, and then his lips slam onto hers, shutting me the hell up.

The kiss is intense, raw, like he's out to make a statement. And damn, it hits harder than I want to admit. I can't tear my eyes away, though. It's like witnessing a wreck—ugly, unavoidable, and somehow it's all I can focus on.

Tia melts into Noah without hesitation, gripping him like she might collapse if he were to let go. The crowd around us goes wild—cheers, whistles, and catcalls ringing out like they're watching a damn show.

Sam grips my arm, pulling me forward, and I let her guide me through the crowd. I keep my chin up, my face set in stone, refusing to give Tia or Noah the satisfaction of seeing how much that little stunt just messed me up.

Sam's voice is steady, low but firm. "He's just trying to fuck with you. Noah doesn't pull shit like that. The only time I've ever seen him kiss anyone is at a party, and that's just when he's hooking up."

I fall silent, my thoughts spinning. My chest feels tight, and I try to steady myself, gripping the strap of my bag like it'll somehow anchor me.

"I don't know," I say finally, my voice quieter than I want it to be. "It looked real to me."

Sam snorts, rolling her eyes. "That wasn't real. Noah's not the type to get all affectionate unless he's after something. He hooks up, then moves on. What he did? That was a statement. He did it to get under your skin. He's fucking with you."

Maybe she's right. Maybe it wasn't about Tia at all. Maybe it was all for me—to twist the knife just a little deeper.

"Well, it definitely worked," I reply, forcing a smile onto my face as we walk through the iron gates. The ache in my chest refuses to fade, but I'm not about to let it take over—not here, not now.

Sam chuckles, nudging me lightly with her elbow. "Honestly, I thought you were gonna march right over there and rip that bitch's hair out just to get her away from him."

I laugh, but it's hollow. "Don't tempt me," I say.

We head up the front steps and into the crowded hallway, dodging elbows and backpacks in the chaos. It's no surprise when eyes turn my way—mostly guys, their gazes following me with that same mix of smugness and expectation. It's clear they've bought into whatever bullshit Tia's been peddling. After the whole condom incident, I'm probably just another easy fuck in their eyes, a rumor they can latch onto to feed their pathetic fantasies.

Sam and I part ways near the lockers. Hers is closer to the entrance; mine's further down, and on the other side of the hall. As I open it to grab my books, the weight of their stares presses on me, intense and unyielding, daring me to make a move. Even with the locker door between us, it doesn't shield me from the whispers, the quiet snickers.

I slam my locker shut with a force that makes the whole row shake and walk down the hallway toward Sam, who's still chatting and laughing with someone by her locker. As I wait for her, I spot Lola heading my way.

"Hey, Aubrey," Lola says, her voice warm. Her face is partially hidden behind those oversized black glasses—geeky as hell, yet somehow, they only add to her charm, making her look even more stunning.

"Hey, Lola," I reply.

"You should probably hate me," she says.

"Why should I hate you?" I ask, frowning.

"Because I prayed someone else would take the heat from Tia," she blurts out, her words tumbling out faster than she seems to expect. Then, she quickly adds, "I didn't mean to throw it all on you, you know? I just... I just wanted someone else to deal with it for a change."

"It's fine, Lola," I say. "I'll handle Tia. Whatever shit she throws at me, I'll deal with it."

Lola drops her gaze, fiddling with the edge of her sweater like a scolded kid. She's not the type to stand up to Tia, and it's obvious. Too damn timid. It's exactly why Tia zeroed in on her, picking her as an easy target, knowing she wouldn't put up a fight. But I'm not Lola. I'm not going to take it lying down.

As Sam comes over and Lola walks away, Sam and I rush down the hall, the bell ringing in our ears, a sharp reminder that we're cutting it close. We enter the classroom just as the bell rings its final note. My eyes immediately flick to the back, where three assholes are tossing a football around, their loud laughs cutting through the air.

Then, the blonde-haired dickhead with the ball locks eyes with me. For a split second, he freezes, his fingers tightening around the ball, and I can already feel the bullshit coming. His smirk spreads slowly across his face.

"Hey, Aubrey," he sneers, his tone thick with mockery. "You gonna hang out with us at lunch? Maybe show us three a good time?" His smirk widens. "I heard you're into all kinds of things. You know, like up the ass, and every other hole."

The room erupts in laughter, the mocking tone echoing off the walls, but it doesn't make me blush from shame—it makes me burn with rage. I shoot him the nastiest glare I can muster, but it does nothing. I slam my books down on the desk, drowning out their taunts. These assholes? They're not worth my time. They don't actually want a response—they just want to show off to their friends, acting like they're untouchable. Well, fuck them.

But then, just like that, the laughter dies. The room goes unnervingly quiet.

I glance over my shoulder, expecting to see the teacher, but instead, it's Noah. He's standing in the doorway, his gaze fixed on the asshole who just spoke, a look so cold it could freeze hell over. The asshole freezes, his smug grin faltering, then completely vanishing as he realizes just how much trouble he's in.

I quickly whip my head back around, pretending I didn't notice, like my heartbeat isn't racing. But all I can think about is Tia—her lips on Noah's, the way they were tangled up. The anger that surges inside me isn't just from that jerk's words. It's the gnawing ache of seeing Noah like that, with her, and realizing just how deep it cuts. I don't need this right now. I've got enough going on.

I sink into my seat next to Sam, doing my best to ignore the pounding in my chest as Noah walks deeper into the room. His eyes flick to mine, and for a split second, everything around us goes still. I look away quickly, pretending I didn't feel the pull, but I can feel the weight of everyone else's gaze on him. It's like he's the damn sun, and the rest of us are just stuck orbiting him, helpless.

I know I shouldn't look back, but I can't help it. His tousled hair falls into his eyes, and his long lashes—everything about him is still beautiful. And then his mouth, that perfect, sinful mouth—the one that used to kiss me like he actually meant it.

I don't get it.

He never wanted to be the center of attention before, but now he soaks it up like he was born for it. Like he needs it.

Noah drops his bag onto the floor just two seats away, and for a moment, he locks eyes with me again. That cocky, infuriating smirk spreads across his face, like he knows exactly what the hell I'm thinking.

Did he just catch me checking him out? I can feel my cheeks flush, my stomach twisting in embarrassment.

I want to crawl into a hole and disappear. What the fuck is wrong with me? And why did I make it so obvious?

Late students scramble to find their seats as the teacher steps in, and relief washes over me when I realize Tia isn't in this class. For once, I can actually breathe for a minute.

I pull my notebook out, flipping through the pages, hoping to lose myself in the work and forget about everything else. If I could just focus, forget about Noah and his stupid, smug smirk. Tia, too—fuck her and everything she stands for. And my mom's messes, always landing on my plate, never my choice.

I can't afford to care about any of it. My future's on the line. My grades. The scholarship I've got for next year—it's my only shot. I can't let anything, especially them, screw it all up for me. I don't have the luxury of falling apart.

The bell rings, and I quickly shove my stuff into my bag and make my way out with Sam.

We head for our lockers, the noise of everyone rushing through the hallway making it feel even more chaotic than the classroom. Just as I'm about to stuff my huge textbook into my locker, the announcement speaker crackles to life.

"Samantha Carter, please come to the admin office."

Sam says a quick goodbye, and before I can even get a word in, she's gone. I head straight for the bathroom, desperate to escape—Noah, Tia, the chaos in my head. I just need a moment of peace.

When I push open the door, I'm met with a group of girls crowded around the mirror, taking their sweet time with makeup, fixing their hair, and snapping selfies like the world revolves around them. I don't have the energy for their nonsense, so I make a beeline for a stall and slam the door shut behind me.

But as soon as I think I can breathe, the bathroom door opens, then the sound of heels click against the tiles.

"Everyone get the hell out of here now," a voice barks.

The words hit the air, cold and final, without a single pause.

I hear the frantic sound of bags being zipped up, the rush of feet pounding toward the door—everyone's scrambling to leave, to escape whatever the hell just happened. But me? I'm stuck. Frozen in this stall, my heart hammering in my chest.

"Are you alright?" the voice asks, and I instantly wonder how many people are standing out there.

"Yeah," comes the reply, cold and clipped. "I didn't expect Noah to pull that shit."

My ears immediately perk up at the mention of Noah.

I'm finished peeing, but I stall, holding off on flushing, hoping they'll just leave. My timing? Perfect, as usual. Wrong place, wrong time—that's my mantra. It's like the universe has a sick sense of humor, always making sure I walk straight into a mess I don't need.

"I know, Nicole. I was just as shocked when he did that."

Nicole. The only Nicole I know is from Tia's crew. Wait—are they talking about the kiss this morning? My heart picks up speed, and I freeze, holding my breath. I stay still, hoping for more, praying they'll say something else.

"Do you think he did it because Aubrey came back? Apparently, they were tight when she was here before," says another voice.

So, there's three of them out there. Fucking great.

"Well, I heard her and Noah were a thing," another one adds, a little too casual for my liking.

"Yeah, but even if they were an item, after that kiss with Tia this morning—I'd say Noah doesn't give a shit about her anymore," someone else chimes in.

That makes five. Five people talking shit about me.

My stomach tightens, the anger swirls inside me.

I can't help but wonder—where the hell is Tia while half her crew is out there spilling secrets about her, me, and Noah? Is she too busy playing the part of the queen bee, or does she not even know what her own people are saying?

Either way, it doesn't matter. This whole mess is spiraling, and I'm caught in the middle of it.

"Sabrina, I told you Nicole doesn't want to hear about that kiss."

"Sorry, Nicole."

Then, another voice jumps in, and I can already feel the headache coming on. "I heard Aubrey banged seven football players at the same time back at her old school."

My heart lurches, a cold, tight feeling spreading through my chest. I can't believe the bullshit they're spewing. I knew Tia's crew loved to spread rumors, but this? This is next-level. The part of me that wants to lash out, to shut them all down, is screaming, but the rest of me is too numb to respond.

"Who told you that?"

"Tia said she heard it from a friend."

Tia, of course. The bitch with her ear to the ground, spreading false rumors like she's some kind of gossip queen. I can practically hear her smug laugh in my head, getting off on the chaos she's causing. This isn't just about me anymore. It's about control—her need to keep me in my place, to make sure everyone thinks I'm just some slut who doesn't deserve anything better.

"Don't worry, Nicole. You might still have a chance with Noah. He's not one to stick around with the same girl for long. You've seen how he moves from one to the next," another voice adds, trying to sound reassuring, like they know everything about him.

"Yeah, but I've never seen him openly kiss anyone like that before," another bitch says, her voice dripping with jealousy. "And even if it was real, I doubt he'd stick with Tia for long. They hooked up once almost a year ago. Just wait for the party this weekend. I bet he won't be with her. You'll see. I think he just did it to say 'fuck you' to Aubrey. That's my take on it."

The words hit like daggers as I repeat them in my head. Is that really what Noah's doing? Just trying to get under my skin?

I'm done with this. I flush the toilet, trying to ignore the bile rising in my throat, and yank open the stall door. Seven girls—well, seven of Tia's crew—are standing there. Some look surprised, others glare at me like they're ready to kill me.

I don't hesitate. With my back straight and my head held high, I meet each of their eyes, not backing down. Let them try me. I'm not going to let Tia or any of her little followers walk all over me anymore.

I step forward, not caring about the tension in the air, not caring about their glaring eyes. If they want a fight, they'll get one.

"Got something to say?" I challenge, my voice calm but sharp.

I stand there for a moment, the weight of the situation settling in. It's hard not to wonder how Tia would react if she knew her own crew was secretly hoping Noah wasn't really into her. Among the group are girls I've never had an issue with—people I've never been a bitch to. But now, here they are, all staring at me like I'm the enemy.

I ignore their glares and walk straight to the sink, not caring that some of them are sitting on the countertop, watching my every move. I turn on the faucet and start washing my hands, the sound of the water filling the silence. Their stares burn into me, like they're just waiting for me to react, but I'm not giving them the satisfaction. They're hesitant, unsure of how to handle me, and it's blatantly obvious.

I dry my hands, taking one last glance at my reflection in the mirror, and then turn to leave. But just as I reach for the door, a voice cuts through the air behind me.

"You know he's over you, right? Just accept it," one of the girl's sneers.

I pause, my hand hovering over the door handle.

Why the hell do they think I'm here just because of Noah? They don't know a thing about my life, about the shit I've had to deal with since I left. And honestly, it's none of their fucking business. All I wanted was to get through this year unnoticed, to avoid their drama and the bullshit. But thanks to Tia and her pathetic insecurities, that's not even an option anymore. I can't stay invisible. Not when she's made it clear she's targeting me.

I glance back at the group, my eyes narrowing as I scan their faces, trying to figure out who had the nerve to talk shit behind my back. Whoever it was didn't have the guts to say it to my face just a second ago, and that pisses me off more than I want to admit.

"Tia might be your queen, but she's just as capable of crashing and burning as the rest of you," I snap, my voice sharp, aimed to make sure everyone who hears feels the weight of it.

I swing the door open and step the hell out of the bathroom, already knowing my words are going to spread like wildfire through this school. It's the same old shitshow—everyone's got an opinion and a rumor to fuel.

The corridor's alive with chatter, students talking over one another, but as soon as I step through, everything goes quiet. Like someone just hit pause on the chaos.

I walk through with my chin up, pretending not to care, but I feel their eyes on me. The stares, the whispers—it never gets easier. I'm a target, picked apart and judged, like they're waiting for me to break. But I won't. Not this time.

CHAPTER 6

NOAH

I fucked up. Completely, catastrophically fucked up. That kiss with Tia this morning? Yeah, the one I thought would mean nothing. Now it's all over the school, spreading like wildfire. And the worst part? I only did it because seeing Aubrey coming my way nearly broke me.

My brain short-circuited, like I didn't know how to breathe, let alone think straight.

Why the fuck is her being back here screwing with my head so much? She's everywhere—under my skin, in my head—and I hate it. I hate that she's still everything.

When I woke up this morning, rock-hard and aching, it wasn't just lust—it was her. Aubrey. Every goddamn detail burned into my brain: her long legs I can't stop picturing wrapped around me, her perfect lips I want to ruin with mine, her laugh, her everything. The whole fucking package. It's like a sickness, something I can't shake, no matter how hard I try.

After I took care of my raging boner, I was pissed.

Pissed because even after all this time, all the heartbreak, I still want her.

Still crave the feeling of her falling apart in my arms.

Her screams, her moans, the way she used to come undone on my cock, my tongue, my fingers—fuck, anything I could give her.

It's all burned into me like a brand I can't erase. My body aches for her like it's some kind of cruel addiction. For the girl who destroyed me. Who shattered my heart into a million pieces and didn't look back. It's pathetic. I know it is. But that doesn't make it stop.

So yeah, when I saw her this morning, I panicked. I kissed Tia like a fucking idiot, thinking maybe it'd make the ache go away. Maybe it'd make me forget—just for a second—that she's still under my skin. But it didn't. It never does. Because no one else will ever be her.

And that's what fucking kills me. It's always her. It's always going to be her. The way she smiles, the way she looks at me like I'm the only one who's ever mattered. Even when she's breaking me, she's the only one. And I fucking hate it.

That kiss with Tia? I only did it to show Aubrey I'm over her—to prove to myself I've moved on, even if my goddamn body hasn't gotten the memo. But now? Now Tia thinks it was some kind of declaration, like I'm all in on whatever the hell this is supposed to be between us. And the fallout? It's a fucking disaster. I've made a mess of everything, and I have no clue how to fix it. How to untangle myself from this without making things worse.

When she grabbed my hand to walk into school this morning, I yanked it back, told her to fuck off, told her it didn't mean shit. But she didn't flinch—just smiled at me, calm and smug, like she knew something I didn't.

"It's fine," she said, like my words were a joke. "It's cute that you're embarrassed about what you did."

I wanted to scream at her, tell her she had it all wrong, that this wasn't some fucking game. But she just kept smiling, like we were in on this together, like the kiss wasn't the stupid, heat-of-the-moment mistake it actually was.

And that look? That smug, knowing look? It told me she still didn't get it. Or maybe she didn't want to.

But shit's only gotten worse.

The rumors are flying, whispers in every hallway, and now Tia's strutting around like we're the new school power couple. She's lapping it up, basking in the attention, while I'm here trying to figure out how the fuck to get out of this mess.

And Aubrey?

God, I can't even let myself think about her without feeling like I'm about to come apart at the seams. Every time her name crosses my mind, it's like a gut punch—a reminder that no matter how hard I try to play it cool, I haven't moved on.

This whole thing has spiraled out of control, worse than I ever could've imagined. And the worst part... I did this to myself. All of it. For what? To prove something to Aubrey? To make her think I'm over her when I'm clearly not. Now I'm stuck in this chaos, and there's no way to fix it.

What the fuck was I thinking?

And as if my mood couldn't get any worse, I walked into the classroom and heard that fuckhead Blane running his mouth, loud enough for everyone to hear. Asking Aubrey if she'd let him and two other dickheads from the football team bang her at once. My blood fucking boiled. Those same idiots who should know by now that she's off-limits. That I don't give a shit about the rumors, about what they think—Aubrey isn't someone you drag into pathetic bullshit. And where the hell is Lucas Simpson? He was supposed to set them straight.

What the fuck is wrong with these assholes? It's like they're begging for me to lose it, and I'm this close.

My anger hit me like a freight train, and I had to clench my fists, my knuckles white from the effort it took not to march over there and beat the shit out of him in front of everyone. Just the thought of him talking about her like that had me seeing red, my pulse pounding in my ears. I wanted to shut him up, make him regret every fucking word that left his mouth. But I couldn't.

I couldn't let myself lose it, because if I did—if I let my emotions slip for even a second—she'd know. Aubrey would know I still love her. And that's a weakness I can't afford to let her see.

So, I forced myself to sit there, biting back the urge to snap, while my jaw ached from grinding my teeth. I'll deal with those assholes later. I'll deal with Blane and his bullshit in my own way, on my own terms. But for now, I have to let it slide, even though it feels like swallowing glass. Because as much as I hate it, as much as it burns me alive to sit still, pretending not to care is the only way to survive her. To survive the wreckage she left behind.

After what feels like the longest hour of my life, the bell rings, and I'm out of that classroom like my ass is on fire. Behind me, I hear Tia calling my name, her voice all sweet and demanding, like she's got some right to summon me, like I'm her damn property.

I stop dead in my tracks, waiting for her to catch up. This shit needs to end. I need to shut this down—shut her the fuck down—before it spirals any further.

She finally reaches me, all confident and smug, and yeah, I can't deny it—Tia's hot as hell. But that's all she's got going for her. She's not my type. Not even close. She's spoiled and opinionated, wrapped up in this bubble of privilege that keeps her cushioned from the real world. She's never known struggle, never faced anything that could leave scars. And that shit just doesn't sit right with me. It's not real, and it never will be.

Not like Aubrey.

Fuck. There it is again. Her name. Her face. The way she's always in my head, no matter how hard I try to shove her out. Tia's standing in front of me, but all I can think about is Aubrey. All I can see is her strength, her fire, the way she's fought through hell and come out on the other side. She's everything real, everything raw.

Tia's just a distraction, a way to fill the empty space left by someone I can't let go of. But it doesn't matter, because as much as I try Aubrey is the one who owns my heart, and nothing Tia does will change that.

"Hey, handsome," Tia purrs, stopping beside me, all sweetness and fake innocence. Her hand reaches for mine.

I yank my arm back, fast and sharp, like her touch has the plague. I can see it on her face—she wasn't expecting that. But I don't care. I'm done pretending, done letting this bullshit go any further.

"We need to talk," I say, my voice sharp, no room for argument. No softening the blow. "I fucked up. Meet me in the gym in five."

I don't have the time or the patience for a scene. If I do this here, in front of everyone, it'll explode, and the last thing I need is for this shit to go viral.

Tia's face falls, and I catch the flicker of hurt in her eyes. But I don't give a damn. I'm done with her bullshit. She's not my problem, and I'm not going to pretend I care about whatever the fuck she's feeling right now.

She knows what's coming. I can see it in her eyes—she's figured it out. I don't care if it fucks with her head, if she's pissed or upset. I'm not here to soften the blow. She needs to understand that whatever this was, it's over. Done. No second chances. No confusion. It's finished.

I turn and walk away, leaving her standing there, frozen in the corridor.

In the gym, I throw on my gym clothes, then take a seat on the bench. Tia still hasn't shown up. The guys are nowhere in sight—thank God. Class doesn't start for another fifteen minutes, but she's still not here. I wanted to get this shit out of the way without any witnesses. My fingers tap on the bench, irritation clawing at me. Time crawls by, and I'm fucking done waiting.

I pull out my phone, my eyes landing on a message from my dad.

Dad: *Your mom just called and asked if she could see you this afternoon.*

I stare at the screen, the knot in my stomach tightening. What the fuck does she want?

I've ignored my dad's message all morning because there's no way I'm ready to see that woman who bailed on me years ago. Fuck her and her perfect fucking family. I couldn't care less about being some afterthought in her shiny new life, especially when she never loved me the way a mother should.

I'm lost in my thoughts, mind racing with anger and confusion, completely unaware of anything around me.

It isn't until a sharp whistle cuts through the air that I snap out of it.

My gaze shifts, and that's when I see her—Aubrey, standing by the volleyball net, surrounded by a few of the other girls on her team.

I should've known she'd be back on the team. Volleyball's always been her thing, something she's never given up on. She's good at it—always has been. And the fact that Tia and her crew couldn't give two shits about the sport, just makes it all the easier for Aubrey to dominate.

I can't tear my eyes away from Aubrey.

My gaze burns as it drifts to those tight-ass shorts hugging her perfect ass. My cock stirs, and I can't stop myself from imagining grabbing that ass, fucking her hard while she screams my name. The thought alone makes me hard, my body betraying me, lost in these filthy, desperate fantasies.

I'm so wrapped up in it, I don't even notice Tia approaching until her hand touches mine. My whole body jerks at the contact. The heat between my legs fades instantly, my dick almost shriveling up as I turn to face her.

"Don't fucking touch me," I growl, my voice cold, pissed off.

"What?" she snaps, irritation flashing across her face. "You had no problem out in that parking lot this morning."

I can feel the storm brewing, the tension hanging between us like a thunderstorm on the brink of breaking. I brace myself, knowing full well that once I spill my guts to Tia, she's going to explode. She's always been a firestorm, a goddamn handful, and I've kept her at arm's length for a reason—because I know better than to get too close. But this? This shit needs to be said.

"I need to talk about what happened this morning," I say, locking eyes with her.

"Yeah?" she replies, her voice sharp, challenging.

"Tia, I need to be straight with you." I don't waste time softening it. "That kiss this morning... it was a mistake. Didn't mean shit. I only did it to piss someone else off."

The second the words leave my mouth; I see her face go from disbelief to hurt. Honestly, I couldn't care less.

"Are you fucking kidding me?" She snaps, her voice sharp with hurt, loud enough to make everyone around us notice.

"Tia," I start to say, but she cuts me off before I can get another word out.

Jace and Reece start to approach, but they stop dead when they hear Tia's voice explode.

"Don't even bother," she spits. "You think I'm that fucking stupid not to know this has everything to do with her? Oh my god, what the fuck was I thinking? You asshole. You think you can just fuck with people's feelings and get away with it?"

I don't flinch. I don't care. But fuck, her words sting.

Her jaw tightens, and for a second, I think she's going to explode again, but then—just like that—she pivots on her heels and storms off, leaving me alone to face the shitstorm of every eye in the room on me.

Jace and Reece stride over with their usual grins, seemingly unconcerned, and plop down beside me on the bench without a word. They know how Tia is—always making a scene. I sit there, stewing in my own damn stupidity, cursing myself for getting caught up in the mess with her.

Reece nudges my shoe with his foot, giving me some kind of silent warning, and I glance up, irritated.

Aubrey's approaching, her frown already twisting her face into that pissed-off expression she wears.

Great. Just what I need—another fucking headache right now.

I take a slow breath, forcing my heart to settle, trying to look like I don't care as I watch her. I hold her gaze, hoping that if I stare long enough, she'll just turn around and leave me the hell alone.

I let my gaze sweep over her, not even trying to hide that I'm checking her out. My eyes trace the curve of her body before deliberately landing on her tits. She doesn't flinch, doesn't even blink, like it doesn't bother her at all—which, honestly, just makes it more entertaining. I've got to hand it to her; she's got nerve.

She stops in front of me, her stance strong, like she knows she has something to prove.

"Can we talk?" she asks, her voice steady.

I smirk, leaning back with an unshakable, cocky grin. Tilting my head slightly, I let my tongue glide over my bottom lip, and I catch the way her eyes track the motion.

"There's nothing to talk about," I say, my tone smooth and dismissive, like she's barely worth my attention. Then, with a smirk that stretches wider, I add, "But if you've got something else in mind for that mouth, I'm all ears."

Jace lets out a quiet chuckle beside me.

She steps closer, her irritation burning in her eyes, and my heart pounds hard against my ribs as she bridges the space between us. When she grabs my hand, it's not soft or hesitant—it's a firm, commanding pull that drags me straight into her gravity. The instant her skin meets mine, it's like a jolt of electricity shoots through me, tearing apart every shred of control I thought I had. My thoughts spiral, wild and chaotic, like I'm caught in a storm I can't escape. And it kills me—how she still has this power over me, like nothing's changed, like I'm still her puppet, tangled in her strings.

She pulls me into the equipment room, and the moment she lets go of my hand, a tidal wave of sensation crashes over me—sharp, jarring, impossible to ignore. My mind snaps back into focus, but it does nothing to steady me. Not even when she turns away, moving away from me in this cramped space. I can't stop myself. My thoughts spiral, dark and raw, consumed by the image of pressing my chest against her back, my lips trailing along the curve of her neck as I fuck her from behind. The way

I want to ravish her has me on edge, every part of me burning to claim her.

"Why are you doing this?" she asks, finally turning to face me. Her voice is quiet, but it slices through me, carrying a blend of frustration and something else I can't quite name.

I force the emotions down, burying them deep where they can't touch me anymore. None of it matters now—not after she made her fucking choice.

"Doing what?"

"Come on, Noah. You know exactly what I'm talking about." Her eyes meet mine, a storm of memories swirling within them—joy and pain intertwined in a way only we could ever understand.

I know her too well to miss it, the faint fracture in her composure, the hurt she's struggling to keep buried.

I straighten, forcing my body to relax, though it's a losing battle with her this close. I can't let myself go there—not with her. Not after everything. Clenching my jaw, I shove down the emotions threatening to surface. "So, should I pull out my cock now, or are you volunteering to grab it for me?" The words drop from my lips, sharp and cold. I want her to feel the sting, to understand exactly where we stand—where she stands. And it's not beside me anymore.

"Noah," she says, her voice softer now, like she's trying to break down the walls I've spent so long building around myself.

She holds my gaze a moment longer, her eyes heavy with things she won't say, and it's unbearable. The tension presses down like a weight I can't shake, so I break it—blunt, cold, and final. I need to shove her as far away as possible, make her understand exactly where I stand.

"Look, if I'm not getting my dick sucked, I'm out of here. Your call, sweetheart."

"Please, Noah, don't be like that," she says, her voice trembling with a hint of desperation. She steps closer, her fingers brushing against my arm as if trying to anchor me, to pull me back to her.

I shake her hand off, the rejection harsher than I intend, but I can't stop it.

The last thing I need is for her to worm her way back under my skin, to make me care again. I'm scared of losing control, of letting myself fall back into something that can never be what it once was.

"Don't fucking touch me," I growl.

"Can we at least try to salvage some sort of friendship after everything we've been through?" she asks, her voice shaky, like she's clinging to something that isn't there anymore.

"Why?"

"Noah," she says softly, and it fucking kills me. I hate the way her voice softens my resolve, like it's dragging me back to a place I don't want to go.

I force down the storm of emotions threatening to break free and meet her gaze. "Trust me, Aubrey, you don't want me as your friend anymore. I don't do friendships with chicks. That shit's over."

She shakes her head, her eyes desperate, like she doesn't want to believe it. "You don't mean that."

I can feel myself starting to crack, her presence pulling me in, tempting me to just give in and be with her again—to laugh, touch, be how we used to be. But I can't. Not after everything.

Deep down, I know she'd leave this town the second she could, and I can't go through that kind of hurt again. It broke me before; it could fucking destroy me this time.

So, I push forward, moving toward her with purpose, each step deliberate as I draw the line. I make it clear—the only thing she's getting from me now is my cock. If that's not what she wants, I'm out.

"Listen, Aubrey," I say, my voice low and hard, each word a sharp jab as I step forward, pushing her back until she's trapped against the cold, damp wall. I lean in close, so she can feel the weight of every word. "The only thing I want from you is to slide my cock into your tight pussy and fuck you like I've fucked every other girl who meant nothing to me."

I lift my hand, pressing it against the wall next to her, closing the space between us. The tension hangs heavy in the air. "Is that what you want?" I ask, my voice steady. "Because that's all you're getting from me."

Her eyes widen, and she takes a sharp breath, like she's fighting to keep herself composed. But when her gaze meets mine, I see it—the impact I have on her. It's exactly what I wanted. To make her feel something, to make her ache for something she can't have, just like she did to my heart when she walked away.

Heat surges through me at the closeness of her, my entire body humming with the charged atmosphere between us. I reach out with my free hand, trailing my finger down the center of her chest, then slipping it between her tits.

Her breath hitches, and I can't help but smirk, feeling the power shift in my favor. I've got her exactly where I want her—vulnerable, wanting, but unable to get what she wants from me.

My presence commands her attention, her gaze locking onto mine, and for a split second, I lose myself in the depth of her brown eyes. The connection is undeniable, but I shake myself out of it, focusing on what needs to happen. Her gaze falls to my lips, and I know we're both playing this silent game. Her hesitation gives me exactly what I need.

With calculated patience, I wait, watching her breath quicken. And the moment she lets her guard slip just enough, I slam my lips against hers, taking what I've been fucking craving.

It's raw, filthy, and needy. The moment I hear a soft moan escape her lips; a wicked, primal satisfaction floods my senses—I've won. I want her to realize exactly what she walked away from. Gone are the days of the inexperienced boy who used to beg for her attention.

I reach out, my fingers skimming across her tit before I grab it, squeezing her nipple hard. She hisses, that sound is like music to my ears.

My cock throbs, desperate, aching to feel her, to fuck her until she knows just how much I crave it. But I force myself to push those urges down, just long enough to regain control.

I turn her around, pressing her back against me, pressing her up against the wall and I bury my face in her neck, kissing her soft skin, breathing her in. Her scent is intoxicating, pulling me under, but I can't let go—not yet. Not until I've made her see how fucking much I've changed. Just a moment longer, and I'll make sure she regrets everything.

"I want to touch you. You have no fucking idea what you're doing to me," I growl, my lips brushing against her skin, the heat of my breath only making it worse. "Let me touch you... Please," I whisper, the desperation in my voice raw as I drag my tongue along the curve of her neck. She shudders, her breath shaky, and when she finally nods, it feels like a victory—a win in this battle between us.

I slide my hand beneath the waistband of her shorts, slipping into her underwear. I run my fingers along her bare pussy and I almost groan. My fingers run through her wetness, feeling how fucking desperate she is, how turned on she is—just as much as I am. Every inch of her screams that she wants me, just like I fucking want her. I press my hard cock against her ass, the heat between us almost unbearable. My fingers find her clit, teasing, circling with a slow, deliberate rhythm. She moans, soft and breathless, and tilts her head to the side, offering her neck like a silent plea.

I fight the overwhelming urge to lose myself in the heat of her skin, the way she smells, the way my fingers slip so easily inside her. My mind screams at me to pull back, to walk away before I destroy everything I've built. If I stay, I'll give in—I'll fuck her, and everything I've planned will be for nothing.

She lets out a soft, breathy moan as I kiss her neck, the sound unraveling me. I move quickly, my lips brushing the shell of her ear, my fingers never slowing down. She closes her eyes, lost in pleasure, her body reacting eagerly, and I can feel her getting dangerously close—so fucking close to her orgasm.

"Listen the fuck up, Aubrey," I growl, my voice dark and heavy with frustration. "This is just a fucking taste of what you gave up when you walked away from me. No matter how much you want it now, know this—you'll never fucking have it again."

In an instant, I yank my hand away, a smirk twisting my lips as I silently declare the end of this encounter. I laugh, the sound rough and mocking as I take a step back. "Too fucking bad, Aubrey. I would've loved to watch you come on my fingers and my cock, but you made your choice ages ago."

Her face flushes with frustration, the desperate ache for release etched across her features. The sight sends a twisted satisfaction coursing through me, knowing I'm the one who's made her burn like this.

Still smirking, I turn away, refusing to give her the satisfaction of more attention. Let her stand there, tangled in her emotions, while I walk away. If she craves an orgasm, she'll have to fucking take matters into her own hands. I'm fucking done with her.

I make my way toward the door, adjusting my hard cock before swinging it open and stepping into the bustling gym.

Jace and Reece are still sitting there glued to their phones.

As I walk towards them, the memory of Aubrey pressed up against me messes with my head.

The sensation of my lips on her warm neck, the heat of her body pressing against mine, and the feeling of my fingers exploring her wet pussy—all of it stirs up a storm I can't shake. My cock is screaming for release, and I need to clear my fucking head. I need to find someone to fuck or just sneak off to the bathroom and jerk off. Anything to get this shit out of my system. I can't keep losing my shit like this whenever she's around.

CHAPTER 7

AUBREY

I'm still fucking grappling with what Noah did to me—how I fell for his bullshit and let him twist me around his finger. I was naive enough to believe he was still the kind, loving guy I once knew, but now I see him for the manipulative asshole he truly is. The worst part? My body still aches for the release he denied me. That fucking prick. But I can't let myself dwell on it—not now, not when there's more important shit to focus on.

My nerves are on edge, anxiety prickling as I stand outside the burger joint Sam told me about. She said they're always hiring, and I'm desperately praying that I land a couple of shifts, maybe more. I need something—anything—to keep me busy, to avoid the stifling silence and half-hearted conversations with my dad at home. Plus, having my own money means I won't have to depend on him for food and basic shit. I need this job, not just for the cash, but for myself.

Taking a deep, calming breath, I step forward and push open the door.

Sam told me the owner, Wes, is a former rockstar who still belts out tunes for his customers. The place looks a little rough around the edges, tucked into a sketchy part of town, but the packed parking lot hints at its loyal fanbase.

As I step inside, the smell of sizzling grease and grilled meat hits me, and I make my way to the counter, bracing myself for whatever comes next.

I glance around, waiting for a server to notice me. The place oozes nostalgia, the walls a chaotic collage of rock band posters from every era. But one band dominates, its presence unmistakable. Broken Oasis. The hometown legends. The golden boys who put this shithole of a town on the map and etched their names into the music scene forever. Xander Williams and Ace Roberts. Their faces stare back at me from framed photos, a shrine to local pride—immortalized not just here but back at school, where they're still revered like gods.

"Recognize those lads?" A deep voice snaps me out of my thoughts.

I turn to see a middle-aged man standing nearby, his bald head gleaming under the neon lights. Chains hang from his neck, and tattoos snake down his arms, each design telling a story I'll never know. He has a roughness to him, like someone who's lived through more than a few storms.

"Xander and Ace," he says with a hint of a smile, his gaze drifting back to the photos. "They used to hang out here all the time. Good kids. Lived and breathed music." He looks at me, eyes sharp but not unkind. "You need a table?"

"Actually, I'm here to apply for a job," I manage, my voice steady enough, though nerves flicker beneath the surface. "I heard you were hiring."

"I am," he says, nodding slightly as he gives me a quick once-over, like he's sizing me up. "You ever worked in a place like this before?"

"No," I admit.

"Alright then... I didn't catch your name," he prompts, his tone casual but his sharp gaze anything but.

"Aubrey," I reply, forcing confidence into my voice even as my nerves kick up a notch.

"Well, Aubrey, you've got five seconds to convince me why I should hire you, considering you've got no experience in a place like this."

My pulse spikes, but I push through. "I need this job, and I'm dead set about proving myself. I'll show up for every shift, always on time. You won't regret it—I'm a fast learner, and I'm ready to give it my—"

He raises a hand, cutting me off mid-sentence. The corners of his mouth twitch, caught between a smirk and a scowl, like he's weighing whether to be amused or unimpressed.

My stomach sinks. I bite back the urge to ramble further, kicking myself for not being more prepared. The fear that I've already blown it creeps in.

His silence feels heavier with each passing second as his sharp eyes bore into me, scanning me like he's trying to figure out what I'm made of.

The pause stretches unbearably long, tension coiling in my chest until, finally, he lowers his hand and speaks.

"So, you're really in need of this job, huh?"

"Yes," I reply firmly, locking onto his gaze with everything I've got, refusing to waver.

He studies me for another agonizing moment before nodding, almost to himself. "Alright. Here's the deal—you've got to prove you can handle this gig. If you can, and only if you can, I'll start you off with three shifts a week—Mondays, Tuesdays, and Thursdays. Weekends are covered for now, but if we're short, I might call you in. Think you can handle that?"

"Yes, weekends are wide open for me," I reply without hesitation, ignoring how desperate I might sound. This isn't just a job—it's a lifeline. I need this to get through the year, no matter what it takes.

"You've got the right attitude. I like that," he says, nodding, his tone softening just enough to feel genuine. "Dedication like yours is exactly what I'm looking for." He extends a hand. "I'm Wes, by the way. When can you come back for a trial shift to see if you're a good fit?"

"I can do the trial now, if that works for you," I offer quickly, trying to sound calm even though my pulse is racing.

A flicker of amusement crosses his face, and he smirks. "Alright then. I'll have you shadow one of the servers, get a feel for the routine and the layout." His gaze shifts to the bustling restaurant floor before landing back on me. "Let's see what you've got."

I scan the room, and my stomach twists into a brutal knot as my eyes land on a face I know all too well—Jace.

Jace, with that infuriating cocky smirk and swagger that screams trouble. The guy who's always treated girls like disposable playthings. Back when I was here with Noah, he was always in the background, Noah's shadow—lurking, laughing, and hunting for his next conquest.

Not him. Please, not Jace, I beg silently, clinging to the faint hope that, for once, the universe might show me some mercy. But deep down, I already know better. Lately, my luck hasn't just abandoned me—it's been laughing in my face at every turn.

And just like that, my fears are confirmed.

"Jace, come on over," Wes calls out.

Jace tosses the damp cloth he'd been using into a grimy water bucket. He takes his time strolling over, his cocky grin growing wider with every step. When his eyes lock onto mine, they glint with a familiar, predatory gleam that sets my nerves on edge.

His gaze drags over me, unashamed and intrusive, and a shiver runs down my spine. I shift uncomfortably under the weight of his stare, hating how exposed and vulnerable I suddenly feel.

"Jace, this is Aubrey," Wes says, his voice steady and authoritative. "She's learning the ropes. Get her up to speed on the basics and keep it professional. None of that inappropriate crap you pull with customers." Wes's tone sharpens, his eyes narrowing. "And if you so much as think about trying anything with her, there will be consequences. Got it?"

A flicker of annoyance flashes across Jace's face, his grin faltering for just a moment before he forces it back into place—tight, insincere, and full of barely concealed irritation.

I can't help the small grin tugging at my lips at Wes's words. He's no fool, clearly well aware of Jace's reputation. It feels like a small, satisfying win—having someone call him out without me needing to dredge up all the inappropriate things I've seen or experienced firsthand.

"Got it," Jace mutters begrudgingly, his tone sour.

"Well, I'll leave you with Jace. If you need me, just come find me. I'll be around somewhere," Wes says with a nod before striding off, leaving me alone with the one person I was so desperate to avoid.

I glance at Jace and catch him blatantly staring at my tits, not even trying to be subtle about it. Typical. Just what I need.

"So," I say, crossing my arms over my chest, "are you going to show me how things work around here, or are you planning on staring at my tits all night?"

His gaze snaps to mine, and a slow, smug smirk spreads across his lips, like he's savoring the challenge I just threw his way. In that instant, it clicks. I finally understand why Jace Cooper's name is whispered in the same breath as Noah's back at school.

His sharply defined jawline, piercing green eyes that seem to dare you to look away, and the way his dark hair falls just right—effortless, like part of some calculated charm—all work together as weapons in his arsenal.

There's no denying his appeal, and I hate that I'm not immune to it. It's the same magnetic pull that's made girls giggle and blush in the hallways, the same pull that's left behind a wake of broken hearts and whispered regrets.

But no matter how undeniably hot he is, none of it erases the truth: Jace Cooper is the living embodiment of everything I despise. The ultimate player. The guy who lives for the thrill of the chase, only to toss girls aside like yesterday's trash once he's had his fun.

Sam's stories about Jace flash through my mind. Three girls at one party. If that's even half true, it tells me everything I need to know about him. Still, I can't help but wonder if some of those rumors—like the ones about me—are just exaggerated bullshit.

Not that it matters. Whatever truths or lies are hidden beneath Jace's smirk, I'm not about to let myself become another notch on his bedpost.

"Only if you're ready to whip 'em out and show me those tits," Jace says, his smirk widening as he gestures crudely toward my chest, every bit the arrogant prick I expected.

My irritation flares into full-blown anger, and I narrow my eyes at him. "Your crude lines might work on other girls, but not on me," I snap, my voice sharp and firm. "Save that shit. I'm not interested, and if you cross any boundaries, I won't hesitate to tell Wes about your behavior toward colleagues."

The words taste bitter as they leave my mouth. I hate even sounding like the kind of person who'd run to the boss, but Jace doesn't need to know that. "I need this job," I continue, keeping my tone steady. "So let's keep things strictly professional, okay? Let's not make this any more awkward than it already is."

For a moment, he doesn't respond. His green eyes wander over my face, lingering too long on my lips, as if he's imagining something I want no part of. My stomach twists as the silence stretches between us. Is this idiot even listening, or is he just another clueless asshole who can't see past his own ego?

Finally, after what feels like forever, he shifts his gaze and shrugs, his tone infuriatingly casual, like I hadn't just called him out. "Let's clean the tables and get them ready for the next group," he says, brushing off the confrontation as if it never happened.

I follow Jace to the tables, frustration bubbling beneath the surface. Working with him is proving to be every bit the nightmare I'd imagined.

Without a word, he returns to the table he was cleaning before Wes interrupted, grabs the damp cloth from the water bucket, and wrings it out. Then he tosses it to me, his smirk all but screaming challenge.

As I lean over to wipe down the table, I can feel his gaze burning into me. I bet the bastards staring at my ass.

I grit my teeth, pushing the thought aside. Focus. Just get through this shift. My hands tighten around the cloth, and I focus on the task, scrubbing harder than necessary as though I can scrape away my irritation.

Jace starts walking me through the restaurant, pointing out the usual shit—where orders go, where the ice machine is, how to restock. His voice, smooth and overly confident, grates on my nerves. But at least, for once, he's giving me actual information instead of a string of sleazy comments.

As we start serving tables together, something shifts. With each trip to deliver plates or clear dishes, he hands me small, practical tips on how to move faster, how to do things more efficiently. He even—God help me—compliments me on my performance.

"You're catching on fast," he says at one point, flashing a grin that feels...almost genuine.

It feels wrong, like a setup. Why would someone like him bother being nice? I brace myself for the usual smirk or a crude comment to follow, but it doesn't come. Instead, the flirting dies down completely, and for a brief moment, it's like I'm just another co-worker to him—no games, no bullshit.

But that only makes me more suspicious. Why the sudden switch? Why can't he just act like this all the time instead of playing whatever game he's got going on?

By the time the night finally drags to an end, I'm utterly spent. My feet throb, my back aches, and every step between the tables and the kitchen feels like I've run a marathon. Jace is somewhere in the background restocking ketchup bottles, and for the first time all night, I'm left alone to clean the last few tables in peace.

As I wipe down the final table, Wes emerges from the kitchen and heads straight for me.

"You did exceptionally well tonight," he says, his voice steady and sincere. "I've been watching you, and I have to say, you've earned the position."

The weight in my chest lightens slightly, relief washing over me. I did it. Somehow, I survived this night.

"Thanks, I won't mess this up," I reply. Having the job sorted means I can stop hunting and start focusing. I'm determined to make this work, even if Jace reverts to being a pain in the ass. If he pulls any shit, I'll shut him down again, no hesitation.

Wes turns, motioning for the other servers to join us. "Alright, I've already split tonight's tips," he announces, then hands me an envelope.

I blink in surprise as I take it. I wasn't expecting to get a share of the tips tonight, especially on my first shift. But hey, I'm not about to turn down extra cash.

"Jace, Susan!" Wes calls out.

Jace saunters over, having just finished arranging the salt and pepper shakers, while Susan follows close behind. I hadn't had much chance to talk to her tonight, with everything being so hectic, but her presence speaks volumes. She's in her thirties, her face marked with stories of hard-earned experience, including a deep scar that cuts across her cheek. Without a word, she snatches her envelope and disappears into the kitchen.

"So," Wes says, turning back to me, "you're scheduled for Mondays, Tuesdays, and Thursdays, five to ten. Paydays are Fridays, but tips get split nightly."

"Thanks, that works perfectly," I reply, grateful for the stability. It's Wednesday, so I'm already thinking about tomorrow's shift and making a bit more cash before the week's out.

"Welcome to the team, Aubrey," Wes greets me warmly, offering a tight smile before turning and heading back toward the kitchen.

I grab the grimy water bucket, preparing to empty it to where Jace had shown me earlier during his rundown of the restaurant.

With the cleaning done and the restaurant spotless, I finally step outside into the cold, dark night. Ten blocks to go. The streets in this neighborhood always put me on edge at this hour, but I have no choice. Three nights a week—maybe more if weekends get added. This is the routine now, and I just have to push through.

The street is eerily silent, the distant hum of an engine starting the only sound. I clutch my arms tighter around myself, silently cursing my decision that I didn't grab my jacket. But I hadn't planned on working tonight—I'd only come to ask about the job.

A car's headlights flare to life in the lot, momentarily blinding me. I shield my eyes with one hand and quicken my pace, my focus fixed on getting home as fast as possible.

Halfway down the block, a chill creeps up my spine like icy fingers clawing at my skin. My heart pounds harder with each step, fear pulsing through my veins. Footsteps echo behind me, too close for comfort.

I force myself to keep my head straight, quickening my pace without breaking into a run. Every nerve in my body is on edge, screaming at me to sprint, but I fight the instinct.

"Hey, Aubrey, wait up."

The voice makes me whirl around, my heart hammering in my chest. "What the fuck, Jace?" I snap; my voice sharp. "You scared me half to death. Don't pull that crap on a girl."

He raises his hands in mock surrender, his expression sheepish. "Sorry. It's late, and you shouldn't be walking home alone. I thought we could walk together."

I hesitate, glancing back at the dark stretch of street ahead. The logical part of me screams to send him away—to walk the rest of the way alone and avoid whatever game he might be playing. This is Jace, the cocky asshole I don't trust. But the oppressive silence and shadows pressing in around me make my stomach churn. The thought of walking ten blocks by myself, vulnerable and exposed, has me nodding before my brain can catch up.

I turn back toward the path ahead and start walking again, my pulse still racing. With Wes nowhere in sight, the question looms: will Jace revert to the smug prick with the sleazy comments? Will I spend the next twenty minutes fending off his bullshit?

He matches my pace easily, his presence too close for comfort. "We work the same shifts," he says, his tone casual. "If you want, I'm happy to walk home together from now on."

His offer sounds almost sincere, like he's doing me a favor. But I don't trust favors from Jace Cooper.

"Yeah, we'll see," I snap, narrowing my eyes at him. "See if you turn back into the asshole I know you are." I keep my tone sharp, trying to sound indifferent, but inside, I'm already bracing for the worst. "Where do you live? Is it anywhere near my place?"

If this is some kind of ploy—a game he plays to get under my skin or, worse, into my bed—he's in for a rude awakening. I'm not one of his easy prey. Tonight, he can go home to his hand and his overinflated ego. That's all he's getting from me, and he better get used to it.

"Nah, I don't live that far, just two blocks past your place," he replies casually, like it's no big deal.

I stop short, turning to him with suspicion carved into every line of my face. "How the fuck do you know where I live?"

A cocky grin spreads across his face—the kind that probably works on every girl dumb enough to fall for his charm. But not me.

"Don't get paranoid," he says, his voice dripping with amusement. "I'm not some fucking stalker. I grew up here. Small town: everyone knows where everyone lives. You're still next door to Noah, right?"

"Yeah," I mutter, my gaze sliding back to the darkened street. The mention of Noah hits me hard—I try to block it out, but all I can see is his hot mouth on my neck, the way he made my legs shake, how he had me so close to coming without even trying. That asshole. Why the fuck did I let that happen?

Jace's voice cuts through my spiraling thoughts. "So, what's the deal between you and Noah?"

I glance over at him, catching the flicker of something in his expression—curiosity, maybe, or something sharper. His gaze flicks away, then back to me, like he's testing the waters, trying to figure something out.

My stomach twists, a knot of suspicion tightening in my gut. Does he know what happened today? Are they all talking about it? Noah, Jace, and Reece—they're always together, always sharing stories. Did Noah tell them how he turned me down? Did he fucking gloat about how easily I let him touch me, like I was some toy he could play with and toss aside?

I clench my jaw, the heat of anger rising to meet the cold dread pooling in my chest. If Jace knows, if he's fishing for a reaction, I won't give him the satisfaction.

I grit my teeth, shoving the thoughts out of my mind. "Why the fuck do you wanna know?" The words come out sharper than I planned, but I don't trust Jace enough to spill any of this shit. Not when I'm still wondering if every word I say will somehow find its way back to Noah.

Jace shrugs, his tone casual, like he's got no hidden agenda. "I thought you two were tight once."

He's fishing, waiting for me to bite. But I'm not that naive.

"Yeah, we used to be tight, but not anymore," I mutter, my eyes flicking to the crescent moon glowing faintly above us. The night feels suffocatingly quiet, and all I really want is to get home. Even dealing with my dad's bullshit seems easier than this.

We walk in silence for two more blocks, then take a right.

Just three more blocks to go, and I can put this whole conversation behind me.

"So, how's school now that you're back?" Jace asks, his voice feigning casual curiosity. Like he doesn't already know the answer. The nerve of him, acting like he's genuinely interested after everything that's gone on. Does he think I'm that stupid?

I can't help the sarcasm dripping from my words. "Oh, it's fucking amazing," I snap, lacing the words with as much venom as I can muster. "But I think you already know the answer to that." My eyes cut to him, sharp and unrelenting. "I've seen you there, right next to Noah, when all the shit went down."

Jace doesn't even flinch. Instead, he tilts his head like he's studying me. "So why do you put up with it? You don't hold back with me, so why let Tia get away with that crap?"

The question hits harder than I'd like to admit. It's the same thing I've been asking myself. Normally, I wouldn't hesitate to call someone like Tia out, but there's this stupid part of me—this lingering echo of who we used to be. Sleepovers, boy talk, and those ridiculous mall trips where we acted like we ruled the world. Maybe that's why it's so hard to cut her off. Because, once upon a time, we used to be friends.

But fuck it. I'm not about to explain that to Jace. Especially not him. Who knows what he might do with the information... From what Sam's told me, Jace doesn't have a great track record with girls. He uses them, then moves on. If I tell him anything, would he twist it to his advantage? Use it as some sick leverage to make me do whatever he wants.

I stay silent, biting back every word on the tip of my tongue. The quiet stretches between us, thick and tense, but I can feel him watching me, waiting for me to respond.

I won't give him the satisfaction. If he wants to pry into my life, I'll turn the tables on him.

"So, you want to talk about rumors?" I say, my voice smooth but cutting. "Let's talk about you. Did you really screw three girls at that party a few weeks ago?"

I watch him carefully, waiting to see if he'll crack. If he's going to pry into my life, I'm damn well going to throw his right back in his face.

A smirk ghosts across his lips, like he's enjoying every bit of his notorious reputation. "Is that what you've heard?" he asks as we approach my street.

"Yeah, and I've seen how you act," I snap, irritation cutting through my words. It pisses me off—this whole double standard. I'm branded as an easy slut when the only person I've ever been with is Noah. Meanwhile, guys like Jace can screw whoever the fuck they want and somehow come out of it looking like gods.

He glances at me, his expression shifting to something surprisingly serious. "No," he says firmly, his tone almost defensive. "I'm not the player everyone thinks I am."

I scoff, not buying it for a second. "So, you didn't hook up with three girls at once at that party?" I press, challenging him to own up to the stories that seem to follow him everywhere.

He doesn't miss a beat. "No," he says, that smirk crawling back onto his face like it belongs there. "I didn't sleep with them." There's a pause, his grin widening, and I know whatever comes next is going to piss me off. "There wasn't any sleeping involved. Just a lot of mouths and pussy."

The anger inside me flares, hot and sharp. I want to scream at him for being such an arrogant asshole, but instead, I let the fury simmer under my skin. He's exactly the kind of guy every girl should stay the fuck away from—cocky, selfish, and completely shameless about using people. And here I am, walking beside him, letting him play the same game with me.

"You make me sick," I bite out, my voice low but seething. "That's literally the definition of a player." The words hang between us, and as much as I try not to, I can't help but wonder if Noah's any different. He and Jace are close, after all. People have whispered about Noah jumping from girl to girl, though Sam's never said anything like what she told me about Jace.

Still, it makes me question everything—if Noah's just better at hiding it or if he's really changed.

Jace lets out a chuckle, his arrogance bleeding into every syllable. "What, you want me to deny it? Pretend I didn't fuck three girls in one night, just to make you feel better? I could lie, tell you what you want to hear, but that's not really my style." He says it so proudly, it's infuriating. And the worst part? There's a part of me still listening.

Finally, my house comes into view, and relief washes over me. I'll be done with him in a matter of minutes.

I don't even look at him when I speak, my voice ice-cold. "And why the fuck would I want to talk to you after hearing that?" Being seen with him will only fan the flames of the rumors, and I won't let that happen. Not when I'm barely holding it together as it is.

"Aub," he says, and before I can make a beeline to my lawn, his hand darts out and grabs my arm, stopping me in my tracks.

"It's Aubrey to you," I snap, yanking my arm out of his grip. Only Noah calls me that, and I'll be damned if I let this asshole think he can too.

His smirk doesn't waver, but the glint of satisfaction in his eyes sets my blood boiling. He's enjoying this—getting under my skin. I hate how much he's loving it. My skin crawls just being near him, but I force myself to stay put, resisting the urge to slap that smug look off his face.

"Just fucking listen, okay?" he says, his tone softening, but not enough to lose its edge of arrogance. "If things with Tia get out of hand at school, you can talk to me."

The way he says it, like he's doing me some huge favor, only makes me angrier. He's not my savior, and I sure as hell don't need him to play the part of some hero swooping out of the sky to save the day. He's as much a part of the problem as the rest of them.

"I'll be fine. I've got Sam," I shoot back, my voice sharp. I'm done with this conversation. I don't owe him anything, and I sure as hell don't need his fake concern.

Jace starts to say something, but I don't bother listening. I don't care what he has to say. I turn and head up the front path, my steps quick and purposeful. All I want is to get the fuck away from him.

As I push the front door open, the sound of the television blaring greets me. My dad's slouched on the couch, a beer in hand, staring blankly at the screen like it's the only thing that matters. He doesn't even glance my way. I might as well not even exist to him.

The urge to scream bubbles up inside me, raw and feral. I want to throw something, break something—anything to release the anger clawing at my chest. But I don't. I swallow it down, just like I always do.

The frustration mixes with the ache that never leaves. The kind that reminds me, no matter how many people are around, I'm always alone.

Chapter 8

Noah

Having Aubrey so close today has fucked me up in ways I can't even begin to explain. The taste of her lips, the feel of her body pressed against mine—it's burned into me like a brand, and no matter how hard I try, I can't put out the fire. I've already jerked off twice today, trying to exorcise her from my head, but it's useless.

When I left the gym, I thought about finding someone else, anyone else, to fuck and drown her out. But I knew it wouldn't work. It's her I'd be thinking about, just like I always do. Every other girl I've fucked becomes her in my head, a stand-in, a pale imitation that only makes the ache sharper. I'm fucking pathetic, haunted by someone who'll never stay.

It took every shred of self-control I had today not to lose it—not to take what I wanted. I felt her everywhere, tight and perfect under my hands, and I knew if I gave in, I'd come apart. She'd worm her way back into my life, tear me apart piece by piece, and then leave in ruin all over again, just like before. That first time? It damn near fucking destroyed me. I barely managed to put myself back together, and I know I wouldn't survive another round.

But the pull is still there—relentless, maddening. It doesn't matter, though. I can't let her back in. So I'll sit here with this torment, this ache that won't go away, because it's better than the pain of losing her again. It has to be.

Sitting in my bedroom, the darkness swallowing me whole, I take a slow drag from my joint, letting the burn in my lungs ground me. I adjust my hard cock, already aching because she's in my head again. Fucking Aubrey. No matter what I do, she's always there, clawing her way back into my mind like she owns it.

I try to shove her aside, but it's a losing battle. So I let my anger shift to someone else: my so-called mother. Or the ghost of her, because that's all she's ever been to me. Ever since I got home, Dad's been on my case about her—about how she's reached out again, wanting to "reconnect." As if I give a shit about her or the half-siblings she decided were worth staying for.

What pisses me off the most is Dad backing her up, acting like it's some noble fucking mission to give her another chance. He knows what she did to us—how she walked away and left us both broken without so much as a glance back. So why the hell is he pushing for this now? Just hearing her name dredges up all the shit I've spent years trying to bury, the same way I've been trying to bury every memory of Aubrey.

But the past never stays buried, does it? It claws its way to the surface, dragging you under until you can't fucking breathe. Right now, it feels like I'm drowning in both of them.

I take another hit from my joint, holding it in until the haze starts to settle over me, softening the edges of my thoughts. It's temporary, fleeting—but I'll take it. Anything to quiet the relentless loop playing in my head.

Then Tia's bullshit flashes through my mind, the way she's been acting toward Aubrey. I don't condone it—it's petty and vindictive—but I'm not about to step into their mess. It's not my place to fix their drama. And Aubrey doesn't need me to. She's always been able to hold her own. She'll stand up to Tia when she's had enough.

Aubrey's strong like that.

Tia lets her insecurities spill out all over the place, so messy and grating it drives me insane.

But Aubrey? She's the opposite. She's composed, a force of nature, and my fucking kryptonite.

She's my one glaring weakness in a world where I've fought so hard to stay untouchable. And that's the worst part. I know how dangerous it is to let her get under my skin again, but it doesn't stop me from wanting her.

I take another drag, letting the smoke escape in slow, curling wisps, like maybe it could carry away some of this pent-up frustration with it. One more year. I keep telling myself that. Counting down the days until I can finally break free and figure out who the hell I'm supposed to be. But no matter how much I want that freedom, the thought of leaving my dad behind hits hard.

Since she walked out and left us shattered, I've been his whole world. He never complained, never crumbled—just picked up the pieces and carried them like they weren't crushing him. He became everything I needed, both parents rolled into one. And I've felt it every step of the way—his love, his pride, his unwavering belief in me, even when I didn't fucking deserve it.

The thought of him sitting here alone after I leave. It fucking wrecks me. Twists something deep inside. He gave up so much for me, and I can't stop wondering how he'll handle it once I'm gone. Maybe I can find a college close by—someplace that lets me come home on weekends, keep him company, make sure the silence she left behind doesn't drown him.

Fuck my mother for what she did to us. For walking away and leaving us wrecked while she built a shiny new life, like we were nothing but a chapter she could rip out and rewrite. She's moved on, but the scars she left... They still ache like fresh wounds—on me, on my dad. She hasn't been a mother to me in years, not in any way that matters. And yet, her shadow still hangs over him.

It drives me insane, the power she still holds over him. Maybe, deep down, he still loves her, no matter what she did to us. Maybe that's what love does—it fucks you up, digs in, and refuses to let go no matter how hard you try to bury it.

I get it. God, do I fucking get it.

It's the same way I feel about Aubrey.

It's not like I want to feel this way. Not after all the ways she cut me open without even trying. But no matter how many times I tell myself to move on, to forget, the feeling sticks. They leave, both of them, and the pain should fade, right? But then they come back, like ghosts stirring up everything you thought you'd buried. And just like that, you're fucked all over again.

I lift the joint to my lips, ready to take another hit, but pause when voices drift in through the open window. Low murmurs, cutting through the stillness. It pulls my attention, and I move closer, leaning against the frame. The streetlights outside cast jagged shadows across the yard, flickering as the leaves shift in the breeze.

That's when I see them—Jace and Aubrey, standing way too fucking close in front of her house.

What the fuck is Jace doing with Aubrey?

My grip tightens around the joint, my chest burning—and it's not from the smoke. Seeing them stirs something sharp and raw inside me, a mix of anger and something worse I can't even name.

My mind spins with infinite possibilities, none of them comforting. If Jace is pulling some fucked-up stunt on her, adding to the shitstorm she's already dealing with, I'll step in without a second thought. The way he looked at her today—like she was just another toy to play with—pisses me off. My fists are already itching, ready to knock some sense into him.

I stand there, tension coiling tight in my chest, as Aubrey steps away, only for Jace to grab her arm, stalling her. The sight of his hand on her twists something ugly in my gut. This damn well better not be Jace doing Tia's dirty work, plotting some bullshit against Aubrey. Knowing the two of them, it wouldn't surprise me. Tia's probably already sucked Jace off to get him to play along. That's their thing, always trading favors for favors, using each other like pawns in some fucked-up chess match.

But not this time. Not with Aubrey.

After the shit that happened between me and Tia today, I won't think twice about telling her to fuck off, no matter how it looks to anyone else—or even if Aubrey finds out how I still feel about her. I can deny that shit in a heartbeat if I have to. They forget who they're dealing with.

I've been ignoring Tia's relentless texts all night. She's been blowing up my phone since this afternoon, flipping between flirting and calling me a bastard because I won't reply. It's exhausting. She's getting bolder too, acting like she's wearing some damn invisible crown, like she's some fucking queen born to rule the world. Well, fuck that. Doesn't she get it? I'm not interested. I never have been, and I never will.

I stub out my joint, ready to storm outside and rip Jace's hand off her myself, but I stop when I see Aubrey yank her arm free and bolt up the front path. Relief barely settles in before my gaze snaps back to Jace, still standing there, still watching her. He's lingering, and it makes my blood boil all over again.

Why the fuck is she even with him in the first place? My thoughts won't stop spiraling, one question louder than the rest: has she changed that much? The girl I knew—hell, the girl I loved—wouldn't have been caught dead with someone like Jace Cooper. I used to know her better than anyone. Every thought, every feeling, every little look she gave me.

But then the rumors start creeping back into my head, like a bad soundtrack stuck on repeat. I can't shake the image of those condoms spilling out of her bag. What the fuck was that about? And the thought of her with Jace—him, with his shitty reputation and the way he talks about girls like they're nothing more than walking orgasms—twists something deep inside me.

A surge of protectiveness tears through me, gnawing at my insides. I don't want her anywhere near him.

But then a voice in the back of my head cuts through the noise with the truth: I've talked about her the same way. Like she's just some easy lay, a quick fuck. I've used the same degrading shit Jace would say, and now I hate myself for it. What the fuck is wrong with me?

From my hidden vantage point, I watch as Jace walks off down the street, disappearing into the shadows. A jagged spike of frustration slams through me. The urge to storm out there, confront him, demand to know why the fuck he was with her, why he dared to ignore my warning after I told him she was off-limits, claws at me. But I hold back.

If I go out there, if I confront him, it'll expose everything—that I've been watching them, that I'm obsessed with the girl next door, that I care way more than I'll admit to anyone.

My gaze shifts to Aubrey's house when her bedroom light flickers on. I edge closer to the window, my body moving on its own, like some desperate stalker. I can't tear myself away. I don't want to. She moves across the room, her steps heavy like she's too exhausted to keep up any walls. My eyes track her every move. She pulls her hair out of its ponytail, the strands falling messily around her face. She's not trying to impress anyone—she's just... her. And I can't look away.

I watch as she tugs her shirt over her head, her movements slow and weary. All I can think is how much I miss her. And how much I fucking hate myself for it.

She's so goddamn beautiful it fucking hurts. Every detail of her is etched into my mind—her eyes, her lips, the way she moves, the way she was. Incredibly fuckable, in a way that makes it hard to breathe. And every time I think about her being with someone else—him—it tears me apart.

The idea that Jace might've touched her, that he might've heard her moan and scream, twists my insides into something ugly and raw. Did I push her toward him? Was it the way I acted—like she didn't matter to me, like she was nothing? I was too proud, too fucking scared to admit how much I needed her. How much I've always needed her.

And the thought of Jace pretending to care, acting like he gives a shit, sets my blood on fire. But the worst part—the thing that eats me alive—is wondering if she's falling for his bullshit.

The Aubrey I knew wouldn't have. She would've told him to fuck off, seen through his bullshit without breaking a sweat. But now? I don't know her anymore. She's not the same.

And that thought... it fucks me up more than anything else.

I stand there, frozen, my gaze locked on her as she slips off her boots, then her jeans. Each movement is slow, deliberate, like she knows the power she holds, making every nerve in my body hum with awareness. My pulse spikes—wild, erratic—as I take in the curve of her hips, the smooth line of her legs, the effortless grace in the way she moves. She's fucking beautiful—no, more than that. She's a goddamn vision, and I'm powerless to look away.

And then, just as I'm losing myself, she looks up. Her eyes meet mine, catching me in the act. The air leaves my lungs in a sharp rush, and for a moment, time seems to freeze.

Surprise flashes across her face, but it's fleeting—replaced by something unreadable. It feels like she can see straight through me, like she knows every dark, twisted thought racing through my mind right now, knows exactly how much I want her. And yet, I'm the one left breathless.

Everything in me aches to fix what's broken.

To end this war we've been waging, to bridge the chasm between us. I want her back. I want to hear her laugh again, see her smile light up the room like it used to, before everything went to shit. But I don't know how to undo the damage I've done, how to rebuild something I've spent so long tearing down.

Memories flood in, unrelenting. Her laughter, her touch, her voice—each one sharper than the last. But the one that destroys me, the one that haunts me, is her walking away. That moment is seared into me like a scar that won't heal.

Her eyes drag down my bare chest, slow and deliberate, like she's trying to carve every inch of me into her memory. But it's when her gaze lands lower that my pulse kicks up. She doesn't just glance—she fucking stares—at the bulge of my cock, thick and throbbing beneath the thin fabric of my grey sweatpants. I don't bother hiding it. What's the point?

The air between us is already thick with all the shit we're too scared to say.

I let my hand drop, fingers brushing against the rigid outline of my cock, a small stroke that feels more like a dare than anything else. My jaw tightens as I look at her, the silence daring her to admit what we both already know—that this isn't just tension. It's years of unsaid words, buried feelings, and all the fucked-up, messy shit that's kept us apart.

The thought of how she felt under my hands today is fucking torture, it spurs my body on. The way her body responded, the soft, breathless moans that came with every stroke of my fingers —they've burned themselves into my brain, a cruel, unrelenting loop. It's not just the memory of her tight pussy or the way her lips parted as she tried to hold back the sounds that killed me. It's what she did to me—how she unraveled every shred of control I had and left me wanting like I've never wanted before.

Now, all I can think about is turning the tables. Making her feel the same unbearable pull, the same aching need that's tearing me apart. I want to strip her bare, inch by inch, until she's trembling, her every thought consumed by me.

The tension between us crackles like a live wire, sparking in the air, sharp and electric. Her gaze holds mine, dark and unflinching, like she's trying to strip me bare.

My hand moves, slow and deliberate, stroking my cock just enough to push the edge—a test, a dare for her to look away, to break first. But she doesn't.

Her gaze remains steady, unwavering, but there's something in her eyes—a flicker of raw, unfiltered need that sets my pulse racing. It's subtle, almost imperceptible, but it's there. A challenge. One I'm more than willing to meet. My hand dips lower, pushing past my waistband, freeing my cock. The air shifts when I do it, her throat working as she swallows, her lips parting just slightly before her tongue flicks out to wet them.

That subtle reaction wrecks me more than it should. A groan rumbles in my chest, low and guttural, as my imagination spirals. I can see it—her lips around me, taking me in inch by inch, the stretch of her jaw as she tries to take more. My fingers tangling in her midnight-black hair, guiding her movements until there's nothing left but the dizzying need to lose myself in her.

My hand moves faster, the slick rhythm filling the space between us. My cock is rock hard, each stroke sending sharp jolts through me, coiling the pressure low in my gut. My breaths come in uneven, shallow gasps at the sight of her—her parted lips, her rising chest—drags me closer to the edge.

Her name tears from my throat in a broken growl as I come, the release blinding, hot, spilling over my hand. "Aubrey." Her name feels like a confession, raw and unguarded, cutting through the layers I've built around myself. My body shudders with the force of it, the pleasure sharp and all-consuming as my strokes slow, dragging out every last ounce of pleasure.

When I finally look back at her, her breathing is uneven, her chest heaving as if she's fighting the same battle I am. Her eyes are unreadable, but the way she stares—like she's as wrecked as I am—tells me I've ruined her, just as much as she's fucking ruined me.

My cock still hangs out of my sweatpants, but I don't give a shit. I move closer to the window, drawn to her like I always am. Her stare pins me in place, unrelenting, cutting through every shitty wall I've put up. Aubrey. Fucking Aubrey. She sees too much. She always has.

No other girl has ever made me feel this exposed, this raw. No one else fucks with my head the way she does.

I reach up, grabbing the curtains in a single sharp move, and yank them shut. The abruptness feels like ripping off a bandage, cutting her off the only way I can. A fucking coward's move, but it's all I have.

For a moment, I stand there, paralyzed, my hand clutching the curtain like letting go of it would mean letting go of her too. Every nerve in my body screams for her, demands I open the curtains again, to see her, to find some proof that whatever this is, it isn't just tearing me apart.

But I don't. I can't.

Instead, I stay there, frozen, the weight of her name lingering in the air, tearing me apart from the inside out.

CHAPTER 9

AUBREY

Seeing Noah jerk himself off in the window shattered any illusion of control I had left. The heat pooling between my thighs wasn't just desire—it was an ache, raw and fucking relentless, crawling through me like it wanted to consume every part of me. My chest felt tight, my breath sharp and uneven, as I stood there watching him, wanting him, hating myself for every second of it.

I shouldn't feel this way. Not after what he did to me in the equipment room. Not after he touched me like that—fucked with my head, left me trembling, exposed—and then acted like it didn't matter. But now? Watching him take what he needed, his head tipped back, his jaw clenched, every movement deliberate and unrestrained... I couldn't think about anything else.

I tried to fight it, but my body betrayed me. The memory of his hands on me, his mouth claiming mine, the way he made me feel like I was burning from the inside out—it all came rushing back, stronger, sharper, impossible to ignore. I didn't want this. I didn't want to feel this desperate, this weak. But fuck, he looked so goddamn good. His muscles taut, his cock in his hand, and I was unraveling just from the sight of him.

If that makes me pathetic, then fine. I'll own it. Because watching him like that wasn't just hot—it was devastating. He wrecked me with just a look, a touch, and now this. And the worst part? I know I'd let him do it all over again.

After barely two hours of sleep—because, yes, I stayed up like a idiot to finish an essay after taking care of myself—I drag my ass out of bed, already wishing the day was over. My body feels like lead, my eyes burn, and every step toward getting ready feels like a goddamn marathon.

I pull on my favorite jeans, the ones that hug my legs just right, and a tank top that's more practical than anything else. Yesterday, I caught a few guys checking me out—Jace being the worst of the lot. After last night, I'm more determined than ever to steer clear of him.

I lace up my old, black combat boots—the ones with scuffed toes and frayed laces that no one else would be caught dead in at school. The girls at school all strut around in branded sneakers or trendy boots with shiny gold logos, and Tia, of course, leads the pack. Always perfect, always at the forefront of whatever glossy magazine told her to buy this week.

It's such a far cry from the Tia I knew years ago, back when she didn't give a shit about appearances or what anyone thought. Now, it's like she's a walking advertisement for everything I'm not.

Sure, my style doesn't match theirs, but at least it's mine. It's real. Back at my old school, there were always girls flaunting their designer labels, sneering at me and my friends like we didn't belong in the same universe. Here, it's different—or maybe worse. The pressure to fit in is suffocating, and everyone's so damn eager to mimic Tia, like she's the standard they all strive to reach.

I grab my homework and cram it into my bag, already pissed off at myself. The essay's shit. I know it. I spent half the night trying to slap something decent together, but between working a shift, watching Noah through the damn window, checking my phone for a text from my mother that still hasn't come, and, well, taking care of myself afterwards, my focus was shot.

Two days. I had two whole fucking days to get it done. And like a complete idiot, I waited until the last minute. What kind of impression is this supposed to make on my teacher? *Real solid, Aubrey. Way to look like you give a shit.*

All I can do now is hope for a passing grade, even though I know it's barely scraping by. The thought of another disappointing result makes my stomach churn, but I shove it down and sling my bag over my shoulder. What's done is done.

As I rush out of my room, the faint sounds of movement from the kitchen stop me in my tracks. My stomach twists. It's been days since I've seen my father, and I'd been counting on that streak continuing. Every morning, I've timed my exit perfectly to avoid him. But today? No such luck.

The old floorboards groan as I step into the kitchen, giving me away. His head snaps up, our eyes meeting for a split second before he glances at the window, like it holds all the answers to the mess we've become.

"Hey," he mutters, voice low and clipped, like even the word takes too much effort.

"Hi," I reply, my voice quieter than I intended, hovering in the doorway. I hesitate, half hoping he'll say something more, half dreading that he won't.

His eyes stay on the window, his tone flat and distant. "Okay, have a good day."

That's it. No effort, no follow-up, not even a flicker of care. I shouldn't be surprised—it's always been like this. We've never been close, not even when I lived here before. He was a shadow back then, especially when he drank. I stayed out of his way, hiding in my room or crashing at Noah's.

Now... Being shoved back into his life, without warning or approval, has only made things worse.

"Yeah," I mutter, forcing the word past the lump in my throat. "You too."

I turn and slip out the door, the silence clinging to me like a ghost.

Outside, Sam's tiny blue car is parked in front of my house, music blasting loud enough to wake the dead. A grin tugs at my lips as I head toward her. She's unapologetically herself, and I love that about her—how she doesn't give a shit what anyone thinks.

I climb into the passenger seat, and she lowers the volume just enough to talk.

"Hey," she says, flashing me a smile. "So, how'd it go last night?"

She's talking about the quick text I sent—about getting the job and, unfortunately, having Jace show me the ropes.

I shrug, keeping my tone casual. "It was alright."

But as we pull away from the curb, my eyes betray me. They flick toward the house just as Noah steps out the front door. His gaze locks onto mine through the car window, and my stomach twists, heat surging through me at the memory of last night.

Him at the window, his cock in his hand. It's seared into my mind, impossible to shake.

Even now, my body betrays me, warmth pooling low in my belly as I force myself to look away.

Once we've passed him, I turn my attention back to Sam, trying to force down the rush of emotions clawing at me. "My feet were killing me by the end of the night," I say, hoping she doesn't catch the slight shake in my voice.

She raises an eyebrow, sharp and curious. "And what about Jace? Was he his usual sleazy asshole self?"

I can't help but laugh, the tension breaking just enough. "Of course he was. Wouldn't be Jace if he wasn't. But Wes—the owner—put him in his place. When Jace tried his shit with me, I shot him down. Then he insisted on walking me home."

Sam's head snaps toward me, her eyes wide. "You're kidding, right? You didn't actually let him walk you home?"

"Well he sort of invited himself. Biggest fucking mistake of my life. The asshole tried to pull some move on me, acting like he's this supportive guy who's there for me if I need someone to talk to about Tia."

She lets out a dry, sarcastic laugh. "Yeah, right. After you give him a blowjob first."

I grin. Sam's bluntness is one of the reasons I like her so much. Since I've been back, she's made me feel like it's okay to be myself—like I don't have to fake my way into a group. Around her and her friends, I can just be me. No pretense. No bullshit.

"It's a wonder he didn't try what he pulled with Jessica," Sam says, her tone darkening slightly.

My grin fades. "And what was that?"

"Oh, girl, you won't believe this crap," Sam says, her voice dripping with disdain. "Bianca was stranded at a football game—car wouldn't start, phone was dead. Jace showed up, and she asked to borrow his phone. You know what he said? That she could—if she gave him a blowjob first. When she said no, he just walked away and left her there. She was stuck for hours."

I shoot her a look, my stomach twisting. "Are you serious? What an asshole."

Sam snorts. "Come on, you've seen the way Jace looks. Him, Noah, and Reece—they're hot as fuck and can practically get girls to do whatever they want. That's why he tried it. He thought he'd get away with it, like he always does."

She's not wrong.

They are hot—hot in that infuriating, unattainable way that makes it impossible to ignore them. Especially Noah. He's always been like that. Even back when we were thirteen, I noticed how girls started looking at him. And now? It still pisses me off.

"Well, Jace didn't try any of that crap with me," I say sharply. "If he had, I would've punched him right in the dick."

Sam bursts out laughing, the sound loud and unrestrained. "I'm sure you would've," she says, grinning as she turns onto the main road leading to school.

I glance out the window, the scenery blurring past, but my thoughts are already drifting.

"Speaking of Reece," I start, keeping my voice casual, "what's the deal between you two?"

Sam's grip on the steering wheel tightens ever so slightly, her eyes fixed straight ahead. She doesn't look at me, and the silence stretches just long enough for me to know I've hit a nerve.

"I don't know what you mean," she finally says, her voice clipped, like she's hoping I'll drop it.

But I don't. "Come on, I've heard him call you *Red*. What's up with that?"

She flicks the indicator, turning left into the school parking lot. "It's just some jerk move to get under my skin, that's all," she replies, her tone deliberately flat, as if trying to shut the conversation down.

I watch her for a moment, noticing the way her shoulders stiffen, how her focus on the road seems a little too intense. It's obvious there's more to the story, but I decide not to push her. Not yet.

Sam pulls into a parking spot and shuts off the engine. She doesn't move right away, just sits there, her fingers gripping the steering wheel tightly, her shoulders tense. Finally, she lets out a long, frustrated sigh and turns to me.

"I just don't want to talk about Reece," she says, her voice quieter now, more raw. "I don't want to revisit that. He's an asshole, just like the rest of them."

I nod, but before I can say anything, the roar of a car engine cuts through the air, drawing both our attention.

My head snaps toward the sound, and my heart stumbles when I see Noah's car pulling in, commanding attention without even trying. He parks near the front gate, and I find myself staring through the windshield as he steps out.

Dark jeans, a fitted black shirt that clings to his chest just right, and that maddeningly effortless way he slings his backpack over his shoulder—it's too much. Then he runs his hand through his light brown hair, pushing it back from his face, and I'm gone, completely lost in the way every little movement feels meticulously designed to undo me.

So caught up in watching him, I don't even notice Sam has already gotten out of the car until there's a sharp knock on the window. I jump, startled out of my trance, and whip my head around to see her standing there with a shit-eating grin plastered on her face.

"When you're ready," she teases, her tone dripping with amusement. Her grin only grows wider when she sees the flush creeping up my neck.

Embarrassed as hell, I grab my bag from the floor and step out of the car, doing my best to ignore the heat still simmering in my chest. Sam's expression makes it clear she's not going to let this go anytime soon, and I brace myself for the inevitable teasing.

"Seems like Noah could talk you into anything," Sam remarks as she steps away from the car, her tone playful but knowing. "They've got all the girls eating out of their hands."

I shut the car door, and she taps the lock button, her smirk widening as she meets my gaze. "Don't worry about it," she adds. "He's one of the hottest guys in school. All the girls can't help but check him out, so you're not alone."

I roll my eyes, but a flush creeps up my neck, anyway. She's not wrong, and the fact that I'm one of those girls isn't exactly a well-kept secret anymore.

As we make our way onto the school grounds, the noise of the crowd shifts, drawing my attention back to Noah. He's striding toward Jace, who's leaning casually against a wall, a cigarette dangling from his lips.

Jace doesn't even flinch as Noah approaches. Without a moment's hesitation, Noah drops his bag and grabs Jace by the collar, yanking him forward until their faces are just inches apart. The tension between them is electric, sharp enough to slice through the murmurs of the crowd now gathering to watch.

I can't hear what Noah's saying, but his body language says everything—rigid, furious, the veins in his neck bulging as he spits out whatever angry words are boiling inside him. I thought they were friends, but this... This is anything but friendly.

Sam's voice breaks through my thoughts. "I wonder what's up with the Fuckboys. Maybe Jace hit his blowjob quota for the month before Noah did," she quips, her tone thick with sarcasm.

I burst out laughing, the sound loud enough to turn a few heads, but I don't care.

As we approach, Noah's voice slices through the air, raw and furious. "Stay the fuck away from her. Got it?" he roars, his tone leaving no room for misinterpretation.

Jace doesn't back down. Instead, he smirks, his words dripping with sarcasm. "Hey, it's not my fault she's all over my cock."

The remark ignites like a spark to gasoline. Noah's fist clenches, muscles coiling as he pulls back, ready to strike. But before he can throw the punch, Jace breaks into laughter—a sharp, mocking sound that grates on my nerves. "Relax, man. Nothing happened. I swear."

Noah's fist freezes mid-air, the tension between them thick enough to choke on. For a moment, he just stands there, his jaw tight and his breathing heavy. Then, slowly, he lowers his fist—but his grip on Jace's collar stays firm, his knuckles white with anger. "You better stay the fuck away from her," Noah growls, his voice low and menacing. With a sharp shove, he sends Jace stumbling backward onto the grass. "That's your final fucking warning, Cooper."

Jace pushes himself back to his feet, brushing off dirt with a scowl. "Alright, I fucking heard you, asshole," he spits, bitterness lacing his words.

Noah's eyes linger on him for a beat longer. Then, without another word, he grabs his bag and stalks toward the school gates. His silence carries more weight than any outburst could.

Sam and I fall in step with the other students heading toward the entrance, the confrontation still buzzing in the air. But just as we near the gate, a voice cuts through the hum of chatter—sharp, cruel, and unmistakable.

"I always knew you were a fucking whore, but now I have proof," Tia sneers, her words drenched in venom.

I stop dead in my tracks, my body stiffening as she steps directly into our path, arms crossed and smirk razor-sharp. She blocks the gate like she's guarding a throne, her head held high with queen-bitch arrogance.

The noise around us dies down, replaced by an oppressive silence as the crowd's attention zeroes in on the brewing chaos. Dozens of eyes lock on us, the weight of their stares suffocating.

I meet her gaze head-on, refusing to back down.

Enough is enough. I've tolerated Tia's shit for days—her snide remarks, her smug little smirks, the way she revels in tearing people down to make herself feel superior. The lies, the manipulation, the cruel games—it's sickening. She's been poking and prodding, begging for a reaction, and now she's going to get one.

I square my shoulders and meet her glare, unflinching. "Say another word, Tia," I mutter, daring her to push me further.

Sam's hand clamps onto my arm, her voice low but firm. "Don't stoop to her level, Aubrey," she says, her tone laced with warning. "As much as I'd love to see this bitch get what's coming to her, she's not worth it."

She's wrong. Tia's been reigning over her little kingdom of lies and cruelty for too long. Someone has to put an end to it. My fists clench at my sides, my pulse roaring in my ears.

Tia's gaze flicks to Sam, her lips curling into a venomous smirk. "Oh, and let's not forget Samantha," she sneers, dragging Sam's name out like it's a slur. "Biggest cock tease in school. Leading guys on and never putting out. Still a virgin, right? That's the word going around."

Sam's grip on my arm loosens. She lets go, her voice raw with anger as she mutters, "Forget what I said."

That's all the fuel I need. I step forward, my pulse hammering, and plant myself directly in front of Tia. "What's your fucking problem, Tia?" I snap, my voice steady despite the storm raging inside me. "What is it? Do you get off on tearing people down? Does it make you feel better about your miserable excuse of a life? Or is this just your sad little way of finding worth in yourself?"

A ripple of murmurs moves through the crowd, an electric current feeding the tension. For a split second, something flickers in Tia's eyes—surprise, maybe even doubt—but it vanishes as quickly as it came. She smirks, her fingers darting over her phone screen.

Then she holds it up, the glow of the screen lighting her smug expression as she spins it toward the crowd.

The reaction is immediate. Faces shift, eyes darting from the phone to me, expressions morphing into judgment, curiosity, and thinly veiled amusement. The whispers follow, quiet at first but swelling into a wave of speculation.

"Holy shit," someone mutters, loud enough for me to hear. His voice carries a mix of awe and disbelief that sends another ripple through the crowd.

My stomach twists into a knot, my nails digging into my palms. I want to know what the fuck is on that screen, but dread coils in my chest. Because deep down, I already know—it's something designed to hurt, to humiliate, to tear me down in the most public way possible. That's who Tia is. That's what she does.

Tia circles back to me, her phone still in hand. Her smirk radiates confidence, as the crowd shifts around us, hungry for the show. Without saying a word, she thrusts the phone toward me, a gesture that feels like a death sentence.

"Go on," she purrs, her voice sweet but poisoned, "Take a look."

Every part of me wants to look away, to turn and walk off, but my eyes betray me, dropping to the screen. The sight slams into me, a gut punch that leaves me breathless. My name is displayed at the top of an Instagram account I've never seen. Below it is a nightmare—a series of photos I don't recognize, photos I never took, ones I wouldn't ever consider taking.

She taps her screen, flipping it back in my direction, her voice dripping with malice. The caption slices deeper, the words stabbing into my skin like a blade: prices for blowjobs, handjobs, every humiliating, degrading thing you can imagine.

The ground beneath me seems to shift, and for a moment, my chest tightens, the weight of the shame sinking deep, suffocating me from the inside out.

This can't be real.

But it is. It's fucking real, and I know exactly who's behind it. Tia. The bitch's cruelty isn't some thoughtless act; it's deliberate, calculated, designed to destroy me in front of everyone. This isn't just some petty rumor or passing insult—it's a public execution.

Tia's voice rings out, light and playful, like she hasn't just destroyed my life. "So, guys," she says, "if you're in the market for a blowjob, it's only eight dollars."

Her words echo in my ears. Laughter starts, cruel and guttural, like the sound of a pack of wolves closing in. It grows, building, feeding off my humiliation.

"Yo, where do I sign up?" someone yells from the back, the comment sparking another round of vicious laughter, a tidal wave of mocking voices that crash into me.

My stomach churns, nausea hitting in waves, threatening to swallow me whole. I can't look at the screen anymore, but it doesn't matter. The damage is done. The whispers and jeers grow into a storm, swirling around me, closing in.

The crowd feeds on my pain, and Tia stands there, basking in the satisfaction of what she's done, glowing with triumph. My skin burns under their eyes, the weight of shame crawling under my skin, settling into my bones. I want to scream, to push through it, but my throat tightens. Tears sting my eyes, hot and furious, but I force them back. I won't cry. Not here. Not in front of this bitch. She doesn't get to see that.

But inside, I'm falling apart.

Every laugh, every whispered comment, every look from the crowd feels like it's suffocating me, like a noose tightening around my neck. I can't escape the images, the captions burning into my mind, each one making me feel filthy, exposed—like I'm drowning in something I can never wash away.

The hardest part? Tia wasn't like this—she was someone I trusted, someone I would've defended with everything I had. That memory makes the betrayal even sharper, the knife she's shoved into my back twisting deeper. Now, all I see is a stranger wearing her face—a monster who's so consumed with hatred that she'll burn everything down just to watch the ashes fall.

And here I am, standing in the fire, choking on the smoke.

I want to scream, to claw back some shred of control, to hurl the truth at her and watch her smug little grin crack. But the words are locked in my throat, crushed by the weight of the shock, the overwhelming numbness pressing down on me. My mind is a battlefield, thoughts colliding like explosions, leaving me standing there like I'm frozen, paralyzed while her vile words keep slicing deeper.

"Twenty dollars for anal? Damn, I thought you'd charge more for that shit," she sneers, her voice cutting through the air with malice, each word designed to draw blood.

The laughter erupts again, louder this time, their laughter a cruel symphony that swallows the air around me. I glimpse Tia's friends—faces lit with amusement, their laughter thick with victory, carving their enjoyment into the space around us like a sick, twisted banner of triumph.

I don't even realize that Sam's hand is on my arm until she's pulling me away, guiding me through the crowd like a lifeline. My legs feel like they're made of stone, heavy and uncooperative, but she won't let go, won't leave me to crumble under the weight of it all. We move toward the school building, but even as we put distance between us and Tia's crowd, her voice still rings in my ears, loud and cutting.

"Forty dollars for two cocks at once!" she shouts, her voice sharp and loud enough to make sure I hear every word.

I flinch, my breath catching, the sobs rising in my throat. I clamp my mouth shut, refusing to let them out. Not here. Not in front of them.

"Are you okay?" Sam's voice is quiet, heavy with concern. She doesn't let go of my arm, her grip firm and steady, grounding me. "God, that girl is a fucking bitch," she mutters under her breath.

She keeps guiding me through the hallway, her hand never leaving mine, like she's afraid I'll shatter if she does.

And maybe I will.

Because right now, it feels like the cracks are already spreading, threatening to break me into a thousand pieces.

CHAPTER 10

NOAH

I was already fucking seething when I walked out the door this morning. My dad's endless bullshit about seeing my mom had me on edge, but seeing Jace with Aubrey last night... That shoved me right over the fucking line. Then this morning happened—catching Jace smirking at me like he had the upper hand, like he knew exactly what he was doing.

People think Jace and I are tight, like we've always got each other's backs. Most of the time, that's true. But we've had our share of problems—more than anyone would guess. We've always managed to work through them, but if he even considers going near Aubrey again, that's it. No forgiveness. Not this time. Not for her.

I lean against my locker, phone in hand, tuning out the hum of voices around me. Then I hear it—whispers cutting through the noise, spreading fast like wildfire.

Aubrey. Her name's everywhere. Something about an Instagram account, some kind of leak. I can't catch every word, but the way people are talking, it's bad. Really fucking bad.

I open the app, my jaw tightening. The rumors swirl in my head, each one worse than the last. And then I find it. The account. The grid fills my screen, and what I see twists my gut: photos of Aubrey—or at least, photos meant to look like her.

It doesn't take long to figure out the fucked-up truth. Her face is pasted onto other bodies, clumsily edited but clear enough to cause damage. It's sloppy, obvious if you know what to look for, but most people won't care. They'll just see what they want to see.

A wave of disgust slams into me, so strong it makes me want to throw my phone against the wall, to break something. This isn't just gossip; this is calculated, vile, and downright humiliating. I keep scrolling, each post worse than the last. Explicit captions, degrading comments, offers for "services" with prices attached. Blowjobs for eight bucks. Anal for twenty. The words are so vile they make my skin crawl, each one designed to tear her down completely. My jaw tightens, and a bitter taste rises in my throat as I stare at the captions, every word dripping with cruelty and degradation. It's a goddamn trainwreck, and I can't look away.

I don't need to think hard about who's behind this. I fucking know. This isn't random. Someone went out of their way to humiliate her, to destroy her. And there's only one person petty and twisted enough to do something this fucked up.

I tap on one of the posts, hating myself for feeding into it but unable to stop. The comments are vile, degrading, a cesspool of strangers reveling in cruelty.

"I'll take two for that price."

"How much for a threesome?"

"Bet she's good with two at once."

My fingers tighten around my phone, and I force myself to breathe, to stay in control. But it's so fucking hard.

I don't know how Aubrey's even holding herself together. How she's breathing under the weight of this storm. But one thing's certain—I can't just stand by. These fuckers with their comments need to learn some goddamn respect, and that bitch behind this is going to pay.

I dim my screen and shove my phone into my pocket, but the images linger, seared into my mind. An urgency clawing, primal and unstoppable. I need to find Aubrey.

Now.

Pushing off the locker, I stride down the hallway, ignoring the noise around me. People calling my name, hands reaching out for attention—it's all meaningless. Right now, there's only Aubrey.

The crowd parts as I move, their stares trailing me, but I barely register it. Up ahead, I catch sight of Sam, her arm around Aubrey, steering her toward the girls' bathroom. Aubrey looks fucking gutted—her shoulders slumped, her face hollow. She's like a shadow of herself, broken under the weight of it all. And seeing her like that. It fucking rips me apart.

I don't even hesitate. Girls' bathroom or not, I push forward. This isn't uncharted territory for me. I've been in plenty of them before, sneaking in for a quick fuck with girls who gave me that look. Fast, rough, meaningless—a way to kill the emptiness for a while. Afterward, I'd leave without a second thought, unless they were up for more. So walking in now? It doesn't faze me. Not even a little.

I shove the door open, boots echoing against the tile. The sharp scent of cheap perfume hangs in the air. Heads whip around, eyes wide with surprise and curiosity. I know what they're thinking—I always do. My presence alone is enough to have some of them imagining what it'd be like to drop to their knees, eager to have my cock in their mouth. It's a look I've seen a thousand times, a perk of being who I am, looking the way I do.

But right now, I don't give a fuck about any of them. My attention is Aubrey, and nothing else exists.

I barely acknowledge the starry-eyed stares lingering as I push forward, scanning the room with a single focus—finding Aubrey. My gaze lands on Sam, leaning against the sink at the far end of the bathroom.

I make a beeline straight for her, my strides quick and purposeful, but there's no sign of Aubrey. My chest tightens, frustration clawing at the edges of my control. Sam glances up, meeting my gaze briefly before going back to inspect her nails. Calm, detached—completely unbothered. That's Sam for you. A sharp contrast to the other girls, who practically lose their shit the moment I enter a room.

"Where the fuck is she?" I demand, my voice low but cutting, sharp enough to get straight to the point.

Sam straightens, her shoulders squaring, her usual air of indifference hardening into something colder. "I'm not telling you shit," she snaps, her tone firm, her glare unwavering. "You're probably in on it with that sick bitch."

Her words cut deep, but I shove the anger down. Now's not the time to lose my cool—not when Aubrey's probably crumbling under the weight of this shit.

Behind me, I feel the stares boring into my back, the room buzzing with silent curiosity.

Normally, I'd bask in it, feed off their attention like the cocky bastard they think I am. But not today. Not now.

I spin on my heels, my jaw tight, and sweep my gaze over the room. "Get the fuck out," I bark, my voice cold and unrelenting. It's not a suggestion—it's a command. The edge in my tone leaves no room for argument.

The girls scramble, grabbing their bags and rushing for the door like their lives depend on it. A few linger, hesitating, their curiosity out-weighing their sense of self-preservation. They're desperate to stay, to soak up the drama and turn it into more gossip. But my glare cuts through, my unspoken message clear: leave.

Most take the hint, shuffling out quickly. But Naomi doesn't budge. Of course not. Tia's lapdog stands her ground, arms crossed and chin tilted in defiance. Her smirk is a challenge, daring me to make her leave.

Fine.

I stride toward her, my movements sharp and deliberate, the tension radiating off me like heat. If she wants a confrontation, I'll gladly escort her ass out myself.

As I close the gap between us, Naomi finally relents, grabbing her bag off the floor. She saunters toward the door, pausing with her hand on the handle. Turning back, she throws me one last smirk, dripping with disdain, a calculated insult that does nothing but pisses me off.

Finally, she huffs, pulls the door open, and saunters out like she owns the damn place.

Good fucking riddance.

Turning back to Sam, I jerk my head toward the door. She doesn't move. The locked stall tells me everything I need to know—Aubrey's not okay. She's hiding, shutting the world out. And fuck, I don't blame her.

Sam's eyes narrow, meeting mine with a sharp, unyielding glare. "I'm not going anywhere," she snaps. "So deal with it, dipshit. Aubrey's my friend. I'm the one who's been here for her, who's had her back since day one. Not you." She steps away from the sink, her voice laced with fury. "You're the asshole who tore her down the second she walked into this school. Don't stand there now and act like you suddenly give a shit."

I flinch—not outwardly, not enough for her to see—but inside, her words gut me. Because she's right. I've been a complete asshole to Aubrey. I made her life hell, tore her apart for no reason other than my own messed-up shit. And worse? I let everyone else do the same, standing on the sidelines like a fucking coward.

But I'm done standing by.

Twisting the lock on the bathroom door, I shut out the world. Let the rumors fly. Let them twist the truth into whatever shit they want. None of it matters. The only thing that matters is Aubrey, behind that locked stall door.

I push past Sam, her glare locked on me but I ignore it. My footsteps echo against the tile as I stop in front of the stall. I stare at the door, willing it to open.

"Aubrey," I call out, my voice sharp and firm. "Open the door and talk to me."

Silence.

Memories claw their way to the surface—her parents' screaming matches, their voices ripping through the walls of her house like they wanted to destroy each other. She'd lock herself away in her room, trying to drown it out. And me... I'd climb through her bedroom window, desperate to pull her the fuck out of that hell.

"Aubrey." This time her name is a plea, raw and broken. "Open the fucking door." I press my palm against the stall, leaning my weight into it. "Don't make me talk to a goddamn door."

Sam shifts beside me, her arms crossed, disapproval still etched across her face. Her glare burns when I glance at her, a silent condemnation for daring to show up. But then she moves closer, standing next to me.

For a moment, neither of us speaks.

The silence is thick, stretching between us. Finally, Sam exhales, her voice quieter but no less sharp. "You don't deserve her forgiveness, you know."

"I know," I admit, my voice low. "But I'm not leaving."

"Aubrey, are you okay?" Sam's voice is soft, careful, like she's trying not to spook her.

"I'm fine," Aubrey says, her voice muffled behind the stall door.

It stings. Fuck, it burns. She ignored me—but she answers Sam like it's effortless. The words hang in the air, but the tremor in her voice betrays her. She's not fine. Not even close.

"Aubrey, come out already," I plead, my voice softer now, fighting to rein in the storm brewing inside me.

Nothing. The silence is harder than any words she could throw at me. My chest tightens, and I rub the ache near my heart, but it doesn't help. The frustration boils over, seeping into my tone.

"Damn it, Aubrey, open this fucking door or I'll do it myself," I snap, my voice sharp, angry, laced with the raw hurt I can't push down.

"Just go away, Noah," she says, her voice brittle and cracking. "Leave me alone. You've made it crystal fucking clear that I mean jack shit to you, so just... go."

My hands curl into fists, nails biting into my palms as I try to stay grounded. I want to yell, to fight back, to tell her how fucking wrong she is—but the truth is? I made her feel like this. Like she doesn't matter.

I glance at Sam, desperate for something—anything. But all I get is her impatient stare, followed by an eye roll that screams get the fuck out of here.

Dragging in a deep breath, I force my voice steady. "Aubrey, I'm not leaving. I know you're hurting."

The faint sound of her shifting on the other side of the door gives me a surge of hope. For a split second, I think—no, I need—her to let me in. But then her voice cuts through, soft and broken, and it fucking wrecks me.

"Don't you think you've done enough, Noah. Just go back to your cheer squad."

My shoulders slump, the weight of defeat pressing down on me like a ton of bricks. I look at Sam, expecting her usual anger, but for once, she just looks... tired. Like she's done with this whole fucking mess.

I hesitate, clinging to a stupid, desperate hope that Aubrey might open the door, might say anything to stop me from leaving. But the silence drags on, suffocating.

With a deep breath that feels like it might shatter me, I turn away. My steps are slow, deliberate, as I unlock the door. I don't look back. I can't. Because if I do, it'll break me.

I pushed her too far. I know that now.

And the worst part? There's no fixing this. No going back.

Chapter 11

Aubrey

This morning's bullshit with Tia burns like acid under my skin. Her humiliating stunt in front of everyone, leaves me raw, exposed. Sam eventually dragged me out of the bathroom, her steady presence the only thing keeping me from falling apart.

I wanted to ditch, flip the entire goddamn day off, and walk out. But when the first bell rang, Sam nudged me toward class, promising that I'm not alone.

I don't hide. At least, that's the lie I've been clinging to. Turns out, I've been hiding my whole fucking life—ducking out when my parents' screaming matches got too loud, disappearing because it was easier than fighting back. And that Instagram account Tia waved around? It shoved me right back into that scared little kid I thought I'd left behind.

But not anymore. Fuck that. I'm not the girl who shrinks while people like Tia get their kicks. Not again.

Sam's the only reason I didn't completely lose my shit. She's been my rock, standing by me when I wanted to shatter. Without her I'm not sure I'd have made it through Tia's crap with my head still held high. But you better believe this isn't over. Not by a long fucking shot.

All morning, it's been the same relentless shit—guys throwing sleazy comments my way, their crude jokes sticking to me like filth I can't scrub

off. Every taunt, every smirk stripping away the parts of me that want to
fight back.

During breaks, Sam, Lola, Liz, and I huddle in the library, desperate
to escape the constant barrage of sexual comments and offers. But even
there, it feels like I can't breathe, like their disgusting demands follow me
everywhere.

All I want to do is scream—to tear into every one of them and tell
them to back the fuck off. But Tia lit this match, and now I'm standing
in the inferno she started. The worst part? I don't even know why she
hates me so goddamn much. But breaking down isn't an option. So, I do
what I've always done: grit my teeth, bury the frustration until it burns a
hole in my gut, and pretend their cruel, degrading bullshit doesn't affect
me. It's the only way to survive. For now.

By lunchtime, things hit a new low. Liz hands me her phone, her face
pale, her hands shaking. I didn't want to look, but I had to. There it
was—the Instagram page: my supposed "sexual services" profile.

Scrolling through the posts, my stomach churned. The comments—God, the fucking comments—made me want to vomit. Guys
bragging about their supposed "great time" with me, leaving vile reviews
like I was some fucking product they ordered online. It's disgusting,
humiliating, infuriating.

Then I see it. The section about anal services. My stomach drops as my
eyes catch the comments—those two assholes from class, the ones always
tossing a football around, leaving their vile, smirking remarks. Bragging
about "tag-teaming" me, about how much I supposedly enjoyed their
cocks. My skin crawls, my hands shake, and my vision blurs.

If it weren't Liz's phone, I'd hurl it at the wall, just to hear the sickening crack of it breaking apart.

Tia has gone too far. This isn't a prank or some petty high school
bullshit. This is cruelty on a scale I never thought possible. Bile rises in
my throat, but I force myself to keep scrolling. I need to see it all—every
disgusting detail, every post, every lie. Twenty vile entries, all crafted
over two days. She's been building this grotesque fantasy piece by piece,

curating it since the day Noah kissed her and their public blowup became the hottest gossip in school.

And why? Was it because she saw me with Noah? Because we slipped into the equipment room together? Was that enough to set her off, to drive her to ruin me like this? I don't know. But one thing is crystal fucking clear—Tia isn't walking away from this unscathed. Not this time.

Each photo I scroll past is another slap in the face. The images are laughably fake—so poorly doctored they're almost pathetic. Almost. But the damage they're doing isn't.

"You shouldn't be looking at it," Sam says, her voice low but firm. Her pen is poised in her hand like she's ready to stab anyone who so much as looks at me the wrong way.

I ignore her, my finger trembling over the screen. "I think Tia started this shit after Noah and I talked in the equipment room," I say, holding the phone out for her to see. My voice wavers, anger and hurt bleeding through every word. "Look. Most of these were posted yesterday. The last two... They went up this morning."

Sam doesn't bother looking at the phone. Her gaze is fixed on me instead, sharp and unwavering.

"Getting hung up on it won't change a damn thing," she says, bluntly.

I grit my teeth, swallowing the lump in my throat before returning the phone back to Liz. "I know," I mutter, my voice heavy and raw. "It's just... I can't understand why someone who used to be my friend would do this to me. I haven't done a goddamn thing to deserve it."

Sam leans back, crossing her arms. "It's because her perfect little world with Noah is falling apart, and she can't fucking stand it. She's been obsessed with him forever, but let's face it, he's never given a damn about her. That kiss. It only happened because you were there. Period."

I shake my head, unsure. "I'm not so sure about that," I say, doubt lacing my voice.

Liz scoffs, her tone sharp. "Oh, believe it. You might not see it, but the rest of us... We do. And just wait—when Tia finds out Noah went into the girls' bathroom to check on you, she's gonna lose her shit. Hell, the gossip's probably already spreading. So, yeah, watch your back."

"God, could this get any worse?" I groan, the frustration twists into a knot in my chest.

Sam's voice is steady but hard. "Yeah. It could. But you're not going through this alone. Got it?"

I nod, but the ache doesn't ease. Tia may have lit this fire, but I'll be damned if I let her burn me to the ground.

Our attention shifts to Lola as she slides into a chair, her books landing on the desk with a casual thud. She settles in like it's just another day, completely unfazed by the storm raging around me.

"How are you holding up with everything?" Lola asks, her voice light, like she's testing the waters.

"I'm fine," I reply, the lie bitter on my tongue.

"God, you're handling it better than I ever did," she says, unwrapping a chocolate bar and setting it in front of me. The gesture feels ironic—something sweet offered in the middle of all this fucking bitterness. "The cruelest thing Tia ever did to me was pour chocolate milk over my head in front of everyone."

I glance at the chocolate bar but don't touch it. It sits there, mocking me with its normalcy.

"Layla mentioned Noah was in a fight earlier," Lola continues, as casually as if she were discussing the weather.

My stomach clenches, but I force my expression to stay neutral. I didn't want to talk to him when he burst into the restroom earlier—didn't want to see his face while I felt so humiliated by that damn Instagram page. I knew if I looked into his eyes for even a second, I'd fall apart.

"Who was it with this time?" Sam asks, her tone edged with curiosity.

"Apparently, he punched Luke and Tory," Lola says, setting a water bottle beside her books like this is just another piece of gossip to dissect.

"What for?" Sam presses.

"Something about the comments on Aubrey's Instagram page," Lola says with a dismissive wave of her hand.

"It's not my page," I mutter, the words sharp enough to sting.

"Well, on that slutty Instagram page then," she corrects, unbothered.

My gaze flicks to Sam, silently pleading for her to dig deeper because I can't bring myself to ask. I can't let them see how much I need to know what Noah did.

"So, what exactly did Layla hear?" Liz cuts in.

"Layla overheard Tia's crew gossiping by her locker. And let me tell you, Tia is pissed," Lola says, flipping open her book with the kind of detached interest that makes it clear she lives for this kind of drama.

Lola's tone is too casual, too rehearsed, like she's narrating the latest episode of a trashy reality show. Not knowing her as well as Sam, I can't shake the feeling that staying in the loop is her lifeline.

"From what Layla pieced together; it all went down in the gym earlier. Noah straight-up threatened the entire football team—told them to delete their comments or else. Apparently, everyone in the gym saw it. Surprised it didn't end up as a live stream."

Her words hang in the air, the weight of them pressing down on me. I can't stop the flicker of something—hope... Anger... I don't know. But it burns all the same.

My fingers tremble as I grab my phone and pull up the fake Instagram page. The cruel, fucked-up comments I saw earlier—most of them are gone now. My eyes zero in on the post that had my stomach in knots—the one with the disgusting "anal" caption. The two worst comments? Deleted.

Noah.

His moods are a goddamn rollercoaster, throwing me into loops I can't escape. One minute, he's distant, like I don't exist, and the next, he's pulling shit like this. Threatening the entire football team. Clearing out the girls' bathroom just to talk to me. Who does that? And yet, beneath the whirlwind of anger and confusion, there's a part of me—a traitorous, pathetic part—that still aches for him. That still wants to believe he's the Noah I used to know.

The Noah who looked at me like I was the only thing that mattered. The Noah who had the right words to cut through all the bullshit.

But he's not. Not anymore.

I squeeze my eyes shut, but his words from the equipment room creep back in, venomous and unshakable: You don't mean anything to me anymore.

Like I was a game to him. A body. A quick fuck.

The sting of it sits heavy in my chest, sharp and unrelenting. Maybe I should've swallowed my pride earlier, should've said something when he barged into the girls' bathroom. But then what? What would it change? I'm just another mistake to him. Another name he probably wishes he could forget.

And yet, here I am. Still hoping. Still stuck.

I shove thoughts of Noah into a mental box and lock it tight, forcing myself to focus on the conversation around me. The girls are talking about today's English assignment, something I know I should be paying attention to—God knows I wasn't during class. I was too rattled, my mind consumed by that fake Instagram page and the fallout. Now I need to catch up, to figure out what the hell I'm supposed to do.

But my concentration wavers. My thoughts keep dragging me back to the chaos I'm trying so hard to ignore.

Get your shit together, Aubrey.

I can't afford to spiral. Academic excellence is non-negotiable if I want to keep my arts college scholarship. It's my ticket out of this mess. If I let my grades slip, if I let this bullshit consume me, it could all fall apart. And I can't let that happen.

The bell signaling the start of the final lesson blares through the halls. Great—another class, another room full of whispers, another round of shitty remarks. I brace myself for it, even though every part of me wants to run and hide.

As we walk down the long, crowded corridor, the onslaught begins.

The loiterers don't hold back, their shitty comments slicing through the air like daggers—snide remarks dripping with innuendo, laughter biting at my heels. Each word chips away at me, but I keep my head high, my steps steady.

At my locker, I fumble with the lock, my fingers stiff and uncooperative. Sam and Liz linger nearby, their presence a small comfort against the hostility that fills the hallway.

Finally, with a sigh of relief, the lock clicks open. I shove my books inside, grab what I need, and slam the door shut. The sound echoes, louder than I intended, and a few heads turn in my direction. I ignore them.

A voice startles me. "Been a tough one, huh?"

Jace leans casually against the locker next to mine, his tone light, almost friendly. He's always had this annoying ability to make his presence feel like it's no big deal, even when it is.

"Yeah, you could say that," I reply flatly, not even sparing him a glance.

He falls into step beside me as I move down the hallway. His proximity grates on me, and I quicken my pace, leaving him behind without a backward glance. He's the last person I want to be seen with in this hallway. I've got enough shit to deal with already and Jace's reputation doesn't need to be thrown into the mix.

Sam and I enter the classroom, Liz peeling off toward her usual spot at the front. We slide into seats halfway down, the safest zone to avoid drawing unnecessary attention. My eyes catch on Luke and Tory as they shuffle in. Their bruises are impossible to miss—Luke's cheek is an angry shade of purple, and Tory's lip looks freshly split. They catch my eye as they pass, and I brace myself for the usual barrage of crude jokes, the sexual comments, the arrogant smirks that make me feel less than human.

But to my surprise, they keep quiet.

They keep walking, silent, their heads low, their energy subdued. It's jarring, almost unsettling, like I've stepped into an alternate universe.

Sam leans over, her lips twitching into a knowing smirk. "Guess Noah really did scare the shit out of them," she whispers.

I barely have time to process her words before the atmosphere in the room shifts.

Tia strides in like she owns the place, her mere presence sucking the oxygen out of the room. Conversations stutter to a halt, the tension palpable. Every pair of eyes, mine included, follows her as she makes her grand entrance.

She locks eyes with me, her gaze sharp and unrelenting. I can feel the heat of it, like a spotlight pinning me in place.

I brace myself. This is Tia, after all. She doesn't just thrive on theatrics and humiliation—she breathes it in, feeds on it.

She drops her bag onto her desk with an exaggerated flip of her long brown hair, a movement so practiced it's almost theatrical. Then she turns, her smirk curling like smoke, and I know it's coming before she even opens her mouth.

"I would've thought you'd be too busy with all your blowjobs and anal bookings to bother showing up to this class," she sneers, her voice carrying just loud enough to command attention.

A few muffled laughs ripple through the room, cutting into the silence like glass shards. I feel the weight of every gaze on me, expectant and hungry. They're waiting for my reaction, for me to crumble under the weight of her words.

But I don't.

I meet her gaze head-on, my jaw tight, refusing to give her the satisfaction of seeing me flinch.

"Oh, Tia, don't be so bitter. Just because the only bookings you get are from your therapist doesn't mean you need to take it out on me."

The silence that follows is deafening. Her smirk falters—just for a second—before she recovers, flipping her hair again like it's some kind of shield.

I turn back to Sam, dismissing Tia's existence as if she's already slipped from my mind. Waiting for her retort, but it doesn't come.

Instead, Noah's voice slices through the charged air like a whip. "Sit your ass down and shut the fuck up, Tia."

The room collectively inhales as he strides into the room, his tone low, firm, and commanding. Every pair of eyes snaps to him, the tension ratcheting higher.

Tia spins on her heels, her irritation flaring into full blown anger as she glares at him. "I don't have to listen to you, asshole. Go fuck yourself," she snaps, her voice biting but trembling at the edges.

The air grows thick, the room transforming into a silent battleground. No one dares to move, their gazes bouncing between the two of them like spectators in a high-stakes match.

Noah doesn't flinch, doesn't even blink. He strides past her to his desk, his voice cold, sharp, and deliberate. "From what I remember, my hand does a better job than that sorry excuse of a fuck we had. So yeah, I'll stick with that rather than waste my time on a lifeless corpse."

A collective gasp ripples through the room, sharp and stunned.

Tia's face drains of color. Her confident posture crumbles, and her lips part as if to retaliate, but no words come. Tears brim in her eyes, the defiance giving way to vulnerability. She glances around the room, her gaze darting desperately from face to face, searching for an ally, for someone to step in. No one does.

For the first time, karma feels tangible, a weight settling on her shoulders that she can't shrug off.

The door creaks open, and the teacher walks in. The sudden flurry of movement—students scrambling to their seats, shoving books onto desks—shatters the moment.

Tia sinks into her chair, her hands trembling as she adjusts her hair and tries to straighten her posture. But her gaze never leaves Noah. It's fixed on him, burning with a mix of anger, shame, and something darker, something raw.

Noah, on the other hand, is calm, composed, his focus entirely on his books as though nothing happened. Her death glare could probably set the room on fire, but he doesn't even notice—or doesn't care.

Noah's ability to shrug off others' judgments like they're nothing has always been something I've envied. He wears it like armor, an impenetrable shield I've never managed to forge for myself. Every whisper, every stare, every word still cuts me in ways I wish it didn't.

I tighten my grip on my pen and force myself to focus on the lesson. This is what matters—my grades, my future—not this bullshit.

But even as I try to concentrate, my thoughts drift back to him. Noah, with his infuriating confidence and sharp tongue. Noah, who's a whirlwind I can't seem to escape. And, God help me, part of me doesn't want to.

In the days following Noah's takedown of Tia, the tension in the air shifts—but not enough to call it peace. More guys shuffle through the hallways sporting fresh bruises and battered egos, their cocky attitudes deflated. The whispers and shit-talking doesn't vanish entirely, but they quiet down when Noah's within earshot. No one's stupid enough to tempt fate twice.

But Tia, though. Fuck. She's relentless. It's like she feeds off her own cruelty, throwing taunts my way every chance she gets. Her little pack of hyenas laugh on cue, their sharp cackles echoing down the halls. She wears her twisted satisfaction like a crown, her eyes glinting with malice every time she lands a jab.

Thankfully, I'm not alone in this. Sam, Lola, and Liz stand firm, forming an unspoken barrier against her constant attacks. They've had Lola's back, deflecting Tia's venom, and now they extend that same loyalty to me. It's a lifeline I cling to, especially on the worst days when the weight of it all feels unbearable.

At home, I bury myself in homework, avoiding my dad like it's a survival instinct. Most nights, I'm holed up in my room, textbooks open but barely touched, my thoughts miles away. When I can't focus on studying, I turn to my sketchbook. Having some money from a few shifts, I finally treated myself to new charcoal pencils. Each night, I lose myself in my drawings, letting the dark strokes and shadows carry away the weight of everything pressing down on me. Drawing is the only thing that keeps me sane, the only time I feel like I can breathe freely. But no matter how busy I try to keep myself; my gaze always drifts toward Noah's window. The curtains are always drawn shut, and every time, disappointment hits like a cold wave. Since the day he stormed into the girls' bathroom and then obliterated Tia in class, he hasn't said a single word to me. It's like I've been erased from his world, and yet I can't stop looking, hoping, waiting.

Things should feel like they're improving—I've got a job now, a small taste of independence. But the silence from my mom cuts deeper than Tia's words ever could. Every ignored call, every unanswered message feels like another knife, twisting further in the same wound.

Today, though, I try to push it all aside.

The sun is out for the first time in what feels like forever, and I'm stretched out on the grass with Sam and Lola. The warmth on my skin, the sound of their laughter—it's almost enough to convince me that things might be okay. But even as I close my eyes and try to soak in the calm, there's a part of me that can't quite relax. A part that knows the storm isn't really over, just waiting to strike again when I least expect it.

Lola shifts beside me and suddenly pops up. "Hey, can you guys watch my bag? I'll be right back," she chirps.

"Sure," I say with a small smile.

She flashes one back before bounding toward the school building, her energy light and carefree.

I glance over at Sam, noticing how quiet she's been. Her fiery red hair glows in the sunlight, but her expression is distant, her attention locked on something—or someone.

I follow her gaze.

Under the shade of a tree, Reece leans in close to one of Tia's bitchy minions, a girl with perfectly styled hair and a smug smile. Her back is pressed against the tree, her face tilted up toward him as he whispers something in her ear. She laughs softly, and he reaches out, tucking a strand of her hair behind her ear with practiced ease. Reece knows how to play the part of a romantic, but there's something about it that feels hollow, calculated.

I glance back at Sam. Her jaw is tight, her lips pressed into a thin line, her hands clenched into fists. There's a flicker of something raw in her eyes, something she's desperately trying to hide.

Something has definitely gone on between them. I don't push, though. The rawness in Sam's expression screams for space, and I know better than to pry. If she wanted me to know, she'd tell me.

It's only when Reece leans in and kisses Tia's minion that Sam finally looks away, her jaw tight as she turns her head.

I quickly avert my gaze too, not wanting her to catch me watching her pain unfold. Instead, I focus on the grass, plucking blades one by one, letting the silence stretch between us.

By the time the final bell rings, Sam is back to her usual self—or at least, the version she wants us to see. She's laughing, cracking jokes, and talking like nothing happened. It's convincing, but I've seen it enough lately to spot the cracks in her armor.

As I stride down the corridor, I head straight for my locker. Sam and Lola are already near the front doors, waiting for me. I grab the homework I need for tonight, determined not to procrastinate like I did two weeks ago. Nearly failing that assessment was a wake-up call I don't plan to ignore. Tonight, it's just going to be me, my notes, and a strong cup of coffee. Tomorrow's work shift will leave me too drained to even think about schoolwork, so I need to knock it out now.

With my bag slung over my shoulder, I walk toward Sam and Lola. They're deep in conversation, but I catch the unmistakable whispers and stares from a nearby cluster of Tia's crew. My steps don't falter.

Instead, I meet their stares head-on, refusing to blink, refusing to give them even the smallest win. Then Nicole steps forward, her voice dripping with mockery.

"Hey, look who's rocking the bargain bin finds!" she sneers. "Raiding the clearance racks again, huh? It really shows!"

The others snicker, their laughter like nails on a chalkboard.

I stop in my tracks and turn slowly to face them. My gaze locks onto Nicole, sharp and unyielding. A sweet smile spreads across my face, the kind that doesn't reach my eyes.

"Wow, Nicole," I say, loud enough for the surrounding crowd to hear. "For someone who spends so much time up Tia's ass, you'd think you'd pick up a better sense of style."

The laughter dies instantly, replaced by stunned silence. Nicole's smirk falters, her cheeks flushing as she glances around, realizing the attention has shifted.

I step closer, my voice dropping to something softer.

"But hey, thanks for noticing my outfit. At least I know someone's paying attention."

Nicole's face reddens, and her mouth opens like she's about to retort, but nothing comes out.

Satisfied, I pivot and keep walking, my head held high. Sam and Lola glance back at me, their eyes wide. Then Sam grins, breaking the tension.

"That was savage," Sam whispers as I catch up to them.

We push through the school gates, the buzz of another day left behind, and head toward Sam's car. She's giving me a lift home, like always. It's routine, comforting even, but the air shifts when Sam casually throws out a question.

"Hey, you going to Chris's party this weekend?"

Before I can even process the idea, Lola jumps in, her voice sharp and decisive. "No way. Not after the shitshow last time."

Sam and I both look at her, surprised. Lola crosses her arms, her expression hardening. "Someone spread this fucked-up rumor that I was gonna give Luke and Tory blow jobs. They hounded me all night about it. I just went home after that."

"Ugh, those assholes," I mutter, shaking my head.

Sam stays hopeful, her tone softening. "But you'll still swing by with us, right? It'll be a blast."

Lola hesitates, her eyes narrowing in thought, chewing on her bottom lip. "I'll think about it," she finally says. "Not sure yet."

Her tone is guarded, the wariness lingering beneath her casual shrug. But she flashes a small smile before heading across the car park toward her beat-up car. The thing's a patchwork of faded paint and a mismatched grey panel, held together more by luck than mechanics. It suits Lola perfectly—scrappy, resilient, impossible to knock down for long.

"See ya tomorrow," she calls over her shoulder before climbing in, the door creaking loudly as it swings shut.

Sam turns to me, pressing the button to unlock her car doors. "What about you, Aubrey? You going to Chris's party?"

"When is it?" I ask, stalling.

"This Friday night." She swings open the door and slides into the driver's seat, the late-afternoon sun catching the strands of her fiery red hair. "It's gonna be a blast."

I climb into the passenger side, the leather warm against my legs, sticking slightly from the heat. "I'll think about it," I mutter, knowing full well that I'm leaning towards no.

The truth is, the thought of walking into a room filled with the same people who make my life hell on a daily basis doesn't exactly scream *fun*. I get enough bullshit during the day; I don't need to volunteer for more.

Sam tosses her bag onto the backseat. "Oh, by the way," she says, starting the engine. "My mom text me. She wants me to pick up my brother's birthday cake, so I've gotta make a quick stop before I drop you off."

"No problem," I reply, fiddling with the strap of my bag. "I need to grab a few things anyway."

"Cool," Sam says, pulling out of the car park. She adjusts her sunglasses, her gaze fixed on the road ahead.

Chapter 12

Noah

Ever since that moment with Aubrey in the equipment room over a week ago, it's like she's taken up permanent residence in my fucking head. The scent of her, the way my cock throbbed at just being near her, and those goddamn sounds she made—they're seared into my brain, playing on a loop I can't turn off.

Every morning, I wake up hard as fuck, my body betraying me, craving her in a way that feels primal. I try to take the edge off, but it's always the same—a pathetic release followed by a hollow ache that never fades. My cock's sick of the routine, sick of my hand. It doesn't want this anymore. It wants her. Wants to be buried so deep inside her that the rest of the world doesn't exist.

Last night, I stood at my bedroom window, smoking a joint, trying to calm the chaos in my head. That's when I saw her coming back from work. Her shoulders were hunched, exhaustion etched into every step, but she still looked like she just walked out of a dream. My dream. She's so fucking beautiful it hurts.

She didn't look up, didn't notice me standing there, but I couldn't tear my eyes away.

Her rejection that day in the bathroom was a slap to the face. I wanted to act like it didn't bother me, like I didn't give a shit, but it cut deeper than I'm willing to admit. Part of me wanted to pull her into my arms, tell her it's going to be okay, just like I used to when her world was falling apart. But things aren't the same anymore. I don't even know if she'd let me touch her like that now. And fuck, that's what scares me the most.

Instead of dealing with her shutting me out, I let my anger take over and turned it on assholes like Luke and Tory. Anyone who thought they could post that fucked-up shit about her got a piece of me. I made damn sure they knew to back off, but it's been exhausting. Trying to keep those pricks in line, trying to keep her life from spiraling further, feels like fighting a losing battle. And the worst part? It doesn't change a goddamn thing between us.

Now I'm stuck hating myself for the way I treated her when she first came back. Like a fucking idiot, I let my pride and the sting of old wounds turn into something cruel, something she didn't deserve. I told myself it was self-preservation, building walls so she couldn't get close enough to hurt me again.

But the cruel irony? My heart aches for her no matter what. Whether she's in the same room or a thousand miles away, it's the same relentless, hollow pain.

The walls between us feel too high now, too solid, and every move I've made since she got back has only built them higher and I don't know how to tear them down.

Every time I try to get closer, I push her further away. Every word I say seems to land wrong—wrong tone, wrong timing, wrong everything. It's like I'm caught in this endless loop of screwing things up, and I don't know how to fix it. Fuck, I'm not even sure if I can.

I push the sheet off and roll out of bed, rubbing the sleep from my eyes. My hand drifts through the tangled mess of my hair, but my focus is already on the window. The curtain hangs there, closed, unmoving, like it does every other morning. But today, something pulls me toward it.

I hesitate for a second, my fingers hovering over the fabric. But then I pull it back. And there she is.

Aubrey, asleep in her bed, bathed in sunlight. It spills into her room, wrapping her in a golden glow that makes her look... serene. Beautiful in a way that twists something deep inside me. I step back quickly, my pulse spiking, afraid she might wake up and catch me standing here like some fucking creep.

It's strange, seeing her there. For the past year, every time I glanced out this window and saw her bed empty, all I could think about was how much I wanted her back. And now she's here.

Her life's always been a fucking mess—chaotic in ways most people can't even begin to understand. And I was the one constant, the one who tried to shield her from it all. Especially when her parents were at each other's throats, tearing into each other like it was some sick sport. I hated their screams, hated how they ripped through her life like a wrecking ball. I wanted to take it all away—the pain, the fear, the weight of it all.

But now that she's back, all I want are answers. Where did she go? Why is she here without her mom? I could've asked, could've handled it like a decent human being, but instead, like a complete fucking idiot, I let my anger win. All that pent-up confusion and hurt exploded the moment I saw her, and I lashed out like a complete asshole. I hurt the one person I promised myself I'd always protect.

Aubrey has always been my safe place, the only person I could confide in without feeling exposed. She knew what it was like when my mom walked out—how it shattered everything. No one at school would get it, and I sure as hell couldn't talk to anyone about what's happening now. But Aubrey? She understood. She was the one who kept me grounded when everything else was falling apart.

I pull on my running shoes, trying to shake the chaos in my head. Maybe if I push myself hard enough, run until my legs give out, I'll find some clarity in the exhaustion. But as I step into the hallway, the smell of bacon stops me in my tracks. Dad's up, cooking breakfast like he does every morning. Some things, at least, never change.

I already know what's coming—another round of the same fucking conversation we've been having for days. Dad keeps bringing it up, hint-ing, pushing. "Maybe you should see her. It might help." And every time, I shut him down. It's a never-ending dance, and I'm so fucking tired of it.

I can't wrap my head around it—his sudden change of heart, like the years of pain she left behind doesn't matter anymore. Like he can just forgive her for walking away without a second thought. It's not that easy for me. It'll never be that easy.

Every time he mentions her, it's like ripping open a wound I've been fighting to close. It hurts. Fuck, it hurts in ways I can't even put into words. And I'm at my limit. I can't keep doing this.

When I step into the kitchen, there he is—Dad at the stove, the smell of bacon filling the air. The radio hums with some talk-show bullshit in the background, the same noise I've been tuning out for years. It's the kind of routine that's kept me steady, a small thread of normalcy when everything else was falling apart.

He glances over when I enter the kitchen, and there it is—his smile. The same one that got me through the worst nights, the hardest days. That smile's like a lifeline, a reminder that even when everything else goes to shit, he's still here, still solid.

"Was that Aubrey I saw yesterday?" he asks, flipping a strip of bacon like he's just making casual conversation. "You didn't mention she was back."

I go straight for the fridge, ignoring the way my chest tightens at her name. "Yeah," I mutter, pulling out the juice. My voice is tighter than I want it to be. "She's been back for a few days."

"Oh." He goes quiet, but I can feel it—the weight of his questions hanging in the air. He's waiting for me to say something more, to give him some explanation, but I keep my focus on the carton in my hands like it's the most important thing in the world. Anything to avoid looking at him. Because if I do, he'll see it. He'll see the mess I've made, the guilt I can't shake, the way I've destroyed whatever fragile connection Aubrey and I still had. He doesn't know how badly I've fucked things up, and I sure as hell don't plan on telling him.

"Son," he says, his voice steady but heavy, "there's something we need to talk about. I can't keep avoiding it."

And there it is. Same shit, different morning. We used to just be us—talking, laughing, just hanging out. I loved that. But now, every moment feels like walking on a live wire, waiting for him to bring her up. And every time he does, I'm right back to being that nine-year-old kid sitting on the front steps, crying my eyes out as I watched her walk away.

"I don't want to hear it, Dad," I snap, shoving away from the counter, my pulse hammering in my ears. "I don't want to see her or her perfect little replacement family. Can we just drop this shit?"

His hand freezes over the frying pan, and for a second, I think he's going to let it go. But then he speaks, his voice clipped and steady. "No, that's not what I wanted to discuss."

I stop mid-step, the tension in the room shifting into something heavier, something I can't quite name.

He finishes with the bacon, placing it on a plate with deliberate care, but I catch the small tremor in his hand, the way he avoids meeting my eyes.

"Dad," I say, softer now, the knot in my stomach twisting tighter. "What's going on?"

He doesn't answer right away. His jaw tightens, and he swallows hard, like whatever he's about to say is too big to get out all at once. My mind races—Is he sick? Dying? Or is this just another way to nudge me toward forgiving her?

"Dad," I try again, sharper this time, my worry morphing into something darker, more desperate. "Just tell me."

"Come on, let's sit down and have a chat," he says, scooping up the food and nodding toward the table.

The weight in my gut doubles as I follow him. This isn't small talk. This is something else. I drop into my usual chair, my fingers tapping restlessly against the edge of the table while I watch him settle across from me. His expression is unreadable, but I can see the effort behind it—the careful control, the way he's bracing himself. My appetite vanishes; I don't even glance at the plate in front of me.

"Just say it, Dad," I push, my voice firm, cutting through the thick silence.

He hesitates, fiddling with the edge of his napkin before finally meeting my eyes. "I've started seeing someone."

The breath I was holding rushes out in one sharp exhale. Fuck. For a moment, I thought he was about to tell me something catastrophic—that he's sick, dying, something irreversible. But this? This I can handle.

A small smile tugs at my lips. "That's great, Dad," I say, leaning back in my chair. "You deserve that. Someone in your life."

He looks up, surprise flickering across his face like he expected me to blow up. "You're not upset?"

"No," I reply, shrugging, forcing the smile to stay. I reach for a piece of bacon, more for something to do with my hands than anything else. "Why would I be upset?"

"I just figured after your mother—"

I cut him off before he can finish the sentence. "Dad, stop. Mom left. She's not part of my life anymore. She made her choice, and I've made mine. So, how long have you been seeing..."

"Simone," he admits, his tone careful. "And it's still early. Just a few months."

I bite into the bacon, the crunch cutting through the heavy silence as I study him. There's more he's not saying—it's written all over his face. The tightness around his mouth, the way his eyes flicker everywhere but mine.

"Want another juice?" he asks, standing abruptly. His chair scrapes loudly against the floor, a clear attempt to deflect.

"What aren't you telling me, Dad?" My voice slices through the air, sharp and demanding.

He pauses mid-step, his back to me. For a moment, he doesn't move, and then he slowly turns around. There it is—the hesitation, the weight of whatever he's holding back.

"Son," he starts, his tone lower now, almost apologetic. "Simone suggested a weekend getaway. But considering the situation with..."

His words hang there, unfinished, as his eyes meet mine. The silence between us is deafening.

"By 'situation,' you mean Mom," I say flatly, the knot in my stomach twisting tighter. Of course it's about her. It's always about her. She always fucking ruins everything.

"Yeah," he says, quieter this time. "What if I'm not here for the weekend and she unexpectedly shows up at the door? I don't want you to have to deal with that."

His words hit like a sucker punch. He wasn't pushing me toward her—he was trying to shield me from her bullshit.

"So that's why you've been asking about her," I say, the pieces finally clicking into place. "To figure out where I stand."

"Exactly," he admits, his shoulders sagging as if a weight's been lifted. "Whether you decide to see her or not, that's your choice. I'd never force her onto you. She left us without a second thought. I just wanted you to be ready... in case she showed up uninvited. Like she did the other day."

The words take a second to land, but when they do, my chest tightens painfully. "Wait—she was here? Inside the house?"

He nods, his jaw clenching. "She walked right in. Made herself a damn coffee. Like the last ten years didn't even happen."

The fury hits, sharp and blinding. How the *fuck* does she think she can just stroll back into our lives? Like she didn't destroy everything when she left.

I slam my hand against the table, the force reverberating through the room. "Are you fucking serious? She just walked in here after everything she's done?"

Dad nods, his shoulders slumping under the weight of his own frustration. "I didn't know what to do. She caught me off guard. I thought I could handle it, but seeing her..."

I rake a hand through my hair, trying to steady the fury surging through me. My thoughts are racing, overlapping, a chaotic mess of rage and disbelief. How the fuck does she think she can just stroll back into our lives, like she didn't shatter them the second she walked out that door?

I should've listened to Dad. Should've stopped shutting him down every time he mentioned her. Instead, I let my anger speak for me, too wrapped up in my own bitterness to see he was trying to protect me. And now? Now she's forcing her way back in, and I'm not ready. I'll never be ready.

"I was going to tell you about Simone and the weekend getaway we planned," he says, his voice tight, "but seeing your mother back in the house... I was too stunned to do anything."

"When is this weekend getaway?" I ask, my words clipped, irritation still bubbling under the surface.

"It was supposed to be this weekend."

"Don't cancel it, Dad. Seriously, don't." I lean back in my chair, trying to force calm into my tone even though my pulse is hammering. "We've both moved on. She's not part of our lives anymore. Go with Simone. I've got plans for Friday night, anyway. If she shows up, I won't have time for her."

I don't say the rest, but it's clear in my mind: if she shows her face, I won't hesitate to tell her to fuck off.

He studies me for a moment, his brow furrowed. "Are you sure, son? You know how forceful your mother can be."

"Yeah, I'm sure," I say.

For the first time in what feels like ages, his face softens into a genuine smile. It's small at first, but it grows, lighting up his features like a weight has been lifted. He stands, already reaching for his phone on the counter, his grin widening.

"Well, I guess I'll give Simone a call and let her know the weekend is still on."

I nod, watching him as he dials. For the first time in days, a semblance of normalcy starts to creep back into the air. Maybe, just maybe, we're finding our footing again.

As he walks out of the kitchen, his voice carries back to me, light and happy. "Hey, honey," he says, his tone warm and relaxed.

I lean back in my chair, exhaling slowly. It's not over—not by a long shot—but for now, it feels like a win.

A grin tugs at my lips. He's found someone. Someone who lights him up like this. I wish he'd told me sooner. Hell, he deserves this. After all the shit he's been through, he's earned every bit of happiness.

I finish my breakfast quickly, skipping the run. By the time I'm stacking my plate in the dishwasher, Dad's back. He moves toward the table, settling into his chair like the world's weight is finally a little lighter.

"How'd it go?" I ask.

"Simone's stoked. Thanks, son," he says, setting his phone on the table. His gaze meets mine, soft and full of gratitude.

"Maybe sometime next week, when you're back, you could bring Simone around to the house," I tell him, my tone casual but sincere. I want him to know I'm cool with this—that all I want is for him to be happy.

His smile widens, and for a moment, he looks younger, lighter, like he's been handed back a piece of himself he thought he'd lost. "I'd like that."

The thought of leaving next year stings less, knowing he won't be alone. Knowing someone else will be here to hold him up when I can't. If Simone's the one to do that—if she's the one who can keep that light in his eyes—then fuck, I'm all for it.

CHAPTER 13

AUBREY

The second I see Noah and Reece sprawled against the school wall, my stomach twists into a knot so tight I can barely breathe. Noah's been avoiding me like the plague since that day in the bathroom—since I told him to back off and refused to talk. And now? Now he's sitting there like nothing happened, like the distance he's put between us isn't driving me insane.

I keep my eyes locked on them. My chest tightens when Noah finally glances up. His eyes meet mine, and for a brief second, everything I've been trying to bury surges to the surface. But I don't let it show. I turn my head away, pretending I didn't see him, like he doesn't fucking matter. Even though he does.

"So, you're still coming to the party tonight, right?" Sam asks, cutting through my thoughts. She's been on me all week about it, wearing me down until I finally said yes. I didn't want to go. I still don't. But Sam's relentless, and honestly, I'm too drained to fight her off anymore.

We head up the steps and into the building, but before we get far, Lola comes flying out of nowhere, stopping us in our tracks.

"Oh my God, where have you two been? I've been waiting forever." She wedges herself between us, looping her arms through mine and Sam's like we have all the time in the world.

I smirk. Lola's different now, more confident. She's come out of her shell since Tia shifted all her bullshit onto me. Maybe not being under constant attack is letting her breathe, letting her be herself.

But then her voice drops, and the look on her face wipes the smirk right off mine.

"Aubrey, there's something you need to know before you get to your locker," she says, her tone sharp, urgent.

My stomach sinks. I glance down the corridor, bracing myself. Whatever it is, it's bad. I can feel it.

Up ahead, there's a crowd gathered by the lockers, their whispers swelling into a hum that gets on my nerves. My heart starts pounding as Lola pulls me forward.

"Alright, let us through!" Sam shouts, forcing the crowd to part.

And then I see it. Red spray paint, dripping down the metal like blood, scrawled in jagged letters across my locker.

SLUT. WHORE.

Fury claws its way up my throat as I stare at the vandalized locker, the meaning sinking in.

Tia. Of course, it's fucking Tia.

I turn around, my eyes scanning the crowd, looking for her smug face. But all I see are her minions—the spineless little shadows who do her dirty work and giggle behind bathroom doors.

I force my feet to move toward my locker like I don't give a fuck, even though my insides are twisted and my hands are itching to hit something. If Tia had been here when I walked up, I wouldn't have thought twice about ripping her apart in front of everyone, showing them just how much of a pathetic bitch she really is. But she's not here. Of course she isn't. So I swallow the anger, shove it down deep, and focus. The words on my locker are just another one of her weak attempts to get to me.

I open my locker, ignoring the burning weight of every pair of eyes glued to me. I drop my bag, pull out my books, every movement deliberate, controlled. Cool. Collected. Unbothered. Then I hear it. That grating, nails-on-a-chalkboard voice that gets my blood boiling.

"Wow," Tia says, her tone dripping with mock sympathy. "Guess your locker finally tells the truth about you, huh?"

FUCK. THIS. BITCH

I slam the locker door so hard it echoes down the hall, silencing the murmurs around us. Turning slowly, I lock eyes with her. She's standing there, her hair pulled so tight it looks painful, makeup layered on like war paint, and that stupid pout she thinks makes her look hot but just screams desperation.

I step closer, my voice steady, sharp. "Here's the thing, Tia—you can spray-paint whatever bullshit you want on my locker, but it doesn't change the fact that you're the saddest bitch in this hallway. And let's be real: no amount of daddy's money or knockoff designer bags is ever gonna fill that black hole where your personality should be."

Her smile flickers—just for a second—but I catch it. So I keep going, leaning in just enough to make sure she hears every word. "Calling me a slut? Babe, I'm not the one throwing myself at anything with a dick and a credit card."

I turn to walk away, tossing a final glance over my shoulder. "Oh, by the way, you might want to fix your tan. Your neck looks real patchy today."

The crowd laughs softly, the sound breaking the tense silence. Tia's jaw tightens, her mask slipping as the attention pins her in place.

"What the fuck did you just say to me?" she snaps, her voice shrill, teetering on the edge of losing control.

I stop mid-step, spin back around, and stalk toward her, my voice razor-sharp. "You heard me, Tia."

Her smirk falters, her confidence wobbling as the crowd presses closer, watching like this is their front-row seat to a showdown. Her eyes dart around, but no one's stepping in. No one's coming to save her.

I close the gap between us, my eyes boring into hers. "You think this shit makes you powerful? Spray-painting my locker and running your mouth like a bitch makes you the queen of this school? Let me tell you something—power isn't tearing people down because you can't face yourself in the mirror. And you, Tia? You're the most terrified little bitch I've ever met."

I take another step closer, and she instinctively retreats, her back slamming against the lockers with a hollow clang. The sound ripples through the crowd, stirring murmurs, but I don't stop. I keep my voice low and sharp. "You don't hate me. You hate that I'm not scared of you. You hate that no matter what you do, you can't break me. And that eats you alive, doesn't it?" I tilt my head, letting my gaze rake over her.

Her pout falters, her too-thick eyeliner smudged just enough to show the cracks in her perfect mask. Her lips part like she wants to retort, but I cut her off before she can even breathe.

Leaning in slightly, I make sure every word lands. "Spraying paint and running your mouth, that's not power, Tia. That's desperation. You're not a queen—you're just a bitter little girl, clinging to whatever scraps of relevance you can find. Keep pulling your stunts, keep talking your shit, but spoiler alert: I don't break. Not for you. Not for anyone. Every time you try, you're just proving to everyone here that you're nothing but a jealous, washed-up bitched who peaked way too early."

Her throat bobs as she swallows, her bravado slipping. I don't wait for a response. I turn on my heels, heading back to my locker, my heart pounding with satisfaction.

I yank the locker open, trying to shake off the tension, when her voice pierces through the air like a dagger.

Fuck me. When will this bitch learn to shut her mouth?

"You can say whatever you want in those pathetic clothes. We all know your family background. A drunken father who—"

The rest of her sentence doesn't register. The world narrows to her voice, her smug tone, and the mention of him. My father. My hands curl into fists, nails biting into my palms as my chest tightens. I spin around, faster than I can think, my vision red-hot and tunneled. Tia's standing too close, that infuriating grin still plastered on her face.

Without hesitation, without a second thought, I pull back and slam my fist into her nose.

She can call me names all day long. Trash my clothes, my hair, my fucking existence—fine. But dragging my life into this? Acting like she knows a goddamn thing about the hell I've been through? That's the fucking line.

Tia's so clueless it's almost laughable. She wouldn't last a second in my shoes, in the chaos of my shitty life. She doesn't know what it's like to be a pawn to parents who stopped giving a shit about you. She doesn't know what it feels like to question if you're enough, if you'll ever be enough.

The impact reverberates through my arm, the sound of bone crunching under my knuckles slicing through the stunned silence of the hallway. Her head snaps back, blood blooming across her face, a vivid red against her pale skin.

The crowd freezes, the chatter dropping to a deafening quiet as everyone processes what just happened. Phones lower. Eyes widen.

Adrenaline surges through me like wildfire, my heartbeat pounding in my ears. I stare at her crumpled form for a second that feels like an eternity, watching her clutch her bleeding nose, tears streaming down her face as she gasps in shock.

And then it hits me.

Shit.

My hand throbs, the sting grounding me as reality crashes down.

What the fuck did I just do?

Blood spills through her fingers like my rage had slashed its own vivid signature across her pale, pristine world. The crimson stains bloom, raw and undeniable, marring the perfection she's spent her life trying to maintain.

The hallway seems to hold its breath. Blood drips to the floor in uneven splatters, each drop punctuating the stunned silence. Tia's muffled cries rise like a siren, shrill and slicing through the air, but all I can focus on is the realization: I did this.

I've never been the type to choose violence. I've always thought I was better than that. But now, standing here amidst the aftermath, I'm not sure who I am anymore.

The weight of every pair of eyes watching me presses down like a boulder, pinning me to this moment I can't escape.

Tia's minions hover around her, their mouths agape as they scramble into action. Some kneel beside her, murmuring in frantic tones, while others raise their phones, the glowing screens capturing my humiliation from every angle. The whispers snake through the crowd, growing louder, feeding on my mistake.

I watch as her friends help her to her feet, their movements deliberate and theatrical, as though staging a scene for maximum sympathy. Blood streaks her face, a stark contrast to the carefully cultivated mask she wears every day. As they guide her down the hallway, their harsh glares stab at me.

My breath turns shallow and ragged as the walls close in. The stares, the whispers, the relentless buzz of phones capturing my failure—it's too much. I glance around, desperate for something solid, something that will stop me from collapsing under the weight of it all.

And then I see him.

Noah.

He's leaning casually against the far wall, arms crossed, his body language untouched by the chaos. His eyes meet mine, steady and unflinching, cutting through the noise like a lifeline. There's no smug grin, no judgment, just a calm that feels like an anchor in the storm.

For a moment, the world narrows to him. The noise dims, the stares blur, and the ground beneath me feels steady again. Noah doesn't say a word, doesn't even move, but his presence speaks louder than the accusations swirling around me.

You've got this. Let them watch.

I take a slow, deliberate breath, feeling the tension melt away from my clenched fists. My heart still pounds, but the panic threatening to suffocate me begins to recede, curling into something I can control.

The storm hasn't passed, not by a long shot. Whatever comes next—the fallout, the judgment, the consequences—I'll face it. But the truth cuts deep than I want to admit: I've fucked up. Tia, the girl who used to be my friend, is the one I've hurt. The guilt digs in like nails under my skin, sharp and relentless.

I tear my eyes from Noah and face the crowd. Their stares are suffocating, like a hundred invisible hands clawing at me, ripping me open to expose every raw, ugly piece of me for judgment. My chest tightens, and suddenly, I can't breathe. Elbowing through the swarm of students, I shove past them, their whispers slicing into me like glass. I don't look back. I can't.

The bathroom door looms ahead like salvation. I don't think—I just move, my heart pounding in my chest like it's trying to escape. I yank the door open and stumble inside, the muted chaos of the hallway replaced by an almost eerie quiet. But the storm inside me doesn't fade.

I rush to the sink, twisting the faucet so hard it protests with a groan. Cold water gushes out, and I splash it over my face, the icy bite shocking against my flushed skin. My breath is jagged, uneven, as if I'm trying to outrun the fire raging through my veins. My reflection stares back at me from the mirror, distorted by droplets clinging to the glass.

My mind spins in a whirlwind of guilt, adrenaline, and dread.

My old man's been keeping his distance lately—like he's done for years, dodging the wreckage of our relationship like two cars swerving to avoid a head on collision. But this? This is different. I can already hear the principal's call, dragging him into the mess I've made. Last time he got one of those calls, it was a disaster—doors slammed, walls shook, and his voice roared like a thunderstorm. This time, it will be a fucking nightmare.

I grip the sink, my knuckles white, and force myself to look in the mirror again. My face is flushed, my hair sticking to my damp forehead. But it's my eyes that stop me—anger, regret, disbelief all swirling together.

What the fuck were you thinking?

The question echoes in my head, bitter and sharp. I squeeze my eyes shut and shake my head, as if I can rattle the regret loose. How did I let Tia drag me down to her level? But no matter how much I want to shove it aside, the truth stares back at me in the glass. I see it clear as day—the same temper, the same reckless anger. The same goddamn thing I swore I'd never inherit from him.

The bathroom door creaks open, and Sam, Liz, and Lola shuffle in, their voices breaking the silence.

"Oh my God, there you are," Sam breathes, relief in her voice as she spots me.

Lola rushes to my side. "Are you okay?" she asks, her voice softer than I deserve.

I grip the edge of the sink tighter, grounding myself. "I shouldn't have let her get to me," I admit, the shame crawling up my throat.

Liz leans against the sink beside me, her arms crossed. "You're like the talk of the school right now," she says, with a grin. "Guys are losing their shit about how badass that was. And honestly? Watching Tia get what she deserves was pretty satisfying."

I shake my head, the bitterness of regret coating my words.

"I don't know. I really hurt her."

Lola places a hand on my arm, her touch gentle. "You're not a bad person, okay? She pushed you, and you snapped. It doesn't mean this is who you are."

Her words hang in the air, but I'm not sure I believe them. Because the person I saw in the mirror? That person looked a hell of a lot like my father.

Sam steps into my line of sight, her arms crossed as she gives me a pointed look. "Yeah, well, after all the shit Tia's pulled over the years, maybe she had it coming."

I shake my head, the weight of it all pressing down on me. "Even if she did, I didn't handle it right. I lost control."

Lola raises an eyebrow, leaning against the wall. "You're seriously beating yourself up over this? Tia's been a bitch forever. Half the school's probably cheering you on right now. Don't let her make you feel guilty for finally standing your ground."

Before I can respond, the bell blares, shrill and relentless, yanking me back to reality. Great. Just what I need. Now I get to walk through the halls, surrounded by stares, whispers, and judgment that'll crawl all over me like spiders under my skin. My books are in my locker, and there's no avoiding it. I'll have to face the storm head-on.

"Come on," Sam says, cutting through my spiral. She grabs my arm, her grip firm as she pulls me toward the door. "You can't hide out in here all day. Tonight's the party—you can blow off steam there."

"You're still coming, right?" Liz chimes in.

"Of course she's going," Sam says, answering for me.

I nod automatically, but it's not the party that has my chest tightening and my heart hammering. It's the waiting.

The loudspeaker. The inevitable crackle of static followed by the principal's voice, calling me to the office. My name, broadcast for everyone to hear, confirming what they all already suspect—that I've officially fucked up.

CHAPTER 14

NOAH

The hallway this morning was fucking chaos —packed bodies, buzzing whispers, and the charged energy of something big about to go down. Through the swarm of students, my eyes locked onto Aubrey and Tia squaring off. There she was—Aubrey, standing her ground for the first time in what felt like forever. A smirk tugged at my lips. She'd finally hit her breaking point, and honestly? It was about damn time.

Aubrey's always had this razor-sharp wit, a way of dismantling people with words that hit harder than any punch. But today? Words weren't enough. She was a fucking storm unleashed, all fire and fury, and Tia? Tia didn't stand a chance. Her smug mask cracked as Aubrey tore through her bullshit like it was nothing. It was raw, brutal, and, let's be real, long overdue.

I didn't catch the whole thing—just enough to piece together what went down. Tia, queen of low blows, had said something about Aubrey's dad, digging deep enough to make anyone snap. And Aubrey? She didn't hesitate. Her fist flew, and the crack of impact echoed through the hallway like a gunshot. For a moment, everything stopped—the noise, the movement, the world itself. Just silence, thick and heavy with shock.

And fuck, it was powerful. Watching Aubrey take back control, watching her refuse to let Tia get the last word—it was gripping, like witnessing something primal and unstoppable. The guys around me were buzzing, hyped over how badass she looked, but I just stood there, rooted in place. She was magnificent—a force of nature, untamed and unapologetic.

This was the Aubrey I remembered, the girl I grew up with. Only now, she was sharper, tougher, and scarred in ways that made her all the more striking. Pride burned in my chest, but it was tangled with something heavier. Because for all the satisfaction of seeing Tia get what she deserved, I couldn't ignore the cost. Aubrey's cost.

The rest of the day dragged on like I was wading through quicksand. Neither of them showed up—no Aubrey, no Tia. Tia's absence was no surprise; she was probably at the nurse's office or hospital dealing with a broken nose. But Aubrey's silence? That hit different. Every class I walked into, every hallway I crossed, I caught myself searching for her, waiting for even a fleeting glimpse.

When the loudspeaker finally called her to the principal's office, my stomach dropped. Suspension was inevitable. There's no way the school would let something like this slide. But it wasn't the school I was worried about. It was what came after. Her father. The hot-headed asshole who doesn't just yell—he fucking explodes.

By the time I pull into my driveway, the weight of the day presses down on me. My gaze drifts to Aubrey's house next door. Her window is dark, the house is too quiet, and my mind won't stop spinning. Is she inside, bracing herself for the fallout? Is he there, pacing, yelling, ready to unload all his rage on her like always?

My jaw tightens, a familiar anger simmering under my skin. Aubrey may have been a storm today, but storms leave wreckage, and I can't shake the feeling that she is dealing with it alone.

The protective instinct I've tried to bury rises like a wave, crashing through the walls I've built to keep it contained. It claws at my skin, this overwhelming urge to check on her, to make sure she's okay, to remind her she doesn't have to face him alone. My knuckles tighten on the steering wheel, my grip whitening, but I force myself to stay put. I know better. Whatever we had—whatever we were to each other—that's gone now.

With a deep breath, I step inside the house and let the door click shut behind me. The silence is instant, heavy, and familiar—the kind that makes it clear I'm alone. Dad's already left for the weekend with Simone.

In the kitchen, a folded note on the counter catches my eye. I walk over, pick it up, and scan the short message in his neat, looping handwriting.

Love you, Son.
Call if you need me.
Love, Dad.

I crumple the note in my hand and toss it into the catch-all drawer—the one messy space in an otherwise perfectly organized kitchen.

It joins the pile of similar notes he's left over the years. They're all the same, variations of him reminding me that I matter.

The fridge hums softly as I pull it open, scanning its contents. I grab an apple from the crisper and bite into it. My phone buzzes where I left it on the counter, and I glance at the screen. It's a message from Jace.

Curiosity tugs at me, and I tap it open. It's a video. Of her. Aubrey.

My thumb hovers over the play button for half a second before I press it, and the screen comes to life. There it is—that moment. Her fist connects with Tia's face, and the sharp crack echoes even through the shitty phone audio. The camera shakes as the crowd reacts, but it doesn't matter. The focus stays on Aubrey, her stance defiant, her eyes blazing.

I watch it again. And again.

I can't look away. The rawness of it, the fire in her—it's electric. She didn't hesitate. She didn't flinch. She just acted. It wasn't pretty or polished; it was raw and real.

Tia had it coming. Everyone knows it. And now everyone's talking about Aubrey. The video's already making the rounds, shared like it's some iconic scene from a fucking movie.

I take another bite of the apple, my mind swirling. Tonight's party is going to be something else.

***

The house is already alive with chaos by the time I pull up. The thump of the bass pounds through the otherwise quiet, polished neighborhood, the thrum vibrating in my chest as I park. Liam's family might have money and the perfect suburban image, but this party is anything but picture-perfect. It's the kind of untouchable chaos only his dad's status as a big-shot lawyer can shield. No one's calling the cops—not when they know who owns the place.

The moment I step inside, the atmosphere hits me like a tidal wave—laughter, music, and that unmistakable electric charge of bad decisions waiting to happen. Eyes are on me before I've even closed the door. The usual suspects—girls with too much makeup and not enough shame—lock onto me like predators, hoping for a piece of my attention. I don't even bother acknowledging them, cutting through the crowd like they don't exist.

On the way to the drinks, I exchange a few fist bumps with the guys. Reece is in the corner, tangled up with some girl who's definitely not Sam—the same Sam he's warned me a hundred times to stay the hell away from. Hypocrite.

In the kitchen, Jace is doing what Jace does best, his hands all over some random girl who's one slap away from teaching him a lesson. When he comes up for air, I give him a nod. He flashes me a shit-eating grin before diving back in like the shameless bastard he is.

Drink in hand, I push through the bodies towards the couch in the center of the room. The party whirls around me in a haze of flashing lights and deafening beats. This is what everyone lives for—nights like this, moments like these.

As I drop onto the couch, the crowd instinctively parts, leaving me some breathing room. The relentless bass drowns out my thoughts, a numbing rhythm I welcome. Within seconds, a few girls drift over, their intentions as obvious as their outfits—curves spilling out of tight tops, eyes gleaming with the promise of a wild night.

They don't wait for an invitation, sliding in on either side of me like they've claimed a prize. Synthia—or maybe it's Cindy, who the fuck knows—makes the first move, her fingers tangling in my hair as she drags me into a kiss that's all tongue and zero finesse. Before she's even done, the other one—name long forgotten—grabs a fistful of my hair and pulls me toward her.

It's a full-blown competition, each one trying to outdo the other, their hands and mouths everywhere. Normally, this kind of attention guarantees a good time. With these two, it's been fun before—wild, even.

But tonight? Tonight, it feels... off.

They pull back, their expectant eyes waiting for my reaction. All I give them is a slow sip of my drink, the burn of alcohol barely cutting through the disinterest creeping under my skin. My gaze sweeps the room, searching for something—someone—worth my time.

And then I see her. Aubrey.

She's across the room, her black hair catching the light, a red plastic cup clenched in her hand like it's the only thing tethering her here. Her body language makes it clear she'd rather be anywhere else, and I'd bet everything it was Sam who dragged her here. Sam and Lola are flanking her, but Aubrey's expression doesn't soften, doesn't wander. Her eyes are locked, her thoughts somewhere far away, and I'd kill to know what's running through her head.

Aubrey's a fucking knockout, the kind of beauty that doesn't even need to try—that's the part that always gets me. She's standing there in tight black jeans that hug her hips like a second skin and a simple top that clings to her curves like it was made for her. It's not flashy or overdone; it's effortless, raw, and so sexy it borders on cruel.

My cock, which had been idly interested in the two girls draped across me, suddenly stirs with a sharper, more focused need. This. This isn't about them. It's about her. It's always her.

I should get up. Go over there. Ask her why the hell she wasn't at school today, even though I already know the answer. But I don't. The idea of her brushing me off, throwing me that perfectly detached look she's mastered, keeps me anchored to the couch. So, I let the girls beside me carry on—one's lips ghosting over my neck, the other's hand rubbing my cock through my jeans. They're distractions, background noise to the real fixation in my head.

When Aubrey's eyes sweep across the room and land on me, my chest tightens. For a second, I think I catch a flicker of something—curiosity, maybe? Annoyance? I can't be sure. What I do notice is the brief glance she shoots at the chick's hand on my cock before her gaze flicks back to mine.

A surge of heat shoots through me, my thoughts dragged straight to that night. The one where she caught me, hand around my cock, stroking to the thought of her. Even now, the memory is enough to make me fucking throb.

Then it happens. That tiny, devastating move that wrecks me every damn time. Her tongue flicks out, slow and unintentional, wetting her bottom lip like she doesn't know the chaos it stirs. My cock aches, and I bite the inside of my cheek hard enough to draw blood, fighting the urge to groan.

The girls beside me could strip naked, and I wouldn't give a shit. My thoughts are tangled up in her—Aubrey. All I want is her under me, her breath hitching as I drag her over the edge, her body trembling as I ruin us both.

One of the girls tightens her grip on my hair, yanking my face toward hers. I let her kiss me, her mouth all heat and hunger, trying to reignite the spark she doesn't realize was never hers to claim. I kiss her back with enough enthusiasm to make her think she's winning. But even as her hands tug at me, I'm somewhere else. In my head, it's not her touch I'm feeling—it's Aubrey's.

I close my eyes and let the fantasy take over. It's Aubrey's hands threading through my hair, Aubrey's lips moving against mine, Aubrey's body pressed so close I can't tell where I end and she begins.

When the girl finally pulls back, breathless and flushed, I sneak a glance across the room, searching for her. Aubrey. But she's gone.

She's not standing with Sam anymore. She's not anywhere.

The realization steals the air from my lungs. The flicker of desire burns out, replaced by a hollow ache I can't shake. She's gone, and it feels like I'm left chasing something I'll never quite catch.

I shove the girl off me, ignoring her whiny protests as she tumbles back onto the couch. My focus is razor-sharp now, cutting through the fog of booze and noise. My eyes dart around, scanning every inch of the room for her. Is she in the bathroom? Did she leave?

A restless energy claws at me, and I down the rest of my drink in one go, the burn sliding down my throat doing nothing to dull the edge.

One of the girls climbs to her feet, sidling up to me. She presses herself against my arm, her tits squishing against me as she leans in close. Her voice is low and syrupy, dripping with calculated seduction. "Let's go upstairs," she purrs, lips brushing my ear. "I'll suck your cock."

Her breath is warm, her tone suggestive, but her words are hollow. Cold.

"Not interested," I snap, shoving her aside.

I don't wait for her reaction as I stride away. She's just another meaningless face in a room full of them.

I move to the far side of the room, keeping a careful distance from Sam while still positioning myself where I can watch. My eyes are glued to the spot where Aubrey was standing, every second dragging by like an eternity.

Five minutes pass—maybe less, but it feels like fucking forever—before I snap.

I cross the room, heading straight for Sam. She's in the middle of a conversation with some guy who looks like he'd rather be studying than partying. I stop beside her, crossing my arms and letting my presence do the talking.

Sam glances up, her smile fading as soon as she registers it's me. Her expression hardens, her guard going up in an instant.

"Where the fuck is she?" I ask, my voice low but laced with frustration.

Sam narrows her eyes, the hint of a smirk tugging at her lips. For a moment, I get it—why Reece is so into her. There's a sharpness to her, something that doesn't bend or break easily. She's gorgeous, too, but that's not why I'm here.

"Who?" she says, feigning confusion. Her brow furrows, but the act doesn't last. I see it click behind her eyes—the realization.

Her gaze flickers around the room, searching for Aubrey. When she doesn't find her, her lips press into a tight, disapproving line.

Without waiting for an answer, I'm already moving, pushing into the next room. My eyes scan every corner, taking in the swirl of bodies, the shadows cast by the dim lighting. Still nothing.

Outside, the storm hits hard, rain hammering against the massive floor-to-ceiling windows. Lightning flashes, illuminating my reflection for a brief second before thunder cracks, rattling the glass and momentarily stealing the crowd's attention.

When I glance back, Sam is gripping her phone tightly, her thumbs flying across the screen in quick, furious taps. Whatever she's doing, she's not telling me, and my patience is running out.

Her head stays down, fingers moving in a blur across her phone screen as I close the gap between us. She's so engrossed, she doesn't even notice when I lean in, catching a perfect view of her messages.

Just as I suspected—she's texting Aubrey.

My pulse quickens, anticipation clawing at me as I watch the exchange. When Aubrey's reply finally comes through, the words make my stomach twist.

Aubrey: Sorry, should've told you. Had to leave. Walking home now.

Walking? In this fucking storm?

Before Sam even looks up, I'm already moving, my legs carrying me toward the front door with purpose. Panic courses through me at the thought of Aubrey out there, alone, soaked to the bone, with thunder cracking and lightning streaking across the sky.

The storm hits like a wall the moment I step outside, the wind howling as sheets of rain drench me instantly. I yank my hood up, not that it helps, and break into a run, my shoes splashing through puddles as water seeps into my jeans. The cold bites, sharp and relentless, but I don't slow down.

Fumbling with my keys, I manage to unlock the car and dive inside, slamming the door against the chaos outside. My breath comes in sharp bursts, fogging up the windows as I dig my phone out of my pocket.

I pause. Does she still have the same number? I've held onto it all this time, even when I told myself to let her go.

With a deep breath, I hit the call button, pressing the phone to my ear as each ring stretches unbearably long. The rain pounds against the roof, matching the frantic hammering of my heart.

One ring. Two. Then the tone shifts—she's declined the call. The beep comes, and I force myself to speak, my voice rough with urgency and emotion.

"Aubrey, it's me. I..." My throat tightens, but I push through. "Where the fuck are you? You shouldn't be out in this storm. Just... call me back, okay? I'll come get you."

I hang up, gripping the phone so tightly it feels like it might shatter. My breath trembles as I toss it onto the seat beside me. Reaching for the ignition, I'm about to start the car when my phone buzzes.

My chest tightens with hope. Aubrey?

I snatch it up, only to see a different name flash across the screen. The momentary disappointment fades as I answer.

"Hey, Dad," I say, trying to steady my voice.

"Noah," he starts, steady and calm, the way he always is. "Just checking in. There's a storm heading your way—they're saying it's gonna be rough."

I exhale, leaning back against the seat, my fingers tapping on the top of the steering wheel. "Yeah, I noticed. It's already coming down hard. Don't worry, I'm fine. Party was shit anyway—I'm heading home early."

"You sure you're okay?" he asks, his voice thick with that fatherly concern that always manages to ground me, even when I'm spiraling. "You sound... I don't know, off."

"I'm good, Dad. Really." For a second, the urge to spill everything claws at me—to admit that my head's a fucking wreck and my heart feels like it's being ripped out of my chest. But I swallow it down. He doesn't need that right now. "I just need to get home before this storm gets worse."

"Alright," he says, though the hesitation in his voice is unmistakable, laced with unspoken worry.

"Drive safe, Noah. I mean it. No rushing, no distractions. Promise me."

"I promise, Dad," I tell him, meaning it. "I'll text you when I'm home."

"Good. Don't forget. And if you need anything—anything—you call me, okay?"

"I will, Dad." I hang up, setting the phone down on the passenger seat.

The silence that follows ringing louder than the storm outside.

The engine rumbles to life beneath me, and for a moment, I just sit there, staring out at the rain-slick streets. The downpour cascades in thick sheets, blurring the world outside.

I'll just head home. And maybe—just maybe—I'll find her.

CHAPTER 15

AUBREY

What a shit day. The absolute fucking worst. First, there's the drama with Tia—her smug face still haunts me—then getting suspended for a week. Like I didn't already have enough shit to deal with. My dad got dragged into school for a sit-down with the asshole principal, and the second we left, he tore into me. His words were like knives, sharp and cutting, telling me I'm nothing but trouble, and that I'll always be a fucking disappointment. That kind of shit hurts, no matter how much I pretend it doesn't.

Now here I am, trudging through this storm, rain pouring down like the universe itself is taking a piss on me. I'm soaked, head to toe, after watching Noah's little circus act with those two girls. He couldn't have made it clearer if he'd had a neon sign flashing I've moved on. And yeah, I shouldn't care—I don't care—but fuck, it stings. Not just the girls. It's him. He's not the same. He's hollow now, like all the parts of him I used to know have been stripped away.

The rain pounds into me, icy and relentless, every drop soaking through my clothes. My boots squelch with each step, water creeping through the seams like betrayal. They were supposed to be waterproof. Figures. Just another lie in a day full of them. Fuck my life.

My phone buzzes in my pocket, the vibration faint under the storm's roar. I wrestle it out, fingers clumsy and wet, almost dropping it before I catch the damn thing.

I mutter a curse, squinting at the screen.

Noah.

You've got to be fucking kidding me.

I stare at his name like it's some kind of sick joke. What the hell does he want? One minute he's putting on a show like he's the fucking king of the world, and now he's calling me? What is this? Guilt? Regret? Or did his little spectacle get boring already?

My thumb hovers over the answer button, indecision gnawing at me. Every rational part of me is screaming to ignore it. Let it ring. Let him deal with whatever shitstorm he's got going on. But there's that other part of me—the pathetic, hopeful part—that remembers who he used to be.

A bitter laugh escapes me as I realize he still has my number. After all this time, he's kept it. But then again, what good is that? He's had it for months and never once used it. Now, out of nowhere, he thinks he can call me. Like I'll just pick up and pretend everything's fine. Fuck that and fuck him.

I jab the decline button with a force that could crack the screen and shove my phone back into my pocket. The rain doesn't let up—it's like the storm knows it's got me beat and keeps hammering down, soaking through every layer until I feel like a walking puddle. My hood's useless, my hair sticks to my face, and every inch of me feels weighed down by wet, clinging fabric. But I grit my teeth and push forward. One goal: get the hell out of this storm.

A bolt of lightning slashes across the sky behind me, lighting up the street in a harsh, white glare. For a moment, everything looks like a scene from a nightmare—shadows stretching into twisted shapes, the wet pavement shining like black glass, the park benches glinting like hollow ghosts. Then the thunder hits, loud enough to rattle my bones and echo in my chest.

I pick up my pace, boots slapping against the pavement, water splashing up my legs with every step. The storm is relentless, the rain icy as it needles into my skin. My jacket is soaked straight through, offering as much protection as tissue paper. Every step feels heavier, colder, like the storm's dragging me down, daring me to stop.

The park looms ahead, dark and deserted. Cutting through it will save me three blocks, and right now, every shortcut counts. I veer into the shadows, ignoring the way the darkness presses in around me. My breath comes in sharp bursts as I jog through, boots skidding against the slick ground. Overhead, the thunder roars again, a jagged crack that feels too close, making my heart jolt.

The wind cuts through me, raw and biting, but I keep moving. I have to. No one's looking out for me—never has been. Stopping isn't an option. If I stop, if I let myself feel any of it—the anger, the hurt—it'll swallow me whole. And I can't afford that. Not tonight.

By the time I reach my street, my legs are burning. The wind howls behind me, like it's driving me forward just to get rid of me. All I can think about is getting inside—away from the storm, the cold, and everything else crashing down on me.

I charge up the front path, nearly slipping on the slick pavement, and grab the door handle with trembling hands. Relief floods through me as I twist it—then it vanishes just as quickly. The handle doesn't budge.

"What the fuck?" I mutter, twisting it harder, my stomach sinking. I yank on the handle again and again, as if sheer force will change the outcome, but it's no use. It's locked. He's locked me out.

I stand there, frozen, rain dripping off my face, my fingers clenched around the cold metal like holding it tighter will make it open. My heart sinks as the truth settles in, cold and sharp. My dad was furious earlier—furious in a way I haven't seen in years. His words from the parking lot replay in my head, cruel and cutting: You're nothing but trouble. A fucking disappointment.

That's why I went to the party, why I stayed out. Anything to avoid being here, facing him when he's like this. But now, standing in the storm with no way in, it feels like there's no escaping it. Not him. Not this. Not tonight.

But locking me out?

My hand drops from the handle, my fingers stiff and trembling from the cold. I don't even realize I'm shaking until I try to steady myself, my breath coming in sharp, uneven bursts.

Lights flash behind me, slicing through the pounding rain. My stomach twists, and I whip around instinctively. A car pulls into the driveway next door.

Noah's car.

Of fucking course.

The universe just couldn't resist throwing one more punch tonight, could it? I watch him park, the headlights cutting harsh beams through the storm. I dart off the front step without thinking, the rain needling into my skin.

As I round the corner of the house, I glance back over my shoulder—a stupid, reflexive move I instantly regret. Through the windshield, his eyes meet mine. I freeze for half a second, every muscle in my body betraying me.

I can feel his stare, sharp and invasive, dissecting me, laying bare all the raw, miserable pieces I don't want anyone—especially him—to see.

The rational part of me waits for the headlights to flicker off, for him to get out of the car and leave me alone. But they don't. They just stay on, burning into me, refusing to grant me even the small mercy of darkness.

Is this some kind of sick fucking game to him? Does he get off on seeing me like this, standing in the freezing rain, drenched and humiliated?

I force myself to keep moving, sloshing through the muddy path to the side of the house. My boots stick with every step, water squelching up through the seams. When I reach my window, my fingers scrabble at the wet glass, searching for any sign that it will open. I know it's locked—of course it's locked—but I try anyway, desperation driving me to cling to the tiniest thread of hope.

It doesn't budge.

"Fuck!"

The word rips out of me, raw and guttural, swallowed immediately by the storm. My teeth clench as anger floods my chest, a sharp, bitter heat against the cold. For a split second, I imagine smashing the window, the satisfying sound of shattering glass. But what then? Bleed out in the rain? Brilliant idea, Aubrey. What the hell am I supposed to do now? Where the fuck am I supposed to go?

I stand there, shaking and defeated, arms wrapped around myself in a useless attempt to ward off the cold. It doesn't help. Nothing does.

The weight of everything presses down on me—the storm, the locked door, Noah's headlights still burning in the background like a cruel spotlight. Every shitty moment in my life feels like it's led to this, dragging me down into this suffocating pit.

For a moment, I consider giving up. Just lying down right here in the mud, letting the rain drown me out. No one would notice. No one would care.

The thought festers for a heartbeat too long before I'm jolted out of it.

Noah's voice cuts through the storm, pulling me back to reality.

"What the fuck are you doing out here in the storm?"

His tone is biting, but there's something else beneath it—concern, maybe. I don't want to hear it. I don't want him here.

Straightening my shoulders, I swipe at my face, pretending the tears aren't there, even though the rain's already taken care of them. He can't know. I won't let him.

"Just go away, Noah," I mutter, my teeth chattering so hard I can barely get the words out. My whole body is trembling, and I hate that he's here to see me like this—raw and fucking ruined.

"Not until you tell me what the hell is going on," he snaps back, stepping closer, his voice cutting through the storm. "Why are you standing out here in the rain?"

I glare at him, my anger rising like a shield to block out the ache inside me. "Why do you even care?"

"Because I give a fuck, alright?" he barks, striding toward me.

The words hit harder than I expect, and before I can shove him away, his hands grip my shoulders. He's strong, his touch firm and grounding, and I hate how it feels like a lifeline I didn't ask for.

His eyes lock on mine. There's no escaping his gaze, no hiding from him, no matter how much I want to.

I hold my ground for a moment, trying to keep the walls up, but they're already crumbling. My body feels heavy, too tired to keep fighting, and the truth slips out before I can stop it.

"My dad lost his shit at school earlier," I admit, my voice breaking as I look down, unable to meet his eyes anymore. "He's locked me out of the house. I can't get inside."

The words feel like shards of glass coming out, each one cutting deeper than the last. I feel so fucking small, so goddamn defeated, like the weight of everything is going to crush me right here. Noah doesn't say anything at first. He just reaches out, his hand wrapping around mine. His grip is steady, solid, and it almost breaks me all over again.

"Come on," he says, like he's already made up his mind.

He pulls me forward, his touch anchoring me as he leads me back down the side of the house. The storm rages on, but with each step, I feel a tiny bit less alone.

When we reach his car, Noah swiftly yanks open the driver's door and cuts the headlights. Lightning rips through the sky, briefly painting the soaked world in stark white light. The storm's fury pushes us toward his house, rain drenching us with every hurried step.

Noah's place is nothing like mine—where mine feels like a prison, his has life, warmth. The sprawling patio is cluttered with chairs and a porch swing that creaks softly under the weight of the storm. It feels like another world; one I don't belong in.

It's the kind of place that feels cared for—everything my own home isn't. A world where people actually give a shit.

We climb the steps, water streaming off us in relentless rivulets, and I let go of his hand, severing the fleeting connection. Noah turns, his expression obscured in the storm's shadows, but the weight of his stare is unmistakable.

"What the hell are you doing?" he demands, yelling out over the storm.

I step further onto the patio, my soaked clothes plastered to me like a second skin. "I'll tough it out here," I manage, my teeth chattering so hard it garbles the words. I try to sound indifferent, but the tremor in my voice betrays me. Wrapping my arms around myself, I brace against the cold gnawing at my bones. It's useless—I'm trembling so violently I can barely stand.

"No fucking way," Noah says, stepping closer. "You're freezing your ass off. You're not staying out here like this. Let's go."

Before I can protest, before I can even think, his hand finds mine again. His grip should burn against my icy skin, but I'm too numb to feel it. All I know is the unrelenting pull as he tugs me toward the door.

He fumbles with his keys, the storm pounding around us, and with a low creak, the front door swings open. Noah flips on the light, flooding the space with brightness, and we step inside.

The warmth hits immediately, sinking into my frozen skin, and for a moment, I just stand there, breathing it in. It feels alien, like I've stepped into another world. Noah's house has always been different—alive in a way mine never was. The faint smell of woodsmoke and something warm—cinnamon, maybe—lingers in the air.

His dad always made this place feel like more than just four walls. When we were kids, I'd watch the way he'd ruffle Noah's hair or call him "kiddo" with an ease that felt impossible in my own home. I'd go back to my house after, pretending my dad might one day do the same. He never did. Love from my dad came with strings, with rules, with impossible conditions I could never meet.

A loud thunk jolts me back to the present. Noah's kicked off his boots by the door, water pooling beneath them in shimmering puddles. Without thinking, I do the same, tugging off my soggy boots and setting them next to his.

Straightening up, I catch his gaze. He's watching me, his eyes steady, unflinching. It's not pity—I can tell that much. It's heavier, sharper, like he's trying to see past the surface, to uncover the shit I've worked so hard to keep buried.

"What?" I snap, harsher than I intend. The vulnerability crawling up my spine is too much, clawing at me, leaving me raw.

He doesn't flinch. "Nothing," he says softly, but his eyes don't waver. They linger, steady and relentless, peeling me apart piece by piece. Like he's trying to figure out what's broken and whether he can fix it.

"Come on," he says, his voice low as he turns and heads down the hall.

I follow, my steps hesitant, unsure, while he moves with effortless confidence. Without a second thought, he pulls off his hoodie and shirt in one fluid motion, leaving his skin gleaming faintly in the low light. My steps falter as he disappears into his room, leaving me stranded in the doorway.

I should look away. I know I should. But I don't.

His wet jeans hit the floor, landing in a careless heap by the hamper. My gaze betrays me, drawn to the hard lines of his body, the way every muscle seems carved, honed. He's all sharp edges and solid strength—broad shoulders, defined arms, the sharp plane of his chest. He's not the Noah I grew up with anymore; he's something darker, more dangerous.

My eyes dip lower, entirely against my will, to where the damp fabric of his boxers clings to him, outlines his cock, leaving nothing to the imagination. Heat surges through me, sharp and unwelcome, stirring something deep, something primal and raw.

Then his eyes snap up to meet mine.

Shit.

I turn away so fast I nearly stumble, my pulse hammering. My chest tightens, and I try to push the heat away, bury it beneath every warning I've ever given myself. He's still Noah—beautiful, infuriating—but he's not mine. Not anymore. He belongs to other girls now, girls I don't want to think about. He's no longer the boy who used to dream too big and make me feel like I could do the same. That Noah is gone. What's left is harder, colder. A man who takes what he wants, no matter the cost.

Wrapping my arms around myself, I turn my focus to his room. It's not the same. The boyish chaos is gone, replaced by something cleaner, more deliberate—but it feels emptier too. Like him.

The sound of the shower starting snaps me back, grounding me for a moment. I should leave. I should. Head back to the patio.

Before I can move, Noah strides back into the room.

My gaze lifts, instinctual, locking with his. There's something there—intense, unrelenting—that pins me in place. He closes the distance between us with the same quiet confidence, and I don't move, can't move.

He stops right in front of me, and his hand reaches out, gripping the edge of my jacket. The fabric clings to me, soaked and stubborn, but he doesn't hesitate. Slowly, deliberately, he peels it away, leaving my skin cold and exposed to the air, to him.

His fingers slide under the hem of my shirt, brushing against my skin—a tease that sends a shiver racing through me—before he pulls it over my head in one fluid motion.

His eyes drop, lingering on my chest, and I can see it—the raw hunger simmering just beneath the surface. It burns, sharp and unapologetic, making my breath hitch in my throat. Fuck him. Fuck this.

He swallows hard, his jaw tight as though he's barely keeping himself together. His hands move to my jeans next, deliberate and unhurried. The button pops open, the zipper dragged down in a way that feels far too intimate. My pulse pounds, a relentless drumbeat, loud and insistent. He's not just undressing me; he's dismantling me, one piece at a time. His hands remain steady as he pushes the wet denim past my hips, peeling it down my legs.

I should stop him. I should say something. But I don't. I can't. My thoughts are a whirlwind, crashing into one another, and his touch only feeds the storm, igniting a wildfire that spreads through me, wild and uncontrollable.

For fuck sake, keep it together Aubrey.

When he drops to his knees in front of me, the air leaves my lungs in a sharp rush.

It's too much. The intimacy of it, the way his fingers skim my skin like he has a right to—it's fucking unbearable. My hands clench into fists at my sides, the urge to push him away warring with the need to pull him closer. Why does he still have this hold on me? Why does the sight of him, like this, on his knees make my heart race and my chest ache all at once?

His gaze is heavy, dark, dragging over every inch of exposed skin like he's memorizing it. It's possessive, infuriating, and all-consuming. My chest heaves, and a scream builds in my throat, aimed at him, at myself, at everything that's brought me here.

Rising to his feet, his hand finds mine, warm and steady, and pulls me toward the bathroom. He doesn't say a word. And I hate that he doesn't need to. The silence between us is louder than any argument, sharper than any insult.

Steam greets us as we step inside, thick and oppressive. Noah doesn't pause. He guides me into the shower with him, my bra and panties still plastered to my body, drenched and heavy with rain and regret.

The water hits me, warm and soothing, cascading over my skin and washing away the worst of the chill. But it can't reach the cold lodged deep in my chest. Noah steps out of the stream, giving me space, but his presence lingers, heavy and inescapable. He's watching me. I can feel it. His gaze burns through the glass panel, as if it can pierce every wall I've built.

And then it fucking happens.

The sob tears out of me, raw and unrestrained, breaking through the barrier I've been struggling to hold together for too long. It rips through my chest, echoing off the walls, ugly and guttural. I'm breaking—splintering under the weight of too much, too fast, too real.

It's everything. Tia. The guilt eating me alive, the shitty choices I've made that turned me into someone I can't even recognize. My father's cutting words that still echo, tearing me open in ways that feel irreparable. The ache of my mother's silence—every unanswered call, every ignored message—that burrows deeper, a constant reminder of my worthlessness.

And Noah. Fucking Noah. Seeing him tonight, laughing, touching those girls like it was the easiest thing in the world, felt like a knife twisting in my gut. It's a reminder of exactly what I am: nothing. Replaceable. Forgotten.

The tears mix with the water streaming down my face, indistinguishable, but I can feel every single one. The sobs wrack my body, pulling me under, and I let them. Because for once, there's no point in pretending. No point in holding it together when I'm already shattered.

The truth is suffocating: I'm fucking alone. No safety net, no one to catch me when I fall. Not even Noah—the guy who once knew every part of me.

The tears come faster now, hot and relentless, blurring my vision and choking the air from my lungs. The weight of it all presses down on me until it's almost unbearable. I don't hear the glass door slide open or feel the change in the air—until his arms wrap around me.

Noah.

He pulls me to him, strong and steady, his chest against my back, warm and solid. For the first time in what feels like forever, I don't feel like I'm about to completely fall apart. He doesn't say a word, doesn't try to fix me with empty promises. He just holds me, anchoring me as my body shakes with the force of my sobs.

I collapse against him, the flood I've been holding back finally breaking free. Every ounce of pain, regret, and heartbreak pours out of me, mixing with the water streaming down my face. I cry for everything I've lost, everything I've fucked up, and every piece of myself I don't recognize anymore.

Noah doesn't let go. His silence says everything his words never could. He holds me like he knows I've already shattered, his face pressing gently into the curve of my neck, his breath warm against my skin. His arms don't tighten; they just hold, steady and unyielding, like he's afraid to let me go

I don't know how long we stand there. Time feels meaningless, the minutes blurring together as I cling to him, letting his presence ground me. Little by little, the storm inside me quiets, the chaos easing until it's just a dull ache in my chest.

His hands don't wander. They stay firm and steady, one flat against my stomach, the other resting lightly on my arm. His grip is enough to remind me that I'm still here. That I'm still standing.

Then, softly, his lips brush against the curve of my neck, careful and fleeting, like he's afraid to break me all over again. His voice follows, low and rough, barely more than a whisper.

"Are you okay?"

It's such a simple question, but it hits me harder than anything else tonight. I swallow against the knot in my throat, the truth burning inside me. No. Fuck, no, I'm not okay. But I can't say that. So I nod instead, the lie tangling in my chest like barbed wire. Noah doesn't push, doesn't call me out on the bullshit. Instead, he leans down, pressing a soft kiss to my shoulder before stepping around me.

I blink, trying to pull myself back into the moment, as he grabs the shampoo bottle from the shelf. The sound of it clicking open feels almost surreal, grounding me in the strangest way. I watch, frozen, as he squeezes a dollop into his palm, setting the bottle back before turning to me.

His hands move to my hair, working the shampoo into my scalp with slow, deliberate care. The touch is gentle but sure, his fingers weaving through my wet strands like it's the most natural thing in the world. It's disarming—intimate in a way that steals the breath from my lungs.

I stand there, rooted in place, my skin tingling under the heat of his touch, my head spinning with the closeness of him.

As he works, I study his face, searching for any signs of tension, anger, or hostility that's defined us for so long. But it's not there. Not even a trace. His calm and focused expression softens the lines of his face, a stark contrast to the tension I've noticed since stepping back into his life.

His eyes meet mine, and everything around us seems to freeze, his hands pausing in my hair. There's something raw in his eyes, something that unravels me. Hunger. Heat. A need that leaves me breathless.

It's like a switch flips inside me. Fuck the mess between us. My hands move with ease, unhooking my bra. As the soaked fabric slithers down my arms and falls in a heap, a heavy silence descends upon us, and it feels like the world has stopped spinning.

Noah's gaze drops, his jaw clenching as his eyes linger on my tits. The sudden hitch in his breath sparks something electric in me—my chest tightens, and the pounding of blood roars in my ears. His throat bobs with a hard swallow, and I have no idea what the fuck I'm doing, but I can't stop. I don't want to stop.

When he reaches out and his fingertips brush against the curve of my breast, I feel a shiver shoot down my spine. There's an electric sensation in his touch, stirring something wild and reckless inside me. As his thumb grazes over my nipple, my breathing becomes erratic, my chest heaving in uneven, shallow breaths.

As he looks up, his eyes meet mine once more, and time seems to freeze. The space between us feels suffocating, as if the weight of un-spoken words and pent-up emotions are fighting to be heard. His lips collide with mine, the impact so strong that I stagger backwards, his hands quickly reaching out to grasp my waist to steady me.

The kiss is raw, desperate, his mouth claiming mine like it's the only thing keeping him alive. My fingers tangle in his hair, pulling him closer.

The first swipe of his tongue ignites a fire so fierce it feels like it could consume me entirely. My knees threaten to buckle, but Noah's palms press firmly against the tiles on either side of me, trapping me against the cold surface. The chill bites at my skin, a sharp contrast to the heat radiating from him. Every nerve in me sparks to life, heightened by the undeniable press of his hard cock against my stomach—a visceral reminder of how far we've crossed the line.

My heart races, frantic and wild, as he alternates between soft, teasing kisses and deep, deliberate strokes of his tongue. It's maddening how well he plays me, how he seems to know exactly where to touch, how to unravel me piece by piece. His rough hands slide up my sides, his calloused fingertips skimming wet skin before settling on my hips. His grip tightens, coaxing me closer, silently urging me to arch into him. I can't resist—I don't want to. My body molds to his like it's where I've always belonged.

Without thinking, my hand moves between us, wrapping around his cock. The groan that rumbles from his chest is low and sinful. His forehead drops against mine, his breath coming in ragged gasps as I stroke him, slow and deliberate, matching the rhythm of his kisses. The way he moans against my mouth sends a fresh wave of heat pooling low in my belly, and I can't stop the guttural sound that escapes me when his hands find my breasts.

His thumb brushes over my nipple before he pinches it just hard enough to make my back bow off the tiles. My head falls back, baring my neck to him, and he takes full advantage of the invitation. His lips trail down, hot and demanding, leaving a path of fire in their wake. Each kiss, each nip of his teeth, draws a gasp from me, my hands clinging to him like he's the only thing keeping me grounded.

I'm a live wire, every inch of me alive with need, every thought obliterated by the feel of his hands and mouth on my skin. It's reckless, dangerous, a line we can't uncross—and I don't care. Not when his touch feels like this. Not when my voice betrays me, whispering his name like a prayer I didn't realize I was saying.

With a wicked smirk playing on his lips, Noah's fingers glide down my stomach, slow and deliberate, stopping just above the waistband of my panties. His touch sends sparks skittering down my spine, my breath hitching as his voice cuts through the sound of the cascading water.

"Take them off," he commands, his tone rough and unyielding, his eyes darkened with lust. There's no hesitation in his words, no room for argument, and the sheer dominance in his voice sends a jolt of heat straight to my core.

I should stop this. I know I should. The memory of him with those two girls earlier tonight flashes through my mind—a cruel reminder of the kind of man he is and the heartbreak waiting for me on the other side of this. But right now, none of that matters. Right now, I don't care about the consequences. I just want to feel something—anything—that isn't the suffocating weight of my own emotions. I want to lose myself in him and let him burn away the ache clawing at my chest.

Tomorrow, I'll face the fallout. I'll deal with the regret, the guilt, the self-loathing. But tonight? Tonight, I need this. I need him.

Noah steps back, his gaze locked on me, unwavering and maddeningly confident. My hands tremble as I hook my fingers into the waistband of my panties, sliding them down my legs and kicking them aside. The sound of the soaked fabric hitting the floor barely registers over the pounding in my ears. When I look up, he's already rid himself of his boxers, his hard cock standing proudly between us and the sight of him steals the air from my lungs. Every ridge, every line of him stands stark under the soft light filtering through the steam, raw and unapologetically masculine.

His eyes meet mine, and his voice drops to a rasp, heavy with unguarded honesty. "Fuck, you're so beautiful, Aub," he murmurs, and the way he says my name undoes me. It's not just a compliment; it's a claim.

Before I can catch my breath, his hands are on me, strong and possessive as they grip my ass and lift me like I weigh nothing. My legs wrap around his waist instinctively, the heat of him pressing against me, branding me. He pins me against the wall, the cold tiles a sharp contrast to the furnace of his body. But all I can feel is him—his strength, his intensity, his mouth crashing into mine with a ferocity that leaves me breathless.

The kiss is wild, desperate, like he's trying to devour me whole. His fingers tangle in my hair, tugging just enough to tilt my head back and expose my neck to him. He doesn't hesitate, his lips trailing fire along my skin, claiming every inch. There's no escape from him, no room to breathe, and I don't want either. Not now. Not when this feels so impossibly good.

Doubt claws at the edges of my mind, whispering warnings I don't want to hear. I know how this ends—with me shattered and him walking away like none of this ever happened.

His lips move with purpose, his tongue claiming mine in a way that leaves me trembling. The sound of my own moan startles me, raw and needy as I press closer to him, my fingers tangling in his hair to keep him near. I don't care that he's not mine to hold onto. I don't care that I'll be left with nothing but memories and scars. All that fucking matters is the way he feels right now, the way he's making me feel.

Noah's hands roam over my body with a purpose that's both maddening and electrifying. His rough fingertips trace over my skin, leaving a trail of fire and goosebumps in their wake. My body arches into his touch, desperate for more—more of him, more of this reckless, consuming need that's burning through every rational thought I have left.

His hips press forward, his cock sliding through my folds, the hard length of him brushing against my clit with each tantalizing thrust. Each stroke sends a sharp bolt of pleasure racing through me, too intense to ignore, and I can't stop myself from grinding against him, desperate for the friction that lights every nerve on fire. Fuck, It's too much and not nearly enough, the hunger inside me clawing at my sanity, threatening to tear me apart.

A low growl rumbles from Noah's throat, rough and primal, sending a fresh surge of heat pooling between my thighs. His hands grip my hips with a possessive force, dragging me closer until there's nothing left between us—no space, no hesitation, no escape. His body presses into mine, solid and unyielding, every inch of him aligning perfectly with me. The hard planes of his chest, the strength of his hands, the unrelenting slide of his cock through my folds—it all consumes me, leaving no room for thought, only feeling.

Every shift of his hips floods me with pleasure, overwhelming my senses as I lose myself in the rhythm he sets. The hot spray of the shower, the slick heat of his skin against mine, the unbearable tension coiling tighter with each movement—it blurs together into a haze of need so powerful it leaves me trembling.

Then he pauses, his hips going still as his hands remain firm on my waist. His eyes lock onto mine, and the intensity in his gaze robs me of what little breath I have left. He looks at me like I'm the only thing in the world, his focus unwavering, his hunger palpable. It's like he's savoring every reaction, every gasp, every tremor, and I feel laid bare under his stare.

Noah moves with a purpose that's both merciless and intoxicating, his cock sliding through my folds with deliberate precision. The slick heat of him teases me endlessly, brushing against my clit, not yet giving me the release I crave. His restraint is maddening, every calculated movement designed to keep me hovering on the edge without crossing the line. His jaw is tight, his breaths ragged, and I can see the sheer effort it's taking him not to bury his cock inside me and fuck me into oblivion.

It's a game of control, and he's winning. The tension he's building feels unbearable, every second dragging out the torment until I'm nearly begging for him. He knows exactly what he's doing, attuned to my every gasp, every shiver, every broken moan. His body responds to mine like he can read the silent pleas I'm too far gone to voice, adjusting his movements to give me just enough to keep me craving more.

The friction of his cock gliding over my clit is devastating, the pleasure so exquisitely torturous that my legs tremble against him. And yet, it's his eyes that undo me—the way he watches me with an intensity that borders on reverence. It's as if he's memorizing every reaction, every twitch of my body, cataloging them for himself. His gaze is a command, an unspoken demand for me to give in completely, to surrender to the tension winding tighter and tighter inside me.

He can feel it, see it, the way I'm unraveling beneath his touch. He's waiting for that moment, holding me there, pushing me to the brink, until there's no turning back. I'm so close—so fucking close—that I can almost taste the release, and I know it will be nothing short of devastating when I finally let go.

CHAPTER 16

NOAH

My eyes stay locked on her face, unable to look away, unable to fucking breathe. She's devastating—beautiful in a way that cuts right through me, raw and untouchable. Every sound she makes, every flicker of her lashes, every goddamn breath. I know what I want. I know how much I fucking love her. And yet, I hold back. Even as every fiber of me screams to sink into her, to lose myself entirely, I hold the fuck back. Because this isn't about me. She needs this—needs the release, the control—and I'll give it to her. I'd set myself on fire if it meant being what she needs right now.

With one final, deliberate glide of my cock against her folds, I see her fall apart. The sound she makes—a raw, desperate moan—hits me, stealing the air from my lungs. Her head falls back, her eyes fluttering shut, her body shattering in my arms. She's perfect, so fucking perfect, and the sight of her coming undone is something I'll never forget. My chest aches, because I know this could be it—the last time I get to touch her, to hold her, to see her like this. And if she walks away after this, I don't know if I'll survive it.

My gaze roams over her, drinking in every detail: her parted lips, the soft flush staining her skin, the way she trembles under my hands. Aubrey, bold and unguarded, is a revelation. I've always known she was beautiful, sexy as hell, but this side of her? The one that lets me hold her together even as she falls apart—It's fucking everything.

I want her so bad it's killing me. Every time her hips roll against mine, every arch of her body, I'm one second away from snapping. My cock aches, the relentless need for her driving me to the brink. I want to bury myself in her, to feel her clench around me, to make her mine in every possible way.

But I don't. I hold back, even though it feels impossible, because this moment isn't about me. It never was. It's about her. It's about drowning out her pain, giving her something to hold onto when everything else feels like it's slipping away.

My hands tighten on her ass, holding her close as we both struggle to catch our breath. Her skin is warm and slick against mine, the water cascading around us like static, but all I can focus on is her. Our eyes meet, and I wonder if she can see it—see how close I am to losing control. See how much I need her. How much I want to slide inside her, to feel her wrapped around me, to take and give until there's nothing left between us.

The need claws at me, overwhelming and insistent, but I say nothing. If I speak, I might ruin this fragile thread holding us together. If she pulls away, if she regrets this, it'll fucking destroy me.

The seconds stretch endlessly, each one marked by the pounding of my heart and the ragged sound of our breathing. Her gaze stays locked on mine, and I see it—fuck, I see it. The same hunger, the same aching desire, mirrored back at me. My pulse hammers in my ears as I shift, my cock brushing against her entrance, teasing us both. It would take nothing—just one push, one movement—and I'd be right where I've been dying to be.

But I wait, even though my body is screaming for release. I wait because I need her to want this as much as I do. I need her to choose me, to crave this moment, to crave me. No other girl makes me feel like this, and I know deep in my gut that no one else ever will. She's it. She's fucking it for me, and I don't even know if she realizes it yet.

Her voice cuts through the haze, soft but resolute. "I'm on birth control," she says, her eyes fixed on mine, and then she nods, giving me permission.

That's all I need. Her words ignite something inside me, a fire that roars to life and burns away every last shred of hesitation, every ounce of restraint I was barely clinging to. There's no turning back now. She wants this. She wants me. And fuck, I'm going to give her everything.

I guide the head of my cock to her tight wet pussy, the heat of her making my breath hitch. The sound of her moan—soft, breathy, and perfect—sends a jolt straight through me. Her body tenses, adjusting to my girth, and the way her eyes flutter shut tells me all I need to know. She's feeling this just as much as I am. Fuck, I've never wanted anything more in my life.

As I push deeper, inch by inch, her tight, wet heat surrounds me, gripping me like a vice. It takes everything in me not to lose it right then and there. I pause when I'm buried to the hilt, savoring the way her body feels around mine. My cock throbs, desperate for movement, but I force myself to hold still, to soak in every sensation, every sound, every heartbeat of this moment.

Her dark brown eyes meet mine, and it feels like the ground's been ripped out from under me. There's something raw, something unspoken, in the way she looks at me—something that cuts through all the tension and bullshit between us. And as much as I want to let go and take her completely, I hold onto this moment, refusing to rush. Not yet.

Slowly, I start to move, pulling out before sinking back in, setting a rhythm that's equal parts torture and salvation. Her walls clutch me with every thrust, hot and impossibly tight, pulling me deeper into her. Her nails dig into my shoulders, leaving trails of fire in their wake, and it only makes me want her more.

"Oh, fuck, you feel amazing," I groan against her neck, my lips brushing her damp skin as I speak. The words are raw, dragged out from the deepest part of me, and I can't stop myself from pressing a kiss there, tasting the water that clings to her.

Years of wanting her like this, of dreaming about her, all come crashing down on me in a way I can't control. She moves with me, her hips rolling in time with mine, her breath hitching with each thrust. Her moans rise higher, raw and unfiltered, and I swear I'm losing myself in her.

Her pussy tightens, pulling me deeper, and I know I'm fucking gone. She's everything—every dream, every ache, every fucking need—and nothing will ever compare to this. To her.

Our mouths find each other in a frantic clash of tongues and teeth, messy and desperate, blending hate and love into something primal, something neither of us can control. Her kiss is wild, just as untethered as mine, as if we're both trying to devour each other, as if we're on borrowed time and this moment could vanish in an instant.

And maybe it will. Maybe this is all we'll ever have. But if that's the case, fuck it—I'll take it. I'll take every raw moan, every breathless gasp, every fleeting second of her.

When I finally pull back, it's not because I want to—it's because I have to. My lungs burn for air, but my eyes stay locked on hers, trying to memorize this moment. Her gaze is unguarded, her expression caught somewhere between vulnerability and defiance. I hold onto this fleeting connection like it's the last thread keeping me from unraveling completely.

Tomorrow will come, and it'll wreck us all over again, resetting everything we've just shared. But tonight? Tonight, she's mine.

With a strained groan, I pull back, the slick heat of her pussy clinging to my cock as I slide out, only to thrust back in deep. The way her body accepts me, the way she molds to me like she was made for this, for me, it's overwhelming. My face buries itself in the curve of her throat, her scent grounding me, steadying me as I lose myself in her.

Every thrust is a crescendo, building until I can barely hold on. The pleasure is blinding, but it's the emotions that wreck me—the years of longing, the bitterness of separation, the desperate need to hold onto her now that she's here.

"Aubrey," I whisper, her name a breath, a prayer, a confession. There's so much I need to say, but the words choke me, caught in the tangle of my emotions. She might leave tomorrow. She might walk out of my life again, and the thought terrifies the fuck out of me.

Her face contorts with pleasure, her nails biting into my skin, and I watch, utterly captivated as she shatters around me. Her body clamps down on mine, pulling me deeper, and it's too much. The way she trembles, the way she comes undone in my arms—it undoes me completely.

My thrusts become erratic as the need for release takes over. With one last deep thrust, I let go, my orgasm ripping through me as a guttural groan tears from my throat. It's blinding, consuming, and somehow not enough. It will never be enough.

I cling to her, holding her close as the waves of pleasure fade, leaving behind an ache I can't shake. I want to tell her I love her. I need to say it. But the words stay lodged in my throat, suffocated by fear and the gnawing uncertainty of what comes next. I can't lose her again. Not like before.

Instead, I press a tender kiss to her lips, letting it linger, hoping it says what I can't. Slowly, gently, I lower her down, keeping her close as the warm spray of the shower washes over us. My hands move on instinct, lathering soap over her skin with a care that feels almost reverent, as if I can somehow anchor her to me.

When I'm done, I wash myself quickly, not wanting to break the fragile connection between us but knowing I need to give her space. Even as I pull away, the thought of her slipping through my fingers again leaves me hollow. But for now, I'll take this moment. I'll take her.

I step out of the shower, the cold air slamming into me like a slap, and quickly wrap a towel around my waist. My chest feels tight as I grab another towel for her and move into my room. Outside, the storm rages on, the rain battering the windows in relentless waves. I pause by the glass, staring out into the chaos, wondering if she's in the bathroom right now piecing together all the reasons why this was a mistake.

The thought fucking kills me.

I pull one of my shirts from the cupboard, the soft cotton something I hope might bring her a little comfort. The lights flicker, the storm's fury outside feeling like a mirror of the storm inside me—chaotic, intense, unrelenting.

The sound of the water shutting off pulls me back, and I head to the bathroom, shirt in hand. When she steps out, the sight of her steals the breath from my lungs. Her damp skin glistens under the soft light, every curve of her body highlighted like a masterpiece brought to life. My cock hardens instantly, throbbing as my gaze drifts over her. Her perfect tits, nipples taut from the cool air; the smooth curve of her hips; and her legs, so stunning they make me want to fall to my knees and worship her all over again.

She's so fucking perfect—every inch of her begging to be touched, claimed, cherished. All I can think is how much I want her. Not just now, not just for tonight, but always. Every fucking day. I want to wake up with her beside me, to hold her, to have her as mine in every way that matters. But for now, I stand frozen, my throat dry, my cock aching, praying she doesn't pull away.

From the moment I met her, she's been my undoing—the quiet storm that slipped into my life and wrecked everything I thought I knew.

I still remember the first time I saw her. She was just a little girl, sitting in her backyard, crying so quietly it made something in me ache. I was up in my treehouse when I spotted her through the branches. She looked so small, knees pulled to her chest, her face buried in her arms like she was trying to disappear.

And then she looked up.

Her tear-streaked face broke something in me I didn't even know could break.

I climbed down, my curiosity dragging me toward her like a magnet. At the fence, I peeked through the gaps, watching as she tried to stifle her sobs, her shoulders trembling while the harsh yelling spilled out from her house. The sound was so loud, so harsh, and she looked so lost.

"Hey," I called softly, trying not to startle her. Her head jerked up, her wide, red-rimmed eyes meeting mine through the fence. "You can come over to my place if you want to get away from the noise."

She hesitated for a moment, her small hands wiping at her cheeks, before climbing through the gap in the fence. Suddenly, she was standing there in my yard, looking at me with this mix of fear and relief that I didn't understand back then.

I was too young to process what I felt that day, too young to grasp why my chest tightened or why I wanted to shield her from whatever had made her cry like that. But now? Now I get it. That day, without realizing it, she became a part of me.

She's carved into me, so deep there's no removing her, no forgetting.

Now that I've had her again—tasted her, touched her, fucked her—there's no going back. Nothing and no one will ever make me feel this way again, like I'm losing control and finding myself all at once.

"Here." My voice comes out rough as I set the shirt on the dresser for her. "You can wear this."

"Thanks," she whispers, her voice soft, almost fragile, as she takes the fresh towel.

I turn to leave, but my body betrays me. I glance back, unable to resist stealing one more look. Her damp hair clings to her shoulders, and the soft light highlights every curve of her body. Her hips, those perfect tits—and fuck, it's enough to drive me insane.

And the thought of this being the last time. Of her slipping away again, like she always does. It guts me. Because I know how this ends. Her mom will show up, or some other excuse will surface, and she'll leave. She always does.

Stepping back into the room, I let the towel fall to the floor and pull on a pair of boxers. The cool air brushes against my skin, but it does nothing to cool the fire raging inside me. My eyes catch the flashing light on my phone, and when I pick it up, my stomach knots. A series of missed calls and texts from my dad light up the screen.

Fuck. I completely forgot to let him know I got home safely.

Sighing, I run a hand through my damp hair and quickly dial his number. The phone barely rings once before he picks up, his voice already thick with worry

"I'm okay," I say quickly, cutting him off. "Got caught in the rain and needed a shower to warm up. Sorry I didn't call." My voice is low, guilt tugging at me.

As I lift my gaze, Aubrey steps into the room. She freezes, hesitating like she's unsure what to do. The oversized shirt I gave her hangs loosely over her frame. But my eyes betray me, trailing down to where her nipples press against the thin fabric, hard and visible.

The heat courses through me again, sudden and undeniable. My cock stirs, the memory of her still too vivid, too fresh. Goddamn it. She has no idea the effect she has on me—how one look, one small movement, can undo me completely.

Our eyes meet, and I motion toward the bed, pulling back the blankets in a silent invitation. She hesitates, her gaze flicking between me and the bed, and for a brief moment, uncertainty cuts through me. What's running through her head? Does she regret this?

"I was worried," my dad says, his voice softer now, drawing my focus back to the phone.

"I'm home, Dad. Everything's fine," I reply, my attention glued to Aubrey as she steps closer to the bed. There's still a flicker of doubt in her expression, but it's fading, her features softening as she inches forward.

"Alright, son. I'll talk to you tomorrow," he says, the worry finally leaving his tone before the call ends.

I set my phone down, my gaze locked on Aubrey. She stops at the edge of the bed, and my pulse hammers in my ears. My cock is still hard, pressing against my boxers, impossible to miss. I don't bother hiding it. Why would I? After the way she fell apart in my arms in the bathroom, there's nothing left to hide. If she wants more, I'm up for it.

"You can sleep on the bed beside me," I say, my tone even despite the tension tightening every muscle in my body. "Or take a blanket and sleep on the floor. Your call." The words taste bitter, wrong. The thought of her on the floor feels fucking wrong. If that's what she chooses, I'll switch places. No question. It'll hurt like hell, though.

She studies me, her gaze flicking between my face and the bed, and I hold my breath, waiting. Finally, she moves, climbing into the bed. Relief floods me, but it's short-lived. She lies on her back, staring at the ceiling, her face unreadable.

The distance between us feels suffocating, and I fucking hate it. "How about tonight we ditch all the bullshit," I say, my voice softer now. "And just go back to being the friends we used to be."

She turns her head to look at me, her eyes searching mine. "Can you do that?"

I nod, the motion small, deliberate. "Yeah," I say, the lie rolling off my tongue too easily. "I can handle it."

The weight on my chest doesn't let up, though. I turn toward her, shifting so I can see her clearly, the need to understand clawing at me. Why is she here? The question has been haunting me since the night I showed up at her window, desperate and reckless, like a fucking idiot.

"Why did you come back?" I ask, my voice breaking the silence between us.

Her eyes flicker to mine, just for a moment, before darting away, her focus shifting to the ceiling. Her face tightens, and I catch it—barely—the flicker of pain she can't quite hide.

The silence stretches between us, heavy, oppressive, and I almost wish I could take the question back. Almost.

Finally, she speaks, her voice trembling as if it's all she can do to hold herself together. "My mom didn't want me around anymore," she says, each word landing like a punch to the gut. "Her new boyfriend decided I was a problem, and she agreed. So, she just... dumped me at my dad's."

Fuck. My chest tightens with a pain that digs deep and refuses to let go. A tear slides down her cheek, and before I even think, my hand moves, brushing it away with my fingertips.

She turns onto her side, curling up slightly, and the sight of her like this—raw, vulnerable, hurting—rips at something deep inside me.

I fucking hate it. Hate that she's in this kind of pain, hate that I can't just fix it. My hand lingers near her face, desperate to do more, to offer comfort, but I force myself to pull back. I can't leave her in this silence.

"My mom's back," I say quietly, my voice rough and strained. "She wants to see me. She's got kids now—two kids with some other guy. A whole new family. I've got a half-brother and sister."

Saying it feels like dragging broken glass across my throat, but if it helps Aubrey, if it makes her feel even a fraction less alone, it's worth it. My voice wavers, betraying how much this rips me apart, but I push through.

"I don't even know them," I admit. "They're strangers to me, but I'm supposed to play big brother now. Like none of the shit she did before matters. Like her leaving didn't fucking destroy me." My jaw tightens as I glance at Aubrey, unsure if I'm helping or just digging us both deeper into this pit.

The room falls into silence, the only sound our breathing, but I can feel her walls starting to crack. Maybe it's small, barely noticeable, but it's there. If bleeding out my own pain makes hers a little easier to carry, I'll gladly rip myself open. That's what you do for someone who owns your heart, even if they don't realize it.

"Wait, what?" Aubrey sits up, her brows furrowed, concern etched into her face. She knows how difficult it is for me to talk about my mom, how much it fucking kills me to reopen that wound. "She started another family?"

I nod, my eyes tracing her face, noting the way her lips press into a hard, angry line. Even pissed off, she's breathtaking. "Yeah, pretty fucked up, huh?"

"You can say that again," she mutters, leaning back against the headboard but keeping her eyes locked on me. "Why did she come back now?"

I shrug, bitterness twisting in my chest. "I don't know. Maybe guilt. Maybe she finally figured out how badly she fucked me up and wants to make it right. But I'm not meeting her." My jaw clenches, the words tasting like poison as they leave my mouth. "She walked out on me, Aub. When I needed her most. I don't need her now. She can try to play happy families all she wants, but I'm not buying it. She doesn't get to come back into my life and act like nothing fucking happened."

The edge in my voice fades as I meet Aubrey's gaze. She's quiet now, watching me, her eyes softening in a way that makes it harder to hold onto my anger. But it's still there, simmering under the surface, because some wounds don't heal. Some scars run too deep.

I pause, my gaze flicking to her lips for a second before meeting her eyes. She's staring at me like she wants to speak but can't quite find the right words. "What about you? Why were you locked out of the house?"

Her face falls, and she looks away, her fingers fidgeting with the sheet. "My dad was so pissed after what happened with Tia," she says, her voice barely steady. Her hands clench into fists, and she swallows hard. "The school called him, and he just lost it. He scared me, and... it brought everything back, you know?" Her voice wavers, and I feel anger rising in my chest—not at her, but at the ghosts that cling to her, dragging her down.

"Remember when he threw that beer bottle at me?" she whispers, her voice so quiet it's like she's afraid saying it out loud will give the memory power.

I nod, my stomach twisting. "Yeah. I remember." How the hell could I fucking forget something like that? Her dad's anger wasn't just loud—it was dangerous. The way his voice shook the walls, the way his hands trembled with fury before he hurled that bottle... It's burned into my memory; a moment of helpless rage I couldn't do anything to stop.

She exhales shakily. "The way he yelled at me in the car after the meeting..." Her eyes drop to the sheet again, her fingers plucking at it like she's trying to distract herself. "He said some really horrible things. Then he pulled over and told me to get out of his car." Her voice cracks, and my fists clench as she continues. "He said if he never saw me again, he wouldn't give a shit. That I'm nothing. Never was and never will be anything in this world."

Her words slam into me, and the anger I've been holding back boils over, hot and bitter. Fuck him. Fuck everything about him—his cruelty, his carelessness, his blind inability to see her for the amazing person she is.

I don't hesitate. My hand moves to her face, cupping her cheek, my thumb brushing softly along her skin. "Aubrey," I say, my voice low and steady. "Look at me."

Her eyes lift to meet mine, and the raw pain I see their cuts, sharp and unrelenting. My chest aches with it, but I hold her gaze, hoping she can feel the truth in my words.

"You know what he's like. His words don't mean shit. They don't define you."

She nods faintly, but there's no strength behind it, no belief. "Yeah, I know," she murmurs, her voice barely audible. But the resignation in her tone says otherwise. The weight of his words is still there, pressing down on her, poisoning the parts of her he doesn't deserve to touch.

"They still sting," she admits, her voice cracking.

"I know they do," I say softly, my thumb tracing gentle circles on her cheek. "But he's wrong. About all of it. About you. You're not nothing, Aubrey."

Her lips press into a thin line, her throat working as she fights back tears. My hand lingers against her cheek, grounding us both in this fragile moment. I want her to feel it—all of it. Comfort. Reassurance. Love. Anything to drown out the echoes of his cruelty.

"You're stronger than him," I say, my voice firm, unwavering. "You've survived everything he's thrown at you. And you'll keep surviving, no matter what bullshit he spews. Because he's fucking wrong. About everything."

I lean in, pressing a soft, lingering kiss to her lips. This isn't about desire, not this time—it's about giving her something real, something she can hold on to when everything else feels like it's slipping away. Her lips press back against mine, warm and tentative, and for a second, I'm tempted to deepen the kiss, to lose myself in her.

But I don't. I pull back just enough to meet her gaze, savoring the tenderness of the moment. This is us—raw, unguarded, stripped down to who we were before the world got so complicated. And right now, that's all I want to be.

I pull away slowly, my hand slipping from her cheek as I force myself to put some space between us. My cock is hard, throbbing painfully, and every nerve in my body screams at me to close the distance again, to lose myself in her like I've done before. But this moment isn't about that. She doesn't need another guy who just fucks her and leaves her feeling hollow. She needs someone who can stay, someone who can listen. A friend. And if that's what she needs, then fuck, I'll be that for her—even if it kills me.

"So," she says, breaking the silence, her voice soft but steady, pulling me from my thoughts. "How did your dad react when your mom showed up?"

I let out a sigh, running a hand through my hair as I lean back against the pillows, my gaze fixed on the ceiling. "He was shocked at first," I admit, my voice tinged with the lingering weight of that conversation. "He asked if my decision to not reconnect with her was about loyalty to him. But once he realized it wasn't about him—that I genuinely don't give a shit about rebuilding anything with her—he backed off. Besides, he's got a new girlfriend now."

Aubrey's eyes widen, surprise flickering across her face in a way that tugs at something deep inside me. "Your dad has a girlfriend?"

I can't help the small smile that tugs at my lips, a flicker of amusement breaking through the heaviness. "Yeah. Her name's Simone. I haven't met her yet, but they're on a weekend trip together right now."

Aubrey's expression softens, her lips curving into a faint smile. "Your dad would never put her above you," she says, yawning. "He's not like my mom."

Her words land with a weighty truth I can't deny. My dad has his flaws, sure, but he's always put me first, even when it wasn't easy, even when it hurt him.

"Can I ask you something?" Aubrey murmurs.

"Sure," I reply, turning to look at her.

"Those two girls you were making out with tonight," she begins, her voice hesitant but firm. "Do they mean anything to you?"

"Fuck no," I answer without hesitation, the words leaving my mouth before I even think.

"Then why do it, Noah?" she asks, her tone soft but carrying an edge of disappointment. "You never used to be like that."

I turn my head back toward the ceiling, my jaw tightening as her question hangs in the air. I take a deep breath, trying to untangle the knot of emotions threatening to choke me.

Do I tell her the truth? Do I admit how fucked up I was when she left, how I used anything—anyone—to numb the ache of losing her? Do I tell her I still love her? But fear creeps in, coiling around my thoughts like a shadow. What if her stay is fleeting? What if I bare my soul, only for her to leave again, taking all of this—whatever this is—with her?

I wrestle with the words, with the urge to tell her everything, and the silence stretches between us, heavy and uncertain.

After what feels like an eternity, I turn my head ready to tell her everything—to spill the truth that's been clawing at my chest—but the words die on my tongue. With her eyes closed and breathing steady, she exudes a rare sense of calm.

Shifting onto my side, I absorb every detail of her, unable to look away from her captivating features. Her delicate nose, perfect lips, and the soft curve of her cheek create a portrait of beauty.

I raise my hand instinctively, the urge to brush her hair away from her face overwhelming me, but I freeze halfway, my fingers hesitating near her cheek. The thought of touching her now would only intensify the desire burning inside me.

Keeping a distance between us feels like torture, but it's necessary. I don't want to screw this up. Being close to Aubrey again, really talking to her, feels like coming up for air after drowning for years. It feels good. It feels right. I don't want my fragile ego to spoil things because she didn't want me the way I wanted her back then.

I want this with her. No, I need this with her. I always treasured her friendship, longing for it deeply, and I fucked it all up by pushing her away. I need to stop being such an asshole to her. She's dealing with enough shit already, and the last thing she needs is me making it worse. If her screw up of a father really did kick her out, I'll talk to mine. He'll help. He'll figure something out. I've always wanted her. I don't think I've ever told her that, and maybe it's time I should.

I quietly ease out of the bed, trying my best not to disturb her. She doesn't stir, her soft breaths filling the quiet room as I grab her damp clothes from where I tossed them earlier.

Tiptoeing out of the room, I head to the dryer. Tomorrow, we'll go to her dad's house together and sort all this shit out. But for now, I can at least make sure she has dry clothes in the morning. It's not much, but it's something.

CHAPTER 17

AUBREY

The soft morning light seeps through the edges of the curtain, casting a muted glow that blurs my vision as I blink awake. For a moment, disorientation grips me, and I don't recognize where I am. Then I feel it: the warmth of an arm draped tightly around my waist. Noah's arm. His scent surrounds me, a mix of soap and something distinctly him, pulling me back to reality.

Last night floods my mind in vivid, merciless detail—the cold tile against me, the desperate way he fucked me, the raw hunger in his eyes that ignited something wild inside me. I swore I'd never let myself go there again, especially not with Noah—the guy who moves from girl to girl like it's a game. Those two at the party? Their laughter, their hands on him, are still burned into my mind like an open wound.

What the hell was I thinking?

But I know. I needed to feel something—anything—to silence the aching void clawing at my chest. To escape the suffocating weight of feeling discarded, unloved, and utterly alone. Noah was my lifeline in that moment, and I grabbed onto him like I was drowning. I shouldn't have let it happen, but I can't bring myself to regret it. For one fleeting moment, he made me feel like I wasn't so invisible.

I shift slightly, trying to slip free of his grasp, but his arm tightens instinctively, holding me in place. He's spooning me, his warm breath brushing against the nape of my neck, his chest firm against my back. And then there's his cock—hard and insistent—pressing against me like it has a mind of its own. My breath hitches, and my traitorous body flares with a spark of desire I wish I didn't feel.

I close my eyes, forcing myself to remember who Noah is. He's the guy who fucks and forgets, the one who never sticks around long enough for it to mean something.

I try again, inching away carefully, but his arm pulls me back, his grip firm and possessive. His face burrows deeper into the crook of my neck, his stubble scraping against my skin in a way that's almost too intimate. Is he awake? I don't know, but I stay frozen, my chest tight and my mind spiraling.

The sharp and relentless sound of my dad's voice echoes in my mind, his words like shards of glass lodged in my chest. There's a stupid, desperate part of me clinging to the hope that maybe it was all a mistake. That maybe he didn't mean it, that locking me out was some kind of accident. But deep down, I know better. I know he meant every single word. The truth sits heavy and cold, a weight I can't seem to carry or let go.

And now, lying here, everything starts to crash down at once. My mind spirals as I think of all the things I need—my clothes, my toiletries, my fucking birth control. That last one hits me, dragging me back to last night. Noah. The way I let him fuck me without a condom, like the reckless, desperate idiot I am.

He's been with half the girls in this town, and now I've got to add "getting tested" to my ever-growing list of problems. And if my dad really kicked me out for good? I'm royally screwed. My mom? She won't even pick up the phone, let alone offer any help.

"Stop thinking so goddamn much," Noah's voice cuts through the storm in my head, low and rough, warm against my neck. His lips brush my shoulder, soft and teasing, and it only makes my chest ache more.

I should push him away, should tell him to back the hell off, but I don't. Instead, his touch feels like the only thing keeping me from completely unraveling.

"We'll figure it out," he murmurs, his tone steady like he actually believes it. "We'll go see your dad, get to the bottom of it, and come up with a plan."

The weight of his arm disappears from my waist as he pulls away, and the loss is instant. Like I've been untethered. He rolls onto his back, the sheets rustling around us, and I wait for it—that moment when he snaps back into the cocky, indifferent asshole. The fragile truce of the night already feels like it's slipping through my fingers.

Noah sits up, the covers sliding down to his waist. My eyes betray me, roaming over him despite my better judgment. Every line, every muscle, every inch of him is a temptation I don't need right now.

He drags a hand through his messy hair, letting out a long, tired breath. For a fleeting second, I wonder—am I too much for him? A burden, just like everyone else says I am. My dad. My mom. They've made it clear enough. Why should Noah be any different? Especially now, when whatever we used to have has been reduced to broken pieces.

I shove the covers off and swing my legs over the edge of the bed, determined to escape the awkward limbo I'm stuck in. My eyes dart around the room, searching for my clothes. I know they're still damp—I should've hung them up to dry last night, but I didn't. Doesn't matter. Wet or not, I'll throw them on if it means getting the fuck out of here.

I feel his gaze on me, heavy and unrelenting, but I refuse to look at him. Instead, I keep moving, my frustration bubbling over when I can't find my clothes. "Where the hell are my clothes?" I snap, finally glancing at him.

He stretches, unbothered. "They're in the dryer," he says casually, his voice calm, like we're discussing the weather.

For a moment, I'm frozen, distracted by the way he moves—effortless, like he knows exactly how good he looks. His body is a masterpiece of lean muscle and effortless sex appeal, his boxers riding low on his hips.

And then there it is, the unmistakable outline of his cock, hard and unapologetic beneath the fabric. Heat rushes to my cheeks, and I force my eyes upward, only to meet his smug, shit-eating grin.

"See something you like?" he teases, his tone laced with that infuriating cockiness that makes me want to punch him and kiss him at the same time.

With deliberate intent, his hand slides down, and he strokes himself, as if it's the most natural thing in the world. His dark eyes lock onto mine, steady and unwavering.

"Feel free to take whatever you want from me, Aub," he murmurs, his voice low and rough, dripping with a confidence that makes my pulse race. That nickname—it cuts deeper than I want to admit, stirring memories of a time when everything between us felt easy, simple, safe.

Now?

It's anything but.

The sight of him, the sound of his voice—it's too much. My body's betraying me, heat pooling low in my stomach even as my mind screams at me to leave, to get the hell out before I lose the last shred of control I have. I know exactly where this is headed if I don't get the fuck out now. In minutes, I'll be under him, over him, tangled in him, and when it's over, I'll hate myself for letting it happen. Again.

It takes every ounce of will power to turn away. My legs feel shaky, but I force myself to move, heading for the door. My hand wraps around the handle, and with a sharp yank, I'm out, striding down the hallway toward the laundry room like I know what I'm doing—like I'm not about to fall apart completely.

Every creak in the floorboards, every familiar corner of this house is a reminder of who we used to be. Back when Noah wasn't this cocky, infuriating asshole.

The soft thud of footsteps behind me sends my heart racing. Noah. Shit.

I can't let him close the distance. If he touches me—if he so much as brushes his fingers against me—I'll crumble. I can already feel it, the inevitability of losing myself in him, the way he's always been able to pull me under without even trying.

I rehearse my plan like a mantra: grab my clothes, leave this house, and deal with my dad. It's Saturday—he'll be home. Maybe I can convince him to let me stay, at least for a little while. I don't have another option. Not when my mom won't even answer her damn phone.

Noah's hand closes around my arm, stopping me mid-stride. His grip is firm but careful, steady in a way that makes me want to lean into him even though I know I shouldn't.

"Don't pull that shit, Aub," he says, his voice rough but not cruel. There's an edge of vulnerability in it, something unspoken that twists my stomach. The way he says my name—it's like he's reaching for the parts of me I've tried to lock away.

"What shit?" I snap, yanking my arm back, though his touch lingers like a ghost.

"Shutting yourself off," he replies, his tone softening just enough to throw me off balance. "I want the truce to hold. I can't fucking stand it when we fight. Just—" He exhales sharply, dragging a hand through his hair. "Just tell me what's going on in that head of yours, because I'm not a fucking mind reader. I need to know what's happening with you."

For a moment, I'm caught off guard. The sincerity in his voice cuts through me, cracking the barriers I've fought so hard to keep intact. But I can't give him what he wants—I can't let him in. Not now, when everything in my fucked-up life is turning to shit.

"I just need to see what's going on with my dad," I say, the lie leaving my lips clipped and hollow. My jaw tightens until it aches, but I keep my chin high, determined not to let him see how close I am to falling apart.

But Noah sees everything.

The way his eyes pierce through my defenses makes it harder to keep standing, harder to pretend like I'm okay.

He steps closer, shrinking the space between us until the heat from his body feels like it's burning straight through me. I stare at his chest, refusing to meet his gaze, because if I do, I know I'll shatter. He'll see everything I've been trying to hide—all the cracks in the armor I've barely managed to hold together.

Noah doesn't let me hide. He never has. His fingers slip under my chin, firm but gentle, tilting my face up until I have no choice but to meet his eyes. That look—intense, unrelenting—makes my breath catch, and I feel the sting of tears threatening to spill. Shit. The last thing I want is to break in front of him, to let him see how much this is fucking killing me.

I swallow hard, trying to shove everything back down where it belongs, but his thumb brushes over my cheek. His touch is a cruel reminder of everything I've been trying to forget, of everything I've buried so deep it's suffocating.

"Let me help you," he says, his voice softer now, almost pleading. "I'll come with you to see what's going on with your dad."

"No, Noah," I snap, sharper than I intend. I need distance. I need space. "I don't need your help with this. I can handle it myself."

He shakes his head, a bitter smile tugging at his lips. "I know you can, Aub. You've always been strong as hell. But I don't give a damn what you say—I'm going with you, whether you like it or not. You can't keep shutting me out."

I flinch at his words, my chest tightening with anger and hurt. "I never shut you out, Noah," I fire back, my voice trembling despite my best efforts to sound strong. "It was you who didn't want anything to do with me. You're the one who pushed me away."

"Because you fucking left me," he says, his voice breaking on the last word.

I hate him. I hate how beautiful he looks when he's this raw, this wrecked. But mostly, I hate that I still fucking love him.

The space between us vanishes entirely, and I'm suddenly hyper-aware of how close we are—his body just barely brushing mine. He leans in, his lips brushing against mine in a kiss so soft, so gentle, it shouldn't destroy me—but it does. It's tender, a fleeting echo of the Noah who used to be kind.

"I'm coming with you to see your father, Aub. So stop talking about doing it alone, because that shit ain't happening," he says, his voice firm, leaving no room for argument. His fingers release my chin as he steps back just enough to give me air, though his eyes never leave mine. He sees it—the way he's unraveling me. And the bastard smirks, that infuriating cocky grin that makes my pulse race even as it infuriates me.

His hand moves deliberately, brushing a stray lock of hair behind my ear. The simple gesture shouldn't affect me, but the light graze of his fingers against my skin sends a shiver racing down my spine. I hate how my body betrays me, leaning into his touch. His smirk deepens, shifting into something predatory, like he knows exactly what he's doing—and that I'm powerless to stop it.

"Noah," I whisper, my voice trembling. I want to tell him to stop, to step back before I lose the last shred of control I'm clinging to. But the words die in my throat, swallowed by the weight of the moment.

Before I can think, he closes the gap between us, his lips crashing into mine with a force that steals my breath away. This kiss is nothing like the first—it's hot, hungry, desperate. One hand cups my face, tilting it to deepen the kiss, while the other grips my hip with bruising intensity, steering me backward until the cold edge of the dryer digs into my lower back.

His body pins me in place, his hard cock pressing against me in a way that's impossible to ignore. Memories of last night in the shower flash through my mind—how he unraveled me, how he fucked me like he had something to prove. The kiss deepens until I'm dizzy, drowning in him.

I kiss him back, letting myself get lost in the chaos of him.

Without breaking the kiss, he grips my thighs and hauls my ass onto the dryer, his hands possessive as they find their place on my hips. "You can't imagine all the fucking things I want to do to you," he growls, his voice rough and dripping with intent. "I want to touch every inch of you. With my tongue, my fingers, my cock—fuck, especially my cock."

He wedges himself between my thighs, spreading them wide, and yanks me to the edge of the dryer until I'm flush against him. The thick, unrelenting length of his cock grinds against my soaked pussy, and the friction draws a gasp from my lips. Every nerve in my body is alight, the hard press of him sending a shiver straight to my core. His eyes—dark, wild, and filled with heat—lock on mine, daring me to push him away. But I can't. I don't want to.

"You're killing me," he growls, his voice dropping to a rough whisper that vibrates against my skin as he buries his face in the curve of my neck. "Fuck you don't even know what you do to me, Aub. I want to make you come so fucking hard you'll forget your own name."

My breath hitches as his lips find the sensitive spot just below my ear, kissing and grazing it with his teeth. Each nip sends electricity through my veins, and I can't stop the shudder that wracks my body.

"You want me," he rasps. His fingers slide higher, brushing over my clit just enough to draw a sharp gasp from my lips. "I can feel it. You're fucking soaked for me." His lips curve into a cocky grin against my neck, and I shiver as he runs his thumb teasingly through my folds. "Tell me you want it, Aub. Tell me you want me to fuck you. Say it."

"Yes," I breathe, the word trembling on the edge of a moan, raw and full of need. "Ruin me. Fuck me as if I was yours."

His mouth claims mine, the kiss desperate and consuming. My fingers tangle in his hair, pulling hard enough to draw a hiss from deep within his throat. His hands roam, unrestrained and hungry, their grip leaving a burning trail in their wake. He strips off my shirt in one swift motion, casting it aside like it's the only thing standing between him and salvation.

His eyes zero in on my tits like he's a starving man, and I'm the feast he's been waiting for. The flick of his tongue wetting his bottom lip, the raw and restrained expression, tells me his holding back, and it makes me ache to know why.

His eyes darken as they rake over me. "You're fucking gorgeous," he murmurs, his voice husky. "Absolutely stunning."

The way he says it—it's not just words. It's reverence. And it hits me, breaking through every wall I've tried to build. For a moment, all I can do is stare, caught in the force of his words and the way they feel like the truth.

Then he leans in, capturing one of my nipples in his mouth.

The warmth of his tongue against the hardened nipple sends a gasp spilling from my lips. He groans low, the sound vibrating against my skin as his tongue flicks and teases, his lips closing around me in a way that makes my back arch and my chest rise to meet him.

His hand presses gently on my shoulder, guiding me to lie back. Even as I shift, his mouth remains locked on my nipple, his teeth grazing lightly, just enough to make me gasp again.

"Later today," he says against my skin, his voice a dark, sinful promise, "I'm gonna shoot my load all over these perfect tits." His words ripple through me, heat pooling low in my belly, and I swear my pussy clenches at the sound of them.

His lips begin a slow, torturous descent, leaving a trail of hot, open-mouthed kisses down my stomach. The scrape of his stubble sends sparks skittering across my nerves, and when his tongue dips into my belly button, I can't suppress the soft, involuntary moan that escapes me.

He kneels between my legs, his breath warm against my soaked folds. The first press of his lips there makes me squirm, and my hips jerk at the contact.

"Fuck, I can smell how bad you want me," he growls, his voice rough, primal, and unapologetically smug. His tongue traces a slow, torturous path along my folds, teasing, testing, making my body beg for him in ways words can't capture.

"Please," I whimper, the word breaking on a desperate sob as his tongue continues its relentless teasing, skillfully avoiding the one spot I'm aching for him to claim. My hips jerk, seeking relief, but he just chuckles, the sound low and dark, sending vibrations through my core. His hands grip my thighs firmly, pinning me down, keeping me at his mercy.

"Patience, baby," he mutters, his lips brushing against my sensitive skin. "I'm gonna make you scream for me. Gonna make you fucking beg for it."

And fuck, I already am.

His tongue flicks out again, barely grazing my clit, and a strangled cry escapes my lips. My fingers tangle in his hair, pulling tight, every fiber of my being demanding more.

It takes every ounce of restraint I have not to shove his face exactly where I need it, to grind against his tongue until the unbearable ache inside me shatters.

"Tell me what you want, Aub," he murmurs, his voice dripping with amusement, dark and taunting. His tongue drags another slow, devastating lick over my clit, the flick at the end pulling an uncontrollable jerk from my hips.

"I want that," I gasp, my voice trembling, breathless, my need consuming me.

He does it again, slower this time, his tongue circling my clit with precision that borders on cruel.

My entire body trembles, each nerve alight with unbearable anticipation. My grip tightens in his hair, and I yank his face up just enough to meet his gaze. His lips glisten with me, the cocky smirk playing on them both infuriating and devastatingly hot.

"You know what I fucking need, Noah," I growl, my voice raw and demanding, every ounce of restraint gone. "Now stop fucking around and give it to me."

His laugh is a low, wicked rumble, the sound alone almost enough to push me over the edge. "So impatient," he taunts, his words sharp and playful, but the look in his eyes is something else entirely. Then he's back, his mouth claiming me with relentless hunger. His tongue presses against my clit with the perfect amount of pressure, obliterating any pretense of teasing.

I lose myself in the rhythm of his tongue, my thighs trembling as he works me with practiced, devastating skill. My grip in his hair eases, my fingers buried there, holding him close as I let go completely. I can't stop myself from grinding against his face, chasing the pleasure he's pulling from me, each movement driving me closer to the edge.

He groans against me, the sound filthy and raw, vibrating through me like a pulse. It's hot as fuck—electric, every flick of his tongue, every press against my clit, driving me higher. I'm unraveling, my body tightening, the release just out of reach but barreling toward me.

He was always good at this—eager, hungry, relentless. But now? Fuck, he's something else entirely. It's like he's been fine-tuning his craft, and the thought of how many others he must've practiced on to get these good flashes through my mind. Jealousy flickers, but it's drowned out by the tidal wave of pleasure.

Noah kisses my pussy with the same filthy hunger he brings to my mouth, his lips devouring me like he's starving. When he slides a finger inside me, my entire body jolts with pleasure, the sensation sharp and overwhelming. His tongue flicks against my clit in a maddeningly fast rhythm, every stroke deliberate, every movement calculated to drive me insane.

When he adds a second finger, the stretch and fullness draw a gasp from my lips, the sound raw and unrestrained. My mind goes blank, consumed by the sensation building deep inside me. His fingers curl perfectly, hitting a spot that makes me see stars, while his tongue dances against my clit, teasing and tormenting me with relentless precision.

Every thrust, every flick, sends me spiraling higher. My moans spill freely, filling the room with the sound of my pleasure. Each wet, deliberate motion of his tongue ends with a teasing flick that sends shockwaves through me, making my thighs tremble and my breath hitch.

It's been so long since anyone touched me like this, but the truth is, no one else has ever made me feel this good. Noah's the only one who knows exactly how to wreck me, and fuck, he's doing it now. My fingers tighten in his hair, tugging hard, and I feel his lips curve into a smug smirk against me. He loves this—loves driving me to the brink, pushing me right to the edge, and holding me there.

"Fuck, Noah," I moan, my voice trembling with desperation. His mouth is pure sin, his tongue and fingers working me over like it's his life's mission to make me fall apart. He sucks my clit harder, his teeth grazing it just enough to make me shudder. The ache between my legs grows unbearable, the pleasure coiling tighter and tighter, ready to snap.

"That's it, baby," he growls against me, his voice thick with desire. He pauses just long enough to glance up at me, his grin wicked. "I want you to come in my mouth, Aub. Then I'm gonna fuck you so hard you'll still feel me tomorrow. Right here on this dryer, like no one's ever fucked you before."

The filthy promise in his words sends my body clenching, my pulse pounding in my ears. The heat in my core coils tighter, ready to snap. He dives back in, sucking my clit with renewed intensity, his fingers curling inside me, stroking that perfect spot.

I lose all control, grinding against his mouth, chasing the high I know only he can give me.

"Come for me, baby," he murmurs, his voice dark and commanding between kisses to my soaked pussy. "Show me how fucking hot you are when you let go."

I'm already there. The tension snaps, and my orgasm crashes over me, leaving me gasping and trembling. My body bucks against his mouth, pleasure rolling through me in waves so powerful I can't breathe. He doesn't stop—his tongue keeps moving, licking, flicking, dragging out every last tremor of my release.

"Oh, fuck," I gasp, incoherent sounds spilling from my lips as he works me through the aftershocks. Each soft, gentle lick sends shivers down my spine, my body trembling and oversensitive. He kisses me one last time, tender and filthy all at once, his lips lingering as if he's claiming me all over again.

A satisfied smile spreads across my face as I catch my breath. No one's ever wrecked me like Noah—no one ever will.

"Shit, that was fucking hot," he says, his voice thick with satisfaction as he rises to his feet, a wicked grin spreading across his face. His lips glisten with evidence of what he just did, and the sight alone sends another wave of heat coursing through me, making my pulse race.

He leans down, capturing my lips in a kiss that's slow and deliberate, like he's savoring every second. I can taste myself on him—dirty, raw, and so fucking hot. The kiss deepens, his tongue sliding against mine, and it leaves me breathless, dizzy, and desperate for more.

As he presses closer, I feel his cock, hard and straining against the thin fabric of his boxers, nudging insistently at my entrance. The teasing contact makes me whimper, my body arching toward him, every nerve screaming for him to close the distance.

"Fuck, Aub," he murmurs against my lips, his voice low and wrecked, like he's barely holding on. "You have no idea how much I need to be inside you right now."

Chapter 18

Noah

With my hands firmly gripping her hips, I lean over and crush my lips against hers, swallowing the soft gasp she makes. The only thing between us is the thin fabric of my boxers, and it's driving me insane. My cock is hard as hell, throbbing, desperate to be inside her, to lose myself in the tight heat that I know only she can give me.

She's fucking beautiful, and the way she rode my face—wild, shameless, and completely her—has my pulse pounding like a war drum. This isn't just want; it's need. It's raw, consuming, and impossible to ignore.

"I'm gonna fuck you, Aubrey," I growl, my voice low and gravelly as I lower my head, taking her hard nipple into my mouth. My tongue flicks over it before I suck hard, drawing a moan from her. "And I want to hear you scream my name when you come on my cock. You hear me?"

I lift my head, my eyes locking onto hers. She swallows hard, her pupils blown wide with desire, her walls crumbling under my touch. She tries to act tough, tries to keep her guard up, but the moment I touch her, she falls apart for me. She fucking wants this—wants me—just as much as I want her. And right now, I want everything. I want her screams, her moans, every damn inch of her.

Screw the distance, screw the past. While I have her here, I'm going to make her mine again. I'm going to fuck her so hard she won't think of anything else.

In one swift motion, I strip off my boxers and toss them aside, no hesitation, no second thoughts. Her gaze drops immediately, locking onto my cock, hard and throbbing, and I catch the way her tongue darts out to wet her lips. The sight alone makes me groan, a deep, primal sound that rips from my chest.

The thought of her mouth on me flickers through my mind—hot, wet, perfect—but not now. I'm too fucking far gone to wait. That can come later. Right now, I need to be buried so deep inside her she forgets every reason she ever left.

With her eyes still fixed on me, I grip my cock, stroking slowly, deliberately, knowing she's watching every move I make. A bead of precum glistens on the tip, catching the light, and I scoop it up with my finger, bringing it to her lips.

"Suck it," I command, my voice rough with desire.

She doesn't hesitate, her lips parting as she takes my fingers into her mouth, her tongue swirling around them like she's savoring every drop. Fuck, the sight alone is almost enough to undo me.

"Good girl," I growl, the words slipping out unbidden as I imagine her talented mouth wrapped around my cock, draining me until there's nothing left. "You're fucking killing me."

Pulling my fingers from her mouth, I shift my attention to the glistening wet heat between her legs. My hands find her hips, pulling her closer to the edge of the dryer until she's perfectly positioned, right where I want her.

My cock presses against her entrance, teasing her. Her breath hitches, and I feel her hips tilt, her body silently begging me to push inside.

"Spread those legs for me," I growl, my voice rough with hunger. She obeys instantly, her legs parting wide, baring herself completely for me. The sight of her, so ready and willing, nearly undoes me.

Slowly, I press the tip of my cock against her entrance, groaning as the tight, slick heat envelopes me. She gasps, the sound soft and sexy. My grip on her hips tightens as I push deeper, savoring every inch as her body stretches to take me. The pleasure starts low, a simmering ache in my balls, and spreads like fire through every nerve.

Once I'm buried to the hilt, I pause, letting the overwhelming sensation consume me. Her eyes find mine, her expression a perfect blend of pleasure and surrender, and I reach down, my thumb finding her clit. I circle it gently, teasingly, as I start to move. My hips thrust slow and deep, each stroke deliberate, every motion designed to draw more of those perfect, breathless sounds from her.

Her head tilts back, eyes closed, lips parted in a silent moan, but I'm not letting her drift away. "Open your eyes, Aub," I command. "Look at me, while I fuck you. Watch who's making you feel like this."

Her eyes flutter open, locking onto mine, and the heat between us burns hotter, fiercer. "Good girl," I murmur, my gaze dragging down to where our bodies meet. Watching my cock slide into her, glistening and wet, is pure fucking heaven. Every thrust makes me want to lose control, to bury myself deeper, to mark her as mine in every possible way.

Her moans grow louder, each one spurring me on. I pick up the pace, driving into her harder, faster, hitting her deeper with every stroke. "Oh, fuck, Noah!" she cries, her voice raw and desperate.

My thumb flicks her clit with precise pressure, coaxing her higher. Her body arches, trembling as she lifts her hips, begging for more. I give it to her, sliding my arm under her back and pulling her up, angling her just right.

The new position lets me hit that spot, and her reaction is instant—her back bows, her nails digging into my shoulders as I pound into her — harder, faster, deeper.

Her moans fuel me, raw and broken, her beautiful face completely lost in pleasure. I can feel her tightening around my cock, her walls gripping me, her clit throbbing under my thumb as she teeters on the edge.

"You're close," I growl, my voice rough with need. "When you come, you scream my name. Tell the whole fucking world whose cocks inside you, Aub."

Her body tenses and then she shatters. Her orgasm crashes, raw and powerful, her pussy pulsing and squeezing as her juices drip down, soaking my balls.

But I don't stop. I keep thrusting, relentless, driving her higher as my thumb works her clit, wringing every last bit of pleasure from her trembling body. Her moans break into gasps, her cries filling the room, and I know I've wrecked her completely.

"Take it, Aub," I tell her, my voice rough and demanding. "Take my cock until you can't take anymore."

Her entire body trembles beneath me, her cries turning into breathless, desperate moans, and I don't hold back. I drive into her relentlessly, my grip firm on her hip as I push her past every limit. Her nails dig into my arms, her legs quivering, but I can't stop—I won't stop—until I've claimed every inch of her. My cock throbs, every thrust the pleasure builds, but it's not enough. I want to ruin her, to make sure she feels me in her very soul.

Her body tenses, her walls clenching tighter, her clit pulsing under my thumb. A second orgasm tears through her, more powerful than the first. Her cries rise into a scream, raw and beautiful, echoing through the room as I keep driving into her, relentless, forcing her to ride the wave with me.

"That's it, baby," I growl, my voice thick as I watch her fall apart. Her face twists in pleasure, her lips forming my name like a prayer, and it pushes me over the edge. Her body milks my cock, stroke after stroke and I let go, groaning as I come hard, spilling deep inside her, giving her every last drop.

Even as my release overtakes me, I keep moving, slow but deliberate, savoring the way her body trembles beneath mine. But I don't stop until the last wave of pleasure has passed, until I've made damn sure she knows exactly who gave her the best orgasm of her life.

Because when she leaves, I want her to remember this. To remember me. To remember the guy who made her scream like that, who made her come undone so completely. That no other guy will ever fucking compare.

Her body comes down from the high of her orgasm, but I keep my movements slow, sliding in and out of her pussy with purpose, savoring every squeeze as she milks the last drop of cum from my cock. Her breathing is ragged, her chest heaving as she floats in the haze of her orgasm. Her skin is flushed, her expression soft, blissed-out, and completely undone—and knowing I'm the one who brought her there fills me with a primal satisfaction. Fuck, the sight of it is enough to make me want to do the whole thing all over again.

I stop moving, keeping my cock buried deep inside her, unwilling to let the moment end. My hands find her face, cradling it gently as I brush my thumbs over her cheeks, damp with sweat and glowing with the aftermath. My smirk widens, knowing I've left my mark on her in every way.

She's the only one I've ever fucked like this. No condoms. No barriers. Just us.

"That was fucking hot," I murmur.

For a second, heavier words hover at the tip of my tongue—words about her being mine, about how no one else will ever touch her like I do. But I swallow them down.

Before I can say anything more, she leans up and kisses me. It's not tentative or soft—it's deep, consuming, and full of something I can't quite name. Her lips mold to mine, her tongue tangling, and I lose myself in her all over again.

My cock twitches inside her, eager for round two, but I pull back, forcing myself to resist. If I fuck her again now, she'll be too sore to handle what I have planned for later. This weekend, with my father out of the house, I'm going to savor every second with her. I'm going to fuck her until she can't take anymore, until her body and mind are so consumed by me that nothing else exists.

Reluctantly, I break the kiss and slowly withdraw, groaning as I watch my release seep from her, glistening against her swollen, tender skin. The sight sends a surge of satisfaction through me, and I can't help but slide my fingers in, pushing it back inside her. Her body is limp, completely spent. She doesn't protest—she doesn't need to. She knows she's mine to take care of.

"Come here," I murmur, slipping my hands under her ass and lifting her off the dryer with ease. Her legs dangle around my waist, and her head rests against my shoulder as though she couldn't bear to be anywhere else.

I carry her toward the bathroom, every step deliberate, savoring the feel of her warmth against me. The shower is next—a chance to clean up, to wash away the evidence of what just happened before we face the inevitable. Her father's bullshit can wait. Right now, with her in my arms, her body trembling in the aftermath of everything I've given her, none of that shit matters.

For now, all I care about is her.

CHAPTER 19

AUBREY

After the shower, I follow Noah back to the laundry room, already pissed at myself for letting this happen again. Why can't I fucking resist him? The second he touches me, it's like every rational thought evaporates, and my good intentions crumble.

But damn, that was the most intense sex I've ever had. Those orgasms hit so hard, I forgot everything—who I was, all the shitty things weighing me down.

And yet, I let him do it without a condom.

Again.

Noah walks ahead of me, completely naked, and despite everything, my gaze drifts over him. The long, lean lines of his legs, the curve of his ass, the defined muscles of his back—it's like he was sculpted by some divine hand just to torment me. Fuck. The heat starts pooling low in my belly again, and I hate myself even more for wanting him.

As much as my body begs for more, my mind knows better. I have to stop this. Sex has always meant something to me—more than just a way to get off. But Noah... he makes it so easy to forget that. The way he touches me, the way he knows exactly how to completely unravel me—it's fucking maddening.

Still, there are those moments—those fleeting moments—when he looks at me like I'm his entire world. Like he sees something in me no one else does.

When we reach the laundry room, he strides in without a glance back. His movements are effortless, each one a reminder of his confidence, his control. He grabs my clothes from the dryer and hands them to me without a word.

I pull my shirt over my head and shimmy into my jeans.

Noah rummages through a basket, pulling out a pair of gray sweatpants. He slides them on with that same easy confidence, then grabs a hoodie, zipping it halfway before turning to look at me.

For a moment, his expression softens. It's so brief I might have imagined it. I hate that I want to believe there's something more to him, to us. But the truth is, I'm probably just another girl who fell for his charm.

And yet, I can't stop wishing things were different.

"I'll meet you at the front door. Then we'll head over there together," Noah says, his voice steady and unexpectedly comforting. He leans down, pressing a soft kiss to the top of my head. The gesture is so small, so out of character, that it leaves me frozen for a moment. Before I can even begin to process it, he's already gone.

As I finish getting dressed, I can't stop the thoughts swirling in my head. Noah coming with me to see my dad—will it make a difference? Will his presence change anything?

A part of me clings to that hope, that maybe having him there will make my dad finally see reason. But then, the memories return of all the times Noah witnessed my dad's rage before. My dad didn't care then, and I doubt he'll care now.

When I step out of the laundry room, I see Noah waiting at the front door, leaning casually against the frame with his arms crossed. His sneakers are already on, and he looks so sure of himself, so solid. I hate how much I need him in this moment. Hate how much I want to believe he'll stay.

I grab my boots and quickly put them on, the damp leather stiff from last night's storm. The laces fight me, refusing to cooperate. "Shit," I mutter, my fingers fumbling as frustration bubbles to the surface.

Noah doesn't say a word. He just watches, that infuriating little smirk tugging at the corners of his mouth.

Finally, the stubborn knots give, and I stand up straight. Without a word, Noah pulls the door open, holding it for me. I step out into the brisk morning air, the coolness biting at my skin.

This is it. Time to face my dad, with Noah at my side.

I'm so nervous. My stomach churns, nerves twisting into tight knots. My heart pounds so hard it feels like it might burst. I don't know what he'll say, what he'll do—and the thought of it terrifies me. I'm not ready to hear what he thinks, to deal with his anger. And what if he won't let me get my stuff? I need my things—my birth control, especially after last night and this morning. The thought sends a cold spike of fear through me, and I mutter a curse under my breath. *What the fuck am I doing?*

The aftermath of the storm is everywhere. Twigs and branches litter the yard, turning it into a chaotic mess that mirrors the tangle of my emotions. Noah strides ahead, calm and controlled, bending occasionally to toss a branch aside like it's nothing. His movements are effortless, so unlike my clumsy, frantic energy.

"What time is it?" I ask, realizing I left my phone behind in the rush.

"After nine-thirty," he replies, his voice even.

His eyes meet mine for a brief second, catching the edge of my nerves. I quickly glance away, forcing myself to act like I've got it together. But I don't. Not even close.

I keep my gaze fixed ahead, trying to summon whatever strength I have left as we approach the house. Each step closer feels heavier, my chest tightening with every inch of distance erased.

When we reach the front step, Noah raises his hand and knocks firmly. The sound cuts through the quiet morning, echoing down the street. I can already picture the nosy neighbors peeking through their curtains, their need for gossip outweighing any sense of shame. The thought of them whispering about me—about us—makes my skin crawl.

The house remains silent. No footsteps, no muffled grumbles of movement. My dad's never been quick to answer the door, but the weight of this silence feels different, heavier. Noah doesn't hesitate. He pounds again, harder this time, his palm slamming against the wood with force. The noise reverberates, loud and demanding, and I wonder if it'll wake him—or just piss him off.

Still nothing.

My eyes flick to the driveway where his car sits, exactly where it was last night. He's in there, no question—probably passed out, too hungover, or just too spiteful to give a shit. I fight the urge to say, screw this. Instead, my gaze darts to the windows, scanning for one that might be cracked open now that daylight makes everything clearer.

Just as I'm about to move, Noah's hand catches my arm, stopping me. "Wait," he mutters, his tone low but firm. His grip isn't rough, like he knows I'm seconds from doing something stupid. His intense gaze keeps me rooted, but before I can ask what he's waiting for, the unmistakable sound of the lock clicking open freezes me in place.

The fucking lock. The one my father never bothered with before. Not until yesterday. That simple sound is its own kind of answer, but it's one I don't want to face.

The door creaks open a fraction, the hinges groaning like they're mocking me. My pulse pounds in my ears, each beat syncing with the rising dread in my chest. I try to steady my breathing, but it's useless. All I can hear are his cruel words from yesterday replaying in my mind.

The door swings wider, revealing my father's face. His bloodshot eyes dart between Noah and me, his expression already twisted with anger.

"What the hell do you want? I told you yesterday—you don't live here anymore," he snaps, his voice a venomous growl. Before I can muster a response, he pushes the door forward, ready to slam it shut. Ready to erase me from his life all over again.

But Noah's quicker.

He throws out his arm, catching the door and holding it steady before it shuts. "So that's how it is, huh?" Noah growls, his voice low and razor-sharp. "You don't give a fuck about your own daughter?"

The words hang in the air, heavy and damning. My dad's face hardens, but Noah doesn't flinch. Instead, he doubles down. With a surge of force, he shoves the door open, forcing my dad to stumble back a step.

Noah strides inside without hesitation, his presence commanding the small entryway, every movement deliberate and unapologetic. He glances back at me, jerking his head toward the door. "Come on," he says, his tone leaving no room for argument.

For a moment, I hesitate, caught between the gravity of what's happening and the fear of what's going to happen.

My father's face twists, his lips tightening and fists clenching at his sides. The fury in him is a living thing, pulsing and ready to explode. The air between him and Noah crackles with tension, but Noah doesn't so much as flinch. He stands firm, calm, and unyielding, staring my dad down like he's daring him to make the first move.

"Go grab your stuff, Aub," Noah says, his tone steady. "You're getting the fuck out of this dump."

I hesitate, shooting him a confused glance. Go where? My stomach knots as the weight of the situation crashes down on me. What's his plan? Where the hell am I supposed to go?

But Noah doesn't look at me—his eyes stay locked on my dad, his expression resolute. There's no room for argument, no time to question him. My dad's silence is like a gathering storm, his fury simmering just beneath the surface, waiting to erupt.

I don't wait for it. I turn and sprint down the hall, my heart pounding. My hands tremble as I throw open my bedroom door, the familiar scent of the space rushing over me. It's not comforting anymore—nothing here is. It's just a reminder of everything I'm leaving behind.

From the front of the house, the sounds of rising voices seep through the walls. My dad's booming threats clash with Noah's calm, razor-sharp retorts. Every word feels like a spark in a dry forest, threatening to ignite something I can't control. My chest tightens with every second that passes, but I keep moving.

My bag lies crumpled in the corner, and I grab it, shoving clothes and shoes inside in frantic handfuls. Essentials. That's all I need. My fingers fumble as I yank open the dresser drawer, snatching my birth control pack. I pop one into my mouth and swallow it dry, the bitterness scraping my throat. My eyes dart around the room, scanning for anything I might have missed.

The clock on the wall ticks like a countdown, pushing me forward.

Then I hear footsteps. I glance up, my pulse spiking, but it's just Noah. He steps into the room, his gaze sweeping over the mess like he's taking it all in. For a second, something flickers across his face—a shadow of memory, maybe, of all the times he's been here before. But he doesn't linger.

"Got everything?" he asks, his voice cutting through the buzz of anxiety in my head.

I nod, zipping the bag shut with a sharp tug. Before I can say a word, Noah slings it over his shoulder and reaches for my hand. His grip is firm, grounding me in a way I desperately need right now.

"Let's go," he says, and I let him lead me out of the room. My legs feel like they're moving on autopilot, my thoughts too scattered to keep up.

The hallway feels longer than it should, each step stretching out into an eternity. As we near the living room, I expect to see my dad looming there, ready to blow his shit. But the space is empty. He's nowhere to be seen.

Noah doesn't stop. He pulls the front door open, the sunlight spilling in and hitting my face. The brightness blinds me for a moment, but I keep moving, following Noah as he steps outside, his hand still wrapped firmly around mine.

The door slams shut behind us, the sound ringing in my ears like the end of something. Reality sinks in: I'm out. Out of that house, out of the chaos, out of the life that's been crushing me for so long.

But as Noah's grip anchors me, leading me into the unknown, a new kind of fear sets in. Because while I'm free of that house, I have no fucking idea what comes next.

As we walk toward Noah's place, uncertainty swirls, tightening its grip like a noose. Where will I go? What the hell am I supposed to do now?

This feeling of belonging nowhere is too familiar, an ache I thought I'd buried long ago. If I could rewrite my past, I would erase the night I left with my mom, rewrite every choice that led to this. Maybe then, I wouldn't be here now. Lost. Stuck. Clinging to the one person who hopefully still gives a shit about me.

Noah.

He walks beside me, my bag slung over his shoulder, his hand steady around mine. Like it's no big deal. But fuck, it is a big deal. It's everything. He's the only steady thing I have right now, and even his presence isn't enough to quiet the panic buzzing in my chest.

I force myself to focus on the basics: finding somewhere to crash until my college scholarship kicks in next year. Survive the next few months, one shitty day at a time. That's all I can handle right now.

When we step into Noah's house, I hesitate just inside the doorway, my feet rooted to the spot. Everything feels too loud, too still, too much. I don't know what to do next, and the air feels heavier in here, pressing down on me like it knows I don't belong.

Noah doesn't stop. He strides down the hallway like this is just another day, carrying my bag, his broad shoulders carrying all the weight I can't. Staying here? That's not happening. Seeing him every day, being in his space—it would fuck with my head in ways I can't even begin to unpack. I've already let him get too close, and every time he's near, my walls feel a little weaker. And then there's his dad. No way he'd be okay with me crashing here.

I hurry down the hall, my steps quick and unsteady, trying to catch up with him. My mind spins with questions, doubts, and the gnawing fear that this isn't going to work.

When I reach his bedroom doorway, I stop short. Noah is standing there, my bag in his hand, his eyes on the bed as he tosses it onto the mattress without a second thought. Like he's already decided this is where it belongs. Like this is where I belong.

Noah grabs his phone from the table beside the bed, his fingers moving quickly over the screen. He looks calm, collected—like this is nothing to him. Meanwhile, my world feels like it's falling apart. When he finishes, he glances up, his eyes locking onto mine.

"I'm starving. Want something to eat?" he asks casually, like we're not standing in the middle of this disaster. Like my life isn't a complete fucking mess.

Before I can answer, he brushes past me, his shoulder grazing mine, and heads down the hall without waiting for a response.

I stand frozen in the hallway, torn between following him and doubling back to grab my phone from his room. My thoughts are a tangled mess, but one thing stands out. I need to let my mom know what happened.

Maybe she'll care enough to help, though deep down, I'm not sure why I keep clinging to that hope. And Sam—she might know someone willing to let me crash on their couch. Just long enough to get through this shit.

I quickly dash into Noah's room and grab my phone off the bedside table. My hands shake as I type out the message.

Aubrey: Mom. I need somewhere to stay. Dad has kicked me out. Ring me, please.

I stare at the screen, willing those bubbles to appear—the ones that mean she gives a damn. Seconds stretch into what feels like forever. The silence is deafening, the screen unchanged, and with each passing moment, my heart sinks lower. She's not answering. Of course, she's not. Why would she?

When I step into the kitchen, Noah is standing in front of the fridge, the door wide open, peering inside. He grabs a carton of milk, his movements casual, and I notice he's already set out two bowls and a box of cereal on the counter.

I hesitate for a second before slipping onto one of the stools at the kitchen island.

Noah doesn't say a word as he pours cereal into both bowls, the sound of it hitting porcelain strangely settles my thoughts. He follows it with milk, sliding one bowl toward me without looking up. Reaching into a drawer, he grabs two spoons and hands me one.

"Thanks," I mutter, taking it from him.

He picks up his bowl, leaning against the cupboard, and shovels a big scoop of cereal into his mouth. He chews slowly, thoughtfully, his eyes locked on me the entire time. It's like he's waiting for something but fuck if I know what.

"Noah, what the fuck are we doing?" I blurt out, breaking the tense silence. My voice comes out harsher than I intended, but I can't help it. "I appreciate you helping me get my stuff, but I have no idea what the hell is going on."

He doesn't even blink. Just keeps chewing, swallows, and replies, "Having breakfast."

He takes another spoonful, shoveling it into his mouth like I didn't just drop a loaded question in the middle of the room.

"Not this," I snap, my frustration bubbling over. "Why did you take my bag into your room?"

Noah shrugs, maddeningly nonchalant. "I don't know. I just did." His words are muffled as he talks with his mouth full. "Now hurry up and eat, because I'm taking you somewhere."

"Noah," I snap, cutting him off mid-chew, my frustration reaching its boiling point. I can't deal with his games right now. My mind's spiraling with uncertainty, and I need answers. I need fucking clarity.

I've always been the kind of person who needs a plan, who needs to know what's coming next. These past three weeks back in this shit hole of a town have been nothing but chaos, and it's messing with my head.

He doesn't answer.

Instead, his phone pings, breaking the silence. He steps forward, setting his nearly empty cereal bowl on the counter before grabbing the phone. His expression doesn't change as he checks the message, his thumb moving quickly over the screen. Then, without a word, he darkens the display and sets the phone face down on the counter like it's nothing.

"Eat," he says, his voice steady but tinged with a strange urgency, like eating is the most important thing in the world right now.

I glance at his phone, my eyes lingering on it for a moment longer than I should. Is it a girl? Someone he's been texting late at night, someone I don't know about. The thought sends an unwelcome pang through my chest, but I shove it down.

With a resigned sigh, I grab my spoon and dig into the cereal. It tastes like cardboard in my mouth, each bite harder to swallow than the last. I feel his eyes on me, steady and unrelenting, but I can't bring myself to meet them. Instead, I let my gaze drift out the window, focusing on the backyard where fragments of our childhood still linger.

The old treehouse his dad built towers over the yard, weathered but standing firm—a monument to countless summers spent hiding from the world. The swing set leans slightly, its chains rusted, a casualty of time. Worn patches of grass mark the places we used to chase each other until we collapsed, laughing and breathless. The memories feel like they belong to someone else, some other version of me. A version who hadn't learned yet that things fall apart.

I force another spoonful of cereal into my mouth, the soggy flakes sticking to my tongue. Noah hasn't said a word about whatever plan he's cooked up, and I'm too drained to ask. If he's got something in mind, I'll hear about it eventually. For now, I just need to get through this moment without losing my fucking mind.

When I finally finish, I glance around and realize Noah isn't in the kitchen anymore. At some point, he slipped out, and I was so caught up in my thoughts that I didn't even notice. Gathering our bowls, I carry them to the sink, rinsing them quickly and setting them in the drying rack.

As I place the last bowl down, I hear his footsteps. Turning, I see him stroll back into the kitchen. He's changed—his gray sweatpants swapped out for black jeans, a fitted black shirt that clings to his shoulders, and scuffed boots that look like they've been through hell and back. The casual confidence in his stride is irritatingly magnetic, and I can't help but check him out.

Fuck.

And there it is—that damn smirk. Cocky and knowing, like he's already pieced together exactly where my mind went.

He doesn't say anything but still I try to keep my expression neutral. I can't let him have the upper hand, not after earlier. Not after catching me staring like some lovesick idiot when he was in his room—when he was stroking his cock.

I can't go there right now. Not when I already feel like I'm standing on the edge of a cliff, and one wrong step will send me plummeting.

He steps closer, holding out a motorcycle helmet, the smooth black surface gleaming under the kitchen lights. "Here," he says, his voice steady. "You'll need this. It's my dad's."

"What are we doing?" I ask, hesitation thick in my voice as I glance between him and the helmet.

"I want to take you somewhere," he replies. "Somewhere to clear your head of all this worry and crap, so you can relax and think straight."

I hate that he still knows me so well. Knows exactly what I need even when I barely recognize it myself. Of course, he sees through all my walls, sees the cracks I've tried so hard to patch. And it pisses me off that he's right.

"I don't have time, Noah," I say, my voice harsh. "I need to figure out where I'm going to crash."

"You're staying here," he says firmly, like it's already decided.

"No." My response is instant, cutting through the air between us. I shake my head, folding my arms tightly across my chest. "I can't, Noah."

His jaw tightens, but he doesn't argue. Not directly. Instead, he thrusts the helmet into my hands with a clipped, "Let's go." His tone leaves no room for debate.

He turns and strides toward the doorway, grabbing a bag he'd tossed on the kitchen table earlier.

I groan under my breath, grabbing my phone from the counter and shoving it into my pocket. A quick glance confirms what I already knew—no response from my mom. The empty screen mocks me, each unanswered message a reminder of just how low on her list of priorities I am.

Why the fuck do I even bother?

I trail after Noah, my steps reluctant. He's already by the back door, holding it open with one hand braced against the frame. His eyes meet mine as I approach, dark and steady, a storm brewing just beneath the surface.

And then his gaze dips, just for a second—lingering on my chest before dragging back up to meet my eyes. It's not subtle. The weight of his stare is almost physical, like I can feel every dirty thought running through his head. And fuck, I know he can sense mine, too.

I force myself to move past him, brushing by as I step outside. The cool air hits my skin, a sharp contrast to the heat radiating off him. Even without looking, I know his eyes are on me. I can feel them, burning a path down my back, lingering on the sway of my hips and devouring every curve of my ass.

At the bottom of the steps, I stop, unsure of where to go next. Noah doesn't pause. He strides past me, heading straight for the old garage tucked at the edge of the yard.

I watch as he grabs the garage door and shoves it open, the sound of metal scraping against metal breaking the quiet. Inside, a sleek black motorcycle gleams under the dim light spilling in. It's the kind he used to dream about when we were kids, back when everything was simpler.

Back then, it was all promises and big plans. Now, it's real.

Even though Noah's a bed-hopping, cocky asshole, it's painfully obvious that he's got his life together more than I ever will.

He strides into the garage, muscles flexing beneath his shirt as he pushes the motorcycle into the yard. I can't take my eyes off him as he swings a leg over the seat, moving with the kind of effortless confidence that makes it look like he was born for this.

With a few swift kicks on the foot lever, the engine roars to life, a low, guttural growl slicing through the quiet of the backyard. He twists the throttle a few times, clearly enjoying the low growl of the machine beneath him. This is Noah—wild, unpredictable, and infuriatingly magnetic.

As I approach, he pulls the backpack from the handlebars and hands it to me. "Wear this," he says, his voice rising over the steady rumble. "Then put the helmet on. I'll help with the straps."

I nod, the vibrations from the bike thrumming in the air around us as I sling the bag over my shoulders. He moves with practiced ease, sliding his own helmet on and securing the straps with a fluid motion. His gaze shifts back to me, waiting for me to follow suit.

I fumble with the helmet, my fingers clumsy against the unfamiliar straps.

"Here, let me," he says, his voice softer now. His hands brush against my skin as he adjusts the straps, and I freeze under the weight of his attention.

His eyes stay locked on mine, steady and unguarded, and for a moment, it's like everything else falls away. The noise in my head, the mess of my life—it all fades under the quiet care of his touch.

"There," he says, fastening the strap securely. "You're good."

I swing a leg over the bike and settle into the seat behind him. He doesn't rush me, just waits with that infuriating patience of his, like he has all the time in the world.

The moment I wrap my arms around his waist, I'm hit with a rush of adrenaline. The solid warmth of him against me, the strength in his back pressing into my chest—it ignites something dangerous and thrilling. My fingers tighten around him instinctively.

Noah twists the throttle, the engine growling louder beneath us. Over his shoulder, he calls out, "Hold on tight."

Then we're moving.

The sudden burst of speed sends a jolt through me, and I tighten my grip, my heart pounding against my ribs. It's my first time on a motorcycle, and it's as terrifying as it is exhilarating.

As we race through the streets, my thoughts drift to when we were sixteen. He used to talk about this—about owning a bike, hitting the open road, and leaving all the bullshit behind. Back then, his dreams always included me. Him and me, taking on the world together.

Even now, it feels like he's trying to pull me into that world, trying to remind me of those dreams. But I know better. No matter how far we ride or how fast we go, the chaos in my life won't disappear. The worries, the what-ifs—they're still there, waiting.

The city fades behind us, the harsh lines of concrete and chaos giving way to rolling hills and open fields. The wind rushes past, cool and sharp, and the hum of the bike beneath us is almost soothing.

For a moment—a fleeting, fragile moment—the noise in my head quiets. The trees blur into streaks of green, the open sky stretching endlessly above us, and I let myself sink into the stillness of it all.

It doesn't fix anything. It doesn't solve the mess of my life. But it gives me a moment to breathe.

And for now, maybe that's enough.

CHAPTER 20

NOAH

I knew I had to drag Aubrey out today, shake her loose from the shit-storm running through her head. But fuck me, having her pressed up against my back is doing things I can't even begin to handle. Every curve of her molds to me, and all I can think about is pulling over and replaying every filthy, desperate moment we had this morning.

She's been gone for over a year and still it hasn't dulled my need for her—not even close. It's sharper now, rawer, clawing at my chest every night.

And yeah, I know she's got a shit-ton of decisions to make about where she's gonna stay. But let's be honest: she's staying with me. She just doesn't know it yet.

My dad's not about to let her end up on the streets—he's not wired that way. Always ready to help someone in need. But before I lay it all out for her, I need to talk to him, lock things down.

This morning, though—fuck. Hearing the shit her father spewed almost pushed me over the edge. Christ. I hope she didn't hear all the vile shit he said. I stood there; fists clenched so tight it felt like my bones would crack. When he looked me dead in the eye and told me to take her off his hands, like she didn't mean a goddamn fucking thing to him, I saw red. I wanted to hit him so bad it hurt, but I didn't. Not for him—for her. She wouldn't want that, wouldn't want me stooping to his level. But it took everything I had not to put him in the dirt for the way he talked about her.

I veer off the road and onto a rough dirt path, the tires crunching over broken branches and debris from last night's storm. The whole place looks ripped apart and forgotten, and maybe that's why I brought her here—because it feels like us. This route's so far off the grid, nobody comes out this way.

The water comes into view, sunlight bouncing off the surface in sharp, dazzling patterns. It's like the universe is trying to remind me that something can still be beautiful, even though it's been through hell.

I roll the bike closer to the bank and kill the engine. The sudden quiet wraps around us, broken only by the soft rustle of leaves. I unclip my helmet and hook it onto the handlebars, but Aubrey doesn't move right away. She's still pressed against me, her arms wrapped tight around my waist, her chest flush against my back. Both of us stealing a moment, holding onto the calm.

"What is this place?" she asks finally, her voice soft, almost hesitant.

Her arms slip away, and the loss is immediate, sharp, like she's taken a piece of me with her.

She climbs off the bike, fumbling with the helmet strap, and I can already tell she's screwed. My dad's safety latch might be practical, but it's a pain in the ass if you don't know the trick. She's not figuring it out on her own.

Without a word, I grab the hem of her shirt and tug her toward me. She stumbles closer, her body brushing against mine, and my fingers move to the latch under her chin. Her eyes flit across my face, lingering in a way that makes my pulse hammer.

I toss a glance up, catching her staring at my lips. She doesn't look away. It's like she's daring me—begging me—to make a move.

Fuck. If she keeps looking at me like that, I won't be able to stop myself.

Finally, the latch gives, and I lift the helmet off her head. Her hair spills out, a wild, beautiful mess, cascading around her face. My hand twitches, the urge to touch her overwhelming, but before I can, she brushes the strands aside herself.

That doesn't stop me.

I hook my arm around her waist and pull her flush against me. My nose grazes the curve of her neck, and she smells so fucking good—like innocence tangled with sin, like she was made to ruin me. My chest tightens with the need to taste her, claim her, wreck her in every possible way.

She gasps softly as my fingers slide up to the nape of her neck. It's all the invitation I need. I crush my lips to hers, tasting her like she's the only thing keeping me alive. It's raw, unrelenting, the kind of kiss that makes the world fall away, leaving nothing but her.

Every thought blurs into a single, unrelenting need. I crave her—every inch of her. My cock throbs, hard and aching, pulsing with the heat of everything I want to do to her.

I break the kiss, pressing my forehead to hers, my breathing ragged. My grip tightens, holding her close enough to feel exactly what she's doing to me. My voice drops, rough and low, brushing against her lips.

"You have no idea how much I want to fuck you right now. How much I want to watch you take my cock like the dirty girl I know you are."

"Noah," she whispers, so soft it's barely there, but it's enough. Enough to shatter the haze of desire clouding my mind.

I press a softer kiss to her lips, lingering just long enough to let her know she's everything I want before I let go.

The heel of my boot kicks the bike's stand into place with a metallic click that echoes in the stillness. When I look up, she's already walking toward the water's edge, her steps slow, hesitant.

I stay on the bike, watching her. The breeze catches her hair, sending it rippling like silk in the sunlight. Even with the sadness etched onto her face, she's breathtaking—the kind of beauty that feels too fragile for a world like this.

The sunlight dances off the water, casting a soft, golden glow around her that feels almost otherworldly—like she's something I'll never quite deserve. She kneels at the shoreline, her fingers brushing sand from a small pebble with delicate fingers. When she flicks it outward, the stone skips once before vanishing beneath the surface, leaving only a faint ripple behind.

Her gaze lingers on the water, strands of dark hair slipping across her face as she searches for another pebble. The slight furrow in her brows says it all—she's lost in her thoughts, the weight of them pulling her further away. She stands, tossing the next stone with a sharp, decisive movement. The quiet is broken by the muted splash as it sinks without a trace.

I ease off the bike, my boots crunching against the sand as I walk toward her. The shoreline is littered with small stones, and my eyes catch on one half-buried in the sand. I pick it up, rolling it between my fingers as I close the distance between us.

I stop beside her without saying a word—words feel too insignificant for the silence stretching between us. Instead, I let the pebble fly. It arcs through the air and skips across the surface, each bounce leaving shimmering ripples in its wake.

Her head turns sharply toward me. "How did you do that?" Aubrey's voice is tinged with awe, her wide eyes meeting mine. A smirk tugs at my lips.

"It's all in the wrist," I say, teasing as I slip the bag off her shoulders and swing it onto mine before she can protest. It's instinct—lightening her load, even in small ways.

Her attention shifts back to the ground, her focus sharpening as she hunts for another pebble. When she finds one, she weighs it in her palm, studying it like it holds some untold secret. Then she throws it with everything she's got. The stone hits the water with a heavy plop, sinking instantly. Not even a single skip.

Disappointment flickers across her face, sharp and unmistakable, and I feel it too, like it's my own failure. I stoop to grab another stone, turning it over in my hand before sending it flying. This one skips effortlessly, bouncing across the water in perfect arcs until it disappears.

Her eyes track the ripples, and she mutters, "Show-off," nudging my shoulder in a playful jab.

The laugh that escapes me is sudden and unguarded—loud and real in a way that surprises even me. She looks over, her gaze locking on mine, and for a brief moment, everything falls away. There's a light in her eyes, a spark of something warm and fleeting, something that doesn't hurt.

The moment feels small, like a whisper in the storm of everything happening around us, but it hits me like the ground shifting beneath my feet. For the first time in what feels like forever, I can actually breathe.

I let myself soak in her smile—a fleeting, rare thing I somehow managed to coax out of her. In the chaos of everything, giving her even the briefest sliver of happiness feels like a fucking victory.

"Let's go," I murmur, turning toward the flat, grassy area that became my haven just weeks ago. It's my place—the one spot where I've managed to untangle my thoughts and figure out how the fuck to survive each day since Aubrey came crashing back into my life.

Her footsteps crunch softly behind me, a reminder that she's close—close enough to touch, though it still feels like she's a world away.

When we reach the spot, I drop my bag and pull out the blanket. A quick shake, and I spread it across the grass before sinking down onto it. I leave enough room for her, hoping she'll sit, and when she does, the air shifts again.

I lie back, staring up at the endless blue of the sky. My hands lace together on my chest—a restraint more than comfort. She's so close I can feel her presence, like every nerve in my body is tuned to her frequency, humming with a need I can't give in to. Not now.

I close my eyes, willing myself to breathe through it, to ignore the thoughts clawing at the edges of my mind. Thoughts of her, of wanting her, of pulling her close and making her forget everything else. But she doesn't need that—not right now. She needs the quiet, the space to figure out her own head. I can't be the one to make it harder for her.

"How'd you find this spot?" she asks, breaking the silence.

I open my eyes, and there she is, leaning back on her elbows, completely oblivious to the way her posture gives me the perfect view of her tits. Damn fine tits, too. No use denying it. The kind that makes it impossible to think straight.

"I just went riding and stumbled across it," I say, shrugging like it's nothing. The truth is a hell of a lot messier—there's no fucking way I'm telling her that seeing her again ripped me apart and left me needing a place to get my shit together before I could even face her.

"I don't know what I'm gonna do, Noah," she says, her voice raw and heavy. "If I don't finish the school year, I'll lose my scholarship to Mayfair."

Mayfair.

Just the name alone brings a smirk to my lips. That school's been on my radar for a while. Tech has always been my thing, and with offers rolling in for my ideas, Mayfair feels like the right fit. Dad and I have talked it over a hundred times, and out of all the options, it's the one that clicks—for both of us.

But hearing Aubrey say it now, knowing she's fighting to keep her future within reach, it hits differently. Like the universe is playing some cosmic joke, twisting our paths closer together in ways neither of us saw coming.

"It won't come to that," I say, my voice firm as I stretch out on the blanket, my gaze tracking a bird cutting lazy arcs across the sky.

"How do you know that, Noah?" she asks, her voice quieter now, edged with something raw and uncertain. She lowers herself onto her back beside me, her words a thread pulling tight between us. "I never thought I'd be here—on the edge of losing everything."

Her vulnerability digs into me, and before I can think it through, I roll onto my side, closing the distance between us until our faces are only inches apart. "Because I know," I say, my voice low but steady.

"You're not losing anything, Aubrey. Not your scholarship, not your future—none of it. Because I won't let that happen."

She turns her head, her eyes locking onto mine, searching for something solid to hold on to. She swallows, the movement drawing my gaze to the curve of her neck, and for a second, it takes every fucking ounce of restraint not to lean in and kiss her. I let out a rough breath and roll onto my back, putting a sliver of space between us. "This morning, I texted Dad," I say, my voice softer now. "Told him you might need a place to stay."

Out of the corner of my eye, I see her shift to face me, her brows furrowed. "And what did he say?"

"He said he'd talk to me about it tomorrow when he gets home."

"Noah, you don't have to do that."

I turn my head, letting a small smirk tug at the corner of my lips. "Got a better offer?"

She lets out a quiet laugh, but it doesn't linger. "No, it's just... things have been a little tense between us. I don't want to make it worse."

"I'm sorry," I say, my voice rough, the words jagged like they're cutting their way out. "For the way I treated you those first few days. I fucked up."

The admission sits heavy in the air between us, the weight of everything I can't bring myself to say pressing down. Like how I've always loved Aubrey more than she'll ever love me. The truth claws at the edges of my resolve, too raw, too real to let out. So instead, I leave it there, unspoken, hoping she doesn't hear it in the silence.

She looks at me, her eyes filled with confusion and hurt. "I don't understand why you did it though. I know I hurt you by moving away, but you just ghosted me. I thought we were friends."

Friends. The word hits like a gut punch. It's almost laughable, how far off that word feels from what we had—what I thought we had. We weren't just friends. Friends don't steal moments like they're the only two people in the world. Friends don't leave you feeling like the fucking ground has been ripped out from under you.

I swallow hard, her words dragging me back to the mess I became after she left. Back to the hollow hookups, the aimless nights, chasing some warped shadow of what I lost.

She didn't just walk back into my life; she brought every shattered piece of me with her. And now she's sitting here, calling it friendship, like it wasn't the most real thing I've ever felt in my fucking life.

I push off the blanket, my chest tight and my head a fucking storm. Moving to the water's edge, I crouch and grab a pebble, gripping it like it might anchor me. With a sharp flick, I hurl it across the water. It skips hard and fast, cutting into the surface, the ripples spreading wide and messy.

My phone buzzes in my pocket, and I yank it out, the screen lighting up with a message from Reece. The usual. He's asking if I'm still on for tonight—game, rally, and the party, where we scope out the next girl to try and fuck.

I stare at the message for too long, Aubrey's words still burning in my chest. If this is where we stand—just friends—fine. At least now I know.

I type out a quick reply before I can second-guess it.

Noah: I'm in.

I'll deal with it the only way I know how.

Sliding my phone back into my pocket, I stare out over the water.

Do I confront her? Do I tell her how she shattered me when she left, how she made me question every fucking thing about myself? Or do I let it go? Would it even matter? Would it change a goddamn thing?

I grit my teeth, the words biting at the edge of my tongue. I know the answer. It wouldn't change a damn thing. She's already decided what we were. What we are. And it's not what I thought. Not even close.

I stare out at the water, as if it's got all the fucking answers. She doesn't see me the way I see her—she never has. That truth, raw and unforgiving, cuts deeper than anything I could ever say.

When I return back to the blanket, Aubrey's sitting up, hunched over her phone. Her fingers move fast, punching out words like she's racing against her own breath. I catch a glimpse of the screen, just enough to see who it's for. Her mom.

It doesn't take a rocket scientist to figure out what's happening—message after message, left unanswered. She's trying so fucking hard, pouring herself out into the void, and it's like her mom can't even be bothered to reply. That kind of silence isn't just an absence; it's a wound that never stops bleeding.

Her fingers hover over the screen before typing out one last desperate plea: Mom, call me. It's urgent. She locks the phone and shoves it into her pocket. When her eyes finally meet mine, the weight of all the unspoken shit between us slams into me, thick and suffocating.

I force a deep breath, steadying myself. This tension, this unresolved mess between us—it's not going to fix itself. And I'm done pretending it doesn't matter. "Pretty sure Dad will let you crash at the house," I say, keeping my voice even but letting the weight of my words hang between us. "But before that, we need to talk. We need to clear the air."

She doesn't respond, just curls into herself, wrapping her arms around her knees like she's bracing for impact. The sight of her like this—small, vulnerable, guarded—it fucks with my head. But I don't back off. I can't.

I exhale shakily, the pressure in my chest building until it breaks free. "You didn't just leave, Aubrey. You fucking left like we didn't mean a damn thing." My jaw tightens as I look away, my hands digging into the blanket beneath me. "Do you even know what that did to me? How it felt? Like I was some fucking disposable thing you could walk away from without a second thought?"

Her silence hits harder than any words could. My laugh comes out bitter and sharp, cutting through the stillness between us. "And now you're here, and we're just supposed to act like it's fine? Like you didn't fucking wreck me? Like we're just friends or something? It doesn't work that way, Aubrey. Not after everything."

The words are out now, raw and jagged, bleeding between us. There's no taking them back, and maybe that's for the best. No more pretending.

No more tiptoeing around the wreckage. Just the truth, ugly and brutal as it is.

"I'm sorry," she whispers, her voice barely audible. Her gaze drops to the ground, and when she speaks again, her words tremble under the weight of everything unsaid. "I fucked myself up too."

She lifts her eyes to mine, and for the first time, I see it—the pain she's been carrying, the regret carved into every word. "If I'd known then what I know now, I would never have left, Noah." Her voice cracks, and she looks toward the water, like the memories are too heavy to face me head-on.

"I thought we were chasing a better life," she continues, her voice soft but weighted with a year's worth of disappointment. "Away from my father and all his bullshit. But it didn't turn out the way I thought. My mom found work at a bar, and I'd be alone at night. Then she started bringing home these guys—one after another. Nothing was stable. Nothing felt right." Her voice wavers, and when her eyes lock onto mine, they're filled with quiet accusation. "I missed you. And you ghosted me."

Her words hit. But I can't let her think I didn't care—not for a fucking second. "You said earlier that I was your best friend, Aub," I start, my voice rough, the emotions clawing at my throat. "But you were so much more than that to me." I hesitate, the weight of the unspoken truth pressing down hard. "You still are."

She has no idea how much she still owns every shattered piece of me, and I can't fucking say it—not when I'm not sure I hold the same weight in her world.

Her gaze softens, tears glinting in her eyes. "I'm so sorry, Noah," she whispers, her voice trembling. "You were so much more to me too."

The word were echoes in my head, sharp and unforgiving. "Were," I repeat, the past tense cutting deeper than I want to admit. My chest tightens, and for a second, I want to demand more. To ask if that's all I'll ever be—some part of her past. But I bite it back, swallowing the frustration burning in my throat.

"We should head back," I mutter, forcing myself to move. I stand, grabbing the edge of the blanket, waiting for her to shift so I can pack it away.

The silence between us is deafening, every second stretching longer than it should.

Just as she moves to stand, her phone buzzes. She pulls it from her pocket, her sigh heavy with disappointment, frustration, and something else she won't name. I glance at the screen, catching the name: Sam. Not her mom. Not the person she's been so desperate to hear from.

Sam: You want me to pick you up for the game tonight?

Her fingers move quickly, typing out a reply.

Aubrey: Nah, not going. Not feeling well.

She slips the phone back into her pocket with a deliberate calm, her movements too measured, like she's trying to keep the cracks from showing. But I see them. I always fucking see them.

I grab the blanket and shove it into my bag, the motion rougher than it needs to be. My jaw clenches as I zip it shut, every small action grinding against the frustration bubbling under my skin.

I glance at her one last time, the words I want to say sitting heavy on my tongue. But they stay there, unsaid, as we both settle into the silence we can't seem to escape.

Chapter 21

Noah

The shower is scalding, steam curling around me as I lean against the slick tiles, letting the water hammer against my back. I scrub at my skin like I can scrape away the weight of the day, but the tension refuses to budge. Aubrey's words keep looping in my head, carving themselves deeper no matter how hard I try to wash them away.

Eventually, I give in—to frustration, to need, to the only thing I can control in this moment. My hand finds its way down to my cock, and I work out the knot of pent-up energy, quick and rough. My body jerks as I finish, bracing myself against the wall, but the release is hollow. The ache is still there, buried under layers of anger, regret, and everything else I can't fucking name.

I dry off, throw on some clothes, and head out. The game's waiting, but my head's still stuck on Aubrey. Maybe I'm just an idiot for holding on to the idea of her, for thinking she's someone I can save. Maybe she's not mine to save anymore.

The carpark is buzzing as I pull in, the usual crowd filtering toward the entrance. Normally, a night like this would be my escape. Fuck the world away until the edges blur. But tonight? The thought doesn't even spark.

Still, I'm here because I told Reece I'd show up. Jace is probably already prowling the lot, sniffing out his next conquest.

Sure enough, I spot him as I park, climbing out of Reece's car with that smug-ass smirk that makes me want to deck him on a good day. But I let it slide, because that's just Jace—an asshole with a knack for making everything worse and somehow getting away with it.

I slam my car door shut, shaking off whatever's left of the hesitation, and slip into the version of myself everyone expects—the guy who doesn't care, doesn't feel, doesn't let anyone get too close. It's easier this way. Because if I don't, if I let myself think about Aubrey for one more second, I might lose my fucking mind.

Jace and Reece are waiting near the entrance, Jace practically bouncing on his heels like he's already ten shots in. He grins wide when he sees me, loud as always.

"Fuck, I've been waiting for this night for fucking forever!"

I shove my hands in my pockets, biting back a laugh. Of course, that's the first thing out of his mouth. Jace has this way of spinning whatever bullshit he thinks will work on a girl—charming lies, fake sincerity, the whole nine yards. And it works. Every fucking time. He'll create some sob story about how those rumors about him aren't true, how he's actually a nice guy. And the fucked-up part? It works. Every fucking time.

I don't need to pull that kind of shit. Girls come to me, plain and simple. They want my attention, my focus, a shot at being the one who sticks around longer than a night. They want my dick, and I don't make them jump through hoops to get it. No lies, no fake charm. Just me.

And if they think it means something more? Well, that's their problem, not mine.

Jace elbows me as I reach them, his grin widening. "You look like you're in a mood, man. Need to get your dick wet tonight to loosen up?"

I smirk, shaking my head. "Let's just get inside. I'm not in the mood for your shit tonight."

The stadium bursts to life as we head in—a chaotic symphony of noise and color. The roar of the crowd, the pounding rhythm of the marching band, and the mingling scents of hot dogs and popcorn slam into me all at once. For a moment, it's almost enough to distract me. Almost.

Out on the field, a group of cheerleaders sprints into formation, a burst of energy and movement that immediately catches my eye. My gaze drifts over the lineup, already cataloging possibilities. There are a few I haven't fucked yet, girls who've been throwing me looks for weeks, waiting for their turn. They wouldn't think twice about making it easy for me. And tonight? Easy sounds good. Anything to quiet the noise in my head.

As my eyes scan the field, I spot Tia standing off to the side. The glaring white nasal splint strapped across her face is impossible to miss, framed by the dark bruises under her eyes that make her look like a pissed off raccoon. She's trying to blend in, but her stiff posture screams discomfort, the awkwardness clinging to her like cheap perfume.

What the fuck is she even doing here?

The other cheerleaders flock to her like moths to a flame, their concerned faces making it clear she's milked her situation for all it's worth. Classic Tia—always the center of attention, no matter how desperate or pathetic the attempt.

Her gaze lands on me, and my gut twists with a familiar sense of dread. Before I can move, she starts toward me, her pace quickening like she's got something to prove.

I curse under my breath and turn on my heel, striding away in the hope that she'll take the hint. The last thing I need tonight is her in my space.

Yeah, I was a dick to Aubrey when she first came back, but Tia? She's a whole different breed of toxic. That Instagram page branding Aubrey a slut... That wasn't just high school drama—that was calculated, insecure-bitch energy, all because Tia couldn't handle someone else shining brighter than her.

In no mood to deal with her bullshit, I stride away, hoping she'll take the hint and fuck off. But, like the relentless pain in the ass she is, she follows, her voice rising with every step I take.

"Hey! Noah!"

I pick up my pace, refusing to acknowledge her.

"Oh my god, will you just stop walking and answer me?" she whines, the pitch of her voice enough to set my teeth on edge.

Then she grabs my arm, her fingers digging in like she thinks she has the right.

Revulsion flares in my chest. I wrench my arm free and spin to face her, stepping closer until she has to tilt her head to look up at me. My glare is ice-cold, my voice low and lethal.

"What the fuck do you want, Tia?" I growl, each word slicing through the space between us.

The way her confidence wavers—just for a second—is almost satisfying. Almost. But not enough to make me forget how much I despise her.

"Stay the fuck away from me, you insecure, whiny little bitch," I snap, my voice low but loud enough to draw a few curious glances from the crowd gathering around us. "I'm done with your pathetic, fucked-up antics. I don't give a damn about you or your crazy shit. Got it?"

Tia's mask slips, and what's underneath is every bit as ugly as I've always known. Beneath the makeup, fake smiles, and the charm she's perfected over years of manipulation, there's nothing but bitterness and insecurity—a hollow shell that thrives on tearing others down to feel important.

I've seen it all before. The way she zeroed in on Lola last year, ripping her apart for nothing but a cheap laugh. And what she did to Aubrey? That wasn't just mean. It was calculated and fucking vile, crossing lines no decent person would ever approach.

"And one more thing," I say, taking a deliberate step closer, my voice dropping into something darker and more dangerous.

"Stay the fuck away from Aubrey. You pull any more of your psycho shit, and it won't be her putting you on your ass. It'll be me."

Tia's eyes narrow, her arms crossing over her chest defensively as she fires back with venom. "So not only is everyone else fucking her, but now you're slumming it with everyone's leftovers?"

The words hit like a blow, but I don't let it show. Instead, I let a slow, deliberate smirk curl across my lips, leaning in just enough to make my words hit harder. "Still better than your sorry, sloppy cunt any day," I say, my tone calm but dripping with venom. "So fuck off and get out of my face."

Her mouth falls open, but I don't stick around to hear whatever bullshit she's about to spit next. Cheers erupt as the teams take the field, and I take that as my cue to get the hell out of there.

I stride toward the bleachers, spotting Jace and Reece where they've staked out their seats. Their conversation stops the moment I approach, Jace's grin growing wide and smug.

"Ah, lovers' quarrel?" he drawls, arching a brow like he's delivered the line of the fucking century.

I flash him a smirk, cold, calculated and empty as shit, more for show than anything real. "Hardly," I snap, my tone like ice. It's a clear warning, but knowing Jace, it'll only encourage him to push harder.

———

As the team roars with victory, the night's next chapter is already written: party time at Dylan's house. Music, booze, and a celebration where getting our dicks serviced is practically a tradition. It's just what we do.

I slide into my car, Jace and Reece piling in after me, their buzz already kicking from the cheap shit they downed in the parking lot. The music blasts as I crank the volume, the cool night air whipping through the open windows. Jace and Reece are hyped, trading crude plans for the night—who they want to fuck, who's the easiest target.

Jace laughs about convincing some chick to try anal, while Reece ticks off names like he's picking from a goddamn drive-thru menu. They're loud, obnoxious, and completely in the moment.

But my mind isn't here. It's on Aubrey. I wonder what she's doing right now.

"Nicole just text," Reece says, yanking me back to reality. "She wants to know if you're coming tonight. Sounds like she's ready to go. Noah's definitely getting his cock sucked tonight," he adds with a smug grin, glancing at Jace for backup.

I force a smirk, pretending to match their energy, but it feels hollow. Normally, the idea of getting my dick sucked would be a no-brainer—a guaranteed distraction. But since Aubrey came back into my life, it's like a switch flipped, and I'm left questioning who and what I am.

She's the one I want.

Not Nicole, not some random girl desperate for attention. It's been clear for a while now that every hookup has been the same—a cheap, meaningless high that fades too fast. And Nicole? She's just another one of Tia's bitchy lapdogs, probably angling for the crown now that Tia's is slipping. The thought of being with her feels like settling for scraps when I already know what I want.

The car slows as we turn onto Dylan's street, and the party energy hits immediately. People spill out of cars, cross the road in packs, and cluster near the house. Dylan's speakers are already blasting, the bass shaking the block.

I find a spot and park.

The second we step out, the sharp smell of weed cuts through the air. Leo, one of the guys from the football team, waves us over, holding out a blunt. I stop to take a few quick hits, the smoke burning my lungs before I hand it back and follow the others inside.

The house is packed, bodies pressed together in every corner, the air thick with sweat, alcohol, and chaos. Colored LEDs flash through the haze, painting everything in deep reds and blues. The bass thunders so loud it feels like the walls are alive.

Reece shoves a drink into my hand as we navigate the crowd, and I down it without hesitation. The alcohol burns its way down, settling in my chest, but it doesn't do shit to quiet the chaos in my head.

Aubrey's still there, her name etched into every thought, impossible to ignore. And no amount of weed, booze, or meaningless fucking hookups is going to drown her out tonight.

I spot Nicole across the room, her eyes locking onto mine over the rim of her cup as she takes a slow, deliberate sip. It's calculated, leaving no room for doubt. She's a sure thing tonight. We've never hooked up before, but I've heard enough stories about her being wild in bed to be curious. Back when Tia ran things, Nicole and her cheer squad stayed in line—probably because Tia threatened to ruin anyone who dared so much as to look at me.

Reece and I grab another drink, settling near a couch as the room buzzes with heat and chaos. Bodies grind together like they're fused, couples tangled in corners, and girls lap-dancing like it's their full-time fucking job. We lean against the armrest, my posture casual but intentional. I make a point of turning slightly away from Nicole—a subtle move, but one that sends a clear message: I'm not easy pickings. If she wants me, she'll have to work for it. And when she does, she'll give in completely. No strings, no games, and no bullshit.

I take a slow sip of my drink, the burn steadying me as my grip tightens on the cup. Reece elbows me in the ribs, sharp and sudden, nearly making me spill my drink.

"Oops, my bad, dude," he says with a laugh, barely glancing my way as his eyes scan the room, already on the hunt.

"Asshole," I say, smirking back, though my mind is elsewhere. It doesn't take long to figure out why he nudged me. Nicole and some other chick are making their way over.

Nicole stops in front of me, her top so tight it's barely holding her tits in place. It's blatant and fucking desperate—exactly what I expected.

But her friend? She's different. My eyes flick to her, taking her in. Long black hair, a fitted black t-shirt hugging her curves, skinny jeans, and boots that look eerily similar to the ones Aubrey wears. She's not from our school—I'd remember someone like her. The fact that Nicole's hanging out with someone like this throws me. She doesn't have a face caked in make-up, like the rest of Tia's crew. It's fucking ironic though, considering how Nicole and her clique love to rip on Aubrey for dressing the same way.

"Who's your friend?" I ask, deliberately ignoring the way Nicole is angling herself closer to me, practically begging for attention.

For a split second, her face tightens, irritation flashing before she forces a sweet tone. "This is my cousin, Nina," she says. "She's staying with us for a few weeks."

Just as I'm about to say hi, Reece beats me to it, sliding off the couch and stepping into the moment like it's his goddamn stage. Of course he does. Reece has that effortless charm that girls eat up, and Nina's no exception. Her lips curve into a smile as he offers to grab her another drink.

I watch as they disappear into the crowd, leaving me alone with Nicole.

Nicole wastes no time. She twirls a lock of her hair around her finger, her eyes locking on me like a predator sizing up prey. Fuck me, could she be any more obvious? I finish my drink, watching her over the rim of the cup, letting her squirm under the weight of my indifference. When I lower it, she steps closer, practically pressing her body against mine.

"You want to find a room and have a bit of fun?" she purrs, her voice dripping with fake seduction.

I let a slow smirk curl my lips, dragging it out, making her wait. "I don't know," I say, daring her to lay it all out for me.

She leans in, lowering her voice to a sugary sweet whisper. "I was thinking we could go somewhere more private." Her tone might be syrupy, but the hunger in her eyes betrays her.

"Why?" I ask, my voice sharp, leaning into the asshole card. If she wants this, she's going to have to work for it. I'm not making it fucking easy— not for her, not for anyone.

Her expression falters for a second—hesitation flickers, then irritation. Nicole's not used to this. I've heard enough locker room talk to know that guys practically throw themselves at her, and why wouldn't they? She's hot, and she knows exactly how to use it. But the way her face shifts, like she's grappling with the effort it takes to spell out the obvious—it's almost enough to make me laugh.

"Surely you don't want me to say it out loud?" she whispers, glancing around as if anyone here gives a shit. The couples grinding against each other in plain view don't give a fuck. She brushes her fingers up my chest, nails skimming over my shirt, her voice dropping lower, oozing with faux seduction. "I thought we could hook up. I could suck your cock, you know."

My gaze drifts past her, spotting Reece and Nina still talking across the room. The contrast between them and this shit playing out in front of me is almost laughable. I shift my attention back to Nicole, smirking, though it doesn't reach my eyes. "Yeah, okay," I say, pushing off the couch and letting my empty cup drop to the floor. "Let's go find a room."

Nicole practically lights up, her eagerness so fucking obvious it's embarrassing. She sways her hips as she leads the way, her skirt barely covering anything, the clack of her thigh-high boots echoing on the floor. It's so exaggerated it feels like she's acting out a scene from some cheap porno.

I trail behind, dragging my feet as she starts testing doors in the hallway, one after another, as if her life depends on it. Open, shut, huff. Locked or occupied. The desperation rolling off her is suffocating.

I lean against the wall, arms crossed, watching the spectacle with barely concealed amusement. She's so caught up in her frantic search for a room that she doesn't even notice. It's pathetic, really.

For a moment, my mind drifts to Aubrey. She never had to try this hard. Everything about her is raw and genuine, unpolished in a way that makes her unforgettable. And yet here I am, stuck in this hallway with someone who couldn't mean less to me, while the one person I actually give a shit about is at my place right now, probably not thinking about me at all.

She finally finds a room, her face lighting up like she's hit the fucking jackpot. With a quick glance over her shoulder to make sure no one's watching, she turns to me, breathless and way too eager. "Come on," she says, grabbing my hand like this is some grand romantic moment instead of the desperate fuck it actually is.

Her fingers curl around mine, firm and insistent, as she tugs me toward the open door. I follow, deliberately dragging my feet, slow enough to make her glance back with a flicker of irritation. She's too eager, too sure of herself, like getting me alone is her big win. It's fucking pitiful.

The room is small, dimly lit by a single lamp on a cluttered desk. The air reeks of weed and stale beer, and the bed's already a mess, blankets half-hanging onto the floor. She shuts the door behind us, leaning against it with a smug smile that screams victory, like she's already sealed the deal.

"Finally," she says, stepping closer, her hands finding their way to my chest. "You have no idea how long I have waited for this."

I stare down at her, letting her think she's in control, but there's a weight in my chest I can't ignore. This isn't going to fix it. It never fucking does.

Her hands linger, sliding over me like she's trying to claim something, but all I can think about is Aubrey. How her touch burned like fire. It mattered. It was real, even if it fucks me up in the end.

I force a smirk, playing the role she wants me to. "So, what now?" My voice is low, my eyes locked on hers, waiting to see just how far she'll go to keep this charade alive.

She steps closer, her body pressing into mine, her hands sliding down to my belt with practiced ease. Her confidence returns, her moves calculated and deliberate, every touch dripping with entitlement. She gazes up at me through thick lashes, her lips curving into a triumphant smirk as she sinks to her knees.

"Let me take care of you," she says. Her hands work quickly, tugging at the button of my jeans, like she's desperately trying to free my cock. Her movements are fast and assured.

This should feel good. It should be exactly what I want—her, on her knees, ready to give me everything she thinks I need. But it doesn't. The moment her tongue flicks out to wet her bottom lip, something inside me twists. Not with pleasure, but with a sick, sinking realization.

I don't want this.

I don't want her.

The way she looks at me, like I'm just another trophy for her collection, makes my stomach churn. I'm standing here, but my mind is somewhere else, my body completely detached. All I can see is Aubrey—her touch, her voice, the way her body fit against mine like she belonged there.

Not Nicole. Not this.

Aubrey.

The thought of her is too strong, burning through me, making it impossible to feel anything but the hollow, undeniable truth:

I don't want this.

I want Aubrey.

"Get the fuck off me," I growl, yanking her back, hard and fast, before she can start anything. The force sends her stumbling, her balance gone in an instant. She lands flat on her ass with a dull thud.

The shock on her face is immediate—wide eyes, lips parted as her breath catches in her throat. It only lasts a moment before her expression hardens, anger replacing surprise. "What the fuck is your problem?" she snaps, her voice sharp as she pushes herself up from the floor.

"My problem?" I bite back, my voice rising as I glare down at her. "I don't fucking want you. So why don't you take the goddamn hint and get the fuck out of here? Go find another dick to suck."

Her nostrils flare, her cheeks burning red with a mix of rage and humiliation. She sneers, trying to hide the sting of rejection under a mask of anger. "Fuck you, you fucking asshole" she spits, venom dripping from her words. She storms past me, her movements jerky and uncoordinated, slamming the door behind her so hard the frame rattles.

The silence that follows feels deafening, the echoes of the door slam cutting through the distant thrum of the party.

What the fuck am I doing here?

The question reverberates in my head, louder than the music, louder than the pointless noise of the crowd outside this room. It's not Nicole. It's not this house full of strangers and distractions that don't mean a damn thing. It's Aubrey. She's the one I should be with. The one who's probably sitting at home, alone.

I should've told her today. Should've stopped being a goddamn coward and laid it all out—how I feel, how she's everything to me. But the thought of her looking at me with anything less than what I feel for her had me choking on the words before they could form.

Fuck that. She needs to know. Even if it means she doesn't love me back the way I love her.

I shove my way out of the room, through the throng of partygoers—couples tangled on couches, groups shouting over music I can't even hear. My chest is tight, adrenaline spurring me forward. By the time I reach the front door, I'm practically running.

Sliding into my car, I grip the steering wheel tightly, my thoughts racing as fast as my pulse.

Pizza. I'll grab a pizza. Something we can share while I finally grow a pair and say what I've been too scared to admit. Pineapple. She used to love pineapple on her pizza. Does she still? Fuck it. I'll get it anyway. If she hates it, at least it'll be something to laugh about.

Twenty minutes later, I'm back home. I toe off my shoes by the front door and walk down the hall, the pizza box warm in my hands. With every step toward the spare room—her room—my heart beats harder, faster.

Her door is slightly ajar, the soft glow of a desk lamp spilling out into the hallway. I stop in front of it, frozen for a moment, trying to get my shit together. My grip tightens on the box as I take a deep breath, exhaling slowly.

Then, steeling myself, I step forward and push the door open gently.

She's there. Sitting at her desk, head bowed over her sketchbook, completely lost in whatever world she's creating. Her hair falls around her face like a curtain, catching the soft glow of the desk lamp.

For a moment, I just stand there, leaning against the doorframe. She looks calm, peaceful—so fucking beautiful it makes my stomach twist. And I can't help but wonder if she's thought about me tonight, even once. If I've crossed her mind the way she's been tearing through mine.

I swallow hard, my throat dry, the words I've been avoiding all night threatening to choke me now. It's now or never.

I let my eyes drift to her hands, watching the way her pencil moves, bringing her sketch to life. The scene she's drawing is so familiar, and it hits me—it's the place I took her earlier today. Every line and shadow, every tiny detail, perfectly captures the moment. It's mesmerizing, the way she sees the world, the way she can make something so ordinary feel extraordinary.

Then she looks up, like she can feel me standing there.

Her eyes meet mine, and a faint smile tugs at her lips. My heart stumbles, my breath catches, and for a second, I can't move.

"I thought I smelled pizza," she says, her voice soft, teasing. Her gaze drops to the box in my hands as she sets her pencil down. When she stands, it's effortless, natural, and somehow more graceful than it has any right to be.

She crosses the room, stopping just short of me, her head tilting as she lifts the lid of the box. "Did you get pineapple?" she asks, her tone light, playful. When she spots the golden chunks scattered across the cheese, her face lights up, her smile stealing the air right out of my lungs. "You did. You remembered."

"Of course I remembered," I say, brushing past her with a smirk, heading for the bed. I sit, dropping the box onto my lap and making sure to leave enough room for her to sit close. The pizza was just an excuse. It's not the food I'm craving—it's her.

I pop the lid open and pull out a slice, taking a bite. The tang of pineapple and cheese hits, but my focus stays on her. Her bag is on the floor, unpacked, her things tucked neatly away. She's settled here, and something in my chest unwinds, like a knot I didn't realize was there.

Aubrey grabs a pillow, propping it against the bedframe before sitting down beside me. She leans forward, grabs a slice, and reclines back, her body sinking into the mattress like it's the only place she's meant to be.

I watch as she bites into the pizza, her soft, satisfied hum breaking the silence. The sound is so simple, so innocent. My dick reacts instantly, heat rushing through me, and I have to fight the urge to groan.

It's ridiculous how much she affects me.

Just her eating pizza, nothing overtly sexual, and yet it's enough to light me up in a way no one else ever has. My mind flashes back to Nicole earlier tonight—her touch, her desperation, how none of it even came close to moving me. But here? Now?

One sound from Aubrey, and I'm fucking gone.

"So, how did the game go?" she asks, her voice casual as she takes another bite of her slice.

"Good. We won," I reply, my tone just as casual.

Her brows knit together, forming that little furrow that always gets me.

It's such a her thing—so naturally Aubrey—that I can't help but smile. That expression takes me back to the first time I saw her through the fence, her face scrunched up in the same way.

"So why aren't you out celebrating?" she presses, her voice light but curious.

I dodge the question, shoving the rest of my pizza into my mouth like it's some kind of shield. The words are there, clawing at the walls of my chest, desperate to escape. I love you. Three fucking words that feel heavier than anything I've ever carried.

"That looks pretty damn good over there," I say instead, nodding toward her sketch on the desk. My voice is deliberately casual, steering the conversation into safer territory. It works. Her gaze shifts to the drawing, giving me a moment to breathe—and to admire her in the soft glow of her lamp. Her neck, her collarbone, the way her tank top clings to her—it's a view I could get lost in, but before I can spiral too far, her voice pulls me back.

"Yeah," she says softly, almost like she's speaking to herself. "Ever since we got back today, I've been wanting to draw it."

"What else have you got in the sketchbook?" I ask, tossing my half-eaten slice back into the box and standing.

As I approach her desk, I wipe my greasy hands on my jeans, and I see Aubrey move. Her body shifts in front of me, her hand pressing lightly against my chest. The warmth of her touch freezes me in place, the moment charged with something unspoken.

"No, Noah," she says firmly, her voice quiet but resolute. Her eyes meet mine, and I catch a glimpse of something guarded, something vulnerable she's not ready to share.

"It's just a sketchbook," I murmur, keeping my tone soft, careful not to push too hard. But her hand lingers, and her gaze flickers.

She's hesitating, her lips parting as if she wants to say something but doesn't know how. She swallows and steps back, turning away.

I think she's about to shut me down completely, to snap the book shut and lock me out. But then she surprises me.

She picks up the sketchbook, clutching it tightly as she walks back to the bed. Sitting down, she flips it open slowly, her movements deliberate.

"I'll show you," she says softly, her tone laced with caution. "But please... don't read too much into it."

Her words are careful, her gaze heavy with uncertainty. Whatever's in that sketchbook isn't just art—it's personal. A piece of her that she's debating whether to let me see.

I circle around to the other side of the single bed, placing the pizza box on the side table to clear some space. The second I sit down beside her, it feels like a live wire ignites between us, crackling and hot. Her scent—sweet and floral—clouding my mind and making it impossible to focus. My body betrays me instantly, blood surging south. I shift slightly, trying to get a grip, but it's a losing battle.

She leans in closer, settling the sketchbook between us. Her shoulder brushes mine, her warmth seeping into my skin. I try—fuck, I really try—to focus on the book, but every nerve in my body is on fire. My thoughts spiral, slipping into places I shouldn't let them go. I picture pulling her into my lap, her body pressed against mine, her breath hot against my ear. My fantasies play out in vivid detail, and the ache in my jeans only gets worse.

She turns her head, her eyes locking with mine, and for a moment, it feels as if the world has stopped spinning. Her lips move, but I barely catch her words. I'm too distracted by the way her mouth curves, soft and perfect, begging to be kissed. My mind is a mess, tangled in the need to feel her against me, to lose myself in her completely.

I grit my teeth, trying to wrestle some control, but it's no use. The fire in me is raging, and sitting here beside her, pretending to care about the sketchbook, feels like torture. Every second is a battle, and I'm losing.

I wonder what she'd do if I kissed her right now? Would she melt into me, give in the way I've been dreaming about? Or would she pull away, haunted by the same doubts and regrets that have kept us dancing around each other for so long?

I lean in slightly, the urge to close the gap between us too strong to ignore. But just as I start to move, she shifts her focus back to the sketchbook in her hands, breaking the moment. The disappointment is sharp, cutting through me like a blade. My body aches, my cock throbs, and the frustration burns hot in my chest.

Forcing myself to focus, I glance down at the sketchbook. And then I see it.

It's me.

She's drawn me with a precision and intensity that leaves me speech-less. Every detail is there—the curve of my smirk, the mess of hair falling over my forehead, the faint shadow along my jawline. It's raw, intricate, and so fucking personal. She must've spent hours on this, maybe even days.

I can't look away. My eyes drink in every detail until I feel her gaze on me, pulling my attention back to her.

She's studying me, her eyes tracing over my features like she's trying to solve some unspoken puzzle. Then her gaze drops to my lips, lingering there just a heartbeat too long.

I don't speak. I can't.

The air between us shifts, heavy and electric, thick with anticipation. When our eyes lock, it feels like time seems to freeze. Everything else fades—the room, the sketchbook, the noise in my head. It's just her. Just us.

Then, all at once, we collide. Our lips meet in a crash of heat and desperation, a spark igniting into an inferno. For a fleeting second, I brace myself for rejection, for her to pull away and rebuild the walls between us. But she doesn't. She kisses me back, her intensity matching mine, her lips soft but insistent, setting my whole body ablaze.

Her hands clutch at my shirt, pulling me closer, and when a quiet, breathy moan escapes her, it shatters something inside me. The kiss is messy, raw, and consuming, like we're pouring every unspoken word, every buried feeling into this one moment. She wants this. She fucking wants me.

The sketchbook tumbles to the floor with a forgotten thud as she melts into me, her body pressing against mine like she's trying to fuse us together. My hands find her waist, sliding over the curves that have haunted me.

When I cup her breast, her soft whimper sends a shockwave of heat, straight to my cock. My thumb brushes over her nipple, teasing before giving it the lightest pinch, and the sound she makes—a mix of surprise and pleasure—fuels the fire raging in my chest—pulling me further under her spell.

I shift, moving to climb on top of her, the need to feel every inch of her body against mine unbearable. My cock throbs painfully, the ache growing sharper as her hips move, grinding against me with deliberate, hungry movements.

A low growl escapes me as my hand slides up, my fingers curling lightly around her throat. It's not enough to hurt—just enough to hold her there, to remind her she's mine.

Her lips part in a breathless moan, her hips rolling with a rhythm that makes it impossible to think straight. She's everything—wild, beautiful, and utterly untouchable, yet here she is, unraveling beneath me. A masterpiece of lust and desire.

"I want you to take my cock," I whisper, my voice rough, barely more than a growl.

The words hit her like a match to gasoline. Her movements grow more desperate, her body arching into mine with a hunger that matches my own.

I trail kisses down her neck, along her collarbone, tasting her skin, savoring every moment. My hands move with purpose, finding the waistband of her jeans, my fingers hovering on the button. But as I pause, a small, stupid detail catches my attention and pulls me out of the haze.

Her boots.

She's still wearing those fucking boots.

Desperate to get her naked, I work swiftly to untie the laces of her boots, throwing them aside, then shifting to her jeans and lace thong. The sight of her wet, exposed pussy leaves me breathless. A surge of desire overwhelms me like a tsunami, my desire to possess her entirely growing stronger. But I grit my teeth, forcing control, knowing the wait will make this moment even more explosive.

"This too," I murmur, as I tug at the hem of her shirt, hungry to expose every inch of her.

As she lifts her arms, I strip the shirt from her body. My fingers deftly find the clasp of her bra, effortlessly undoing it to reveal her beautiful tits.

I don't hesitate. I eagerly suck on one puckered nipple, savoring the taste as my tongue dances over the sensitive peak. Her throaty moan is like a drug, consuming and captivating, stirring a deep desire for more. Fuck, that sound—her sound—is everything. Each moan is sending a searing heat through every inch of me.

I trail kisses down her trembling abdomen, each press of my lips driving me closer to madness. The warmth of her skin against mine, her breath hitching with each kiss. The scent of her arousal fills the air, intoxicating and undeniable, and I know I can't stop myself from tasting her. The urge to consume her, to lose myself in the intoxicating sweetness, the sinful flavor of her, is almost unbearable.

"Spread your fucking legs for me," I growl, the words rough and dripping with hunger.

Without hesitation, she complies, parting her thighs, exposing herself fully. Her bare and glistening pussy is the epitome of perfection.

"Fuck," I mutter, the word barely audible over the pounding of my heart. Ever since I laid eyes on her again, this image—her like this, spread open and ready, needy—has been consuming me. And now that she's here, so vulnerable and so fucking perfect, I know I'm done for. Nothing will ever compare to this. Nothing will ever compare to her.

With a shuddering breath, I lean in, my tongue teasing her clit with slow, deliberate strokes. The way her body reacts—arching off the bed, her hands gripping the sheets—is enough to make me lose my fucking mind. Her moans are like fuel to a fire that's already raging, each sound sending a jolt straight to my cock. I keep going, licking, sucking, tasting every inch of her. She's so fucking perfect and I can't get enough. Sliding two fingers inside her only makes it better, her slick walls clenching, pulling me deeper into her. The sensation drives me wild, my hunger for her growing with every gasp and cry of pleasure that spills from her lips.

The room is filled with the sultry sounds of her pleasure as I explore her clit, my fingers moving with precision, bringing her to new heights. Her hips buck against my face, desperate and demanding, her movements telling me exactly what she craves. I give her everything, swirling my tongue in slow, teasing circles before sucking her clit harder. She's close—I can feel it in the way her pussy pulses around my fingers, her breaths coming in ragged gasps. And then it happens.

She shatters beautifully, her body quivering as her pussy tightens around my fingers, her moans reverberating around the room. But I don't stop. I continue to tease her clit, savoring the moment and prolonging her ecstasy. Her taste is addictive, and the way she grinds against my face, taking everything she needs, is so fucking hot I feel like I might explode just from watching her.

Her movements slow, her body trembling as the waves of her orgasm begin to ebb. Her fingers tangle in my hair, pulling urgently, her touch burning as she yanks my head away, her body overwhelmed with sensation. I press a soft, lingering kiss to her pulsating pussy, unable to resist one last taste of her before I pull back.

When I look up, I see her chest heaving, her skin flushed a deep crimson, her eyes heavy with a drowsy satisfaction. A smirk slowly spreads across my face as I wipe my chin; her juices linger on my lips, a messy but beautiful reminder of what I've just done to her.

"That was so fucking hot," I groan, my voice thick with desire and pride. Her parted lips tremble, unable to form words, but all she can do is stare at me, her body still trembling from the aftershocks. And fuck, I've never seen anything more beautiful.

Rising to my feet, I yank my shirt over my head and toss it carelessly across the room. Her eyes immediately lock onto my chest, and I see the hunger in her gaze as it sweeps over me. With quick, deliberate movements, I kick off my shoes and peel away my jeans and boxers, letting them fall to the floor. My cock stands erect and eager for her touch, and the way her eyes linger on it sends a shiver down my spine.

As she moves onto her knees on the bed, her gaze fixed on my cock, a primal and irresistible urge stirs within me. And then she moves, sliding off the bed and standing right in front of me, so close I can feel the heat radiating from her skin.

The mere thought of Aubrey on her knees for me, surrendering completely, fills my mind with images so filthy they make my cock throb. I can't help it—I want her like that. No, I fucking *need* her like that. My thumb grazes her bottom lip; its softness contrasts sharply with the overwhelming need that thrums through me.

"Now open that fucking mouth and take my cock," I growl, my voice low and raw, thick with urgency. The command leaves no room for hesitation, no room for second-guessing. My need for her, for the feel of her lips wrapped around me, is all-consuming.

Dropping to her knees, her dark hair falls around her, she tilts her head up to look at me, and the sight takes my breath away. The raw, primal need inside me stirs as my cock twitches.

Fuck, she's perfect—so willing, so ready—and I feel like I might lose it just from the way her eyes flick between my face and my cock.

CHAPTER 22

AUBREY

I know I shouldn't be doing this with Noah again, but logic is a faint whisper, drowned out by the deafening roar of desire. I'm consumed by him, every rational thought obliterated by the fire that burns. My body still quivers from the way he just made me come—like he unlocked a part of me no one else has ever touched. The raw need in his touch, the relentless intensity of his demands, has me aching to give him everything. To watch him lose himself in me, to see him fall apart in my hands.

Our eyes lock, and I surrender completely. The way he looks at me—dark, hungry, and possessive—sends heat pooling low in my belly. A growl rumbles from his chest. The sound alone sets my pulse racing, my body yearning.

"Open," he commands, his voice rough and low, thick with unspoken promise.

My gaze drops down to his cock—long, thick, and veined, standing proud and pulsing with need. A bead of pre-cum glistens at the tip, and I can feel the restraint in him, every muscle coiled tight as he fights for control. If I don't give him what he wants soon, it will be agonizing, and fuck I want to be the one to shatter him, to push him over the edge.

I lean forward, my tongue flicking over the tip, tasting him. The salty-sweetness lingers on my tongue as his groan rips through the silence, raw and guttural. His fingers weave into my hair, gripping tightly, holding me in place as if letting go isn't an option. This side of Noah—assertive, commanding, his dominance razor-sharp—has me breathless, craving more. I've never seen him like this, and it's dangerous. Addictive. Irresistible.

I glance up, meeting his gaze as I take him into my mouth. The moment our eyes connect, something shifts. His groan deepens, rough and desperate, and it fuels me. Slowly, he pushes forward, sliding deeper, testing my limits. I hollow my cheeks, taking him further, my tongue tasting the underside of his cock.

His grip tightens in my hair, his restraint slipping with each passing second. I'm completely his in this moment, surrendering to the way he commands, the way he looks at me like I'm the only person who matters. Every inch of me burns, desperate to please him, to drive him to the point of no return.

"You look so fucking hot with my cock in your mouth," he growls, his voice rough, his words sending a shiver through me. He pushes deeper, hitting the back of my throat, holding me there. His head tips back, eyes fluttering shut for a moment as he lets himself sink into the sensation. When his gaze comes back to mine, it's raw, unrelenting, blazing with need.

Without breaking eye contact, he pulls back only to thrust forward again, the movement deliberate and desperate. He fucks my mouth with a rhythm that leaves me breathless, every thrust sending a jolt of heat straight through me. I lose myself in him, in the way he grips me, the way he claims me, the way he unravels me completely.

His grip tightens, anchoring me in place, and I surrender completely, letting him take what he needs. I relax my throat, yielding to his relentless thrusts as his groans wash over me—low, raw, and utterly unrestrained. They fuel me, each sound a spark that sets my body ablaze. I glance up, catching the way his face contorts in pleasure, and it's breathtaking. In this moment, with him unraveling above me, a truth I've buried deep rises to the surface: I've always loved him. Always. No matter how broken we are, no matter the tangled mess of our past, I always will.

I feel his cock throb against my tongue, the pulsing rhythm perfectly in sync with the guttural groans spilling from his lips. His release comes in a powerful rush, warm and unrelenting, as his thrusts slow to a deliberate, almost reverent pace. He groans my name, rough and wrecked, and the way he says it sends a sharp ache through my chest—a want, need, craving. I want him. All of him. Inside me. Around me. Until there's nothing left but this raw, consuming need.

His grip on my hair loosens, his fingers relaxing, but he doesn't let go entirely. He holds me there, his touch gentler now as he rides out the last waves of his release, every drop spilling down my throat. His gaze stays on me, heavy with something deeper—something unspoken. Even as the moment begins to fade, I feel it settling between us, an undeniable truth neither of us can say.

For a brief moment, he stills, his cock softening against my tongue as tension coils thick in the air. His fingers slide from my hair to cup my cheek, the gesture tender and fleeting. And there it is—something familiar and haunting. The look he gave me before I left, before I shattered us into pieces.

A question arises: Has he forgiven me?

The silence stretches before he finally pulls away, withdrawing from my mouth and pulling me to my feet. His arm circles my waist, firm and possessive, pressing our bodies together as though he can't bear to let go. His hand brushes the hair from my face, his thumb tracing my cheek with a tenderness that nearly undoes me. I see it—the hesitation, the flicker of vulnerability. He swallows hard, his throat working as if he wants to say something. But nothing comes.

Then, the softness is gone. His hand shifts to my throat, his dominance reasserted, as his lips collide into mine. The kiss is frantic, all-consuming as my body melts into his. His need is wild, untamed, and I'm swept away by it.

He guides me to the bed, his grip unyielding, his intent clear. He lays me down, positioning himself at my entrance, and before I can prepare, he thrusts forward in one powerful, unrelenting motion. A sharp hiss escapes me as he fills me completely, stretching me, consuming me. The sensation overwhelms my body, a mix of pain and pleasure that leaves me trembling beneath him.

He doesn't give me a moment to adjust, doesn't hold back. His hips snap against mine, his pace primal and punishing. Each thrust is a surge of raw, unchecked power, driving into me. Pain and pleasure blur into something electric, sparking through my body with every relentless stroke. I gasp, back arching as I lose myself in the storm of him.

His gaze locks onto mine, intense and unyielding, and I feel it—the way he claims me, body and soul. Every motion, every thrust, is a declaration, a reminder that no matter what's broken between us, this fire will never burn out.

My nails dig into his thigh, and the sharp sting only seems to drive him harder, faster, each thrust more brutal than the last. I can't think—there's no space for anything but him, no room for rational thought. Every movement tears me apart and puts me back together again. My body trembles as he stills for a moment, leaving me gasping, desperate for more.

"Noah, please." The words tumble from my lips, raw and broken, heavy with the weight of everything I feel. Desire, hunger, need—it all bleeds into my voice, a plea I don't fully understand. I'm not even sure what I'm asking for. More time? A deeper connection? Just him, every part of him.

His voice cuts through the charged air like a blade, low and commanding, a dark promise woven into every word. "If you want it..." His hand grips my chin, tilting my face so I'm forced to meet his gaze. "Then take it."

Before I can process his words, he flips us with a swift, fluid motion. A startled squeal escapes me, and my heart pounds as realization hits—he's giving me control. Daring me to take it. The shift in power ignites something wild within me.

I don't hesitate. My hips roll, taking in every inch of him completely, every movement driving me deeper into a haze of pleasure. Each shift sends jolts of arousal as my body finds its rhythm.

"Fuck," he groans, the sound guttural and unrestrained, his hands sliding up my body, claiming me inch by inch. His fingers pinch my nipple, a sharp jolt of pleasure tearing through me, and I can't help the moan that spills from my lips. His voice drops, darker now, dripping with authority. "Play with your pussy," he orders.

My hand moves instinctively, sliding between my legs, and the instant my fingers find my clit, the intensity spikes. Each stroke sends sharp bursts of pleasure through me, the sensation of his cock filling me mixing with the heat of my touch. It's too much and not enough all at once.

"That's it," he urges, his voice strained as he watches. "Rub that little clit. I want to feel you fucking explode."

I'm lost in the sensations, my body moving on autopilot as I chase the release dangling just out of reach. His hands grip my waist, guiding me. His groans fill the air like music. His words are like gasoline poured on the fire raging within me.

"Yeah, ride me just like that. Fuck yourself on my cock—take it all. You know this pussy's mine, don't you? Show me how bad you fucking want it."

His dominance, his raw, unfiltered need, pushes me over the edge, my hips moving faster, my fingers working my clit with frantic urgency. Wet sounds fill the room, the heavy slap of our bodies colliding in rhythm with his deep, guttural groans. Sweat slicks over my skin, my muscles trembling, but I don't stop. Can't stop.

Each thrust drives me higher, his cock hitting places so perfect, so deep, I lose myself in the spiral of pleasure. My finger moves faster, winding me to the breaking point. I'm teetering on the edge, and when it snaps, it's going to destroy me.

I'm close.

So fucking close. One more stroke, one more thrust, and I know I'll fall apart completely in the fiery chaos of him.

With a low, feral growl, Noah pushes my hand away, replacing it with his own.

His fingers move with precision, finding a rhythm that consumes me. A desperate moan tears from my lips, raw and unrestrained, as he strokes with skill and relentless focus. My hips buck against him, chasing the pleasure he's expertly drawing out of me. And then he finds it—that spot that makes me cry out, a sound so primal and needy it shocks even me.

"More," I gasp, the word barely audible over the pounding of my heart. My voice is ragged, dripping with desire, and he doesn't hesitate. His pace quickens, his touch rougher—exactly what I crave. My body burns, building higher and higher. I ride the wave, clinging to him, until it finally crashes down.

My orgasm hits me, ripping through me with devastating force. My back arches, my body trembling and shuddering as I call out his name, loud and unfiltered. There's no stopping it, no containing the ecstasy. My walls tighten around him, pulling him deeper, as I shatter completely, coming undone in his hands.

Before I can catch my breath, Noah flips us over with effortless strength. His hands grip my ass, and he takes control. I spread my legs wider, surrendering to him, offering myself completely. My eyes lock onto his, and I can't look away.

His face is a mask of raw desire, his lips parted as deep, guttural sounds escape him. He pushes back inside, filling me completely, claiming me with every rough, perfect thrust. And I think I might just break apart.

His mouth crashes down on mine, fierce and demanding. It's not a kiss—it's a storm. All-consuming, leaving me dizzy, trembling beneath him. I yield completely, lost in the fire of his touch, the way his body commands mine without hesitation.

Each thrust feels like a declaration, a conquest. He's marking me, claiming me as his. I moan into his mouth, swallowing the savage groans spilling from him. His need is palpable, reflected in every kiss, every bite, every rough stroke.

Noah moves faster, harder, his body driving into mine with a force that makes the bed creak beneath us. My legs tighten around his waist, pulling him deeper, and I lose myself in him—his heat, his power, the way he knows exactly how to fuck me.

Finally, with one last, brutal thrust, he pulls out, a sharp growl tearing from his throat. His hand moves over his cock, pumping it as he releases over me, marking my stomach with his cum. He groans, the sound guttural, animalistic, as his gaze locks onto the mess he's made.

"Fuck, look at you," he says, his voice rough and low, still heavy with arousal. He strokes himself one last time, pumping out every drop, his eyes fixed on me. "So fucking hot dripping with my cum like you were made for it. I'd cover every inch of you if I could. That's my mark on you."

For a moment, he stays there, staring at me, his chest heaving with every breath. His gaze is unreadable, and an icy dread grips me in an instant. My mind flashes back to the equipment room, to the second he walked away. The second he treated me like nothing more than a fleeting moment. A mistake to be left behind.

My heart sinks as he turns away, reaching down to grab his shirt from the floor. *This is it. He's going to leave again, just like before.* That hollow ache creeps in, familiar and unwelcome, wrapping around my chest like a vice.

But to my surprise, he turns back.

Without a word, he kneels by the side of the bed. I blink at him, caught off guard, as he uses his shirt to wipe the streaks of cum from my stomach. His touch is soft, the fabric dragging gently over my skin. It's such a simple act, but the tenderness in it stirs something deep. Like he's taking care of me in a way I didn't expect, in a way I didn't know I needed.

When he's done, he doesn't pull away immediately. Instead, he leans down, pressing a tender kiss to my bare pussy. The touch is light, reverent even, and just when I think it's over, his tongue flicks against my swollen clit—teasing, taunting. A low groan escapes me before I can stop it, my body arching involuntarily toward him, desperate for more of his touch.

He pulls back just enough to look up at me, his dark eyes glinting with satisfaction. That sexy, infuriating smirk spreads across his face—the one that says he knows exactly what he's doing, knows exactly the effect he has on me. And damn it, he's right. My body responds to him like it's his to command, and the worst part is, I don't want to fight it. Not now. Not with the way he's looking at me.

And fuck, I hate how much I love it.

I don't move, my body heavy with exhaustion, every limb feeling weighted and slow. My chest tightens, and my vision blurs as tears threaten to spill over. The ache in my chest feels unbearable, an emptiness so vast it swallows me whole.

Noah's hard to read now. Once I knew every nuance of him—his thoughts, his fears, his dreams. Now, he's a puzzle with too many missing pieces, a mystery I can't quite solve, no matter how hard I try. And that realization only makes the ache worse.

I watch as Noah climbs back into the bed. Without hesitation, he wraps his arms around me, pulling me into him like I belong there, like he needs me just as much as I need him. I close my eyes, letting the warmth of his embrace calm me.

There's something unspoken in this moment, something fragile and achingly real. I don't dare move or breathe too hard, afraid it might shatter.

Our eyes meet, locking in a silent conversation that feels heavier than anything words could carry. His gaze softens, and in it, I see a flicker of something I can't name—something I don't dare hope for.

Then, without warning, he leans in. His lips brush against mine in a kiss so soft, so tender, it makes my chest ache in a whole new way. This isn't hunger or lust—it's something deeper. A connection. A solace. It cracks something open inside me, stirs emotions I've buried so deep I didn't think I'd ever feel them again.

A tear slips silently down my cheek, and I don't bother to wipe it away. I *love* him. I always have. And as much as it terrifies me to admit it, I can't keep it locked inside anymore. My heart aches with the weight of everything I want to say, with the fear that he'll never feel the same way. But I can't hold it back. I need him to know. Even if he doesn't reciprocate. Even if this moment is all we'll ever have.

"I need to tell you something," I whisper, my voice trembling. My heart pounds, each beat a desperate plea for courage. "Noah... my heart has always belonged to you. Even when I left. Even when I tried to forget. It's always been you. I love you, Noah." My voice cracks, the words carrying a lifetime of emotions.

Noah lifts his hand, his fingers brushing a tear from my cheek, the touch so gentle it almost breaks me. I hold my breath, my heart pounding like a fucking drum in my chest as I wait for him to say something—anything. The silence stretches out, each second dragging me deeper into uncertainty, like the moment could shatter if I breathe wrong.

His expression shifts, the hard edges of his face softening just enough for something real to bleed through. His hand lingers on my cheek, trembling slightly, and for a second, I think he might pull away.

"I..." He pauses, his throat working as he struggles to find the right words. Then, finally, he exhales sharply, like he's ripping off a Band-Aid. "I love you too, Aubrey. I never fucking stopped loving you."

His voice is low, just above a whisper, but it crashes into me like a wrecking ball, knocking the air from my lungs. Relief hits hard and fast, that makes my head spin. I search his eyes, desperate for confirmation that this isn't just a moment, a slip of vulnerability he'll regret later.

And there it is.

The truth. Bare and raw, staring back at me like it's been there all along, waiting for me to see it. He's always loved me. Even through the shit we've been through, even when we were apart and everything felt broken—he still loved me.

"You... you mean that?" I whisper, my voice breaking slightly, still scared to believe it.

Noah's thumb grazes my cheek again, his gaze locked on mine. "Yeah," he says, his voice low but steady. "I mean it. I've always loved you, Aub. Even when everything turned to shit."

"I thought you hated me," I whisper, my voice barely holding steady.

"I tried to, at first, but I can't, Aubrey. No matter how hard I tried, I just couldn't." Noah's voice is rough, edged with the kind of honesty that hits me right in the chest. "You've always been it for me. Even when I was too much of an asshole to admit it."

I can't breathe. The vulnerability in his voice, the unguarded truth—it's like nothing I've ever heard from him before.

Before I can find the words to respond, he leans in. His lips capture mine in a kiss so tender, so real. His mouth moves against mine slowly, deliberately, like he's trying to tell me everything he's never been able to say with words.

The kiss deepens, and I feel it—the weight of his love, his regret, his need—all wrapped up in this moment. It's not just a kiss. It's a confession, a plea, a promise.

I wake earlier than usual, my body still sore from another long night of hot, heated sex. The ache is a sweet reminder of everything Noah did to me—every touch, every kiss, every filthy word whispered against my skin. Since I told him I loved him, everything feels different. Deeper. Rawer. It's like we're channeling every unspoken emotion into each other, carving it into our bodies with every moment. I see it in the way he fucks me—with passion, with purpose, with love.

Rolling over carefully, the sheets slide against my bare skin, cool and soft. I smile when I see him still sleeping. My eyes roam over his face, memorizing every detail—the strong line of his jaw, the faint scruff dusting his chin, the curve of his lips. God, those lips. The same ones that worshipped me last night, that kissed every inch of me with a devotion so dirty, it still sends heat flaring low in my stomach.

My gaze drifts lower, the steady rise and fall of his bare chest as he breathes. The early morning light filters through the curtains, casting shadows over the hard planes of his muscles, making him look impossibly beautiful. He's at peace, utterly at ease.

In this moment, he's everything. Perfect and real, raw in his stillness. Like the world narrows to just this—just us.

The sudden urge to capture him, to immortalize this exact moment, grips me fiercely. I need to draw him. Noah stripped down to his raw beauty.

Carefully, I slip out of bed, my movements slow and deliberate so not to disturb him. The coolness of the floor contrasts with the warmth of the bed, but I barely notice it. My eyes sweep the room, searching for my sketchbook. Then I remember—last night.

I was showing Noah my sketches, and in the heat of the moment, I didn't care where the book ended up.

Scanning the room, I spot it half-hidden beneath a tangle of discarded clothes near the bed. I kneel, reaching for it, my fingers brushing the pages with a rush of relief. I flip through the drawings quickly, checking for any damage, but every line, every shadow remains untouched. Perfect.

Just like him.

I move around the room quietly, gathering my clothes from where Noah tossed them in last night's haze. Pulling on my shirt and jeans, I grab my notebook and charcoal pencils before settling at the end of the bed.

Exhaling, I flip open the book to a blank page. My fingers take over, moving instinctively as if they've been waiting for this moment. The first lines are light and tentative, outlining the gentle slopes of his face and the strong angles of his jaw.

Line by line, shadow by shadow, I lose myself in the process. I blend the charcoal, perfecting the delicate curve of his lips, the faint scruff along his chin, the unruly strands of hair that fall across his forehead. With each stroke, Noah's image emerges on the page, just as he is now.

I'm so immersed in the drawing that I don't notice he's awake until I glance up. His eyes are open, watching me, his expression soft and unreadable. That look—it's the one that undoes me every time. It's not just heat or desire; it's something far deeper. Like he's peeling back every layer of me and loving what he finds.

"Hey," I say softly, a smile tugging at my lips.

He doesn't respond right away, just keeps staring at me, his gaze flicking from my face to the sketchpad in my lap. A slow, lazy smile spreads across his face—pure Noah.

"You couldn't resist, huh?" His voice is rough with sleep, teasing but tender.

"Stay still, or I'll have to start over," I murmur, trying to fight the heat rising in my cheeks.

But Noah just stretches, his smirk deepening. "Come here," he says, his tone low and inviting.

Without hesitation, I set the sketchpad aside and crawl back onto the bed. He pulls me against him, his arms wrapping around me in that effortless way of his, and I melt into his warmth, letting the world fade away.

The sound of the front door opening shatters the moment. My stomach drops. Shit. It's Noah's dad—and he's not alone. I can hear his voice, low and steady, mingling with someone else's. Probably his girlfriend.

I freeze, staring at Noah, who's still sprawled across the bed like nothing's wrong.

"You should get up. Now," I hiss, panic clear in my voice.

Noah just smirks lazily, as if I'm overreacting.

"Seriously, Noah," I snap, grabbing his arm and tugging him upright. My pulse is racing, and I'm already mentally bracing for the fallout if his dad walks in and finds us like this.

Noah groans in protest but doesn't fight me. I toss his jeans at him, my movements frantic. My eyes scan the room, searching for his shirt, and then my heart sinks. I remember exactly where it is—used to wipe his cum off my stomach last night. Great. Just fucking great.

When I glance up, Noah's already buttoning his jeans, his smirk as casual as ever. He steps toward me, so composed it's almost maddening, and presses a kiss to the top of my head like we're not in the middle of a damn crisis.

"Don't panic," he says, his voice low and steady, like he's got everything under control. "He won't come looking for us while he has Simone here."

With that, Noah slips out of the room and heads across the hallway into his bedroom. I stand there for a moment, my nerves still on edge, and turn to face the mirror above the dresser. My hair is a mess, my cheeks flushed from the rush of everything. I run my fingers through my hair, trying to smooth it down, as if that'll somehow make me look more put-together.

I'm still trying to get my breathing under control when I spot him in the reflection, moving back into the room with a fresh shirt pulled over his head. Before I can say anything, he's right behind me, slipping an arm around my waist, pulling me back against his chest.

His mouth finds the side of my neck, his breath warm and teasing as he presses a soft kiss to my skin.

"We should probably go out there," he murmurs. His lips brush against my neck one last time before he pulls back slightly. "Relax, everything will work out."

I nod, though the tightness in my chest and the unease twisting in my stomach don't go away. Noah squeezes my waist gently, his touch grounding me, and I feel my pulse settle just a little.

"Trust me," he says, his voice firm, the assurance in it something I can't quite argue with.

CHAPTER 23

NOAH

I knew Dad wouldn't have a problem with Aubrey staying. He's always had a soft spot for her, like he sees something in her that most people miss. I don't know why she was so nervous—he'd help her in a heartbeat, no questions asked. And seeing him with Simone. It actually made me happy. She's good for him, the kind of genuine nice that doesn't feel forced. That afternoon, the four of us just hung out—simple, easy, no drama. Dad even pulled out an old board game we used to play when Aubrey stayed over as kids. It was like stepping into the past, only now, everything between us is completely different.

Ever since Aubrey told me she loved me, something shifted. Something deeper, more intense, and completely undeniable. Those three words hit me like a punch to the chest, knocking the air right out of me. When she said it, time froze. I had to make sure I wasn't dreaming because hearing her say it... Fuck. Her love is all I've ever wanted, even when I was too much of a goddamn idiot to admit it to myself.

There's no way to describe how it feels to know the one person who's owned your heart all these years feels the same. What we have now... it's more than it ever was. It's no longer innocent; it's raw, consuming, and fueled by everything we've been through. Our love burns hotter, and every time I'm with her, I'm reminded of how good it feels to lose myself in her completely.

I crave her touch like it's the only thing keeping me grounded, and I know she feels it too. It's in the way her hands cling to me, desperate, like she can't get close enough. It's in the way her eyes hold mine, like I'm her whole world. I'm addicted to her—every smile, every sound, every fucking inch of her—and I know, without a doubt, Aubrey is just as addicted to me.

Yeah, even on the day when my dad came home with Simone, I couldn't resist, fucking her until the early hours of the morning. Couldn't get her out of my head, couldn't stop thinking about all the filthy things I wanted to do to her. The way she moves on me, the way she gives herself over to it completely, it's fucking intoxicating. She comes alive on my cock, moaning uncontrollably even when she's trying so hard to keep quiet.

I had to cover her mouth with my hand when she came, her body trembling against mine. God, it was everything. I'm pretty sure my dad must've heard her—there's no way he didn't. Not that he'd ever say anything. That's not his style. He knows we're together anyway. Saw us holding hands when we came out to meet Simone. I could feel his eyes on us, watching, probably connecting the dots.

I know how this works. He'll want to have a talk soon, pull me aside for one of those fatherly conversations about respect and responsibility.

It's been a few days, and Aubrey and I are starting to find our rhythm again. It's far from perfect—hell, it's messy and complicated—but there's something steady beneath it all. Like we're learning how to be us again. Piece by piece, we're rebuilding what was broken. And I'll take it, no matter how slow the process.

I can tell she's worried about going back to school, even if she won't say it outright.

It's there in the way her shoulders stiffen when she thinks I'm not paying attention, in the way she changes the subject anytime it comes up. No one at school knows about us—what she means to me. And while she's been sitting out her suspension, the rumors have already started swirling.

I've heard the shit people are saying. Every word makes my blood fucking boil. Tia, Nicole, and their crew of bitches are behind it; I'd bet my life on that. The nasty shit they're spreading about Aubrey makes me want to march right up to them, slam their faces into their lockers, and tell them to shut the fuck up. Maybe even leave a dent in the metal, just to make sure they get the message.

But I didn't. Not because I didn't want to, but because Aubrey wouldn't want me to fight her battles for her. She's strong like that, even when she shouldn't have to be. Still, when she walks back into that school tomorrow, I'm going to make sure those assholes have something real to talk about.

I've never given a shit about petty high school drama. Making statements isn't my thing. But this? Us. It's different. I want Aubrey to know I've got her back, no matter what. And I want everyone else to understand one simple truth—she's mine. So fuck Tia. Fuck Nicole. Fuck their jealous, petty bullshit, and fuck anyone else who has a problem.

I'm sitting in my car outside Aubrey's workplace, staring at the empty parking lot, my thoughts spinning. My phone buzzes on the seat next to me. I glance at the screen—an unknown number.

My jaw tightens. *Who the fuck is texting me?*

I open the message, and the second I read it, anger tears through me like a raging storm.

How the fuck did this bitch even get my number?

I grip the steering wheel hard, my chest heaving as I try to keep my cool. But the words are already burning in my brain, lighting a fire I can't put out.

Unknown Number: Noah, please, I want to talk to you. You have a brother and a sister who want to meet you.

The text makes my pulse pound. My thumbs fly over the screen, hammering out a response: Fuck off.

I hover over the send button, my finger twitching with the urge to hit it. To throw the words back at her and let her know exactly what I think. But then I pause, my hand shaking as I hesitate.

Why give her the satisfaction of knowing she got to me?

With a frustrated exhale, I delete the message and block her number. She can crawl back to wherever the fuck she came from. I wish she'd stop pretending like she suddenly gives a shit, like she wants to play happy fucking families.

My grip tightens on my phone before I toss it back onto the passenger seat. The lingering anger refuses to fade, buzzing under my skin like a live wire.

Voices pull me out of my spiraling thoughts, and my gaze snaps up. Aubrey's walking toward me, her stride confident, but my focus immediately locks on the person beside her. Jace. That smug asshole.

They're deep in conversation, her face turned toward him as she talks, her body language relaxed. My jaw tightens. I trust Aubrey—of course I do—but Jace? Not a fucking chance.

I've seen the way he operates, the slick smile, the smooth lines, the calculated charm he uses to manipulate girls into giving him exactly what he wants. My stomach twists at the thought of him trying that shit on Aubrey. She's too smart to fall for it, but that doesn't mean I don't hate the idea of him trying.

Then it fucking happens. The bastard reaches out, his hand landing on her shoulder. My fingers curl around the door handle, itching to step out and handle it. I could use the release—a fight would burn off the frustration still boiling from hearing from my mother.

But I don't move. Not yet.

Because before I can react, Aubrey does. She steps away from him, sharp and deliberate, brushing him off with a precision that makes me pause. I freeze, watching as she speaks to him, her stance tense but unshaken. Whatever she says makes his smug smile falter, and then she turns, walking straight toward the car.

Jace doesn't follow. He doesn't move at all. He just stands there, watching her, his gaze lingering far too long. Like he has any fucking right.

Anger surges through me, clawing at my chest as Aubrey slides into the passenger seat.

"What the hell was that about?" I snap, my voice sharper than I intend. My eyes are locked on Jace, his figure still frozen in the distance. "What did that asshole say to you?"

Aubrey exhales sharply, her tone calm but firm. "I told him to keep his hands off me and that he's not to do it again."

Her answer satisfies me, but it doesn't douse the fire raging inside. I nod, gripping the steering wheel as I turn the key. The engine roars to life, the sound matching the irritation simmering just beneath my skin.

I throw the car into gear and pull out of the parking lot, the tires squealing slightly against the pavement. Every move I make is laced with the anger I can't quite shake, the image of Jace's hand on Aubrey replaying in my head like a fucking taunt.

It's not just Jace's hand on her—it's everything. The message from my mother earlier, the way she keeps clawing back into my life after disappearing for years. After all this time? What the fuck makes her think she can waltz back in like nothing happened?

Aubrey's hand finds the back of my neck, her touch soft, grounding. Her fingers move gently, easing the tight knots of tension there. My hold on the steering wheel loosens slightly as her hand slides into my hair, her fingertips working their way through the strands. It's such a simple gesture, but it pulls me out of my head for a moment—just enough to breathe.

"What's wrong?" she asks quietly.

I take a deep breath and let it out slowly. There's so much I want to say, but I hold back on mentioning Jace. Aubrey's already handled him, and I'll deal with that fucker tomorrow. Instead, I shift my focus to the other thing gnawing at me—the thing that feels like it's going to split me open if I let it.

"I got a text from my mother tonight," I begin, the words feel heavy in my mouth. "She wants to see me. Apparently, I should meet my brother and sister."

The car falls into silence, the only sound the rhythmic clicking of the turn signal as I pull onto our street.

It's the kind of silence I hate—the kind that presses down on my chest like a weight.

I pull into the driveway, the tires crunching softly against the gravel. Killing the engine, I sit there for a moment, my hands still on the wheel. Aubrey unbuckles her seatbelt and turns toward me, her gaze steady and searching, like she's trying to figure out the best way to navigate the minefield I've just laid out.

"Maybe you should meet up with her?" she suggests gently, her voice careful, like she knows she's treading dangerous ground.

I slowly turn to look at her, my jaw tightening.

"She fucking walked away, Aub," I snap, the heat in my voice sharp, though it's not meant for her. It's for my mother. "She didn't care then, so why the fuck does she care now?"

The thought of seeing her again feels like ripping open a wound that never fully healed. And now, she wants to come back with her shiny new family, expecting me to play along. No. Fuck that.

"I know she did," Aubrey says softly, her voice calm despite my anger. "But maybe if you see her face-to-face…" She pauses, choosing her words with care. "You could ask her why. Why now, after all this time, she suddenly wants to reconnect. Why does she think it matters?"

Her words sink in, stirring something I don't want to confront. Without thinking, I reach out and pull her toward me, shifting her so she's straddling my lap. Her presence steadies me in a way nothing else can.

I press my forehead against hers, closing my eyes as I grip her hips tightly.

All I want is to lose myself in her, to drown out every fucked-up thought in the heat of her body, to make it all disappear, until the ache in my chest fades.

My hand moves to her throat, firm but measured, a possessive grip that steadies me as much as it grounds her. She's mine—every inch, every breath—and I never want to let her go.

Moonlight spills through the car windows, casting a soft glow over her face, illuminating the curve of her lips and the hunger smoldering in her eyes. She holds her breath, her gaze locked on mine. Her body trembles, heat radiating from her, her entrance achingly close to my throbbing cock.

"Fuck me, Aubrey," I rasp, my voice raw and desperate. "Please... I need you." It's not just her body I'm pleading for—it's everything. The release, the salvation only she can give me. She knows that ache, that hollow void. Aubrey always understands.

With deliberate slowness, she reaches for the seat adjustment, lowering it with a smooth motion. The seat reclines, giving us more space, and she moves with it, her body pressing closer to mine.

As my hand falls from her throat, she takes charge without hesitation. Her hands move to the buttons of her work shirt, unfastening them one by one. She shrugs it off with confidence. Her bra follows, and the sight of her bare tits under the moonlight is nearly my undoing.

"Fuck," I mutter, the word catching in my throat as my gaze drinks her in. The way her nipples harden under my stare, the way her chest rises and falls with each breath—it's intoxicating. And yet, I crave more.

She moves to unbutton my jeans, her fingers deft and quick, and when she pulls my cock free, a rush shoots straight through me. My head falls back against the seat, my eyes closing as her hand wraps around me, her touch firm but teasing.

She strokes me slowly at first, the steady rhythm making my cock throb with need. Every movement pulls me further away from the weight in my chest, closer to the only escape I trust—her.

"Kiss it," I growl, my voice frayed with desperation. I move my hand to the base of my cock, aching to feel her mouth.

Aubrey doesn't miss a beat. She shifts beside me, her weight leaving my lap, and the loss is a hollow ache. But then her hand is back, firm and deliberate around my shaft. When her lips press a soft, teasing kiss to the tip, it's like lightning crackling through my veins. Her tongue flicks out, catching the bead of cum, and my breath catches.

Watching her like this, confident and utterly in control, leaves me undone in the best way. Powerless, yet utterly consumed by her.

"Keep going," I murmur, voice strained and thick with need.

I don't have to say it twice. Her lips curve into a knowing smirk, that glint of mischief in her eyes.

Her tongue swirls slowly around the sensitive tip, her movements deliberate and teasing. Each flick sends a surge of pleasure ripping through me. My stomach clenches, a guttural groan tearing free as I fight to keep my composure. It's agony and ecstasy, an exquisite torment that strips away every thought but her.

When her lips wrap tighter around the head of my cock and she sucks, a shudder ripples through me. I swear I lose a part of myself to her in that moment. The sharp throb toes the line between pain and pleasure, but it's the kind I'd surrender to again and again. My hand slides into her hair, tangling in the soft strands as I hold her steady—not just to guide her, but to anchor myself to the earth.

She parts her lips wider, stretching them around me, taking me deeper with every deliberate motion. Her tongue presses against the underside of my cock, the wet heat of her mouth drawing me further into her spell. My jaw tightens as I watch her, utterly transfixed.

I push deeper, and her throat tightens briefly before she relaxes, her resilience cutting through my control. Her eyes flick up, meeting mine, and I see the fire there—determination mixed with challenge. My restraint frays, unravels entirely.

"Fuck, Aub," I growl, my voice rough and broken. "Take it. Take all of me."

I pull back, then thrust forward again, the tension in my body coiling tighter with every movement. My head falls back briefly, my eyes squeezing shut as I savor the raw pleasure, but I force them open. I need to see her—see the way she takes me, the way she owns every second of this.

Her gaze locks with mine, and a low, growl tears from my throat. My hand tightens in her hair, a silent warning. And then I slam into her mouth, the rhythm relentless, driven by pure, aching need. She doesn't flinch, doesn't falter. Instead, she matches me, her mouth opening wider to take me deeper, her resolve unshakable.

"Holy fuck," I gasp, my chest heaving as my hips snap forward. "It feels so fucking good. I could do this every day—feed you my cock, lose myself in you." The words spill out, unfiltered and raw, because with her, there's no holding back.

She sucks harder, her lips sealing tight, her tongue working in perfect rhythm. The pressure builds, unbearable and intoxicating, until I'm trembling. My hips jerk, the pace frenzied, as I teeter on the edge.

"Fuck—Aubrey," I hiss, my voice barely more than a rasp. "You're going to make me come so fucking hard."

The tension snaps, pleasure ripping through me like a lightning strike. My body convulses, my cock pulsing as I spill into her mouth. My hips drive forward one final time, every nerve alight, every sensation magnified. She doesn't stop, her mouth working me with relentless precision, coaxing every last drop as if claiming a part of me I'll never get back.

As I collapse back against the seat, my chest heaving and body trembling—the way she's left me undone, completely and utterly hers.

I glance down at her, and the sight unravels me all over again. She's still moving, still breaking me apart piece by piece, her lips and tongue working me dry with an almost maddening precision. When her motions slow, she looks up at me, her eyes gleaming with satisfaction. She's utterly breathtaking, a fucking masterpiece.

"Fuck, Aub," I rasp, my voice hoarse, my fingers still tangled in her hair.

With a soft pop, she releases me, her lips swollen and glistening as she leans back, her breaths uneven. The sight of her—disheveled, flushed, and marked by what we've just done—sends another jolt of heat surging through me.

She shifts, climbing up to straddle me, her knees pressing into my thighs, her body warm and flush against mine. Her hands brace on my shoulders as she sits up, capturing my mouth in a kiss. It's softer than I expect, a lingering tenderness.

Between kisses, she murmurs, "We should head inside before your dad wonders what we're up to."

She grabs her shirt, pulling it on, leaving her bra forgotten on the floor. As she moves to climb off me, to open the car door, I grab her wrist, yanking her back into my arms. Our lips collide in a kiss that's anything but gentle—it's raw, desperate, a chaotic clash of teeth and tongues as I pour every messy, fucked-up feeling into her.

My hand cups the back of her neck, holding her in place like letting go would shatter me. "You have no fucking idea what you do to me."

She lets out a soft laugh, her lips brushing mine one last time before she leans back. "If your dad sees us out here too long, he'll start asking questions. And I can't mess this up, Noah. I don't want to screw this up."

Reluctantly, I shove my cock back into my jeans and step out of the car, following her into the cool night air. I watch as Aubrey straightens her clothes, her hands smoothing over the fabric like she's trying to erase the evidence of what just happened.

Her gaze flicks to mine, and I catch the flicker of worry there—the fear of fucking this up. She doesn't need to stress; my dad would never kick her out.

CHAPTER 24

AUBREY

Sleep was a fucking joke last night. My mind wouldn't shut up, replaying every worst-case scenario on an endless loop. Going back to school after my suspension? Yeah, that's the kind of shit that keeps you staring at the ceiling, chest tight, wondering what fresh hell's waiting on the other side of those doors. Halfway through the night, I couldn't take it anymore. I snuck into Noah's room—the guy with a PhD in destruction, who can wreck me in every way imaginable and put me back together with a mind-blowing orgasm. He didn't disappoint.

Now, I'm lying in his bed, his arm locked around my waist like I'm some possession he refuses to let go of. His face is buried in the crook of my neck, his breath warm against my skin. And for a moment, I let myself sink into it. Into him. Because, fuck, being here feels like everything I've ever wanted. Safe. Wanted. Loved.

It takes everything in me to pull away, to slide out from under his arm as his fingers twitch like they want to pull me back. My feet hit the floor, the cold seeping through, but I keep moving. Every step away from him feels like I'm ripping a part of myself off and leaving it behind.

But I can't stay.

Not when Ken's just down the hall. If he catches me sneaking out of Noah's room, it's game over. Ken's been too good to me—giving me a place to stay, a chance to finish school, and maybe even a shot at getting out of this fucking mess. I can't risk screwing any of that up.

Last night, after we fucked and collapsed into each other, Noah opened up about his mum. The pain in his face, the way it still lingers after all this time, cut deeper than I expected. I want to help him, which is why I suggested he meet up with her. I get it—I know what it's like to be abandoned.

Watching him wrestle with his own demons drags my own to the surface, especially the mess with my mother. I'm so fucking angry at her and that pathetic excuse for a boyfriend she clings to. They deserve each other. When he inevitably dumps her for someone else—because he will, given his track record of his womanizing bullshit—maybe she'll finally realize the mistake she made.

But I'm done.

If she ever tries to crawl back into my life, she'll get the same treatment she gave me. I'll treat her like someone I used to know. Noah feels the same way about his mother, and honestly, I can't blame him. You can only take so much before you stop letting people in.

Dressed and ready to face the day, my bag slung heavily over my shoulder, I step into the hallway. The aroma of cooking hits me instantly, a punch of nostalgia I wasn't prepared for. It pulls me back to those nights I spent crashing at Noah's house as a kid. Back then, waking up to the smell of breakfast felt like magic—like the world wasn't such a shitty place after all. Now, living here, that familiar scent has taken on a bittersweet edge, a reminder of the safety I once felt under this roof.

I make my way into the kitchen and spot Noah perched on a stool by the island bench, deep in conversation with his dad. Ken's busy at the stove, spatula in hand. Their heads turn toward me as soon as I step through the doorway.

"Good morning, Aubrey," Ken says, his voice warm and caring, the way it always is.

"Good morning," I reply, heading toward the stool beside Noah. But before I can sit, he's already on his feet, crossing the space between us. His fingers thread through mine, his touch grounding me as he leans down to press a soft kiss to my lips. It's not the usual fiery, desperate kind of kiss we share, but something quieter. Gentler. Because Ken's just a few feet away.

Without a word, Noah slides the bag off my shoulder like it's his job to carry the weight for me. He guides me to the counter and settles back into his seat, pulling me into the space beside him. It's such a small thing, but it feels massive—like he's telling me, in his own way, that I belong here. Even if part of me still struggles to believe it.

"You nervous about going back to school today, Aubrey?" Ken asks, glancing over his shoulder after he flips something on the stove.

"Yeah, a bit," I admit, fidgeting with the edge of my sleeve. "I just hope everything goes smoothly."

"It will," he says, his voice steady, reassuring. "You'll be fine. I just know it." He flashes me one of those warm, unwavering smiles that only Ken can pull off, the kind that makes you believe everything will be okay.

He plates the last pancake and carries the food over to us—pancakes, eggs, bacon, the works. "Hope you're hungry. I might've gone a little overboard this morning."

Noah snorts, a grin tugging at his lips. "He's a little nervous. Simone asked him to stay at her place this weekend and he thinks we'll starve to death while he's gone." His tone is teasing, but there's a glint of affection in his eyes when he looks at Ken.

Ken chuckles, rubbing the back of his neck in a way that betrays his unease. "You know, I am a little nervous," he admits, trying to brush it off, though the worry is written all over him.

"You'll be fine, Dad," Noah says, piling an ungodly amount of bacon and eggs onto his plate like he hasn't eaten in weeks. "It's Simone. You two have practically been glued together lately. What's there to worry about?"

Simone. She's been here nearly every afternoon when Noah and I walk through the door, her warmth and easy smile filling the space like she's always belonged. She's kind, but it's more than that. There's a steadiness to her, something that feels right. And then there's the way Ken looks at her—like she's the missing piece he never knew he needed. Like this could be it for him.

Ken lets out a long breath, his shoulders relaxing slightly. "Yeah, you're right. Everything will be fine." He grabs a pancake from the stack, rolls it up, and bites into it like he's trying to convince himself as much as anyone else.

I watch their exchange quietly, a strange warmth blooming in my chest. Moments like this—simple, easy—make it feel like maybe, just maybe, things don't always have to be so hard. Even if it's just for a little while.

I help myself to a couple of pancakes, drizzling them with maple syrup before taking a bite.

Ken mentions a few places he and Simone want to visit, and Noah nods along, tossing in a few comments to keep the conversation flowing.

What surprises me is what Noah doesn't say—there's no mention of his mom reaching out yesterday. Not even a passing reference. I can't tell if he's avoiding it or if the words are stuck somewhere he can't reach.

When Ken finishes his coffee and loads the last plate into the dishwasher, he claps Noah on the shoulder. "You two have a good day," he says, flashing me a kind smile before heading out.

Noah pockets his keys, and we follow suit.

In the car, the silence stretches thin and taut.

I sit stiffly in the passenger seat, my fingers digging into my thighs to keep them from trembling. My mind is a chaotic mess, spinning through every worst-case scenario. Tia's not going to let last week slide—there's no way. She'll retaliate, humiliate me, make sure I know exactly where I stand.

But I can't let her drag me down again. I can't afford to lose control like that, not with everything riding on me keeping my shit together. If I screw up again, it won't just be my reputation on the line—it'll be my future. My scholarship. My one shot at getting out of this mess. And losing that tuition would ruin me.

Noah pulls into the parking lot, and my stomach twists as I take in the scene. Students are scattered across the courtyard, laughing, chatting, moving toward the gates like it's just another day. For them, it probably is. For me, it's a battlefield.

The engine cuts off, and the silence in the car is deafening. Noah doesn't move. Neither do I.

He knows. I can feel it in the way he glances at me, his hand lingering on the gearshift. He can probably sense the tension radiating off me, the way my anxiety hums like static in the air.

"You ready?" he asks, his voice low, careful. He opens his door but stays put, waiting for my answer.

I take a deep breath, forcing my hands to relax. "Fuck no," I mutter, my voice low but steady. "But when has that ever stopped me?"

Noah raises a brow but doesn't say anything, his hand brushing mine briefly before he steps out of the car.

I nod to myself, swallowing the lump in my throat that feels like a goddamn rock. Stalling isn't going to make this any easier.

Sam texted me earlier this morning—buzzing with excitement about me coming back. She's been texting every day, just like the other girls in the group. This morning, she said things were "different" now. Whatever the hell that means. She wouldn't elaborate, just promised to explain when I return. Does "different" mean Tia's gone nuclear? Has she been out for blood while I've been gone? I wish Sam had just told me outright so I'd know what kind of shitstorm I'm walking into.

Noah grabs his bag from the backseat and circles around to my side. By the time he opens my door, I'm already fumbling with my own bag. Get your shit together, Aubrey. If Tia sees you cracking, she'll smell the blood in the water. Noah slides his hand into mine, his grip firm and steady.

We step into the school grounds, and immediately, I feel it—the weight of their stares. It's suffocating, pressing down on me from every direction. People always watch Noah, especially the girls, but this? This is different. It's like I've got a bullseye painted on my back, and everyone's taking aim. Even the groups lounging on the grass freeze mid-laugh to gawk, their whispers chasing us up the front steps.

I keep my eyes forward, jaw locked so tight it might crack. Fuck them. Fuck their stares, their gossip, their bullshit.

I focus on the sound of my boots against the floor as we enter the building. One step at a time. Keep moving. Keep it together.

The corridor is alive with noise—clusters of students gossiping, laughing, slamming locker doors. Others linger by their lockers, casually rummaging through their stuff like they don't have a care in the world. My gaze flicks ahead, and then I see her. Tia.

She's standing near the lockers, something white plastered to her face—probably trying to cover the bruise I gave her last week. Her little clique is gathered around her, orbiting like she's the sun in this twisted solar system. The second Noah and I come into view, all their eyes lock onto us, their stares sharp enough to cut.

As we approach, the air grows heavier, the tension thick enough to choke on. I brace myself to walk right past her, to ignore whatever venom she's about to spit. But Noah has other plans.

He stops dead in the middle of the hallway, yanking me toward him so abruptly I let out a startled gasp. Before I can ask what the hell he's doing, his arm loops around my waist, pulling me flush against him. And then his lips collide with mine.

The kiss isn't sweet or gentle. It's raw, possessive. My head spins as his tongue claims my mouth, the faint sounds of whistles and murmurs around us barely register over the blood roaring in my ears. My fingers clutch his shirt, desperate to steady myself as my knees threaten to give out.

When he finally pulls away, I'm left breathless, my lips buzzing, heart thundering. His forehead rests against mine, and his voice drops to a low, dangerous whisper.

"No one will fuck with you now that I've marked you as mine."

Those words send my pulse into overdrive. My heart slams against my ribs, the echo of his declaration still ringing in my head. I try to speak, but my throat tightens. All I can do is nod, my body betraying me as I stand there, caught in his gaze.

"Breathe," Noah murmurs, his lips brushing mine in a softer kiss, a quiet reassurance before he pulls back. "Fuck them." His hand slips into mine, tugging me toward my locker. He doesn't look around, doesn't care about the stares. He owns this fucking school, and now, somehow, I'm part of that.

As the haze from the kiss fades, I catch Tia's glare, cold and relentless. Her posse mirrors the venom on her face, but I don't care. Suck it up, bitches. He's mine. He just made that crystal fucking clear. Their scowls can't touch me—they fuel me. They can keep their judgment to themselves because they aren't winning this.

The sound of hurried footsteps draws my attention, and I turn to see Sam and Lola rushing toward me. Sam's eyes are wide, practically glowing with curiosity, while Lola watches with a faint, teasing smirk. Before either of them can speak, Noah leans in for another quick kiss—this one light but deliberate, like a promise.

"I'll catch up with you later," he says, his voice warm, that tone that makes my knees weak all over again. He gives me a quick smile before turning and heading off, leaving me standing there, Sam and Lola staring at me like I've just dropped the juiciest secret of the century.

Sam grabs my arm the second he's out of earshot. "Okay, spill. Since when are you and Noah a thing?"

I open my mouth to explain, the words right there, on the tip of my tongue. I want to tell her it's new. How I haven't had the chance to mention it yet, or bring up the fact that my dad kicked me out. But before I can speak, Reece's voice cuts through the moment.

"Hey, Red."

I catch the embarrassed flush coloring Sam's face, and my gaze shifts to see Reece walking by, his dark hair messy in a way that looks intentional, his piercing blue eyes locked on Sam. She immediately drops her gaze, refusing to look at him. No response. No acknowledgment. Just silence.

What the fuck? Sam doesn't back down from anyone. It's clear something happened between them.

"Yeah, you need to tell me about that," I say, watching Reece as he continues down the hall.

"Come on, just tell us about Noah," Sam says, her voice rushed, clearly trying to redirect the spotlight.

I narrow my eyes at her, noticing how she waves my question off too easily. Her posture is stiff, and she avoids my gaze—obvious signs that I've hit a nerve.

Bullshit. I smirk, watching her attempt to dodge. "Really? That's your move?" I challenge, but she stays silent, her lips pressed together, resolute. Fine. If she's not going to spill, I know who will. I turn to Lola, my instincts telling me she's not the type to let a juicy detail slip by without adding something. "Lola," I ask, "what's the story?"

Lola doesn't hesitate, blurting out the answer like it's no big deal. "Sam and Reece had a thing once."

"Lola!" Sam snaps, spinning toward her, panic flashing in her eyes. "Shut up!"

"What? She was going to find out eventually," Lola replies nonchalantly, pushing her glasses up the bridge of her nose, as if it's just another fact.

Before I can respond, Lola adds with a grin, "So tell me...you're hitting that, right?" She gestures toward where Noah disappeared. "Because, honestly, I'd be hitting that every second of every day and night if I had the chance."

"Oh my god, Lola," Sam groans, rolling her eyes. "You seriously don't know when to shut up."

"What?" Lola shrugs, completely unbothered. "I'm just stating facts. You ask any girl here and they all wish they were Aubrey right now."

The bell rings, loud and sharp.

Lola bolts, muttering something about not wanting another tardy slip.

Sam stays behind, leaning against the lockers, shaking her head. "I'm telling you, that girl doesn't know when to shut up."

As I grab my books, I feel it—the stares. The eyes boring into my back, like daggers. I glance over my shoulder, and there she is—Tia, standing with a few of her loyal followers. Not as many as before, though, and that's when it clicks. I remember Sam mentioned earlier that things had changed.

I slam my locker shut and turn to Sam, the question already on my lips. "So, what's been going on while I've been gone? What did you need to tell me?"

Sam gives me a sly glance, her lips twitching into a smirk. "Oh, you're going to love this," she says, practically grinning from ear to ear. "Since you practically shut Tia the fuck up, Nicole's decided it's her time to shine. Half of Tia's bitches have jumped ship and gone with Nicole. It's turned into a full-on bitch battle for the crown."

I blink, caught somewhere between disbelief and amusement. "You're kidding."

"Not even a little," Sam replies, her grin widening. "It's like Mean Girls on steroids out here. And the best part? You're the one who kicked it all off. Tia's been scrambling to hold onto her power ever since you knocked her on her ass."

A small, wicked grin spreads across my face. Maybe this day isn't going to suck after all.

CHAPTER 25

NOAH

It's lunchtime, and I'm at our usual table with Reece and Jace. They're talking, but I'm barely paying attention to the shit coming out of their mouths. Reece is rambling about some party, and Jace—predictably—won't shut the fuck up about some new girl he's obsessed with. Something about her tits, because that's apparently the only thing his brain can process. I'd tell him to shut it, but I'm too busy scanning the cafeteria, waiting for Aubrey to appear.

Then "*she*" shows up.

Tia struts over with her little clique in tow and slides into the seat across from me like she owns the fucking place. Seriously? After everything that's happened, you'd think she'd have gotten the hint to fuck off. Even Reece and Jace don't acknowledge her—too wrapped up in their own bullshit. None of us care. Hell, we've all been there with Tia, and trust me, it wasn't anything worth bragging about.

"Did you see the way she looked at me?" Tia pipes up, her voice sharp and irritating as hell.

I keep my eyes on the cafeteria doors, pretending not to hear her, but my ears are tuned in. If she's talking about Aubrey, she's playing with fire. One wrong word, and her food tray might end up being a new fashion accessory.

Tia doesn't notice my growing irritation and keeps running her mouth, her voice like nails on a chalkboard. "I can't believe she has the audacity. How dare she go against me," she whines, stabbing at her food like it personally offended her.

"So, how long do you have to wear that thing on your nose?" Elice chirps, her voice entirely too cheerful for Tia's current mood.

Tia freezes, her icy glare snapping to Elice like a viper. It's the classic Tia death stare—the one that screams, "fuck off or die". Elice shrinks back, her confidence evaporating in an instant. I can't help but smirk. Yeah, that's about right. Tia's always been too obsessed with her looks to care about anyone else.

"How long is that shit stuck on your face, anyway?" Jace asks, leaning back with a smug grin. He doesn't even bother hiding his amusement, clearly enjoying the chance to poke at Tia.

Her head snaps toward him so fast it's a miracle she doesn't sprain something. The look she gives him? Pure venom. It's the kind of glare that could stop most guys cold, maybe even make them rethink their life choices. But Jace? He just grins wider, completely unfazed, practically daring her to take a swing.

Nicole strides over to the table, her glare locked on me like she's been sharpening it for days. All because I wouldn't let her suck my dick the other night. Classic Nicole—if it wasn't me, it was someone else's cock keeping her busy. Her frosty stare shifts from me to Tia, and just like that, the tension skyrockets. I give it ten seconds before we're in full bitch-fight territory.

Ever since Aubrey knocked Tia off her pedestal, Nicole's been circling like a vulture, ready to pick up the scraps and claim the crown. It's pathetic, really. Get a fucking life, Nicole.

Her little entourage crowds around the table, all radiating that fake mean-girl energy. The kind that's all smoke and mirrors, nothing real behind it. The air's thick with glares and hostility, a powder keg waiting to go off. Meanwhile, Reece leans back, completely unfazed, hitting on some chick named Lilly with one of his signature bullshit lines. I can see it in her face—he's already won her over. By the end of the day, he'll have fucked her and moved on. Same old shit.

Then it starts.

Words fly across the table, sharp and aimed to kill. Snide comments about Nicole's weight, which, honestly, is ridiculous.

Nicole fires back with something about Tia's face, and the whole thing spirals. Every word is a dagger, meant to cut, to pierce, to leave scars.

"For fuck sake, shut the fuck up," I snap, my voice slicing through the chaos.

The table falls silent, their eyes snapping to me. I don't have the patience for this shit anymore. The toxic back-and-forth, the endless drama—it's fucking exhausting.

Without another word, I shove my chair back and stand, scanning the cafeteria. Sure enough, in all this bullshit, I missed what I've been waiting for—Aubrey. She's already here, sitting at her table.

I don't waste a second. I start walking, and Jace and Reece follow without question, like always.

Nicole's voice rises behind us, sharp and demanding, but I don't bother looking back. Neither do the guys. Whatever she's shouting, it doesn't matter. If she thinks I'm sticking around for her and Tia's bitchy back and forth, she's delusional. I'm done.

As we weave through the crowded cafeteria, conversations stall, heads turning to follow us. Like we're their personal entertainment. I block it all out, zeroing in on Aubrey's table.

She's mid-laugh, listening to something Sam's saying, her smile widening with every second. That smile—it's a fucking showstopper. The kind of smile that makes you freeze like a complete idiot, staring because you can't help yourself.

Her eyes flick toward me the moment and for a second, everything else fades—the noise, the drama, all the bullshit. It's just her.

I squeeze in beside Aubrey, the warmth of her presence grounding me as I slide closer. Reece and Jace follow suit, wedging themselves into the group, and the shift is immediate. The buzz of the cafeteria dies down, replaced by a heavy silence as everyone stops to wonder what the fuck we're doing. But I don't care. Let them watch. Let them speculate. None of it matters.

Across the table, Jace plants himself between Lola and Liz, a shit-eating grin stretched across his face. I know neither of them is falling for his smooth lines—they're not the type to make it easy. But that won't stop Jace. If anything, the challenge will just fuel him. Reece, on the other hand, slides in next to Sam, and the energy at the table shifts immediately.

The fiery, no-nonsense Sam, who stood her ground when Aubrey locked herself in the bathroom, suddenly disappears. Her confidence dims, replaced by something quieter, almost shy. She keeps her gaze down while Reece looks at her like she's the only person in the room.

"Hey, Red," Reece finally manages, his voice softer than usual, testing the waters.

Sam's eyes flick up for a brief moment before darting away, and there's something unspoken hanging in the air. It's subtle, but I feel it. Maybe something's already happened between them. If it has, he hasn't told me or Jace, and that's not like him. Reece shares everything.

Well, most of us do. Jace? He shares way too fucking much.

The scent of her perfume floods my senses as I wrap my arms around Aubrey's waist, pulling her closer. I bury my nose in the side of her neck, letting myself get lost in the soft, familiar warmth of her. I don't give a fuck about the people watching. Let them stare. They're used to seeing me act like I don't give a shit about anyone, so let them choke on the truth. If anyone's got a problem with it, they can take it up with my fist.

"You want to go to the lake this afternoon?" I ask, pressing a kiss to the side of her neck. Her skin is warm, and she shivers slightly under my lips.

"Yeah," she says with a small smile, her voice soft. "I want to sketch the lake while I'm there."

Before I can say anything else, Jace jumps in with his usual bullshit.

"What about Nic's party, man? Don't tell me you're not going. It's going to be fucking epic."

I lift my head and catch him grinning at me like the smug asshole he is. The look I shoot him would make most people back off, but not Jace. He thrives on pushing buttons.

"Apparently, there are going to be chicks from Westside Hill," he adds.

Lola beats me to it before I can even open my mouth to shut Jace down.

"All you do is think with your dick, Jace," Lola says, rolling her eyes so dramatically it's a wonder they don't get stuck in the back of her head. "Surely one day, you'll find a girl who wants more than a five-minute ride on the Jace express. Or, you know, maybe one who doesn't fake it just to get it over with."

The table erupts in laughter. Jace's grin falters for the first time, though he tries to mask it with his usual bravado. "What can I say, Lola? My dick knows what it wants," he mutters, but the flush creeping up his neck betrays him.

Lola doesn't let up, leaning forward with a smirk that's equal parts savage and amused. "Surely one day, you'll realize there's more to life than chasing tail. Or maybe you won't, and your dick will catch something so exotic, even antibiotics won't know what to do with it."

"Jesus, Lola," Jace mutters, shaking his head as the table bursts into fresh laughter.

She sits back, completely unbothered, her grin widening. "Don't say I didn't warn you. Evolution's a bitch, Jace. Even for fuckboys."

I can't help but notice how much Lola's changed. She's not the same girl who used to shrink into herself whenever Tia tore into her. That defeated look, like she was bracing for impact every time someone spoke, is gone. Now, she sits taller, holds her head higher, and doesn't take shit from anyone. It's a hell of a transformation, and I respect it.

The conversation shifts to something else—something I barely register because I'm too caught up in Aubrey. The way her lips curve when she smiles, how her eyes light up when she talks about things that matter to her—it's impossible not to get lost in her.

The bell rings, signaling the end of the break, and I groan inwardly.

I don't want to go back to class. My instinct is to grab her hand, skip the rest of the afternoon, and head straight for the lake. Just the two of us, no noise, no bullshit. But I already know what her answer will be.

Aubrey's too focused, too determined to keep her shit together for her scholarship next year. She's not about to let anything mess that up—not even me. I overheard her talking to my dad about it the other day when I came in after my workout. She's got her priorities straight, and I respect the fuck out of that. But damn, it's hard not to want to be selfish. To steal her away, just for a little while.

The rest of the afternoon drags on like a goddamn eternity. Mr. Wheeler's class is a bore fest—a combination of monotone lectures and dry material that could put a hyper-caffeinated kid to sleep. By the time the final bell rings, I'm practically out of my seat before the sound finishes echoing through the halls.

I snap back to life, ready to get the hell out of here and back to what actually matters.

I lean against the lockers, waiting for Aubrey as she stuffs her books and homework into her bag. Honestly, homework's the last thing on my mind—if it weren't for my dad constantly on my ass about my grades, I wouldn't bother with it at all.

The hallways thin out, students rushing past, slapping high fives and shouting over each other as they head toward freedom. Aubrey shuts her locker with a soft click, and we start walking toward the front of the school.

But then, as we reach the steps, I freeze.

I stop breathing.

She's there. My mother.

Standing right in front of the school, blending into the crowd of parents and students like she belongs. She's watching the passing faces, her gaze skimming the crowd, but it's obvious she's here for me. My stomach twists, and my blood runs cold as anger claws its way up my chest.

How dare she? What the fuck does she think she's doing, showing up here? I made it crystal fucking clear—I want nothing to do with her. I ignored the calls, the texts, every half-assed attempt she's made to slither her way back into my life.

The fucking audacity.

My dad's voice echoes in my head, telling me about her sudden reappearance. He said it caught him off guard. That's putting it lightly. How does someone like her, someone who left without looking back, think they can just waltz back in like nothing happened?

Fuck that.

She doesn't get to do this. Not after the shit she put us through.

My mind flashes back to those early days—me, sitting on the front steps as a kid, waiting for her to come back. My dad beside me, his arm around my shoulders, trying to convince me it was going to be okay, even though he knew it wasn't. I can still see the look in his eyes. Helpless. Defeated. He tried. God, he tried. But it was never enough. She left a void behind that not even time could fill.

I glance at Aubrey, my chest tight. She squeezes my hand, a silent reassurance, but it doesn't help. I can feel the storm building, the anger bubbling up, threatening to spill over. I want to scream. To march right up to her and tell her to fuck off. To leave. To never come back.

But instead, I stand there. Frozen. Watching her.

Aubrey pulls me forward gently, trying to guide me away, but my feet feel like they're stuck in cement. My mother's eyes lock onto mine the second she sees me moving toward her, her expression softening, hopeful. Like this is a goddamn reunion. Like she's waiting for me to forgive her.

The air feels heavy, suffocating. I take a shaky breath, trying to ignore the fury clawing at my chest. But the moment she opens her mouth, all that anger comes flooding out.

"Noah," she says softly, her voice laced with some bullshit tenderness. Like she has any right to say my name.

"Fuck off."

The words come out sharp, loud, and final. I don't hesitate, don't flinch. I want her to feel every syllable. To know that whatever she thought this was, it's not. She doesn't mean anything to me anymore. Not now. Not ever.

"Please, Noah, let's just talk," she says, her voice edging on pleading as I push past her without a glance. I don't stop. I don't even hesitate.

I hear her voice again, sharper this time. "Aubrey."

That one word, spoken so desperately, sets my blood on fire. She's trying to use Aubrey, trying to pull her into this mess. As if she has any right. As if she can guilt me into giving her a second of my time. How dare she speak to Aubrey like that? How dare she even say her name when the last time she saw Aubrey, she was just a little girl?

It's manipulation. All of it. Classic fucking power play.

I stop dead in my tracks, my rage boiling over. I spin on my heels and storm back toward her, the crowd of students still lingering on the school steps can get fucked. Let them watch. Let them see. I don't give a damn.

I close the distance, stopping inches from her, my voice low and sharp. "Don't you ever fucking talk to her," I growl. "You don't know her. You don't know me. So back the fuck off and don't come near either of us again."

Her face crumples, her mouth opening like she's about to say something, but I'm done. I'm so fucking done. I turn away, leaving her standing there, her presence like a stain I can't scrub off fast enough.

I make it to my car, my anger coursing through my veins. I throw my bag into the backseat with a force that rattles the entire car. My hands are shaking, my chest heaving as I grip the steering wheel, trying to keep myself from losing it completely.

Out of the corner of my eye, I see Aubrey crossing the parking lot. She slips into the passenger seat, her movements calm, steady. The complete opposite of what's going on inside me.

"Are you okay?" she asks, her voice gentle, like she's trying to keep me grounded.

I drag a hand down my face, exhaling hard. "I don't know why the fuck she came back," I mutter, my voice rough with frustration. "This shit is fucking with my head."

She doesn't answer right away. Instead, she reaches over, her fingers lacing through mine. She doesn't need to say much—she knows me too well. Knows when to talk and when to let me stew in my anger.

Finally, she speaks, her voice steady. "I know how hard this is for you. I saw what it did to you as a little boy, the day she left... and every day after that."

Her words cut deeper than I want to admit, yanking me back to places I've spent years trying to bury. That kid who sat on the steps every night, waiting for his mother to come back. He's gone. I killed him a long time ago. Or at least I thought I did.

"She asked me to tell you she'll be at the park on East Side this Saturday," Aubrey says after a pause, her words careful. "With Lilla and Cole. If you'd like to meet them."

Her words land heavy, like a blow I wasn't braced for. Lilla and Cole. The names twist in my chest, sharp and unfamiliar.

I glance at Aubrey, my throat tight.

"It's your choice, Noah," she says, her voice soft but firm. "You don't have to go if you don't want to."

I don't even know what to say to that. What the fuck can I say? I turn my head away, staring out the side window as my mind spirals. Everything feels like it's caving in—spinning out of control. Part of me wants to scream, to say fuck that and walk away from this shit for good. But then there's the other part... the part of me I've spent years trying to bury. That little kid still clinging to the hope she'd come back. Still waiting on those fucking front steps. That part of me doesn't know what to do.

I look out through the windshield, watching cars pull out of the lot and students rushing to leave, their laughter and voices blending into a distant hum. It all feels so far away, like I'm stuck underwater, drowning in memories I never wanted to resurface.

"I don't know if I can do that, Aub," I finally say, my voice thick and raw, like the words are fighting their way out of me.

"I know," she murmurs, her thumb brushing softly over the back of my hand, keeping me in the present, even as my mind keeps pulling me back to the past.

I don't want to face my mother. I don't want to give her the satisfaction of thinking she can just show up and act like everything is okay. But there's a small, nagging part of me—one I fucking hate—that's telling me to go. Telling me to hear her out, just to see if she's got anything real to say.

"Do you think I should go?" I ask, my voice breaking in a way I didn't mean it to.

She doesn't answer right away. She just squeezes my hand, her silence steady and reassuring.

When she does speak, her voice is soft but sure. "I think you should do what's best for you. But I won't pretend to know what that is, Noah. I just know this... I'm here. Whatever you choose."

Chapter 26

Aubrey

The change in Noah over the next few days was impossible to miss—he was there, but not really there. It was like he was stuck in his own head, chasing some thought or memory he couldn't outrun. I felt it the second I got in the car with him: the air was heavier, tense. The way his hands gripped the steering wheel like it was the only thing keeping him from spiraling. The way his eyes stayed glued to the road, avoiding me.

He didn't know what to do and watching him wrestle with it hurt like hell. And fuck, I didn't know how to help him.

Even when he took me to the lake that afternoon, his silence screamed louder than anything he could have said. I sat with my sketchpad in my lap, trying to lose myself in drawing—the soft ripples of the water, the trees framing the shore—hoping I could capture the calm I wished he felt. But every time I glanced at him stretched out on the blanket beside me, staring blankly at the sky, I could see it. The tight set of his jaw. The restless tapping of his fingers against his stomach. His thoughts running wild, dragging him somewhere I couldn't follow.

I thought maybe that night he'd tell his dad. Tell Ken about his mom showing up, about how it was fucking him up inside. But he didn't.

And I get it. Ken was in a good mood, laughing, smiling like everything was perfect. And Noah, being Noah, wouldn't ruin that. He wouldn't unload something so heavy, even when his dad asked if everything was okay—again and again. But I saw it. I saw how much he wanted to say something. How hard he was fighting to hold it together, even as the cracks started showing.

Days passed, and that tension didn't let up.

It's been another grueling night on my feet, and I'm beyond relieved to clock out.

My pockets are stuffed with tips, and there's a quiet sense of accomplishment in knowing I've earned my keep for another day. The cool night air hits me as I step outside, and my eyes immediately find Noah's car parked in its usual spot. He's waiting for me, like he always does.

Despite all the shit he's dealing with about his mother, we've settled into a routine. It's simple, steady, and it feels so damn good to have a slice of stability in my life. For once, I'm part of something that isn't crumbling under its own weight—no yelling, no shattered bottles, no drunken fathers waiting to explode.

My nerves, the ones that always have me on edge, feel like they're settling for the first time in what feels like forever. All because I know I have somewhere safe to stay.

Ken has reassured me more times than I can count that I'm welcome to stay as long as I want. Those words... they mean everything. They give me the breathing room to focus on what's important: keeping my grades up, securing my scholarship for next year, and holding on to the one thing I can't imagine losing—Noah.

I head toward the car, my muscles aching with every step. Even though Noah's expression is unreadable, just seeing him there, waiting for me, brings a strange sense of calm. I slide into the passenger seat, and the soft glow of the interior light flickers on.

My gaze goes straight to him. His hair's a mess, the way I love it, but not because he styled it that way. No—it's from him running his hands through it over and over, like he always does when he's overwhelmed.

I shut the door and lean toward him, pressing my lips to his. The warmth of his mouth against mine, the way his hands immediately reach up to pull me closer—it's intoxicating. In this moment, I could lose myself in him completely. But even as I savor the kiss, I can't ignore the tension still radiating from his body. His shoulders remain rigid, his grip on me almost desperate, like I'm the only thing keeping him together.

It's time. Time to stop holding back. Time to say the thing he doesn't want to hear but needs to. He can't keep going like this, carrying his mom's bullshit, pretending it isn't tearing him apart.

"Noah," I say, my voice soft but steady as I reach out, my hand resting on his cheek. His skin is warm, but the tension beneath my palm feels like a wall he's building brick by brick. "You need to decide. You can't keep drowning in this, pretending you're fine. It's killing you, and I can't just sit here and watch."

His eyes snap to mine, and what I see there almost shatters me. Conflict. Pain. Anger. It's a storm that's been brewing for too long, and it's finally reaching its breaking point.

"I know," he mutters, his voice rough, low, almost like he's admitting defeat.

"Then talk to me," I plead, leaning closer, desperate to reach the part of him he's trying so hard to lock away. "Please, Noah. Tell me what's going on in your head."

He lets out a sharp, shaky breath, his jaw tightening as he fights against the words clawing their way out. Finally, he speaks, his voice a mixture of anger and vulnerability.

"I'm so fucking pissed at myself," he starts, his tone bitter. "Because I don't want anything to do with her. I've told myself that a thousand times. But then there's this part of me... this stupid, pathetic part that just—" He breaks off, his voice cracking as he tries to push through. "This part of me that needs to know why. Why she fucking left. Why I wasn't good enough for her to stay." His words hit hard, but he's not finished. "And what happens when I see her with them—those other kids—and she's being a mom to them, Aub. A real mom. It's like I never fucking mattered. Like I wasn't enough for her to stick around for. How fucked up is that?"

My heart aches for him—for the boy he was, for the boy who deserved so much more than this crushing weight. I can hear the hurt in his voice, feel the confusion that's been eating away at him for days.

He's unraveling right in front of me, and it's fucking breaking my heart to see him like this, to see the pain he's been carrying for so long.

"It's not fucked up, Noah," I say gently. "It's human."

"No, Aub" he snaps, his voice rising as the anger in him boils over. "It's weak. It's fucking weak, and I hate it. I hate that I care. I should be able to just shove her out of my head, like I've been doing for years. She doesn't deserve a second of my time, but now she's here, and—" His voice breaks again, and he turns his head away, like he can't bear to look at me. "She's stirring up all this shit I thought I buried," he says quietly, his voice so raw it almost breaks me. "And I fucking hate her for it. I hate that I can't stop thinking about her."

I watch as his shoulders slump, the exhaustion etched into every inch of him. He's a mess of anger and grief, and it's tearing him apart.

"Then go see her," I say firmly but softly, my words steady. "Go meet her and get the answers you need, Noah. Because you can't keep doing this to yourself. You deserve better than this."

His head snaps toward me, his eyes locking on mine. There's so much there—anger, confusion, fear. A storm raging behind those dark eyes, daring me to take it back. But I don't.

"You think it's that easy?" he says, his voice low but sharp, each word dripping with bitterness. "You think I can just show up, hear whatever bullshit excuse she has, and then what? Just move on."

"No," I reply, keeping my voice steady even as the weight of his pain presses down on me. "I don't think it'll be easy, Noah. I think it'll fucking hurt. But you deserve to know. You don't have to forgive her," I continue, softening my tone as I lean closer. "You don't have to keep her in your life after this. But you deserve the truth, Noah. You deserve to stop carrying all this shit around, wondering why you weren't enough. Because you are enough."

He swallows hard, his jaw tightening as his eyes dart away from mine, locking onto the windshield.

"I'll go with you if you want," I add gently, my voice barely above a whisper. "But you need to do this. Not for her—for you."

He exhales sharply, the sound more like a hiss than a breath. "I don't know if I can, Aub," he mutters. "I don't know if I'm ready to hear whatever bullshit excuse she's got. Or if I even want to."

"But maybe you need to," I say, leaning closer, my words soft but firm. "Even if it's bullshit. Even if it doesn't fix anything. Maybe hearing it will help you finally let go."

All night, Noah's been off—silent, lost in his own head, barely speaking as we sat together in his room.

Every time I tried to reach out, he'd just shake his head, run his hands through his hair, muttering words I couldn't make out. It felt like he was holding himself together with nothing more than sheer willpower, on the verge of falling apart.

And now, the day has come.

I sit in the passenger seat of Noah's car, watching him grip the edge of the seat like it's the only thing keeping him from shattering. His jaw is clenched so tight I can practically hear his teeth grinding. He hasn't said a word since we parked, but the storm brewing in his eyes speaks volumes, saying everything his lips can't.

From where we sit, I can see her—his mom. Sitting at a bench under a tree, looking so goddamn calm, so perfect, like she hasn't been nothing but a ghost in his life for years. Two kids sit with her, a boy with his face buried in a game, and a girl, both laughing, carefree. They don't know what this moment is doing to Noah. How seeing them so normal, so whole, is like a dagger twisting over and over into a wound that's never really healed.

It's so fucking clear from here—they've got the mother Noah never had. A mom who stayed. A mom who actually gave a shit. A mom who's there for every little thing, every milestone, every goddamn moment. A mom who didn't just fucking vanish without a trace.

And it pisses me off because Noah deserved that. He deserved that kind of love, not the hollow bullshit he got. The rage building inside me doesn't even come close to what he must be feeling.

I glance over at him. He's staring at them, his leg bouncing, his fingers twitching on the wheel like he wants to smash something.

"You don't have to do this," I say softly, breaking the silence that's stretched too long between us. "We can just go. Fuck her, Noah. You don't owe her anything."

He doesn't look at me, eyes still locked on the scene in front of us, but I see his throat tighten, the way he swallows hard. "I fucking hate this," he mutters, voice rough with anger. "I hate that I'm here. But I need to know, Aub. I need to fucking know why she left. Why she stayed for *them*."

The way he says them—it's jagged, raw, like just speaking the word rips him open. I reach over, my hand finding his arm, and I squeeze gently. "I'm here, Noah," I tell him. "Whatever happens, I'm here with you."

Finally, he looks at me and I see the pain in his eyes. Then, with a deep breath, he opens the door and steps out.

I follow him, stepping out of the car and walking beside him as we cross the park. His body's stiff, radiating tension, like he's bracing for a blow that's coming. I slip my hand into his, squeezing it, a silent promise that he's not alone in this. His fingers curl around mine, tight

As we get closer, I see her look up. Her face lights up, relief washing over her as if she has been waiting for this moment—for this joyful reunion. She stands, her smile too bright, too forced, as she smooths her hands over the front of her jeans, like she's trying to look put together.

The two kids beside her stop what they're doing, their attention snapping to Noah, curiosity flickering in their eyes.

But Noah? He's a different story. He's rigid, tense, like a coiled spring ready to snap. Every step he takes is heavy, like he's walking into a warzone, the weight of everything he's carried pressing down on him. I can see the storm inside him, brewing with anger and pain, and I can't help but hope he makes it through this—hope he survives whatever the hell happens next.

CHAPTER 27

NOAH

It hurts. God, it fucking hurts. It's like a knife to the gut, seeing her there on that bench, laughing with the girl—my half-sister. The sight claws at something raw, something I thought I'd buried years ago. All I want is an answer. Why? Why the fuck did she leave me, only to stay for them?

Earlier, through the windshield, I studied the boy. He looks about nine—older than I was when she walked out. Which means within a year or two of leaving, she started over. A whole new family. A family she fucking chose.

Now, standing in front of her, the anger rises, threatening to pull me under. I want to scream, to hurl every ounce of hurt and fury at her, to make her feel the way she made me feel. I want her to understand how deeply she fucked me up. But I don't. Because as much as she broke me, Dad was the one who picked up the pieces. He gave me something she didn't—a good life. A life full of love. The kind she's clearly giving them now.

I glance at the boy and girl. Their eyes are on me, and the boy's face delivers a jolt—features we both share, unmistakably hers. Then there's the girl, clinging to her hand, her wide, innocent eyes staring up at me.

My chest tightens. She doesn't know. She has no idea what it's like to be left behind.

"Noah," my mother says, her voice hesitant, cracking like she's afraid of what I might say.

My eyes snap to hers, and it feels like the air's been sucked out of the world.

"I'm so glad you came," she says softly, carefully, like she's walking on glass. "Cole and Lilla have been excited to meet you."

I don't respond. I just stare at her, my grip tightening on Aubrey's hand as rage simmers beneath the surface, threatening to erupt. What does she think she can say? Standing here, face-to-face with her, I wish now I hadn't come. There's nothing she could say to make it better. Nothing that could undo the silence, the absence, the damage.

She opens her mouth, probably gearing up to spew some bullshit about how sorry she is or how much she's missed me. I don't let her.

"Why?" I snap, my voice low but sharp enough to cut.

She freezes, her mouth still slightly open, staring at me like she doesn't know what to say.

"Why the fuck did you come back?" I spit, my voice shaking with the weight of years spent swallowing this pain. "You think you can just show up now and fix everything? Say a few pretty words and worm your way back into my life? Fuck that. Fuck *you*."

Her face crumples, but I don't care. Let her feel even a fraction of what I've carried all these years. Let her know what it's like to hurt like I did. There's no apology on Earth that could erase the damage she left behind.

She glances back at the kids—the ones she chose. "Why don't you two go play on the equipment while I talk to your brother," she says, her voice soft, sweet, like this is some kind of happy family reunion instead of the train wreck it is.

Brother. I didn't even know these kids existed until Dad told me she was back. Maybe I should've told him what I was planning, let him come here to get his answers too. Or maybe he's better off not knowing. Better off not reopening the wounds she left behind.

The kids nod and run off toward the playground, casting curious glances back at me—their so-called brother. My stomach churns as I watch them. They don't have a clue who I am, and I don't want to know them. They're living the life I should've fucking had.

She turns back to me, a tentative smile on her lips, like she's trying to soften the blow.

"Noah," she starts, her voice careful.

"Don't," I snap, cutting her off. "Don't act like we're some happy fucking family. You made your choice a long time ago."

Her smile falters, and she looks down, her hands twisting together nervously. "I know I hurt you," she says softly.

"Hurt me?" I repeat, letting out a sharp, bitter laugh. "You didn't just hurt me. You fucking abandoned me. You left me and Dad without a second thought, and now you show up with your shiny new family and expect me to play big brother. Fuck that."

She flinches, tears welling in her eyes, but I don't stop. I can't. The anger's been building for too long to hold it back now.

"I'm sorry," she whispers, her voice cracking.

"Sorry doesn't mean shit," I snap, the words like fire on my tongue.

She nods, wiping her eyes like that'll make a difference. "I understand," she says quietly. "I just... I wanted to see you. To explain—"

"Explain what?" I cut her off again, my voice rising. "That you traded us in for them. That we weren't good enough for you. Save it."

Her lips press together, and the guilt in her eyes is almost satisfying. Good. She fucking should feel guilty. But then she opens her mouth, and I know she's about to try justifying it all—like there's some magical excuse that could make up for the years she ripped away.

"Noah, please—"

"Do you know what it's like," I cut her off, stepping closer, "to sit on the front fucking steps every night, waiting for someone who never comes back? To watch your dad, try to pick up the pieces, pretending it doesn't kill him every time your name comes up? You wrecked us. For what? So you could go play mom somewhere else?"

Her tears spill over now, and she raises a trembling hand to her mouth, like that'll stop the truth from cutting her. But I'm not done. Not even close.

"And don't you dare stand there crying," I say, my voice quieter now but no less venomous. "You don't get to cry. You don't get to act like the victim here. You left us. And now you've got them." I jab a finger toward the playground, where Cole and Lilla are climbing on the jungle gym, laughing like their lives aren't a shattered mirror of mine. "Maybe they'll never know what it feels like to be left behind. Good for them. But you know who does? Me. And Dad."

Her shoulders start to shake, and she's barely holding it together, but I don't feel a shred of pity. How could I, when I've spent years clawing my way out of the shadow she left? The kid who waited on those steps every night, hoping for a miracle? That kid's dead, buried under years of silence and disappointment.

"I shouldn't have come here," I mutter, shaking my head. "This was a fucking mistake."

I turn to leave, my chest tight and heaving, the weight of everything threatening to crush me. But I can't stay here. Not with her. Not with them.

I've barely taken two steps when her voice stops me. It's raw and broken, just like the memories she left behind.

"Noah, please. Don't go."

I freeze, keeping my back to her. Every instinct is screaming at me to keep walking, to leave her here the way she left me. But there's another part of me—the part I fucking hate—that can't quite let go yet.

"I'm sorry," she says, and her voice cracks under the weight of the words. "I'm sorry I left. I'm sorry I wasn't there for you and your dad. I know I can't change it, Noah. I know I can't fix what I did."

Slowly, I turn just enough to look at her, and the sight of her knocks the wind out of me. She's standing there, arms wrapped tightly around herself, tears streaming down her face. She looks... smaller. Fragile. Weak.

"Why?" The question escapes me before I can stop it, quieter now but sharp enough to cut. "Why did you leave us? Why did you stay for them?"

She takes a hesitant step closer, and this time, I don't move, don't flinch. "Because I was a coward," she admits, her voice barely above a whisper. "I was young and scared. I thought if I left, it would be better for both of you. I thought I could start over, be a better person. But I didn't. I just made it worse."

Her words linger in the air, heavy and bitter, and I can't decide if I want to scream at her or laugh at how fucking pathetic it sounds.

"You have a brother and a sister, Noah," she says, her voice trembling like it might crack in two. "Cole and Lilla. They'd like to get to know you. They've heard about you. They've asked about you. And I know I have no right to ask, but... please. Give them a chance. Give *me* a chance."

I stare at her, my chest tight and my mind racing.

She's asking for something I don't know if I can give—forgiveness, a chance to rewrite the past, something that feels impossible.

A brother and a sister. Cole and Lilla. They've heard about me. Asked about me. And now she wants me to just step into this picture-perfect family she built after ripping mine apart.

My gaze shifts to the playground, where Cole and Lilla are laughing together, their joy so effortless. They look... happy. The kind of happy I was supposed to be. And maybe that's why I can't bring myself to hate them, even as the sight of them tears me up inside.

Dragging my eyes back to her, I let the coldness in my voice do the talking.

"Fine. I'll meet them. But you?" A bitter laugh escapes as I shake my head. "I don't want anything to fucking do with you."

Her face crumbles, and for a moment, I think she's going to say something, to plead her case, but I cut her off before she can.

"You don't get to walk back into my life like nothing happened. You don't get to pretend that you didn't fuck me up when you left. I'll meet them, but that's it. You and me. We're done."

Her shoulders slump, and she nods, her lips trembling as she swallows down whatever words she was about to say. "Okay," she whispers, her voice breaking. "I understand."

"Get them," I say, jerking my head toward the playground. "If they want to meet me, let's get this shit over with."

She hesitates for a moment, as if she's unsure whether I mean it, then nods and turns toward the playground.

As she walks away, I feel Aubrey's hand wrap around my waist, holding me steady. She steps in front of me, her presence the only thing keeping me from bolting. I glance down at her, unsure of what's coming next.

What the fuck do you say to two kids you didn't know existed until a few weeks ago?

"Are you okay?" Aubrey asks softly, her voice steady even though I can feel her watching me like I'm a bomb about to go off.

"No," I mutter, dragging a hand through my hair for what feels like the millionth time. "I'm not fucking okay, Aub. None of this is okay. But it's not their fault." The words sting as they leave my mouth, bitter and sharp. "I have no fucking idea how to deal with this."

Aubrey rises on her toes and presses a soft kiss to my lips, her touch gentle, grounding. "I know," she says quietly. "But you'll figure it out as you go."

Before I can respond, I hear the quick slap of sneakers on pavement. Cole and Lilla come running toward me, and every muscle in my body locks up. My jaw tightens as they skid to a stop a few feet away, both staring up at me like I'm some kind of big deal. What the fuck am I supposed to do?

Aubrey steps aside, slipping her hand into mine, her grip firm but reassuring.

"Hi," Lilla says, her voice soft and unsure. "Are you our brother?"

Brother. The word hits harder than I expected. I swallow hard, forcing the lump in my throat back down. She's so small, so fucking innocent, and for a moment, the storm inside me quiets.

EVE CAMPBELL

"Yeah," I say finally. "I guess I am."

Cole steps up beside her, taller, older, but just as uncertain. "Mom told us about you. Not a lot, but... we've wanted to meet you for a while."

There's something about the way he says it, like he's genuinely excited to see me, even though he doesn't know shit about who I am.

I glance back at Aubrey. She's standing just behind me, her eyes steady and calm, her expression soft. She doesn't say anything, just gives me a small nod, like she's silently telling me I've got this.

Turning back to Cole and Lilla, I take them in—open faces, hopeful expressions, like they actually want me in their lives. And as much as I want to hold onto the anger and the hurt, I can't aim it at them.

They didn't choose this. They didn't do any of it.

***

My dad leans against the counter, coffee mug in hand, watching me pace the kitchen like I'm trying to wear a hole in the floor. He doesn't say a word, just tracks my movements with his steady gaze, waiting for me to speak. The silence feels heavy, like it's pressing on my chest, but I don't know where to start. How the fuck do I put today into words?

"I met them," I finally say, dragging a hand through my hair as the tension in my chest threatens to suffocate me. "I met her kids"

Dad freezes, his mug halfway to his lips. He doesn't take a sip. Instead, he sets it down on the counter with a quiet clink. "You saw your mother today?"

I stop pacing and lean against the fridge, like it's the only thing keeping me upright. "Yeah. Her too."

His jaw tightens, and he swallows hard before speaking. "And?"

"And she's full of shit," I say. "She tried to explain why she left, like there's anything she can fucking say that makes it okay."

"Did she give you any kind of answer?"

"Not one that makes any sense," I say bitterly. "She said she was young and scared, but she wasn't too scared to have another kid—two fucking kids—not long after she left. She stayed for them, Dad. She built this whole new life with them..." My voice falters, the words catching in my throat.

Dad steps closer, his expression hard to read. "Why didn't you say you were going?"

"I didn't think you'd want to know," I mutter, staring at the floor. "Maybe I should've. Maybe you deserved to hear her excuses, too."

He lets out a bitter laugh, shaking his head. "I've heard enough excuses from her, Noah. I don't need to hear more."

I finally meet his eyes, the weight of the day crashing down on me. "She said they want to know me. Cole and Lilla. She said they've been asking about me."

Dad's face softens, just a little, but his voice stays steady. "And what do you want?"

My throat feels tight, and it takes me a moment to answer. "I don't fucking know," I admit, my voice breaking on the last word.

He steps closer, placing a hand on my shoulder. "You don't have to decide anything right now," he says firmly. "But whatever you do, make sure it's for you, Noah. Not for her. Not for them. For you."

CHAPTER 28

AUBREY

It's been a few days since Noah met his mother, and things between us have been... off. He's quieter than usual, more withdrawn, like he's carrying something too heavy to put down. I see it in the way his jaw tenses, the way his hands flex at his sides like he's itching for a fight with something he can't name.

He hasn't said much about what happened that day. I haven't pushed, even though it's been eating me alive to sit back and wait. I know him, though. Noah doesn't respond well to pressure—it's like trying to hold a flame in your hands. He'll talk when he's ready, but the silence. It's fucking killing me.

I head out to the garage, where he's been spending most of his afternoons. The faint sound of tools clinking filters through the open door, and when I step inside, I see him. He's shirtless, his back to me, earbuds in, completely immersed in his motorcycle.

I lean against the doorway, taking him in. The way his muscles flex as he tightens a bolt, the grease streaked across his skin—it's mesmerizing. His cap is on backward, and there's a smudge of oil on his shoulder. He looks raw, rugged, and heartbreakingly beautiful.

"Noah," I call out, but he doesn't hear me over the music.

I stay where I am, watching the way he moves with that quiet intensity of his. Here, in the garage, it's like all the chaos inside him finds an outlet. It's focused, controlled—a sharp contrast to the storm I know he's bottling up.

When he finally glances up and notices me, he pulls out an earbud, his lips curling into that lazy smirk that never fails to make my heart skip.

"Enjoying the show?" he teases, wiping his hands on a rag before tossing it onto the bench.

"Maybe," I admit, stepping further inside. "You're kind of hard to ignore."

He laughs out loud. "You just gonna stand there and stare, or are you gonna help?"

"Help with what?" I challenge, raising an eyebrow. "You look like you've got it all under control." I take another step closer. "You've been out here a lot."

"Yeah." He picks up a wrench and turns it in his hands. "Gotta keep busy, you know? Better than sitting around, thinking about all the shit I can't change."

"You don't have to do this alone, Noah," I say softly, keeping my voice steady.

He pauses, his fingers tightening around the tool. "I know," he says, his voice rough and quiet. "But some things, Aub... some things are just too heavy to share."

I step closer, close enough to touch him, but I don't. Not yet. "You're strong, Noah, but even you can't carry the world on your shoulders forever."

I lean in, pressing my lips to his, and Noah melts into me. The kiss is wild and unrestrained, like he's pouring every ounce of himself into it—every flicker of anger, every shred of pain, and every raw drop of love. When he finally pulls back, his forehead rests against mine, his breath hot and uneven against my skin.

"Fuck, Aub," he mutters, his voice low and rough, every word igniting something deep inside me. "If my dad wasn't inside right now, knowing he could walk out here any second, I'd fuck you right here on that bench—make you scream so loud the whole neighborhood would know exactly who you belong to."

My heart stumbles, heat surging through me as I meet his smoldering gaze. I smirk, my voice dipping into a teasing tone. "Then maybe we should go somewhere you can."

Noah doesn't hesitate. He tosses the tool in his hand onto the workbench with a loud clang, grabs his shirt, and pulls it over his head in one smooth, almost aggressive motion. Without another word, he grabs my hand and leads me out of the garage, his grip firm and unrelenting.

The engine roars to life as I slip into his car, and before I can ask where we're going, we're flying down the street, the wind whipping through the open windows. I barely manage to keep my hair out of my face, but my attention isn't on that. It's on him.

Every now and then, I catch him glancing at me, his eyes dark with unfiltered need.

The way he keeps shifting in his seat, his jaw clenched, tells me everything I need to know. His cock is hard, straining against his jeans, and it's driving him crazy. It's like he's fighting the urge to pull the car over, drag me out, and fuck me.

He looks over and catches me, my gaze locked on him. Noticing the way I'm watching, his smirk widens. It's that cocky, knowing grin that tells me he's fully aware of the effect he's having on me. He owns me in this moment, and he knows it.

"I can pull over here," he says, his voice thick with amusement and something darker, rougher. His gaze flicks to mine, daring me, taunting me. "If you can't fucking wait."

My heart hammers, a thrill rushing through me at the raw challenge in his tone. I know exactly where he's taking me—to the lake. But the way his voice drips with promise makes me wonder if we'll even make it there.

"So impatient, eh?" I tease, my voice light but tinged with heat, each word laced with challenge.

My pulse thunders in my ears, my skin buzzing under the weight of his gaze.

His lips curl into a smirk, his focus shifting back to the road as the muscles in his jaw flex. "When I know what I want, I don't fuck around, Aub," he growls, his voice a deep rumble that makes my stomach flip. "And right now, I want to fuck you."

The raw intensity of his words hits like a lightning bolt, sending a surge of heat straight to my core. My breath hitches, and I press my thighs together, trying to anchor myself. But I don't back down. Instead, I lean closer, my voice dropping to a whisper, deliberately provocative. "Then stop talking about it and show me."

His smirk sharpens, dark and feral. "Careful what you wish for," he warns, his voice a low growl that vibrates through me.

Without another word, Noah slows the car, his foot easing off the gas as he steers us toward the side of the road. The tires crunch over gravel, and he pulls us behind a cluster of trees, the cover just enough to shield us from prying eyes.

The car jerks to a halt, the engine cutting off with a jolt. Before I can react, his door flies open, slamming shut with a force that echoes through the stillness.

I watch him stride around the car, his movements deliberate, every step radiating a quiet, searing intensity. When he reaches my door, he yanks it open, his eyes blazing as they meet mine.

"Out," he commands, his voice rough, leaving no room for argument.

His hand clamps around mine, his grip firm, and he pulls me from the car like he can't stand another second of distance between us.

Noah doesn't stop—he leads me to the front of the car, his pace unrelenting.

Before I can catch my breath, his hands are on my waist, strong and sure, lifting me like I weigh nothing. He puts me down on the warm metal of the hood.

His lips meet mine with a ferocity that steals the air from my lungs. There's no hesitation, no gentle buildup—just raw, unfiltered hunger as his tongue slides past my lips, claiming me like I'm the only thing that matters.

One hand grips my waist, his fingers digging into my skin possessively, while the other cups my face. His touch is firm, not rough, a deliberate statement that I'm his.

The scent of him—oil, and pure, unadulterated Noah—wraps around me, clouding my senses until all I can focus on is him. His body presses against mine, his heat bleeding into me, his movements demanding yet utterly intoxicating.

I surrender, my body arching into his, my hands clutching at his shoulders like he's the only thing keeping me tethered to the earth.

Every touch, every kiss, ignites my skin like wildfire, and I can't stop myself from melting under him. Noah knows exactly what he's doing—how to make my body respond with a precision that leaves me trembling. I let him. Fuck, I want him to. Because when Noah touches me, the rest of the world fades to nothing.

He pulls back slightly, his eyes locked on mine, burning with raw intensity. His hand moves to my shirt, yanking it over my head in one swift, fluid motion. "Take it off," he growls, his voice rough and commanding as his gaze drops to my bra.

There's no mistaking the hunger in his eyes, like he's already seeing through the thin barrier of my bra.

I bite my lip, as I reach behind to unclasp it. The second the straps slip loose, he's on me, tugging it off and tossing it aside without hesitation. His tongue swipes across his bottom lip, and the simple gesture sends a shiver racing through me, tightening the knot of desire coiled in my chest.

Without breaking his gaze, he crouches down, his hands moving to my boots.

One by one, he pulls them off, taking his time like he's savoring every second of stripping me.

When he's finished, his hands are on me again—rough, deliberate—pushing me back until my spine meets the metal of the car hood.

His fingers find the button of my jeans, the practiced flick of his hand undoing it in a heartbeat. The zipper follows next. Then he grips the waistband firmly, dragging both my jeans and panties down my legs in a slow, unhurried motion that makes every inch of uncovered skin feel like it's burning.

As he tosses the fabric aside, his eyes drop to my bare pussy, and the way he looks at me—like it's his favorite fucking meal—sends a jolt through me. His lips part slightly, his tongue darting out to wet them as his gaze rakes over me, dark and insatiable.

"Goddamn," he mutters, his voice low and gravelly, dripping with unrestrained desire.

His hands grip my knees, spreading my legs wide. He doesn't look away—doesn't even blink—as his eyes take in every inch of me. The heat in his stare burns like a physical touch, leaving me raw, exposed, and completely at his mercy.

"You're fucking perfect," he growls, his voice thick and rough, his fingers pressing into my thighs just enough to make me gasp. "And I'm gonna make sure you feel every fucking second of this."

His fingers slide through my slick folds, slow and deliberate, teasing me with a maddening precision that leaves me arching off the car hood. A sharp gasp escapes my lips as the ache intensifies, and he lets out a low, feral sound, his jaw tightening like he's barely keeping himself in check.

"Fuck," he hisses, his voice raw as his dark, wild eyes lock onto mine. His fingers move deeper, spreading my wetness, and a wicked smirk tugs at his lips. "You're so fucking drenched for me," he murmurs, his tone rough and filled with dangerous satisfaction. "This pussy's begging to be fucked."

He leans forward, pressing a soft, almost tender kiss to my stomach, and the contrast only makes the ache worse.

"You're mine, Aubrey," he whispers, his voice dark and possessive, every word a claim that sinks deep into my soul. His lips brush against my skin again, his breath hot and tantalizing. "And I'm gonna take my time fucking you."

CHAPTER 29

NOAH

The sight of her glistening pussy turns me fucking feral, making me lose every shred of control. It's dripping—soaked, desperate—like it's calling out to me to claim it, wreck it, worship it. Mine.

I drag the pad of my finger through her folds, the action slow and deliberate, savoring the feel of her hot, soaked flesh. "Fuck, Aub," I rasp, my cock throbbing with an ache so sharp it's almost unbearable. She bites down on her bottom lip, a soft moan slipping free, and it's so fucking sexy that all I can think about is burying myself inside her—right fucking now.

Sliding a finger into her, I feel her tight, wet heat clench around me like it's never letting go. The sensation nearly wrecks me on the spot

"Fuck, you're so tight," I growl, my voice thick with need as I push another finger inside her, stretching her inch by inch. She arches her back, her hips rolling into my touch, chasing the friction like she can't get enough. The sight of her—head thrown back, lips parted, body moving for me—is enough to drive me to the fucking brink.

My thumb grazes her clit, slow and deliberate, drawing teasing circles that make her whole body jerk beneath me.

That's it," I murmur, my voice rough and raw, dripping with desire. "Take it. Show me how much you fucking want this." I thrust my fingers deeper, curling just right, and her hips buck wildly against my hand, her body writhing as she chases the pleasure I'm giving her.

"You're so fucking wet," I rasp, my voice barely recognizable, thick with lust. "This pussy's begging for my cock."

Her moans only get louder, and I swear to God, every sound she makes drives me closer to insanity. I lean in, letting my breath skim over her skin, my lips brushing against the curve of her chest.

"Fuck, Aubrey, you feel so fucking good," I groan, my voice tight with hunger. "I'm gonna make you come so hard, you'll scream my fucking name." I press a soft kiss between her tits. "I'd burn the whole fucking world for this pussy."

Her voice is soft, breathy, dripping with need as she whispers, "Noah."

Hearing her say my name like that—so desperate, so full of want—makes me feel unstoppable. She's right there, teetering on the edge, every part of her begging for release. And I'm not stopping until I take her over it.

"That's it," I growl, my voice rough and thick with lust. "Just let go for me, Aubrey. Let me feel it."

And she does. Fuck, she does. Her face twists into the most breathtaking expression of raw pleasure and surrender, her body giving in completely, no barriers, no holding back. Every gasp, every filthy moan spilling from her lips is intoxicating as fuck. Her head tilts back, lips parting as wave after wave of her orgasm crashes through her. I swear I've never seen anything hotter in my life.

I can't tear my eyes away, watching her ride it out. Her body trembles beneath my touch, every inch of her unraveling for me.

But I don't stop. I keep my fingers moving, sliding back into her, drawing out every last tremor. Watching her fall apart like this—completely fucking lost in the moment—is addictive. She's perfection, and she's mine.

When her breathing starts to steady, I pull my fingers free. They're glistening with her arousal, her pleasure slick on my skin. I bring them to her lips.

"Open. Taste how fucking good you are."

Her lips part without hesitation, her tongue darting out to swirl around my fingers.

"Fuck," I mutter, my cock throbbing at the sight. Watching her eagerly suck her own arousal sends a searing rush of heat straight through my body, every muscle taut with need.

When I pull my fingers free, I don't give her a moment to recover. I lean in, crash my lips against hers, devouring her in a kiss that's fierce, hungry, and all-consuming. She tastes like heaven, her scent and warmth pulling me deeper, driving me mad. I grind my hard cock against her, letting her feel exactly how much I fucking want her.

"I'm going to fuck you now," I growl against her lips, my voice heavy with promise. I pull back just enough to take her in—sprawled across the hood of my car, every inch of her fucking perfect. Her nipples are hard, her chest rising and falling as she fights to catch her breath, her body practically begging for me.

Her legs are spread wide, her glistening pussy on full display, wet and ready to ruin. The sight alone sends a feral growl rumbling deep in my chest.

I step closer, towering over her, gripping her knees and pushing them even wider. "Fuck, Aubrey," I rasp, my voice thick with reverence and raw need. "You look like a fucking dream. All spread out and dripping for me. You want this cock, don't you?"

"Yes," she breathes, her voice trembling with desperation. Her body arches off the hood, reaching for me, her need as undeniable as my own.

I reach down, undoing the button and zipper on my jeans with rough, impatient movements, shoving them down just enough to free my cock. It's rock hard, thick, and ready, and the way her eyes drop to it—her lips parting slightly, her breath hitching—sends a jolt of want, stoking the fire already raging inside.

"You see what you do to me?" I growl, my voice low as I wrap a hand around my length, stroking it slowly, deliberately, letting her watch every movement. "This cock's been aching for you all fucking day. I need to fuck you. It's driving me insane."

I press the tip against her entrance, dragging it slowly through her slick folds, teasing her, pushing her to the edge without giving her what she's begging for.

Fuck, the way she moans, her body shuddering beneath me, is like a drug I'll never get enough of.

"You're so fucking wet," I say, my voice low and dripping with raw hunger. "This cock's yours, and you're gonna take it like the good girl you are."

Her eyes lock on mine, dark and wild, a daring smirk playing on her lips. "Then stop talking," she breathes, her voice trembling but bold, "and fuck me already."

My grip bruising as I grab her hips and slam into her with one hard, brutal thrust. She cries out, her back arching off the hood as I bury myself deep, the tight heat of her wrapping around me, perfect and maddening.

I don't wait, don't hold back. My hips move in a relentless rhythm, my cock pounding into her with raw, unyielding force. The sharp, rhythmic sound of skin meeting skin fills the air, mixing with her moans—louder now, filthier, like she's coming undone beneath me.

"You like this, don't you?" I rasp, my voice rough, dark, and full of hunger as my hands slide down to grip her thighs, spreading her wider. I thrust harder, deeper, claiming her with every movement. "You like being fucked out here, where anyone could see, like the dirty fucking girl you are."

Her nails dig into my arms, sharp and relentless, her cries raw and desperate, spurring me on. "You're fucking mine, Aubrey," I rasp, my voice thick and possessive as I drive into her, her slickness coating every inch of my cock. "Say it. Tell me who owns this pussy."

"You," she gasps, her voice cracking as I thrust harder, deeper, her body shaking beneath me. "You, Noah. Fuck, it's yours. All yours."

Her words ignite a deep, feral hunger I can't contain. I give her everything—every ounce of raw, unrelenting intensity, claiming her completely. Her pussy tightens, gripping like it never wants to let go, pulling me deeper with every thrust.

Her desperate cries push me further, wrecking what little control I have. My hands clamp down on her thighs, giving me the perfect view of her pussy swallowing every inch of my cock. The sight of her—wet, tight, and taking me so perfectly—combined with the way she clenches around me, sends a deep, guttural growl tearing from my chest.

"You feel that?" I rasp, my voice raw, unhinged, teetering on the brink of control. "Feel how fucking perfect you are for me?"

She nods frantically, her nails scraping against the hood of the car as I slam into her again, harder, rougher, my body demanding everything she has to give.

Her back arches beautifully, her breasts rising like an offering, and I can't fucking resist. I lean down, capturing one in my mouth, my tongue flicking over her hardened nipple. Her sharp gasp melts into a moan—raw and desperate, fueling the inferno inside.

"Fuck, Noah," she cries, her hands tangling in my hair, tugging as I nip and suck at her skin, leaving marks that scream she's mine. Mine to take. Mine to ruin. And I want the whole fucking world to know it.

My hips don't falter, driving into her with raw, relentless intensity.

Her body begins to quake beneath me, her cries shifting into wrecked, desperate moans. "I'm gonna come," she gasps, her voice trembling, her grip on me tightening.

"Good," I growl, pulling back just enough to watch her break. My thumb finds her clit, pressing quick, filthy circles that have her entire body jerking under me. "Come for me, Aubrey. Let me feel this pussy squeeze my cock."

She screams as her orgasm crashes over her, a breathtaking, chaotic masterpiece. Her body writhes, her head thrown back, her cries echoing around us as I keep moving, thrusting through her climax, drawing out every delicious second of her pleasure.

I drive into her with reckless abandon. Each thrust is harder, faster, the tension in my body coiling tighter, pushing me closer to the edge.

My grip on her hips tightens, my hold possessive, grounding her as I pound into her, relentless and wild. My breaths are jagged, my jaw clenched against the ferocious need clawing its way free.

"You feel that?" I snarl, my voice dark and frayed. "Feel how fucking close I am. This pussy's got me losing my goddamn mind."

Her gasping cries are a melody I can't escape, her voice trembling as she whispers my name like a prayer. But I'm too far gone to hear, my pulse roaring, my cock pulsing, the heat coiling tighter and tighter until it finally snaps, dragging me under with it.

My body locks up as my release hits like a lightning bolt. It's blinding, consuming, my cock jerking violently as I spill into her, thick and hot. My head falls back, a guttural growl tearing from my throat as wave after wave of ecstasy crashes through me, leaving me trembling, raw, and utterly wrecked.

I keep moving, shallow and desperate thrusts, wringing out every last ounce of pleasure, refusing to let it fade, emptying everything I have into her.

Panting, I collapse against her, my chest pressed to hers, both of us fighting to catch our breath.

I stay buried inside her, twitching faintly, and fuck I'd love to stay here forever, lost in the way her body clings to mine, warm and perfect.

"You're fucking perfect," I murmur, my voice hoarse and heavy with satisfaction. I press a lazy kiss to her jaw.

The aftershocks ripple down my spine, every nerve alight, still humming from how incredible she feels.

As the intensity slowly ebbs, I pull back just enough to meet her gaze. Her eyes are soft, full of something so deep and consuming it makes my chest tighten. I brush her hair back from her face, my fingers lingering against her cheek, memorizing every detail, every curve, every breathtaking inch of her. Then I lean down, capturing her lips in a kiss—slow, deep, and raw, pouring every unspoken feeling into this moment.

"I love you," I say, my voice rough and stripped bare. "Fuck, Aubrey, I love you so much it scares the shit out of me."

Her eyes shine as she looks up at me, her lips trembling with emotion. "I love you too, Noah," she whispers, her voice soft but unwavering. "I always have."

I straighten up slowly, withdrawing from her with deliberate care. My cock slides free, and I watch the way her body trembles beneath me, my cum slipping out of her, dripping onto the hood of the car. The sight makes a wicked smirk tug at my lips. She's utterly wrecked, trembling, and undeniably mine.

———

The weeks roll by, and for the first time in what feels like forever, life isn't trying to knock me on my ass. Aubrey and I? We're solid—fuck, we're better than solid. We've found this rhythm, this unspoken thing that just clicks. She's happy, working at the diner, coming home with that soft smile and a pocket full of tips. And me? I'm not drowning in the bullshit anymore. Not constantly clawing my way out of the wreckage of my past. Well, mostly. Some shit's harder to shake than others, but with Aubrey, it doesn't feel so heavy.

The stuff with my mom still lingers, like a splinter I can't dig out. She keeps pushing, asking me to get to know Cole and Lilla, but I can't. Not yet. Just thinking about it makes me want to hit something, anything, just to let it out.

Dad told me to take my time, to face it when I'm ready, and for once, I'm actually listening. Maybe someday I'll figure out how to deal with it—how to untangle the shit in my head—but not now. Not yet.

Aubrey's been the one keeping me steady. She's glowing these days, smiling more, like she can finally breathe easier, finally relaxing. She knows she has a safe place to fall now, and that's all I want for her. We spend as much time as we can at the lake. The place is our spot now.

Sometimes she sketches while I sit back and watch her. Other times, we're tangled up in each other, fucking under the open sky.

A few weeks back, I took her out of town for her volleyball competition. She rode on the back of my bike, her arms wrapped tight around me, her body pressed so close I could feel every curve. It was fucking perfect—the wind whipping past, her laughter in my ears, her warmth against my back.

At the game, I was the loudest guy in the stands, shouting her name every time she scored. She'd roll her eyes at me, but I caught the smile she tried to hide. That was my girl, kicking ass on the court, and I was so damn proud of her.

Then everything fucking changes.

It's a normal night. Aubrey's curled up next to me on the couch, the glow of the TV painting the room in soft, flickering light. It's easy. It's right. And then her phone pings.

She picks it up, and the second her face shifts, I know something's wrong. She stiffens, her eyes glued to the screen like it's a countdown to a bomb. Her breathing changes—shallow, uneven—and the room feels too quiet, like the calm before a storm.

"What is it?" I ask, my voice rough, my chest tightening with this sinking feeling I can't shake. Like the ground's about to fall out from under us.

Her fingers tighten around the phone, her breath hitching. It's a long moment before she finally whispers, "It's my mom."

And just like that, the world shifts. Fuck.

The room feels like it's closing in, the air too thick, too heavy to breathe. My stomach twists, my chest locks up so tight it hurts. Every alarm in my head is blaring, a screaming red light I can't ignore. Whatever this is, it's bad. Worse than bad. I can feel it in my bones.

It's going to fuck her up. It's going to fuck us up. I know it.

The urge to rip that phone out of her hand is overwhelming. Toss it into the yard. Smash it to pieces. Do anything to make this moment go away. I want to tell her to forget it—pretend it doesn't exist, pretend we're untouchable. But I can't.

Because I've been here before. I know this feeling—the weight in my chest, the pit in my stomach that's already swallowing me whole. I know exactly how this ends.

It's that slow, brutal unraveling. The kind that sneaks up on you and rips everything apart piece by piece. And fuck, I can't survive it again. Not this time.

Not when the time comes for her to leave.

CHAPTER 30

AUBREY

The text has been sitting there since last night, staring back at me every time I unlock my phone.

Mom: Aubrey, I really need to see you. I'm sorry for everything. I shouldn't have done what I did. Please, can we meet?

I've read it at least a hundred times. Each word feels heavy, as if designed to fuck with my head. Not because I don't know what to say, but because I don't know how I feel about saying anything at all.

Do I even want to hear what she has to say? Part of me wants to delete the text and pretend it never existed. But then there's the other part. The stupid, fucked-up part of me that needs answers.

I sit on the edge of Noah's bed, my phone clutched in my hand, staring at the message like it might change if I just look hard enough. The words blur the longer I focus on them, my thumb hovering over the screen. But I can't bring myself to type a single thing.

The door creaks open, and Noah steps in, fresh from the shower, his hair damp and messy, a towel slung low on his hips. His eyes find mine instantly, narrowing when he spots the phone in my hand.

"Still haven't responded?" he asks, his voice careful but clipped.

I shake my head, looking down at the phone like it's some kind of bomb about to go off. "I don't know if I should."

He exhales sharply, the sound tight and sharp, then grabs a pair of jeans. "It's your mom, Aubrey. I get it. But you know how she is. Unpredictable. In and out of your life whenever it suits her."

"I know," I say softly, my voice barely above a whisper. "But... what if this time is different?"

He freezes for a second, his hand still on the shirt he's picked up. When he turns to face me, his jaw is tight, his eyes darker than usual. "And what if it's not? What if she says all the right things, makes you believe it, and then fucks off again? What happens to you then?"

I can hear the pain woven through his words. This isn't just about me—it's about him too. He's lived this cycle with me, watched it break me more times than I can count. And now I'm dragging him into it again.

"I don't know," I whisper, my voice trembling. "But she's my mom, Noah. I have to try, don't I?"

His shoulders sag, his frustration melting into something softer, something I don't deserve. He steps toward me, sitting down beside me on the bed. His hand brushes against mine, grounding me. "Just... don't let her hurt you again, Aubrey. I can't fucking stand to see you like that."

"I know," I say, forcing a small smile for his sake. I don't know if I'm trying to reassure him or myself.

He studies me for a moment longer, his gaze soft but unreadable, before leaning in to plant a gentle kiss to the top of my head. His lips linger there, warm and steady, and I close my eyes, holding onto the fleeting comfort. Then, with a quiet sigh, he pulls back.

"I'll be outside if you need me," he murmurs, his voice low, almost hesitant. Without another word, he turns and heads for the door, leaving me alone in the room.

I stare down at the phone in my hand, the text glowing on the screen like a taunt. I read it again, letting the words burrow deeper, twisting something sharp and raw inside me.

Taking a deep breath, I start typing.

Aubrey: I can meet up. When and where?

My heart pounds, heavy and erratic, as I stare at the message, my finger hovering over the send button like it has the power to hurt me. Every instinct screams at me to delete it, to shove this mess into some dark corner and pretend it never existed. But I can't.

With a sharp inhale, I hit send before I can second-guess myself. My hand trembles as the weight of what I've just done settles in, cold and unrelenting.

The message delivers, the screen staring back at me, unfeeling and final. I let out a shaky breath and toss the phone onto the bed, like putting distance between us will somehow make it all easier. But it doesn't. The heaviness stays, gnawing at the edges of my resolve.

And now, all I can do is wait. Wait and pray I haven't made the biggest fucking mistake of my life.

The soft ping of a notification cuts through the silence, sharp and jarring. My stomach lurches as I snatch the phone back, my hands shaking as I unlock the screen. There it is—her reply, clear and undeniable.

Mom: At the coffee shop on Elm Street at 3PM today. It's important.

Of course, it's today. Of fucking course. She can't wait—can't give me time to think or breathe. When it's about her, it's always urgent, always immediate, as if the world revolves around her schedule.

I read the text again, the words blurring as heat rises to my face, anger boiling beneath the surface.

I think back to all those months ago—to the nights I sat in the corner of my dad's house, broken and desperate, tears streaming down my face as I reached out to her. Begging. Pleading. Crying into the void for her to care, to notice, to fucking say anything. To actually give a shit about me.

But she didn't.

Not a single fucking word. Just silence. Cold, empty, deafening silence. Like I wasn't worth even a half-assed response. Like I didn't fucking matter.

And now, she expects me to show up. Just like that. Now she's got something "important" to say. It's such bullshit.

The selfishness of it—it's so fucking her, and it cuts deeper than I'll ever admit out loud. She's always been like this. Picking and choosing when to give a shit, when to show up, when it benefits her, when it makes her feel better about herself. It's never about me. Never has been. It's always about her. Always.

I clutch the phone so hard my knuckles ache, the urge to hurl it across the room burning in my chest. But what would that solve? She'd still be her, and I'd still be the one standing here, drowning in this endless, hollow ache, trying to figure out why I even give a damn.

I start pacing, my thoughts spiraling into darker and darker places. Part of me wants to call her out, scream into the void, and tell her to fuck off, make her feel even a fraction of what I've felt these last few months. To remind her that she's the one who left, the one who made me feel like I was nothing.

I stop in my tracks, glaring down at the phone like it's the root of all this pain, the text carved into my mind like a scar. "Why now?" I mutter under my breath, the words trembling with rage. "Why the fuck now?"

Leaving my phone behind, I head off to find Noah.

The midday sun is blinding and hot, beating down relentlessly and shimmering off every surface. Noah is in the middle of the back yard, slouched in one of the old chairs by the firepit, his phone in hand. His cap is pushed back, the sharp angle of his jaw tight with tension.

I clear my throat, and his eyes flick up, meeting mine.

"Hey," he says casually, but I can see it—the concern etched into his brow, the way his gaze sharpens. He knows something's up. He always does.

"I'm going to see her," I say, my voice quieter than I mean it to be. I try to sound sure of myself, but it comes out shaky and small. "This afternoon. She wants to meet up."

For a moment, Noah doesn't move, doesn't speak. His expression doesn't change, but I see it—the flicker of hurt that flashes in his eyes before he reins it in, masking it with calm.

He stands, slipping his phone into his pocket and stepping closer, his movements slow and deliberate.

He's not angry, not disappointed—just resigned. Like he knew this was coming and hates every second of it.

He exhales, the sound heavy and measured, before finally speaking. "Whatever you decide, Aub," he says, his voice low but steady, "just know... it doesn't change anything for me. I'll always fucking love you."

The lump in my throat grows unbearable, tears pricking at my eyes as his hand reaches up to cup my face. His thumb brushes against my cheek, a soft, grounding touch that almost makes me fall apart.

Then he kisses me. It's tender and slow, but there's a weight to it, something unspoken and final, like a promise he's afraid to make. Like he's letting me go, even though it's killing him. It feels like goodbye.

The realization hits me, sharp and unforgiving, leaving me stripped bare. My chest aches with a rawness I can't explain, like something vital has been ripped away.

"Noah," I whisper, the word barely escaping my lips, trembling under the weight of everything I can't bring myself to say.

His hand lingers on my face, warm and steady, in a way that only makes the pain worse. But then he steps back. His jaw tightens, his movements stiff, every step like it's costing him something he doesn't have to give. And then he's gone.

I stand there, frozen in place, my heart pounding so hard it feels like it might shatter. The world around me is quiet, unnervingly so, until the muffled sound of a car door closing breaks the stillness.

My head snaps up, panic surging through me. I run to the side of the house just in time to see him backing out of the driveway.

"Noah!" I call out, my voice cracking, desperation spilling out of me. He doesn't stop. He doesn't even glance in my direction.

The engine growls as the car picks up speed, pulling away. I break into a sprint, my feet pounding against the pavement, the burn in my chest intensifying with every step.

"Noah!" I scream, the sound ripping from me, but it's useless. He's already gone, his car shrinking into the distance until it vanishes entirely, swallowed by the horizon.

I stop, gasping for breath, the emptiness inside me expanding until it feels unbearable.

He's gone. And it feels like he's taken the last piece of me with him.

The coffee shop hums with quiet conversation, but it feels like the noise is muffled, like the world knows there's a storm brewing inside me. My mom sits at a small table near the window, her hands clasped tightly around a mug. She looks smaller than I remember—fragile almost—but still the same.

It's only been three months since she left me at my dad's and walked away, but it feels like a lifetime ago. Like years of anger and hurt have been condensed into every second since she left.

Her eyes find mine as I step through the door, and she forces a soft, hesitant smile. Like that's going to fix everything. Like that smile could erase all the pain, all the betrayal. Like I'm supposed to just forget how she abandoned me.

"Aubrey," she says, standing up, her arms twitching like she's about to pull me into some big, heartfelt hug.

But I don't move.

I stay rooted where I am, crossing my arms over my chest and stopping a good few feet away. The message is clear: she doesn't get that from me anymore.

Her hopeful smile falters, the light in her eyes dimming as she slowly sits back down. Her fingers tighten around the mug, twisting it like she's searching for something to hold onto, something steady in the storm she created.

"What do you want?" I say, my voice flat, cold, cutting through the quiet like a blade. No softness, no warmth. Just the raw edge of all the shit I've been carrying.

I see it land exactly the way I want it to, see the flinch, the way her shoulders jerk slightly, like I've hit a nerve. Good. She deserves to feel that sting.

She takes a deep breath, her gaze dropping to the coffee cup in front of her as if the right words are hidden somewhere in its depths. But it's too fucking late for that.

"I'm sorry," she finally says, her voice trembling. "I made a mistake—"

"A mistake?" I cut her off, my voice rising just enough to draw a few curious glances from nearby tables. "You call what you did a fucking mistake? You knew what he was like, and yet you still left me there so you could go play house with your asshole boyfriend. You left me, Mom. You dumped me at Dad's place, knowing exactly how he is, all so you could shack up with some cockhead who promised you the world. That's not a mistake—that's a choice. You chose him over me."

Her face crumples, tears welling in her eyes, but it doesn't do a damn thing to ease the knot in my chest.

If anything, it twists tighter, stoking the anger simmering just below the surface.

She looks down at her hands, twisting them like she's trying to wring the guilt out of her own skin. When she finally speaks, her voice is quiet, barely audible over the clatter of dishes and the low murmur of conversations around us.

"I thought he was the one," she says, shame thick and heavy in her words. "I thought he was going to give me the life I always wanted."

I laugh bitterly, shaking my head. "The life you wanted. What about me? Did I factor into that perfect little life of yours, or was I just some inconvenience? Leaving me with Dad—who, let's not forget, drinks himself into a fucking rage most nights—was an improvement compared to me hindering your freedom?"

Her shoulders shake as she struggles to hold back her sobs, her breath hitching with each broken attempt. "I thought I was doing the right thing," she says, her voice trembling as a stray tear slides down her face. "I thought he was what I needed. But I was wrong, Aubrey. I was so wrong."

"No shit," I snap, my voice sharp as the anger bubbling finally boils over.

Her lips quiver, and her voice cracks as she continues. "I thought he loved me. I thought he loved us."

"Us?" The laugh that escapes is cold, and bitter. "Don't even try to include me in that shit. There was no us. There was only you and him, and you know it. I was just in the way." My voice rises. "And how'd that work out for you? Did your knight in shining armor live up to all those shiny promises?"

Her sobs grow louder, and a barista glances our way, hesitating like they might step in. But I don't care. The words are out now, raw and vicious, years of hurt spilled out onto the tiny coffee shop table between us.

She stares at her hands, now stained with the salty evidence of her grief, wishing the tears could cleanse her regret. "He cheated on me," she whispers, her voice cracking under the weight of the confession. "I found him with another woman. He left me."

"And now what?" I spit, my anger sharp. "Now that he's out of the picture, you want to come back into my life. You want to play mom again, and act like the last three months didn't happen? It's a little late for that, don't you think?"

Her shoulders hunch, as if bracing for a physical blow, her voice a mere whisper as she confesses, "I know I don't deserve your forgiveness, Aubery," the words heavy with unspoken regret. "But I'm trying. I'm trying to make things right. I want to go back to how things were," she says, her voice cracking, a single tear tracing a path down her cheek. "I want to be your mom again."

"You're not my mom!" I snap, the words like shards of ice, each syllable sharp and cold. "What you did is not something a mother would do. A mother doesn't pick some asshole over her kid and call it love."

The anger is a pressure cooker threatening to burst, simmering beneath my skin as I stand there. Her tear-streaked face is almost pitiful; her eyes, red and swollen, search mine desperately for a glimmer of hope. But it doesn't soften me. It makes me fucking angrier.

"Why didn't you text me back?" I demand, my voice rising. "When I needed you. When I told you I had nowhere to live."

Her face crumples, hot tears streaming down her cheeks. For a moment, she stares, her mouth working soundlessly, as if searching for the right words, her expression a mixture of surprise and bewilderment. Her hands tremble as she wipes at her tear-stained cheeks, her voice barely a whisper as she mumbles a pathetic excuse.

"I thought you'd be okay," she whispers, her voice trembling.

"Okay?" My voice cracks, rising in pitch as fury boils over. "That's your excuse? That's all you've got?"

"I made a mistake, Aubrey" she says again, her voice pleading. "I didn't know—"

"You didn't know because you didn't fucking want to," I cut her off, my chest heaving. "You didn't care."

Her sobs grow louder, her shoulders shaking uncontrollably, but I don't let up. She needs to understand she's the one who broke this, not me.

"I'm happy now," I state, the words sharp, cutting through the tension between us. I can feel eyes on me, but I don't care. "I have Noah. I have Ken. They've given me more love and stability in these last few months than you ever did. They're my family now. Not you."

Her eyes widen, the shock clear on her face, and she stands, the chair screeching over the tiled floor. She reaches out like she's desperate to close the distance between us. But I step back, putting up the wall she should've seen coming long before this moment.

"Aubrey, please," she pleads, her voice cracking. "I can change. I can—"

"No," I snap, cutting her off, my voice cold and final. "You don't get to try now. You don't get to pretend to be something you're not. You made your choice. You chose him. And now I'm choosing me. I'm choosing my happiness. So leave. Leave and don't ever contact me again."

I turn on my heels, my heart pounding in my chest, my hands shaking as I walk away. The weight of the tears stinging my eyes threatens to break me, but I refuse to look back. I can't.

"Aubrey!" she calls after me, her voice breaking with desperation. "Please, don't do this. Please, don't do this to me, Aubrey."

I don't stop. I don't look back. I keep walking, the murmur of her voice blending into the background of the coffee shop as I leave.

I exit the building, each step carrying me further away from the woman who left me behind.

Fuck her and her pathetic excuses. I'm done.

CHAPTER 31

NOAH

I sit on the hood of my car, staring out at the lake. The water's calm, reflecting the late afternoon sun, but it doesn't do a fucking thing to quiet the storm inside me. My phone is in my hand, the screen black, and I keep checking it every five minutes like some desperate idiot. But there's nothing. No text. No missed call. No sign she's even thinking about me right now.

Still, I don't text her. I can't. I refuse to be that guy—the one begging for attention, asking if she's staying or leaving. But the thought of going back to the house and finding it empty, finding her gone... It's a knife straight to the chest, and it cuts deeper every time I think about it.

Hours. It's been hours of this—of sitting here, watching the sun dip lower, convincing myself she'll come back. That she won't leave with her mom. But the truth is... I don't fucking know.

And that uncertainty? It's tearing me apart, one piece at a time.

I rake a hand through my hair, gripping it like it'll somehow loosen the tension that's got this stranglehold on me. It doesn't. My head's a fucking disaster, thoughts ricocheting in every direction, each one worse than the last.

What if she chooses her mom? What if she decides to start over with her, to rebuild whatever they used to have? What if I'm not enough to make her stay?

The bitter laugh that slips out feels hollow, even to me. Fucking pathetic. That's what this is. Sitting here, unraveling over something I can't control. Over some girl who might not be mine to keep.

But she is mine. At least, I want her to be. Even now, when she's not here and everything feels like it's falling apart, I can't let it end like it did last time. I can't be the asshole who ghosted her, who left her wondering if I ever gave a shit. I won't do that to her again.

The buzz of my phone jolts me, my heart leaping into my throat. I unlock it so fast I nearly drop it, but it's not her. Just some notification I couldn't care less about. I toss the phone onto the hood, leaning back with a heavy sigh, my eyes fixed on the sky above me.

"Fuck," I mutter, the word breaking the suffocating silence. It feels like I'm on the edge of something, teetering between waiting and breaking.

I don't know how much longer I can sit here. I don't want to go back—to walk through that door and find out she's gone.

Because if she's gone... God, I don't know what I'll do.

The sun dips lower, casting long shadows across the lake, its reflection on the water so serene it feels like a cruel joke.

It's the kind of scene people write about, the kind that's supposed to stir something, but right now, it's just a cruel backdrop to the storm raging inside me. I've been sitting here for hours, dragging out the inevitable. But I can't do it anymore. It's time to face it—whatever the fuck it is. I have to go home, to see if she's still there or if she left, taking a piece of me with her.

The drive feels endless. Every mile stretches on forever, the road ahead blurring as the knot in my stomach tightens. Each second feels like it's dragging me closer to my own execution.

When I finally pull into the driveway, the house looks exactly the same as it always does. Quiet. Calm. Like nothing's changed. But it doesn't feel the same.

The air feels heavier, oppressive, like the house already knows something I don't.

My heart pounds in my chest, erratic and frantic, and I hate it. I hate this fear—this uncertainty that has me frozen in place.

I kill the engine and sit there, my hands gripping the wheel so hard my knuckles turn white.

I've been in fights that left me battered, bruised, bleeding, but this? This is a different kind of pain. It's the kind that doesn't heal, that cuts deeper than fists or words ever could. The kind that leaves you gasping for air, feeling like you'll never be whole again.

I force myself to breathe, to move. My boots crunch against the gravel as I climb out of the car, every step toward the front door heavier than the last, like gravity's working against me.

When I open the door, my eyes instinctively dart to the spot by the entryway—the place where Aubrey always leaves her boots.

They're not fucking there. I freeze. The sight hits me as if my heart has been ripped out of my chest. She's gone. No message. No explanation. Just fucking... gone.

I step further into the house, every movement heavier than the last. The silence is deafening, pressing in like a living thing. Each room I pass feels emptier than the previous, as if her absence has sucked the life out of the space.

And then, out of the corner of my eye, I catch movement.

I turn my head toward the back window, my gaze landing on the patio. There they are—my dad and Simone. They're sitting together, his chair tilted back as he listens to her talk. His face is relaxed, his posture easy, and then he smiles.

At least one of us is happy.

I linger there, watching them through the glass. My dad deserves this—deserves some kind of peace after everything he's endured.

I tear my gaze away from the window, trying to swallow the pain, bury it where it can't touch me, but it's no use. It's there, raw and relentless, clawing at me with every breath.

I don't know if she's coming back. And that thought, that's the one that fucking breaks me.

My steps down the hallway are slow, every movement heavy like I'm trudging through quicksand. My head's a mess, my chest tight, and each step feels like it's leading me closer to the moment when my heart shatters completely.

I stop outside her door. It's cracked open slightly, not enough for me to see inside, but I don't move. I can't. My heart is pounding, my pulse loud in my ears, and the thought of seeing that room empty is almost enough to undo me.

But I force myself to breathe, to take one step forward, and then another. My hand brushes the door, pushing it open just a fraction more, and my gaze locks on the room.

And there she is.

Aubrey's sitting at her desk.

For a moment, I can't breathe. I stand there, frozen, half convinced my mind's playing cruel tricks on me. But then she moves—her head tilting as her pencil glides across the page, completely absorbed in her sketchbook. She's there, completely oblivious to the storm she's left me drowning in.

It's her.

It's really fucking her.

Relief hits, so overwhelming my knees almost give out. My chest loosens, and for the first time in what feels like hours, I can finally fucking breathe.

My eyes sweep the room, needing proof that she's not some mirage. Her bag's leaning against the wall. Clothes are draped over the back of the chair. The bed is just as it was this morning, unmade and perfectly Aubrey.

She shifts in her chair, the soft movement catching my eye as the light glints off her hair. She's so fucking beautiful, so completely her, that I can't look away. It's like she's a magnet, pulling me in without even trying.

I don't even realize I'm staring until she looks up, her eyes meeting mine.

A slow, easy smile spreads across her face, and just like that, the room isn't so heavy anymore. She lights it up, the same way she always lights up something inside me.

"Noah?" she says softly, her voice cutting through the chaos in my head, pulling me back to solid ground.

I push off the doorway, my legs finally moving even though they feel like lead. My throat's tight, and I shove my hands deep into my pockets because I don't trust them not to fucking shake.

"Hey," I manage to get out, my voice rough, low, like it's all I'm capable of.

And just like that, everything I've been holding onto—the fragile, crumbling pieces of me—finally feels steady again.

She stayed.

She fucking stayed.

She chose me this time.

Her pencil hovers over the page, forgotten, as her eyes stay on me. Her smile softens, something quieter but just as warm.

"Are you okay?" she asks, her voice gentle, steady, like she doesn't realize she's the reason I am.

I nod, swallowing hard against the lump in my throat. "Yeah," I say, my voice firmer now, but still raw. "I am now."

MORE FICTION BY EVE CAMPBELL
<u>FIVE SUMMERS</u>

Indulge in the ultimate bad boy romance with "Five Summers"! Get ready to swoon as the brooding heartthrob meets his match in the good girl next door.

His heart may be cold, but when it comes to her, he would set the world ablaze...

The task was simple.

Finish school, get discovered, and then I'd have it all. The fame, the money, and the hordes of groupies.

That was until I noticed Poppy Reeves, the girl who lived two doors down. All these years, and I can't believe I never saw her.

I never thought my black heart would feel something. Especially for a girl who constantly gets bullied for her looks.

Out of everyone, she is the only person who truly understands the real me.

Now, I have to choose - Do I follow my heart or stick to my plans?

Perfect for fans of...

  - MF (Male/Female) Romance
- **Bad Boy Vibes**
- **Good Girl**
- **Opposites Attract**
- **Touch Her And Die**
- **Teenage Crush**
- **Enemies To Lovers**
- **Burn The World Down For Her Vibes**
- **Dual POV**

Full Story - No Cliffhangers.

SIXTY DAYS OF SUMMER

She might be Nate's little sister... This might break up the band... But that doesn't stop me from wanting her...

I've always played by my own rules, kept everyone at a distance, but then there's Scarlet. She's off-limits, the one girl I can't have, yet every time she's near, it feels like I'm one step closer to breaking every rule I've made.

She's Nate's sister, and crossing that line could destroy everything—my friendship with Nate and Theo, the band we've built, and the fragile control I'm barely holding onto.

But Scarlet sees me—the real me—and the closer I get, the harder it is to stay away.

I know I shouldn't want her... but I do.

Sixty Days of Summer is perfect for fans of...

- MF (Male/Female) Romance

- Bad Boy Vibes

- Opposites Attract

- Touch Her And Die

- She's Off Limits

- Burn The World Down For Her Vibes

- Dual POV

Please Note: This book has flawed characters and contains material that may elicit a strong emotional response for sensitive readers.